Don't Mess with the Carter Boys:

The Carter Boys 3

Don't Mess with the Carter Boys:
The Carter Boys 3

Desirée

www.urbanbooks.net

Urban Books, LLC
300 Farmingdale Road, N.Y.-Route 109
Farmingdale, NY 11735

Don't Mess with the Carter Boys: The Carter Boys 3

ISBN 13: 978-1-945855-55-9
ISBN 10: 1-945855-55-X

First Trade Paperback Printing December 2018
Printed in the United States of America

10 9 8 7 6 5 4 3 2 1

Distributed by Kensington Publishing Corp.
Submit Orders to:
Customer Service
400 Hahn Road
Westminster, MD 21157-4627
Phone: 1-800-733-3000
Fax: 1-800-659-2436

Don't Mess with the Carter Boys:

The Carter Boys 3

by

Desirée

Tia

"Well, I'm glad you're out now," Porscha said as we opened the door to my apartment.

I had just got released from fucking jail Monday afternoon after waiting a whole weekend to get processed and to see the judge. Regardless of whether we had bail money or not, they weren't letting us out until Monday, just because they could. I was angry. I was pissed. I wanted to shower, fix my hair, and eat. Never had I been through anything like that, and I hoped to God I wouldn't go through it again.

Glancing at my phone as I set my stuff down, I waited for the call from Jahiem. Shit, I couldn't believe that on top of my parents knowing I was pregnant by this nigga, I got arrested with him too.

"Girl," Porscha said with a small laugh as she sat down on the couch in the living room, going through her phone. "Y'all two might as well be Bonnie and Clyde," she joked as I went to my room with a roll of my eyes. "Getting arrested together and shit. It's cute!"

"Shut up, Porscha!" I laughed as I quickly grabbed my things and went to the bathroom, hopping in the shower and letting that hot water hit my dirt-filled skin. *Ugh! This was what I needed!* My hair was drenched in shampoo as I washed away the stress of the weekend.

Looking down at the suds hitting my feet, I felt my growing belly and smiled. Jahiem turned me into a ride or die chick without me even realizing it. I was right there by his side, fighting with this nigga. I couldn't even believe it. I did it all for someone I couldn't stand in the beginning, a man I could barely hold a conversation with without arguing over something petty. Yet, there was something about his mean, goofy ass that I was falling for. Even his wild-ass family was something I saw myself being a part of. *Shit, I don't know.*

I had already missed my classes for the day, so I just decided to say fuck it. Stepping out of the shower, I let out a sigh of relief. Feeling clean, hair pulled into a ponytail, I wrapped a white towel around my body after rubbing shea butter on me.

"Porscha!" I called out and heard no response. She must have left. Grabbing my phone, I saw Jahiem had called me twice. *Damn!* I quickly dialed his number, keeping the towel tight around me as I sat on the arm of the sofa. Jade was probably out on the yard or with Trent, soaking up that Greek attention. *Bitch.*

"Aye," Jahiem answered as I smiled. "You at home?"

"I am—"

"Open the door. I'm in the hallway now," he rushed, hanging up.

Damn, nigga. I opened the door and stood in the hallway, waiting in anticipation to see him. With the towel still wrapped around me, I watched him cut the corner and start a light jog toward me. Even though we were arrested together, we had been immediately separated once we were processed. In the car ride over there, I hated that I cried, because I wanted to be strong for him, but he kept me calm the entire way, telling me what to say, what not to say, and that he wouldn't let nothing happen to me. I'd been through more shit with this nigga in months than mothafuckas I'd been with for a year.

"What are you running for?" I called out with a laugh as he came sprinting down, wearing sweats, a long-sleeve white thermal, a skull cap with the cute fuzz ball at the top and ATLANTA going around the rim of the cap. He was so damn cute with his facial hair, gripping the middle of his pants, walking like he was about business.

"When did you get out?" he asked, immediately hugging me tight as I wrapped my arms around his neck. "I been up there trying to see when they released you. When did they let you go?" he asked again, holding me close as if this was the last time he would see me.

"Not too long ago," I said in his chest, feeling him bend down before lifting me off the ground. He closed the door with his foot and took me to my room. "Nigga, what are you doing?" I laughed.

"I gotta be at the airport in an hour," he breathed, closing the door to my room. "I can't believe yo' mean ass held a nigga down at the movie theater."

"Nigga, you ain't the only thug." I laughed, letting him lay me back on the bed before climbing on top of me, peeling my towel away. His eyes immediately went to my stomach with a huge grin, placing the most delicate kiss on it. Looking at me, he came up and kissed me hard on the lips as I wrapped my arms around his neck. We really couldn't get enough of each other. You know those moments when you about to fuck someone who got that good shit? You excited just thinking you about to get an automatic nut.

"Nobody hurt you? You good? None of them fucking pigs touched you inappropriately, right?" he questioned, eyes searching my body for marks.

"I'm good, Jahiem." I smiled, taking his hat off. "I'm good, baby. Nobody is going to touch me. They not stupid. I would have fucked them up on sight, nigga," I stated as he smiled at me while kicking his sweats off. "Why are you looking at me like that?"

"Because," he said, smoothing my wet hair back as he looked me in the eyes. "I think I just fell in love with yo' crazy, thugging ass."

My eyes grew wide, trying to hold back this weak-ass smile as I felt my heart grow, my cheeks flush, and my body tingle in hope. Shit, I couldn't believe I was about to say this, but it was the only other way to describe it.

"I love you too, Jahiem," I admitted right before he kissed me again.

Stay Strong or Not

Taylor

"Girl, I don't know what I'm going to do," I said to Amira, walking in my house on a late Tuesday evening. I was fresh from my 9 to 5. I was on the phone with one of my sorors from back in California, talking about the craziness of this past weekend. Definitely needed to take my mind off of the chaos, from fucking Olivia's boyfriend up to Trent and I having sex. I hadn't spoken to him since Sunday, since everything went down. Olivia hadn't been home, because she'd been staying with Shiloh and probably would be there for the next week or so, until things blew over. It must have been nice knowing couldn't nobody really fuck with you without fucking with yo' brothers.

"You know what you gotta do," Amira continued as I rolled my eyes, closing the door and popping the lights on in the dark living room. "You fucked Trent, and it's probably going to happen again."

"It was just a one-time—"

"Nuh-uh, ho. You've been in love with this guy since God knows when. When we met, that's who you used to always talk about when we talked about boys. Now you moved back to Atlanta, and what do you do? Sleep with him." She laughed as I dropped my head in shame, slipping my heels off. "Sex was good, right?"

"It was amazing." I smiled to myself, enjoying that small feeling down below, like he was still inside of me.

"You kissed his ass, too?"

"I did."

"Mm-hmm, so you know what you have to do now. You gotta act like you don't want him. Act like he's replaceable, because in reality, he is. You haven't spoken to him since, right?"

"Nuh-uh," I said, thinking about how I'd been tempted the night before to call him. I had to keep telling myself he had a girlfriend.

"Good," Amira stated, getting into her manipulating mindset. "So, I give it three days before that nigga starts clinging to you, calling you, wanting to know what you're doing, trying to stick it in again; but you don't let him do it!" she warned as I nodded, taking mental notes. "Don't hang out with him. Don't give him the time of day until he gets rid of the New York bitch," she stated.

I spotted headlights flashing through my window. As she continued to talk, I looked through the window and saw Trent's car pulling up. *What the fuck?*

"Are you listening, Taylor?"

"Girl, he just pulled up to my house," I said with a laugh, opening the door.

"He what? Girl, let the clinginess begin. That nigga is going to be on you like white on rice."

"I don't think so," I said, watching him get out of the car. He always knew how to dress to impress. "Damn . . ."

"Nuh-uh! Don't do that! Not on this damn phone. If I can't see how fine he is, don't rub that shit in my face over this phone," Amira snapped, and I laughed.

"Girl, bye. I'll call you later and tell you what happened," I said as we hung up, still laughing.

He was on the phone himself as he closed the door, adjusting his tie while talking business. Looking him over, I smiled, seeing he was dressed in his usual black dress slacks, slick shoes, and black dress shirt with a thin black tie. All-black against the light complexion caused his light brown eyes to pop from a distance. With his fraternity's letterman jacket on, I could see he was bleeding that crimson and cream. Same as me.

"Yeah, I can get with John tomorrow and discuss what we can do about his lack of papers. Hopefully, we can come to some sort of deal or arrangement," he said, sounding proper as he walked slowly up to my door, smiling at me.

Damn, Trent. As if you wasn't fine as hell in high school, you got to be fine as a grown-ass man and look sexy in a suit. Not a lot of men can pull that shit off. Just imagine Elijah dressed up. I can't even picture it.

"Yeah, will do," he said, nodding his head as he checked his nails. "Yeah, okay then. I'll see you at the office tomorrow. All right." Hanging up, he smiled at me. "You not gonna let a nigga in?"

"Really, Trent?" I laughed, seeing how he switched it up from uppity to hood in a matter of seconds. I stepped aside so he could come in, catching a whiff of his lovely scent. He always smelled good.

Closing the door, he looked around as if it was his first time being here, before turning to me, smirking with a sneaky grin.

"What, Trent?"

"You trying to fuck again?" he asked, and my mouth dropped. He shook his head, laughing while holding his stomach.

"I'm playing. I'm playing, Tay." He laughed.

"Oh, I was finna say, nigga, you must have lost yo' damn mind." I laughed. "What are you doing here?"

"I need a favor," he said, looking me over, already making me feel self-conscious. Since I was just getting off work, I had kept it simple with a blouse, slacks, and blazer. Nothing fancy. My hair was pulled back in a tight ball.

"What's that?" I asked.

"I got a formal event tonight that I gotta go to with my fraternity, and I need a date," he said, and I quickly shook my head.

"Nigga, I just got off work. I'm tired. And where the fuck is yo' girlfriend?" I asked, hand on my hip.

"She's not Greek, and I don't feel like hearing her complain about being the only girl that's not Greek. You know?"

"Mm, so tell her to pledge," I mumbled, walking in the kitchen.

"She's not that type of girl. Come on, Taylor. Do me this one huge favor. This is an opportunity for me to network a little, get my resume out so I can have something serious when I graduate next month."

Looking back at him, I sighed. I never turned down an opportunity to network my damn self, since I had just graduated that past spring.

"What type of event? What's the dress code? Who all is going to be there, and will I be on my feet all night?"

"Charity, most of the top elite people in Atlanta, black and white. Dress code is formal as fuck. Everyone who is anyone will be there, and I will rub your feet when or if you ever get tired," he pleaded, and I smiled. Shit, that was all I needed to hear. "It's a charity event my fraternity chapter is hosting, and I'm not trying to be the only nigga without a date."

"What time does it start?" I sighed as he smiled, coming over to me to hug me hard as I laughed.

"We got to be there in about an hour," he said, and my mouth dropped.

"Nigga! Why are you just now telling me this?"

"Come on. While you doing all this yacking, you could be getting dressed. Hop in the shower. I'll pick out what you're going to wear," he said, rushing to my room.

Oh my God. I quickly jumped in the shower, washing up, trying to think of what to do with my hair. How was I supposed to introduce myself? "Hi, I'm his friend, Taylor Rowan. I'm his date for the night, Taylor Rowan."

I shook my head as I wrapped the towel around me, after showering and drying off with some lightly scented lotion. Opening the door, I headed to my room, seeing him go through my closet like a mad man. A red quarter-sleeve dress that went just below my knees with a wrap going across the waist was laid out on my bed. I wore that shit to church. Hell, that was my "I'm feeling like a ho" church outfit because it was so body-hugging. He had jewelry picked out next to the dress, and even picked out a backup dress that was pushed to the side. I smiled, watching him look at my collection of flats and sneakers.

"Why you got so many damn shoes?" he pressed, closing one shoe box only to open another. "Where are your heels at?" He turned to look at me before letting his eyes look me over slowly.

"Nigga, it's in the box over there," I said, pointing at the huge box in the corner next to my bed. "I haven't had a chance to unpack them because it's so many."

He stood up, proceeding to go through my dresser, pulling out black seamless boy shorts and a matching strapless bra.

"Here," he said, tossing it on the bed as I laughed.

This nigga here. I know some women would be disturbed by the fact that he was picking out my outfit, but Trent had always been that way. He liked to look good and liked women around him to look good. Olivia was the same way. She was constantly telling someone what they should or shouldn't wear.

"Trent, you cannot be serious! I'm not wearing this! It's too body-hugging!"

"Just try it on for me," he begged, going through the shoes.

I sighed, waiting until he had his back turned before slipping on my panties and bra. I still wasn't comfortable standing completely naked in front of him, but as I put the dress on, he turned around, eyeing the fit.

"See! My ass looks like a fucking monster back here," I said, turning to give him a view. "I can't scare none of those old niggas there."

"Yeah, you right." He laughed, going through the closet again. "Take that off. We can find another one."

After about three dresses, a lot of turning in circles, walking toward him and standing in the mirror together to see if we looked good, we settled on a dark navy-colored dress with long sleeves, just barely above the knee. It was still body-hugging, but it left me some room to breathe. With my hair in a high bun and makeup done to perfection to make my small eyes pop, we were soon on our way.

As we headed to the event, I thought about his girlfriend and the real reason he didn't want her to come.

"If it's all of Atlanta, technically this isn't some Greek event," I pressed, watching him drive with ease.

"You right."

"So, your girlfriend could have came, nigga." I laughed, watching him smirk as he licked his lips at me.

"She wouldn't know how to act around people like that. Shit, you don't either probably, but at least you can turn it on and off."

"I do know how to act," I said, smoothing my dress out, looking at the silver bracelet that decorated my wrist. "Have you spoken to Olivia ever since the whole incident happened?"

"Maaaan," he let out, shaking his head as he dragged a slow hand over his low haircut. "I don't think I will ever get over the sight of seeing my brother aim a gun at some kids. That shit is wild to me. I try not to think about it," he said, looking back before switching lanes.

"Well, Olivia told me Shiloh spared his life because of some girl?" I questioned, wanting to know more.

"Yeah, whoever the chick was, he knew her. That's all I know about it. I honestly don't even like talking about that shit. I hate that I was even there in the first place."

"Defending your sister's honor," I reminded him, but he shook his head.

"Not like that though, Taylor." He sighed. "I'm far from a killer, and you know I'll only fight if I have to defend me and mine, but that shit? Fucking with the grandma and the kids? Trell wanting to fuck with the girl? I mean, that ain't my life. Never was, and never will be."

"Amen," I agreed with a small smile, looking at Trent.

He grew quiet as we drove in peace through the lit streets of Buckhead, seeing the tall buildings, people walking on the sidewalk, restaurants live with chatter and noise on a Tuesday night. It was definitely one of the posher areas of Atlanta. For those reading this who have no idea about Atlanta, just think Lenox Square Mall. Everyone knows about that place at least. If not . . . shit, look it up.

When we arrived at our destination, he had a valet park his car. I watched him quickly change from the letterman's jacket to a matching black blazer, buttoning it closed as he checked himself. He was nervous for some reason. I couldn't figure out why, though. I walked over to him, grabbing his hands to keep him from fussing over himself.

"You good, pretty boy?" I teased, adjusting his tie as he looked down at me, smiling.

"Nothing on my face, right?" he asked, trying to touch his face.

I smacked his hand away as I looked him over. "You're fine, Trenton Michael. Let me see your teeth," I said, and he smiled. I nodded, letting him check mine before laughing to ourselves. We were too much for each other, clearly.

"You ready? I'm not going to embarrass you. I'll make you look good if you do the same for me," I told him as we walked toward the door.

"I got you, Big Tay," he said, and I playfully punched him in the shoulders before entering the huge building.

The moment we stepped inside the ballroom where a live orchestra was playing, we saw everyone standing in their finest attire, dressed to impress. He was greeted by some of his professors from school.

"Trent, can't wait to hear this speech of yours," an older man said as they shook hands.

"You won't be disappointed, sir. I can promise you that." His hand slipped to my lower back with ease.

A speech? Really?

"Let me introduce you to my date for the night, Taylor Rowan," he said, and I smiled, shaking the man's hand as he looked me over.

"Oh, well, you look lovely as all get out. How did you manage to get caught up with this kid here?" he teased.

"To be honest, sir? I have no idea," I said, and we all laughed, playing our part.

That night was almost too perfect to count. The food was amazing, but I barely ate because I had a thing about eating in front of people. Trent's speech about this charity in front of hundreds of people was brilliant, almost to the point where I knew he didn't write that shit. I, of course, collected business cards and handed out some. I was definitely ready to put my business degree to use in any field—as long as I was making money.

The live orchestra had a soloist that was featured, and the moment I saw who it was, I nearly screamed. Elijah's girlfriend stood in front of everyone, playing the fuck out of that violin. Even Trent didn't know about it, but she was dubbed one of the top violinists in the country. Who would have thought? Standing there in her long red gown, she stood out against the orchestra members, who were dressed in black. She was playing straight from memory with no sheet music.

By the end of the night, I had met Trent's frat brothers, who were teasing him about not bringing this Jade girl because she wouldn't fit in. I met new sorority sisters of my own, and I even got a chance to stop by and chat with Jordyn, who looked shocked to see me.

"Why didn't you tell Elijah to come?" I asked as we walked to the table to grab a drink.

All eyes were on her because she was literally stunning in her dress, hair pulled back in a high ponytail that swung when she walked, and her gray eyes shining. She was gorgeous. Whoever did her makeup needed to be awarded, because she looked like a pure model. Unlike Olivia, she didn't carry herself like she was beautiful. She barely recognized it, but the eyes on her were definite.

"He wouldn't come to something like this." She shrugged. "I'm constantly asked to play for events and weddings, but Elijah coming? I don't know if he would know how to act."

"I think he would love to see you play," I said, watching Trent walk over, smiling at me before looking at Jordyn.

"Aye, I wish my brother could have seen you play," he said as she gave him a short, brief smile before walking off suddenly. He dropped his head with a small laugh.

"What did you do to her, Trent?" I pressed with a laugh.

"Told her about herself one day, and she hasn't messed with me since. I told Elijah to tell her I apologize, but she—" He stopped, shrugging. "I don't know, but you got my whole frat asking about you."

"I bet!" I laughed, looking at his brothers, seeing they were all grouped together, taking pictures.

"Oh!" he let out, looking around quickly before waving someone over. "My mama came too. She wanted to see you."

"Oh, where is Ms. Ava at?" I asked excitedly, seeing a short, dark-skinned woman walk over in a long, black dress. She had those signature low-lid eyes, few wrinkles, and a smile that was identical to all of her kids. Elijah, Olivia, and Shiloh pretty much could never be denied by her, but Trent looked like his daddy with those hazel eyes. She made sure she kept youthful. Ms. Ava barely looked like she was over fifty.

Meeting her halfway, I immediately wrapped my arms around my second mama. She had practically raised me alongside my own.

"How are you doing, baby girl?" she asked, patting my edges down. *Of course she would*.

"I've been doing good, hanging with your character of a son," I teased, and she smiled sneakily at Trent.

"I see." She smiled before playfully cupping his chin in a motherly fashion. "I'm so proud of my baby."

"Mama, come on now," he said, moving her hand as I laughed.

"He gets embarrassed, but he has to know I'm proud of him. Stayed out of prison, stuck with his studies, and now is going to graduate and go off to be a lawyer. I can't believe I'm getting a lawyer in the family," she cooed, eyes watering up. He dropped his head in utter embarrassment before pulling her close for a hug. "You make me so proud, Trenton. You know that?"

"I know, Mama," he cooed, kissing her cheek. "But you can't be crying like this, now. I got people watching me."

"Boy, shut up," she quipped, playfully pushing him back. "I'm glad one of the boys actually made something of themselves. Elijah was too busy running behind Shiloh's ass that he got caught up in the same foolishness. Should have been following you," she continued, expressing her favoritism toward Trent. I knew Shiloh hadn't spoken to her in years for some unknown reason, and Elijah definitely had a love/hate relationship with her, but Trent would always be her favorite, while Olivia was a daddy's girl.

"I don't know why Olivia wasn't here for this. I know Elijah is busy with his music thing with the boys, but Olivia could have made it."

As we all spoke, remembering the old days when we were kids, Jordyn walked over with her violin case in hand and coat on, like she was ready to go.

"Hey, I just wanted to stop and say bye," she said quickly, and we hugged.

"You're leaving so soon?" I asked, peeping Trent whisper something in his mom's ear. *Ohhh, shit, here we go.*

Let me tell y'all something about Ms. Ava. She did not play when it came to her kids. Trent was her obvious favorite, of course, but let her find out about a girlfriend of one of the boys. She was quick to slice through them with ease and not think twice about it. She was very protective over them.

"Really?" she said, eyes wide as she looked Jordyn up and down. "So, you're dating Elijah? My son?" she started.

Here we go.

Jordyn's eyes lit up as she looked at the woman, mouth slightly open. "I wouldn't say dating—"

"Sleeping with my son? Sound better for you?" she asked, and I nearly choked on my spit, watching Trent smirk from behind his mama. "My question to you is, why? You seem like a nice young girl that's too good for him."

Jordyn cocked her head back.

Oh, shit.

"What exactly does that mean?" Jordyn asked, setting her violin case down. "I never understand when someone says you're too good for another person."

"Oh, okay, since we want to get smart with ya elders, I'll bring myself down to your level then," Ms. Ava said with her neck rolling.

Biiitch! She's about to go the fuck in!

"Why are you fucking around with my no-good son? Clearly you—and take this as a compliment if you want—but you have something going for yourself. It's only a matter of time before he gets arrested and gets locked up for good, knowing his stupid behind. So, with all this money he's making with his music, clearly you must be in it for something other than attraction."

Jordyn smiled politely as she picked up her violin case. "I'm going to tell you like I told Trent. Your son is the only person that likes me for me. Take away the makeup, take away the fancy name brand clothes and looks, and nobody paid any attention to me. No one looked twice at me. I'm so used to being called ugly, lame, annoying, and a nerd that I almost started to believe that, until I met your son," she said as my mouth dropped. "So, me being too good for your son, who you obviously have no faith in as a mother, is false. Regardless of how you feel about your own child, I would like to say you did a fantastic job raising him, yet I can't say the same about this one standing behind you, who blatantly disrespected me by telling me had he known I was pretty all along, he would have tried to talk to me," she let out.

I gasped. Shit, that sounded like something Trent would say. Why the fuck was I gasping?

"And with all due respect, I'm not dating your son. I told him I was in love with him, and unfortunately, he didn't feel the same way, so . . ." She shrugged. "Have a fantastic night," she said, flipping that ponytail off her shoulders as she walked off.

Clap back like hell! I looked at Ms. Ava, who stared at her, watching her, before turning to look at Trent.

"What did I do?" He laughed with his hands up.

She just turned her attention back to Jordyn, who was shaking hands and hugging people as she made her way out.

"You good, Ms. Ava?" I asked, wondering what was going through her mind. She just smiled at me, low eyes, looking freakishly like Elijah with that complexion and those features.

"I like her. Bring her by the house this weekend so I can talk to her privately," was all she said before looking at Trent. "You too. Bring this Jade girl by the house so I can meet her."

"How you know about—"

"Men gossip worse than women, boo boo." With a wave of her hand, she walked off to mingle in the crowd, thinking she was cute.

I looked at Trent's face, laughing my ass off. *That's what he gets.*

When we got in the car, it was all laughs all the way back to my place. Jordyn had slick went the fuck off on his mama without two thoughts about it, like it was nothing. So, you know we had to call Elijah, putting his ass on speaker.

"Hello?" he answered in a groggy voice, sounding like he was asleep.

"Bruh! Jordyn met yo' mama," Trent said as I laughed. "And that shit did not go well at all."

"I heard. She called me and told me what happened." He sighed, coughing. "What did Mama say?"

"She likes her," I chimed in, hearing Elijah laugh.

"Jordyn be snapping, though. Don't let that nerdy-ass look fool you, nigga. She's protective as fuck over me," he let out. "I know Mama be bashing me when she get in front of her golden boy."

"Nigga, shut up," Trent, aka Golden Boy, retorted.

"But she play nice when she got her hand out for some money, though. I ain't tripping, though." He sighed.

"How can you not love her back? Jordyn told her that she was in love with you but you didn't feel the same way!" I shrieked.

"I don't."

"Nigga, you lying!" I laughed. "That shit is going to catch up with you, Elijah, if you don't tell her how you feel. All it takes is one dude to sweep her off her feet."

"It ain't happening."

"Mama wants to meet Jade too. Wants both of them to come over this weekend so she can talk to them."

"Man, what the fuck?" Elijah snapped. "Why she give a fuck who I'm dealing with all of a sudden? I'm not bringing Jordyn over there, especially if you bringing yo' bitch."

"Now, what's yo' problem with his girlfriend?" I let out, wondering how these two even were related half the time.

"I don't have a problem with her," Elijah said simply. "If Jordyn ain't fucking with her, neither am I."

"But you don't love her," I mumbled with a shake of my head. *Men.*

Once we made it back to my place after fooling around on the phone with his brother, Trent, ever the kind gentleman, walked me to my door. We stood in the cold night, with him towering over me and my hand on the knob, ready to push it open.

"Well, I had a nice time." I sighed with a content smile. "Hopefully, I can put some of these business cards to use," I said, waving my clutch.

"Yeah, me too. Your feet didn't get tired, I see," he said, looking down at my heels.

"Bruh, my feet are in pain and probably swollen from being on them all damn day and night." I laughed. "Oh, best believe I'm going to make you rub them one day."

"I got you," he said, cheesing as we stood awkwardly, staring at each other.

"Well, good night," I said, pushing the door open.

Feeling his hand grab my arm, I stopped to look at him, seeing he was trying to say something but couldn't figure out how. "What?"

"I really don't want to go back to my girl tonight," he said, smiling sheepishly.

I rolled my eyes. "Nigga, you look like Elijah with that face right now," I said, and he laughed. "What do you mean you not trying to go back to her tonight? What are you telling me?"

"Let me spend the night with you," he stated, clear as ice with his words.

I licked my lips slowly, and he watched the movement with his eyes before slowly leaning forward to kiss me. For a second, our mouths didn't move, until I gripped the back of his neck to bring him closer. His hands came to my waist. Right there in the open night, we were making out in front of my door.

"One last time, Trent, and then no more. I'm serious," I breathed against his mouth.

"I'ma make it count then," he replied, picking me up in one easy move before carrying me inside.

Fuck!

Now, you all know as well as I know that it wasn't the last time we had sex. The next night, he came over after work and waited up for me, bringing food, a couple of bootleg DVDs, and a case of beer. We were laid up on the couch, eating and watching the worst bootleg movie I'd ever seen. It didn't matter, though, because we were more in tune with each other than the movie. He lay shirtless and pantless on the opposite side of the couch, with me lying on the other end. Our legs were intertwined. All I had on was a basic-ass yellow shirt. No panties, no bra, nothing. My hair was wild and all over the place in a huge 'fro.

"Aye," Trent said, slurping up his noodles as he grinned at me. It had to be going on 9 o'clock, and Olivia was nowhere to be seen. She was probably still crashing at one of the other brothers' houses.

"What, big head?" I cheesed, and he playfully kicked me, causing me to laugh.

"You ever thought this would happen to us?"

I smiled, thinking to myself before shaking my head. I'd been damn near obsessed with Trent since I could remember, but never in my wildest dreams did I think this would happen between us.

"What about your girlfriend, though? She has to know something is up if you not spending the night with her," I let out.

He rolled his eyes. "Why you gotta bring her up now, Tay?"

"I'm just saying!" I laughed with a shrug, putting my plate down. "You ain't shit, nigga, for cheating on her. Might as well break up with her and just be with me. Shit," I mumbled, watching him smirk.

"Everyone likes you better than her. I can't even bring Jade around my brothers without some shit being started." He sighed. "None of my friends rock with her, and she don't even try to make that shit better. Don't even like being seen with her no more."

"Well, what do she look like? What's she like?" I asked curiously as I cut the TV off. *Fuck-ass movie.*

I watched Trent put his plate down, rubbing his head as he thought about it, almost as if he forgot what his girlfriend looked like. Elijah had told me he didn't like her, and Olivia said she automatically hated her because of how she talked to him and how they met.

"She's . . ." he started, looking up as he thought about it. "Dark skin with blond dreads."

"What?" I spat out with a laugh as I looked at him, eyes wide. "You? Dreads? Girls?"

"I know, Tay," he said, shaking his head. "I hate that shit. Hair looks fucking disgusting at times. I tell her she would look better with it cut off, but she not trying to hear that."

"Damn." I laughed, playfully touching my own hair. I automatically knew I was cuter than her. I had the education, the Greek behind me, and looks. Side chick: one. Main ho: zero.

"She got tattoos all over her body, piercings, and she got a mouth that just—" He stopped as he stared at his hands in deep thought before smiling to himself.

I felt my heart stop in that moment, just seeing him smile off a basic memory of her. I didn't like that.

"She's fucking crazy, Tay. Never met no girl like her. Drives me insane. Can't hardly take her no fucking where because she will act up."

"Sounds like Elijah." I laughed. "You dating yo' own brother."

"That's what that shit feels like at times." He sighed. "I tell her to act more ladylike, but she thinks I'm saying that shit just to fuck with her."

"Well, what is she into? What does she do? Who does she usually surround herself with on the yard?" I asked.

He looked up at me suddenly, slow smile. "If she's not with me, shit, I don't know who she be with. She got her own li'l friends, but they lame as fuck, so I don't fuck with them like that."

"You a mess, Trent." I laughed as I stood up. "You need to break up with her."

"I might just do that shit this weekend," he said, standing up as he followed me to the room. "You gonna be my girl, Big Tay?"

"Boy, stop." I laughed, looking back at his fine ass as he tucked that lower lip in, grabbing on his dick and giving me that "you about to get this dick in you" look.

The moment we entered my room, closing the door behind us, he leaned in, kissing me hard as he backed me up against the door. His hands slipped underneath my shirt.

"You and me are meant for each other," he said against my lips. "You know that, right?"

"I always knew that." I smiled, feeling my heart nearly skip a beat. It's amazing what good sex can do.

The next night was no different. We were laid up in the bed, with him giving me the business as I gripped his back, arching my own in response to his stroke. He was telling me all the good shit a girl loves to hear.

"You're my girl now, Tay," he breathed against my ear before biting it, causing me to moan out loud. "You hear me?"

"Yes, baby," I moaned, feeling him go faster. Tightening up around his body, I closed my eyes to focus on what was happening below.

"You can't fuck with nobody else but me." He pumped harder.

I just nodded, enjoying the ride. All the while, his girlfriend kept popping into my head. I didn't even know the bitch, but I knew what we were doing was wrong. I just felt like she was more so the side chick than I was.

"Shit! You feel so good, Tay," he moaned, slowing down as he worked his hips in a circle.

I dropped my head back, feeling my body jerk quickly in response to the change of stroke. Nigga did it every time. He knew I couldn't handle that. Once I got mine, just like almost every time, he was a second behind me, getting his. Letting him collapse on top of me, bodies sweating, I glanced at the time, seeing it was going on 3 o'clock.

Breathing heavy, he placed a delicate kiss on my shoulder. "I gotta get ready to go." He sighed, sitting up as he took care of the condom.

"Were you serious about me being your girl?" I asked, sitting up as we stared at each other. "And not messing with no one else but you?"

He just smiled sheepishly with a shrug.

"Soon as I break up with Jade, you're mine, Tay. You know how I am, being territorial as fuck. You know I don't play that shit," he stated, and I nodded, knowing all too well.

Trent, when he had a girlfriend in high school? Nigga was straight crazy, overprotective, easily jealous, and would get petty as fuck if you didn't clear it up for him. I could only imagine if we were out in public, if he caught another man looking at me, what he would say. All of the Carter brothers were like that, though, protective over their women.

"Aye," he said, looking at me with a teasing grin, hazel eyes glistening. Trent sat on the edge of the bed, checking his phone while I kept my same spot, feeling too comfortable to move.

"What, nigga? You smiling like you up to something."

"Wanna give me head?" he asked, and my mouth dropped before laughing. "Ah, come on, Tay!"

"Nigga, why y'all be so pressed for some head? I'm too cute to do that shit," I said, smoothing my hair back.

"You about to be my girlfriend, though. You gonna eventually end up doing that shit anyway." He laughed as I rolled my eyes. "Come on, baby," he begged, leaning in as he kissed my bare stomach, rolls and all, knowing I loved that shit. "Just one time, Tay. Let me just see what that mouth feel like. It can't be better than this beautiful thing between yo' legs," he said, touching my spot. I hiked my knees up, spreading my legs wide instantly, like it was a button he just touched.

"You are so fucking beautiful, Taylor. You know that? Taylor Carter," he continued, laying that game on thick as I gushed.

"So, I get yo' last name now?"

"We getting married, and we having kids. You already know this, though," he said, kissing my stomach again.

I shook my head slowly as I shrugged. "Bring it here, nigga," I said, watching his eyes light up. *The things you do for the ones you want.*

Once that was said and done, giving this nigga the head game of a lifetime, hearing him tell me I was better than Jade did boost my confidence up. I'm not going to even lie. Yet, as I watched him stand up, getting himself together, a part of me felt used. A small part of me should have known better. But, I wasn't too worried, because he couldn't stand his girlfriend. Shit, I hated her just from hearing him talk about her mean ass.

"So, when are you going to break up with her?" I asked, watching him get dressed, tossing on his coat and shoes.

"Soon, Tay. Just wait on me," he said, blowing an air kiss to me. "Come walk me out."

Jah & Jo

Jade

It's been a minute since I've been in the book. I know y'all mothafuckas probably didn't miss me. Whatever. We got a bigger problem to fuck with.

For those who don't remember me, let me reintroduce myself because the bitch you met in the book earlier did some growing up, you know? So, as you know, I'm Jade, Trent's soon-to-be-ex-bitch. I'm a dark-skin beauty with honey-blond locs officially hitting my shoulders, tattoos lined up on the arms, cute petite curvy frame, double piercing on the tongue, one on the nose, and a lovely one near the brow, nipples, and clit. I'm straight from New York, all day every day. Only been in Atlanta for a few months, and let me tell you about this fuck-ass, gay-ass, trifling-nigga-having-ass city. If the nigga ain't gay, he's cheating. If he ain't cheating, he don't have no fucking job. If he don't have a job, he selling dope out his mama basement at thirty years old. If none of that fits for yo' nigga out of Atlanta, then I'm sorry, but he *still* a fuck nigga in my book, son. Real talk.

I sat on the edge of my bed, looking hard at my phone. It was Thursday night, with my boys, Chris, KD, and Mo—you know, my regular niggas I stayed rolling with. It was barely midnight, and we all sat there debating on what the next move was.

Tia was in her room for the night, running her mouth on that phone, being loud as ever. I occasionally looked across from me, seeing the empty space my roommate Jordyn once occupied. If I had the bitch's number, I would have called to apologize. I wished I could take it back. Tia and I both had a sit-down about that, and we both regretted ever even laying hands on Jordyn. One, it was too easy to fuck her up because she wasn't going to fight back, and two? We did it for the wrong reasons. All that shit mixed with jealousy and petty hating is what really got her jumped. I had no real beef with ma, but I hadn't seen her since. I used to ask Trent where she be at, but she didn't fuck with him like that either, so he never knew. The way Elijah defended her that day, came and pretty much moved her the fuck out this apartment and away from us, said a lot about their relationship. I somewhat wished Trent would do that for me if I was ever in a situation like that, but I doubted it.

"Aye, so what's the move?" Chris asked, snapping his fingers in my face to snap me back at attention. "We rolling up on this nigga or nah?"

"We need to make sure he's fucking around on her before we do anything stupid. Nigga could just be working late," KD reasoned as we all looked at him stupidly.

"Nigga, you already know he's fucking around on li'l ma," Mo snapped angrily. They were just as mad as me, if not more, because they spent the majority of the time defending his ass when I thought he was in the wrong. Trent wouldn't have no clue because he didn't fuck with my friends like that.

"I never rocked with dude in the first place, but he made you happy, so that was all that mattered. But now, shorty?" Mo retorted, looking hard at me as I nodded. "We trying to make some moves. What you want to do, Jade?"

"Let's go roll up. I want to see this for myself to make sure," I said softly, tying my locs up in a short ponytail. "Where my shoes at?"

Soon as we stepped onto the yard, walking over to the boys' dorm where Chris parked his car, I slipped my hands in my coat pocket, thinking. My heart was pounding with anxiety against each step. I had first got hit up with the news of Trent going out to some event earlier this week with another bitch who was all over him, and how he so carelessly didn't ask me to attend instead. He used the excuse of thinking I wouldn't be comfortable doing stuff like that with him. *Nigga, I'm barely comfortable around yo' friends, but I'm at that frat house night after fucking night.* It just goes to show he really didn't even know me.

"Aye, let's stop by the store and grab some rellos and some snacks. The café ain't had shit in there to eat today," KD complained as we stepped onto the parking lot. The yard was empty, with a few people walking around or hanging outside their building. It was just too damn cold to be doing anything as we piled into the small black Mazda.

"When's the last time you saw Trent?" Chris asked as I put my seatbelt on, sitting up front with him as he cut the heat on.

"Shit, I haven't seen him since this morning. Nigga has been ghost all week. He works and doesn't come back to the yard until the next morning," I said, realizing he had settled down with the side ho. Got comfortable as fuck. "He told me he was hanging with his sister until she got better from whatever the fuck happened, but we already know what's up," I said.

Chris nodded, backing out. "You know where his sister stay?"

"I got her address on my phone," I said, showing Chris, and he put it in his GPS.

Yeah, I looked that shit up on the internet. Whoever the bitch was that went to the event with Trent stayed with his sister. I'm not stupid, never will I play stupid, and never will I be made to look stupid.

"So, what the fuck we doing? Posting up? We walking up on the nigga?" Mo asked, ready for battle as we hit the streets.

"Right now, let's just cut the music on and ride out, B," Chris said, hooking his phone up to the radio dashboard.

The moment I heard "Ms. Fat Booty" by Mos Def, I was lit. We were officially jamming in the car, and for a second, my mind was taken off Trent fucking another girl. All four of us in the car, citing lyrics to old school New York hip hop, I felt like I was back home with my boys. Streets were damn near empty, with a few cars passing by as we pulled up to the gas station.

"Aye, everybody but Jade put they money in," Chris demanded as he turned around, hand out.

I smiled as I got out of the car with my money in hand, ready to buy the rellos and snacks, since they was putting the money in for gas—all so we could chase after this fuck-ass pretty boy. In my black leggings, snow boots, black hoodie, and cream-colored coat with the fur on the hood, I walked up to the store like I had business to take care of. Locs were up, piercings out, as I played with the two rods in my mouth, snatching up what I could get from the store. I stuffed a few inside my coat and only bought the cheap shit like chips, candy, and honey buns. I knew KD's country ass was a fan of the bun, so I got a couple just for him.

"Aye, shawty," I heard someone say.

I looked back, seeing this old nigga with a missing tooth in the front, extra-long-ass blue tee, with jeans sagging so low I almost thought we were back in 2002.

"Damn, you look good as fuck. Where you from, baby?"

"I don't respond to shawty," I said coolly, paying the man while I kept a close grip on my coat so my other goods wouldn't fall out.

"Anyone ever tell you you look like Lauryn Hill?" he continued.

I rolled my eyes. I got sick of hearing that, because then they started pointing out differences.

"Except she didn't have the piercings, and her hair wasn't—"

I walked out, hearing the bell chime as I rushed back to the car with a Kool-Aid grin, knowing I had gotten away with my snacks.

"Where the lighter at?" Mo asked, feeling around the seats as I dumped all the snacks out on my lap. I could smell the weed in the air as KD began to roll up with the rellos I bought.

"Yo, everybody is good? We ready?" Chris called out, looking at me specifically as I took a lighter to go over the perfectly rolled blunt.

"Let's do it," I said.

The moment we found his sister's house, I immediately spotted Trent's white car parked outside. Looking at the time, I saw it was going on 2 o'clock. We got lost like hell and had stopped again for some drinks at the liquor store. So, with Chris cutting his lights and car off, we sat in the cold car, waiting, wondering, and thinking what the next move was. I was high as fuck, but I still felt my heart beating faster and hands becoming weak with a slight tremble. Anxiety was trying to eat at me at the thought of this nigga fucking around with this girl.

"Call that nigga, Jade," Mo snapped, and I pulled out my phone.

"What if he's sleep—"

"You are his girlfriend. It don't matter if he's 'sleep or not. Yo, call that nigga!" Chris put in.

I sighed, dialing his number. He hadn't texted me not once that day. I put it on speaker, and we all watched the house for any sign of movement as the phone rang twice before going straight to voicemail.

"Ahhh, that nigga pressed ignore on yo' ass, bruh!" KD laughed, falling back in his seat. "I say we knock on that door."

"And then what?" I pressed, looking back at him. "What if he's actually doing what the fuck he said he was doing, which was being with his sister?"

"You know that's not what he's doing," Chris mumbled. I turned to look at him. "You in denial, Jade. I know you be playing tough, like you don't give a fuck, but even you know better than most. This nigga is fucking around on you, ma."

"She need to see it for herself," Mo stated as I looked hard at the small brick house. With the street lamp near us going off completely, we seemed to be shielded by the darkness, while the house was well lit from the lamp posted next to it. How convenient.

"So, we waiting?" KD asked, passing the blunt to Chris, who took his pull on it before passing it to me.

"We waiting," I repeated in confirmation, taking a long pull on it before getting comfortable in the seat.

My eyes never left that house. Occasionally Chris would cut the heat on, but we were trying not to cause too much noise, so we stuck it out in the cold car, high as fuck, laughing at nothing in particular, with KD falling asleep. Even fucked with him for a little bit before finally, the door opened.

"Yo, yo yo, look," Chris said quickly, throwing a plastic bottle at KD to wake him up.

I sat up in the seat, seeing Trent step out of the house, smiling hard. With the lamp post shining perfectly on the house, I could see him as clear as day.

"Try calling him now, Aria," Chris demanded, using my first name.

I quickly tried calling him again, watching his phone light up. The moment he glanced at it, I saw the girl coming behind him, wearing nothing but a T-shirt and some house shoes, looking like she was freezing. She had a huge ball of hair that was wild and all over the place as she laughed at something he said.

"Nigga, answer the phone!" I could hear her joke. "Tell her you were with me."

"Hey, this is Trent. Sorry I missed your ca—"

I hung up, feeling my blood nearly boil as I watched them hug and kiss affectionately on the mouth.

"Oh my God," I breathed, gripping my stomach as I kept my eyes hard on them, watching them kiss.

"I told you," KD mumbled.

Mo hit him in the chest. "Nigga, what the fuck did I say?"

"Aye, you good?" Chris asked, grabbing my arm, but I snatched it back as I started to button up my coat, ready to get out. "Whoa, whoa, hold up, ma. You can't—"

"Why I can't?" I snapped angrily as I looked at Chris, who had a look of pity in his eyes.

"Not like this. Catch that nigga off guard, Aria."

"Trent, I'm serious!" The girl laughed as he smacked her on the ass before walking to his car with her following behind him, all googly-eyed and shit over my nigga! My man! He backed her up against his car, slowly making out with her like they'd been together for years. This wasn't no ordinary side ho. She had history with him.

I took a deep swallow, trying to hold back tears as they kissed one last time before he got in the car and she walked back to the house, closing the door. It wasn't until then that my phone lit up with him calling me.

"Answer that shit!" Mo called out.

"Nah, let me answer—"

"Hold up. She gotta be the one to answer the phone," Chris demanded as they began fighting over what I should do.

"All of y'all shut up!" I snapped, wiping my eyes before sliding to answer. "He—hello?"

"My bad I missed your call. What's good?" he said smoothly as I watched him pull out of the driveway and drive off.

"Nothing," I mumbled, trying my hardest to hold it in, to keep it together. "I . . . um . . . I'm going back to sleep."

"Aye, leave the door unlocked for me. I'm staying with you tonight," he said before hanging up.

The car became deadly silent as I looked at my boys.

"So, what are you gonna do?" Chris asked, starting the car.

I felt my face slowly scrunch up as I let the tears break free. Leaning forward on the dashboard, I cried hard.

"Aye, fuck that nigga, Jade! Don't waste yo' tears over someone like that! Nigga don't know shit about you, never tried to even get to know you like that! You were the one that changed for that nigga! I bet he don't even know what the fuck yo' favorite color is, or what you like to eat."

"Or yo' favorite movie," KD threw in.

"*The Breakfast Club*," they all chimed in before laughing.

I sat up, wiping my face, trying not to laugh.

"Nigga never did shit for you but tell you about yo' self and make you hang out with his friends. Make you dress a certain way so you could look good next to him. Bruh!" Chris snapped, looking back at Mo and KD. "You know how many niggas hit me up on a regular, asking about her ass? None of these niggas is scared of Trent or his brothers. They still want to snatch you away from him."

"No they don't," I said, wiping my eyes as more tears came down.

Without warning, all three of them reached in and hugged me hard and cussed me out at the same damn time.

"Aye! You are a beautiful woman who is stupid talented with the paintbrush and pencil. You—"

"Do he even know you do art, Jade?" Mo retorted.

I shook my head no, still locked in their embrace.

"Nigga lost out; not you, mama," Chris cooed, kissing me on the side of the head. "Let that nigga go. He ain't doing nothing but dragging you down. He don't appreciate what he has, so let him go fuck with that bitch then. Shit, help that nigga out and cut him loose so he can fuck around with whoever while you move on to better things. You feel me?"

"Yeah," I mumbled, wiping my eyes as I looked at my three boys. My amigos. "I swear I love y'all more than you will ever know."

"Ahhh!" they all let out, hugging me harder as I laughed.

"Love yo' mean ass too, shawty," KD said, rubbing my locs. "Fuck that nigga, bruh, real talk. Nigga was slick gay anyway."

Back in my room, I took a shower, still crying, still replaying the scene of him kissing that girl like he was in love with her. He never kissed me like that. Never. I almost forgot he was supposed to be on his way over, because I ended up lying in the bed, crying to myself, ignoring that nagging knock on the door, until I heard Tia answer it, going off on him in the process.

"My bad," I could hear him say before walking to my room. Opening the door slowly, he came in, keeping the lights off as he slipped out of his clothes and lay in the small bed next to me, wrapping his arm around my waist.

"You 'sleep, Jade?" he whispered, kissing my shoulder.

I cringed, more silent tears coming down.

"Jade?"

"What, Trent?" I mumbled in a shaky voice.

He sat up quick, popping the lamp light on, and leaned over to see my face. His hazel eyes were wide in horror and shock.

"Shit," he hissed as he quickly got up to get on my side of the bed, bending down to eye level to look at me. "What's wrong? What happened, baby?"

I just stared at him, wiping my eyes. "Don't worry about it—"

"I ain't never seen you cry before, and you telling me not to worry about it? Did someone say something? Are you hurt?" he asked, checking underneath the covers like that was the cause of all my pain.

I stayed quiet, just looking at the man I thought I was falling for—beautiful, perfect face with those eyes that could melt your heart.

"Jade, baby, talk to me," he pleaded, trying to look concerned. "You not pregnant, are you?"

"No." I barely mumbled the response.

He took his thumb, wiping the fresh tears as his face furrowed in confusion and uncertainty. "I can't really handle you crying on me, Jade. I'm not sure how to take this shit right now. Seeing you like this," he said softly. "Can you please tell me what's wrong, baby? Did I—"

"What's my favorite movie, Trent?" I asked.

His eyes grew wide, mouth slightly open, like he was searching for the answer. "I . . . uh . . . I don't know," he admitted.

"My major? What I want to do in life? Do you know?" I asked, and he shook his head no. Unbelievable. I knew everything about this man. Everything and more. He didn't even know why we were going to the same damn school.

I slowly got up from the bed and went into the closet, grabbing my giant canvas book to hand to him. It held my paintings, pencil work, photography, everything. I watched him go through the book in awe, and then he looked at me, smiling.

"You did these, baby?" he asked, sounding shocked.

I nodded. "I've been working with my professor so I can have an art show in the spring," I said softly. "My first show in Atlanta."

"Aye, this is beautiful," he said, looking at one in particular.

"Thank you."

He looked up at me as we locked eyes, just staring.

"What?" I asked.

"Why were you crying, Jade?" he pressed again in a serious tone. "You never do that. What's wrong?"

I slowly smiled, thinking I was going to let him hang himself before completely ending it. He was so used to me popping off at the mouth and talking shit constantly. Not anymore. All I saw now when I looked at him was that girl, him kissing and touching up on her like they'd been together for years. If that was the kind of girl he wanted to be with, be seen with, and have everyone like, then I'd let him get to it, nigga. I would take my leave, but not before giving him hell for the next few days before cutting him loose.

"Nothing is wrong, Trent," I said, wiping my face one last time. "Just having a girl moment is all."

Welp

Noelle

"So, you haven't heard from him since?" Layla asked as her, Tyree, and I sat in the living room late Friday night. It was going on a week since that violent incident had occurred. He hadn't texted me, or called, or come over. I hadn't seen him since, and we lived right next door to each other.

"I haven't," I answered, looking at my nails. It was supposed to be girls' night out, but clearly, we weren't doing any of that. Waiting on the pizza that we ordered, we sat in tattered clothes, basically bumming it out on the couch, with two of Tyree's friends on their way to my place to join in on the men bashing. I sat in basketball shorts that I was just now realizing were Shiloh's, and a shirt that had my church from back home on it. My hair was hanging freely, nowhere near done. I felt like a fucking wreck on the inside and looked like one on the outside.

Even after witnessing everything for myself, I had still told the police I didn't know who the guys were, and I felt awful about lying. Yet, here I was thinking I was going to get an explanation from Shiloh, but nothing. Not even a text message to see if I was okay. Aunt Alice had been knocked out to the point where her memory was completely gone, and the kids were too terrified to speak. They reported what they saw, but they each had their own version of the story, giving the police nothing to work from. The guys in the house said nothing, and whoever Lee's friend was ended up being shot directly in the head as he was walking out of his house two days later. Just the thought of Shiloh killing someone made me cringe in regret that I had even entertained his crazy ass.

"Hellooooo," Tyree waved, throwing one of my pillows at me as he smirked, drink in his hand. "Bitch, you stay daydreaming. Why don't you just call him?"

"And say what, Tyree? Hmmm? You were going to let your brother rape me? I saw you pull a gun on someone?" I questioned, thinking back to how he and I had first met. I could feel tears start to come down. I should have known he was off his fucking rocker to begin with when he pulled that stunt with me.

"Honey, I told you those brothers are not to be played with. Hell, Trell used to stay being caught up in some mess when we first met."

"Have you spoken to him?" Layla asked as Tyree rolled his eyes, rubbing his bald head while sipping his wine, sitting there in a small T-shirt and even shorter shorts.

"Chile, no. I hear he's been trying to get my new number, though, from some of my clients. I told them, 'If y'all love me, you won't give my ex-boyfriend the number, no matter how much he tries to pay you.' Nigga lost his damn mind, talking about, 'I'll be back.' Yeah, I miss him, but I don't miss having to worry about who he's sleeping with and who he's talking to on the phone, with me trying to listen for a bitch's voice. He wasn't ready for a relationship."

"How can you be with someone who's like that? Who's so . . . violent and—"

"Noelle, you are going to have to toughen up, boo boo." Tyree laughed. "Trell never put his hands on me in a violent way, never threatened me, and never let nobody fuck with me. Yeah, they are rough as fuck, but as long as that shit isn't directed towards you, I don't see the problem."

"Mm-hmm," Layla chimed in.

My mouth dropped as I looked at them. I couldn't believe they were condoning this.

"I'm still a little mad you didn't get a chance to test that dick game out," Layla said.

"Biiitch! You too?" Tyree laughed as they slapped hands. "Girl, I've been wondering about Shiloh's fine ass since he first got out of prison. I was like, please let this man be into niggas too, because I will gladly cheat on Trell for Shiloh. I was hoping his fine ass got turnt out."

"I can't believe I'm hearing this," I mumbled as they continued, alcohol definitely influencing the conversation.

"Shit, I was telling her that he probably can eat, stroke, and pound like a champion! Like, bam!" Layla let out, standing up as she twerked. "Have a bitch looking back at it like, ooooh-wee!"

"Hold up, trick. Let me show you how Shiloh looks like he get down," Tyree said, getting up and lying flat on the carpet. He began grinding slowly, humping the air with one leg up as Layla screamed.

"Yes, baby! Yaaaaas!" she said as they laughed.

I tried my hardest not to smile, but I could see why Shiloh didn't like staying over here when Tyree was here. He was too much.

Suddenly, there was a knock on the door. Tyree got up to answer it, letting in two girls who had drinks in their hands. One of them was pregnant like she was about to pop, and the other looked like she ran her mouth too much, like Layla.

"Welcome! Welcome! I was just telling them how we think Shiloh be having sex, how he be stroking," Tyree said, and they laughed. "Niya and Tiffany, meet Noelle and Layla. My work bitches meeting my ride-or-die hoes."

Once the greetings were out the way and everyone became comfortable with each other, the drinks were passed around to everyone, minus Tiffany, since she was pregnant. Somehow the topic of me not having sex with Shiloh continued to come up. It seemed like everyone wanted to know what he was like, not caring that I was still traumatized over this past weekend.

"Well, before you cut that nigga off completely, you need to go ahead and fuck him one good time. You know how many girls would kill to be with that nigga?" Tiffany asked, rubbing her belly as I rolled my eyes.

"She don't even realize how good she got it," Tyree said, shaking his head. "I be telling her all the time that he don't do that girlfriend shit, so you know he really liked her."

"Whatever. I don't do killers and convicts," I mumbled just as Tyree's phone blared loudly on the coffee table, showing an unknown number.

"Who the fuck is this calling me from . . . probably one of these sorry-ass females in Atlanta, calling me from a house phone, trying to get done up for a club. Honey, I don't do fashion charity," he groaned, answering the phone as he clicked speaker. "Hello?"

"So, you changed yo' number on me, nigga?"

Tyree's face dropped as we all looked at each other, hearing the voice. I recognized it immediately as the one who'd had his hand over my mouth. Tyree's face quickly softened up, and for the first time, the always overly confident, bald-headed gay man I knew him to be looked vulnerable, weak, and afraid to even respond. I'd never seen him like this, but Niya took the phone, seeing Tyree was too shocked to speak.

"Why are you calling him?" Niya asked. "He said he was done. You should be happy now that you got a chance to sleep around without hurting his feelings in the process. Go back to being a ho and leave my nigga alone."

"Niya, get the fuck off the phone and put him back on—"

"You're on speaker!" Layla called out.

"Who the fuck is—"

"Do it matter?" Tiffany chimed in.

"How many of y'all is it? Like, damn! I'm trying to talk to him in private!"

"Tyree, do you want to talk to him?" I asked softly, seeing his eyes about to water up as he shook his head no. He was quiet as a mouse. Unbelievable.

"He said he ain't trying to talk to you," Niya said.

Trell sighed. "Ty, please don't do this to me," he begged softly. "Why you got me on speaker for all these fuck bitches to hear?"

"Who you callin' a bitch?" we all shrieked at the same time before laughing. We definitely weren't going to make it easy for him.

"Whatever you gotta say to him, you can say it to all of us, because guess what, Ontrell? Every time you fucked him over, he came running to us, crying about yo' sorry ass, so you owe us all some type of an apology, explanation, and another apology just because we don't like yo' dog ass," Niya snapped. I wished I had a friend like that.

"Can he hear me at least?" Ontrell asked.

We looked at Tyree, who kept his gaze to the carpet, stuck on sad.

"He can hear you," I said.

"You got a nigga freaking out right now. I thought you would have . . . I don't know . . . called me or something, but I gotta find out you changed yo' number on me? Why won't tell me where you staying at? And you still won't come home?" he asked, voice getting weak.

"I'm sorry, Tyree. You know I am. We got two years of being together. Why you trying to leave me after all that we been through? I don't even know how to fucking function without you, bae. I woke up the other night sick as fuck, and I'm so used to you knowing what to do, telling me what medicine to take and nursing a nigga back to health, but I . . . I don't . . . can you come home, please?" he begged, voice shaking.

I felt my eyes watering up. I started to fan my face, keeping the tears from escaping, seeing the other girls were shaking their heads. Tiffany wiped her eyes, while Layla went to comfort Tyree, who started to cry.

"Ontrell, Ty isn't saying anything right now," Niya said softly.

"Is he still there?" he asked.

Tyree looked at the phone. "I'm here," he answered, voice cracking.

"Come home, Ty. Please come back home. I can't sleep by myself, I can't eat, I can't fucking think without you," Trell begged.

I heard the sounds of a familiar car engine from afar. Shiloh was home. He should have been over here begging for my forgiveness like his younger brother.

"I'm done, Trell. I'm so done. I can't let you put me through the same shit you been doing again—"

"I learned my lesson! I'm done with it. I'm done talking to these bitches and fucking around. None of them can replace what you and I have."

Tyree got up and grabbed the phone. "What we had, nigga," he corrected before hanging up and turning it off altogether.

"That's what the fuck I'm talking about!" Niya cheered. She went to hug him, but he pushed her away.

"Don't do that. I still love that nigga more than I love life itself," he snapped, wiping his eyes. "Shit, we need to go out tonight. And I'm not talking about no local-ass teen club or dry-ass lounge. I want something that is turnt the fuck up before we get there. I ain't got a nigga holding me back, and all y'all bitches single as hell, so let's go."

I groaned, not wanting to leave the house. I was comfortable, and it was cold outside. I didn't feel like stepping out. "Y'all can go ahead," I said, waving them off.

Tyree pursed his lips, taking my hand and yanking me off my seat.

"I don't want to go!" I laughed with a whine.

"Bitch, you already done fucked up with me by not having sex with Shiloh before you decided to cut him off."

"I didn't cut him off! He hasn't called me!"

"Maybe he's waiting on you to call him," Layla suggested.

I rolled my eyes. It was amazing how they stuck up for him because he had a dick that they themselves wanted. Unbelievable.

"Look, we not about to worry about it no more. As far as I know," Tyree started, hand on his chest as he looked at all of us, "we are the finest mothafuckas in Atlanta. We are single, sex game is on point, and we deserve it with all this shit we been through. Let's get out this damn depressing-ass house."

"Hey!" I chimed in, but he waved me off. "My house isn't depressing. It's the people."

"Let's go fuck some shit up!" he continued, stepping onto the couch, drink raised in the air as we looked at this fool. "Let's go take these fuck niggas of Atlanta for everything they got!"

"Whooo!" Niya screamed in agreement. "Preach!"

"We are young, fine as shit. We don't, and will never, settle for anything less!" Tyree screamed out as they all cheered him on.

I stood there, arms crossing over my chest, trying to resist the power of the turn-up speech. I had a sour facial expression.

"I've been living in Atlanta long enough to know that when all else fails?" he screamed out in anticipation. "Nigga, y'all turning the fuck up!"

"Amen!" Tiffany screamed as they laughed.

I shook my head with a smile before walking back toward my room.

"Where you going, chocolate? Don't fight it, boo!" Tyree laughed as I waved him off.

"I'm about to find me an outfit!"

"Aye! Now we got Noelle prude ass on one! Leh go!" Tyree shouted. "Turn that radio on. Let's see where all the parties at in the city tonight."

So, with the music blasting from the DJ on the radio, playing live from a party, I took a much-needed shower, thinking about what to wear. I wanted to take my mind off Shiloh, and if a mindless party was going to do it, by all means, I was down for the cause.

Niya and Tiffany went home, deciding to meet us at the club. Tyree had outfits already picked out from his collection for Layla and me, so once I was done with my shower, I let her take hers, with Tyree following soon after. I definitely needed a music change. With TLC's "No Scrubs" playing throughout the house, I peeped the extremely short dress Tyree had picked out for me. All red—Shiloh's main, and only, color.

"What the fuck is this, Tyree?" I pressed, holding up the silk teddy dress. He stared at me, smiling, with the towel wrapped around his chest like a woman. Layla held up her lace black dress with a smile. It was all see-through.

"Where we going is a lingerie theme party, boo," he said, taking the dress and holding it up to me with a smile. "Girl, trust me! I style women for a living. I know what I'm doing. Hurry up and put y'all shit on so I can do y'all hair and face. I don't let females roll with me looking average, boo." Snapping his fingers, he walked out the room. "Clock is ticking, ladies!"

"Layla, is he serious?" I pressed, looking at her as she smiled.

"Bitch, I like my outfit. I don't know about you, but I love mine." With that, she immediately started to change into hers while I stared at mine.

Fuck it.

Before long, we were both sitting on the edge of the bed, fully dressed, with him finishing up our hair and makeup. Layla had braids, so she just threw her hair into a side ponytail coming down her shoulder. My hair was given a side-swoop bang, with the rest coming to my shoulders. Makeup was flawless. Tyree was definitely an artist with his work. He wore his black, grey, and white skinny harem pants, nearly showing his underwear, and a simple blazer jacket, shirtless underneath, showing off his cut body.

"Damn, look at my bitches," he said, looking back at us both. "Layla, you look like you been fucked too many times and still look good, bitch. I see you!"

"Nigga, shut up!" she snapped as they both laughed.

Then his playful eyes came to me, shaking his head slowly.

"What?" I asked, looking down at my silk dress, barely covering my thighs. My ass pretty much poked the dress out in the back, and my breasts were so out, nipples piercing through. I looked like a sexy porn star with the red heels to match. "I still don't understand why I can't wear a bra."

"Honey, you might just turn a nigga straight for a night," Tyree said, looking me over with his tongue sticking out. I immediately hit him on the chest, and he laughed. "Take it as a compliment, bitch. Damn! I'm not about to actually try you. Vaginas and me don't mix, boo. Something nasty about females."

"Ain't nothing nasty about mine," I retorted, and he smirked at me.

"Oh, I bet," he said.

I hit him again, causing him to laugh. "Can we go? I'm so ready to get the fuck out of here before I break down and start crying over this nigga again."

"We can go," I said, grabbing my house keys. "Whose car are we taking?"

"We can take mine since y'all both staying here," Layla said as we walked toward the front door, coats put on over our scandalous outfits.

Of course, our night that was supposed to be filled with turn-up and forgetting about crazy men turned into the worst night of our lives. We ran out of gas in the middle of the highway. Layla thought it was funny, but Tyree went off on her while we waited for help. I kept checking my phone for any messages from Shiloh. Nothing. Oh! Then, of course, when we got to the party, it was the most freaky, sex-craved, white-people-infested type of party. We were the only blacks there, and Tyree was the only gay there—the only one that was open, at least. He claimed he got somebody's number, but I didn't believe him.

So, we were now at a gas station, parked, going through Facebook and Instagram, trying to find another party to go to. I just wanted to go home. I hated being the one out of the group that was the sulky worry wart, but I was tired. I was too old for this.

Niya and Tiffany had decided to stay in, never even bothering to show up, so it really was just us three.

"Okay, how about this?" Tyree said, popping Skittles into his mouth as he read the party flyer out loud from his Instagram. "Ladies free all night. Dress code is ultra-sexy. It's going to be—ah, hell nah. Nuh-uh, we not doing this one," he said, shaking his head suddenly.

"What does it say?" Layla asked with a laugh before she read the screen. "Fuck no, we not doing that one. Africans are crazy. They party too hard for me."

"Let me text a few people," Tyree said, typing fiercely on his phone.

I sighed in the back seat.

"Bitch, let me hear you sigh one more time and we putting you out this damn car."

"Why can't we just go home?" I flipped. "Obviously it's not meant for us to be out like that!"

"Pass her a bottle," Tyree demanded.

Layla handed me a bottle of vodka. "Drink it and just be chill, Noelle. Relax for once and have a little fun for the night."

I took the bottle but didn't drink it as they continued to look for a party to hit up. When we finally found one that was close by and worth going to, we started the car up and rolled out.

Now, you would think the night would get better, right? Fuck no. The moment we walked in, coats off, looking like we just came from a slumber party for adults, I immediately spotted familiar faces.

"Shit!" Tyree hissed as we entered the small room. "It's packed as fuck in here!"

It seemed like the crowd was at a standstill, with everyone shoulder to shoulder, lights flashing and DJ hollering out to the crowd as "Touchin', Lovin'" by Trey Songz played loudly. It was so hot in there I almost forgot I had taken off my coat already.

"Aye!" Tyree yelled close to my ear. "Let's go stand over there! It's room over there!" He pointed.

We followed his lead, hand in hand, linking up as we maneuvered through the crowd, with me catching the eyes of the familiar faces. Shiloh's friends were there, which meant he was there. I thought he was at the damn house. Looking around, I tried to see if I could spot him, all while keeping up with Tyree and Layla. The moment I saw him, smiling in the face of another girl as he leaned in close, whispering something in her ear, I nearly fell out.

"Do y'all see that?" I screamed, pointing at Shiloh as Ty and Layla looked back, mouths dropped.

"See, I told you you should have called that nigga up," Tyree sang with a laugh and a shrug. "Girl! When I say that nigga is wanted by every bitch in Atlanta, and you were the only one lucky enough to have his attention? You think he was going to wait on you? You see those girls surrounding him?" He pointed as I eyed the girls who were hanging around him, watching, waiting, and looking thirsty. "Bitch! Those are the hoes in line just to get that nigga to smile at them!"

"You should have at least slept with him!" Layla let out. I damn near had to stop myself from hitting her in the face.

"Aye!" Ty called out, getting my attention as he wrapped his arm around my neck, coming down to my level to whisper in my ear. "You see all these niggas that are following behind yo' ass, though?"

I looked around, seeing guys literally watching and waiting for me to break free from Tyree as they started making their way closer to me.

"Bitch, you know they not here for Layla's short ass. They got their eye on you. If you want Shiloh's attention, then, bitch, get that nigga's attention. Keep it classy and cute." With that, he let me go and walked off with a laugh, following behind some man before dipping into a hallway.

Layla turned to me with a wide smile. "I'm about to go get me something to drink. You want anything?" she asked over the music.

I shook my head no, watching her walk off, leaving me alone. The club was so damn packed I couldn't tell who was who, because people were starting to blend in together. Feeling a hand on my lower back, I turned around to see this tall, light-skin guy smiling down at me, wearing all black with a NY fitted cap tipped up.

"Yo, what's good, beautiful?" he asked against my ear. I smiled, loving the northern accent. "I see you got fans, ma," he pointed out as I looked at the guys who couldn't take their eyes off me.

"I guess I do." I laughed with a shrug. He was definitely young in the face, probably younger than me.

"What's your name?" he asked, standing close by me with his arm slinking around my neck.

"Noelle," I told him.

I guess he couldn't hear me, because he bent down to put his ear close to my mouth so I could repeat it.

"Noelle!"

"Ah, shit, that's a beautiful name, baby. Where's yo' dude at? I know you didn't come here by yourself."

"I did," I mouthed.

He dropped his head in a dramatic tone, making me laugh. "Nah, that nigga is gonna pop out somewhere and try and fuck me up for talking to you. Ain't no way you came here with nobody, ma."

"I did!" I laughed. "I'm single for the night."

"Ah, for the night." He nodded, rubbing his chin playfully as I laughed. He was definitely cute. Young, but cute.

"Yo, this for all my wild ATL girls out there that's trying to get down! Here we go!" the DJ yelled as the song switched to Travis Porter, "Make it Rain." Ohhh! I had my hand in the air ready like I was about that life.

"You about that life, ma?" he teased, already coming behind me with his hand on my back, ready to push me forward. His dick was pressing hard against me.

Fuck it. What the hell? Why not? While in Atlanta, right? I bent down and started going slow, waiting for that beat to drop. He had already lifted my dress up to where it was just my ass showing. He was grabbing onto my hips just as Layla came back with her guy, and two drinks in her hand.

"Bitch, I knew you had it in you!" she screamed, handing the two drinks off to the guy as she started dancing.

It was all fun and games until I stood back up, turning around to see NY guy nearly mesmerized.

"Yo, I'm not letting you out of my sight, chocolate! Not for a second, ma!" he let out with his arms wrapping around me, hand gripping my ass.

To say I became uncomfortable was an understatement, but I spotted Shiloh's friend Lamar eyeing me hard before walking back, disappearing into the crowd.

Good. Go run and tell your friend.

"Aye!" I looked up at NY guy, licking his lips as he looked down at me. "You trying to bounce tonight, ma? You want to leave with me for the night?"

"Where would we go?" I questioned, knowing good and well I wasn't going anywhere with him.

"Anywhere you want, ma. I don't see no other female but you tonight," he assured me.

I looked around one last time, hoping Shiloh would at least see me before I decided to take NY's hand, letting him lead the way.

"Noelle!" Layla shrieked, mouth dropped as I followed behind NY, hand in hand, waving at her shocked expression. "Bitch, I know you not about to walk off with this nigga of the minute! You—"

"I'll be back. I'm just stepping outside real quick!" I yelled back over the music before disappearing into the crowd behind him. Looking to my left, I spotted Shiloh, who was definitely looking around with one of his friends, pointing in my direction.

"What up, playboy?" Someone greeted NY as they slapped hands, coming in for a hug with me standing by his side, trying my hardest not to look back. "This you for the night, bruh?"

"Hell yeah. You know I got a thing for chocolate girls," NY said with a laugh as he winked at me.

I put on a fake smile before looking back, seeing Shiloh standing right behind me, eyebrows coming together in confusion. NY didn't even freaking see this man and his crew standing heavy behind him, because he was too busy running his mouth, trying to show me off to his friends.

"So, this how we doing it, Noe?" Shiloh asked, barely audible over the loud music.

"This is how you're doing it, Shiloh! Not me!" I flipped, letting go of NY as I turned my full attention to him. "You didn't call me, you never came to see me, and the first time I'm seeing you, you smiling in the face of another girl!"

"Noe, we not—"

NY guy immediately pushed me behind him as he stepped to Shiloh, who just looked annoyed, head tilting to the side.

"Yo, we got a problem, B? You fucking with my girl?" NY pressed, back hunched over as Shiloh's lips pursed, expression beyond irritated. I tried to step in between, hoping not to let this get any further than it already had.

"Wait, don't—"

"Nah, baby, I got you! These niggas down here be disrespectful as fuck! You seen me with her. Why the fuck you trying to come at her like—"

"Bruh, you making me uncomfortable. Back up," Shiloh said calmly before looking dead at me. "Noe, if you want to talk, want me to explain everything, then we can talk. But I'm not doing this shit in front of everybody."

I stepped in between them, putting my hand on NY's stomach to back him up, because I already knew what Shiloh was capable of.

"It's fine. I know him," I told NY, trying to calm him down.

"I don't give a fuck if you do or not. That was straight disrespectful, son!" He flipped.

Shiloh cocked his head back slightly, almost smirking, like he was trying to keep himself from laughing. I rarely say the N word, but this nigga was sick in the head, and I couldn't believe I still liked someone like him.

"I don't play that shit! You saw her with me and you still—"

"I'm a disrespectful-ass mothafucka, bruh. Fuck you still in my face for?" Shiloh retorted as his friends laughed.

Oh, Lord. It was my first time hearing him be sarcastic. At least I hoped it was sarcasm. Either way, NY didn't take it too well.

"You think you funny, nigga? You think—"

"Aye!" Lamar snapped, stepping up. "Nigga, this is his girl in the first—"

"Ohhh! So you do got a nigga!" NY laughed, looking hard at me as I swallowed a pit of nerves. I wasn't even fucking drunk, so I couldn't blame it on the alcohol like I wanted to. I had caused all of this.

"I am so sorry," I told NY, hoping he would drop it, because I could see his friends start to round up behind him. "I didn't mean to lead—"

"Noelle?" Shiloh called out, hands in his pockets. "We leaving." With that, he walked off with his crew, and I shamefully followed behind, with a few of his friends keeping me close. No doubt, the whole club was watching about thirty-something guys slowly make their way through the crowd with ease as we walked out the main doors after grabbing my coat.

Waiting by his car as he finished up talking, I texted Tyree and Layla that I was leaving with him. I hated that I even . . . Why was I still entertaining this man even the slightest bit after what I saw? He was crazy, mean, ruthless, and reckless with his anger, yet here I was, waiting by his car like a fucking idiot.

Watching him walk back with that strut like he was cool with his life, I pursed my lips together with attitude as he unlocked the doors. Slipping inside, he cut the car on, letting the engine roar before cutting the heat on. He reached in the back seat, grabbing my pink blanket, and handed it to me.

"Thanks," I mumbled, covering my legs as I looked at him, watching him look at me with those low eyes.

"Why the fuck you wearing that?" he asked.

I looked down at myself, wrapped in the pink blanket. He couldn't even begin to think about all the questions I had for his ass.

"Why did you threaten to kill someone with a gun? Why when I first met you, you put a gun to my head? Why do I see you after a week of ignoring me, smiling in another girl's face at a club? Huh?" I snapped, looking hard at him. "Why, Shiloh, do you smile so easily with other girls, but not with me? Why?" I shook my head as I looked out the window, trying to hold back tears. "Why the fuck am I still in this car with you even through all of that? Why do I still like you?" I mumbled, more to myself than him.

Feeling the car move, I looked at him, watching him back out of his parking space. "Where are we going?"

"We just riding, Noe," was all he said, cutting his radio on.

With him slowly trying to explain himself and the situation with his sister, I somewhat understood his actions. Somewhat. Yes, if that was me, I would want someone to defend my honor as much as he did his younger sister. Occasionally glancing at him, watching him play with a toothpick in his mouth, leaned back in the seat with a gun in his lap and one hand on the wheel, I sighed. We had to be on the highway for at least a good hour, maybe even more. I had no clue where we were going, but it was definitely away from the city life. People think of Atlanta, and only Atlanta, when they think of Georgia, not realizing there is no difference between Alabama and South Carolina. It was nothing but fields, dirt roads, and peach trees if you drove through Peach County. It's a typical country state.

Sitting up, I rolled the window completely down, letting my hair whip in the cold wind, smiling as I took in the smell of clean air. Cold, but clean. I was feeling closer to home than ever. I looked back at Shiloh. He gave me a side glance and a small smile.

"What you feeling right now, Noe?" he asked softly as I rolled the window back up.

"Like I'm home. I've been homesick for the longest," I told him, and he nodded.

"You want to drive?"

"I don't know how to drive this thing." I laughed, watching him pull over on the side of the road. "Shiloh! I'm serious! I don't know how to drive this thing!"

"You can drive a car, shawty. This is no difference. Just more powerful," he said. "You can drive stick, right?"

"Yeah, but—" I watched him get out as I hopped over to the driver's seat, forgetting about the blanket as I closed the door.

Oh, Lord. Hearing the cars zoom by fast had my nerves on an all-time high as he got in the passenger's seat, putting the blanket over him, leaning the seat back even farther. "Shiloh, what if I—"

"Just drive, baby," he said calmly, opening the glove compartment to pull out a small bag of weed.

I checked to make sure signal lights were working, then cut the lights on and off before finally merging back onto the highway, driving like a slow grandma. The gas pedal was so strong. I blinked and it jerked forward.

"Where are we going?" I asked, watching him light up his joint.

"Wherever you want to go, baby," he said, smoke pouring out of his mouth.

I smiled, hearing the radio softly play throughout the car. I looked over at him, seeing he was looking at me, watching me drive.

"What, Shiloh?" I smiled softly, seeing him return the smile, eyes heavy.

"You still fucking with a nigga," he said in a low voice.

I just nodded. I had no other response, because I didn't halfway understand why I would even entertain someone as dangerous as him.

"Even after what you saw, and knowing how I am, you still down for me."

"I guess so." I shrugged, looking in the rearview mirror. "I like you. You might be a little scary at times, but . . . you're no different from the rest of us. You have feelings like everyone else. You just hide it better."

"Yeah," he agreed in a low voice, taking a pull on his joint. "You out of my league, Noe. I never dealt with a girl like you before. Make a nigga nervous being around you."

"Me? Make you nervous?" I laughed, glancing at him, seeing he was serious. I could feel the cold air hit hard as he rolled the window down. "How is that even possible?"

"I don't know, but I want to be honest as fuck with you about everything," he said, turning the radio down a little bit as I began to cruise comfortably on the two-lane highway. "Ask me anything, and I'll tell you."

I looked at him as he leaned back in his seat, comfortable, joint already finished as he tossed it out the window, blowing a thick white cloud of smoke out his nose before rolling the window back up.

"Why did you get locked up?" I asked suddenly, lining up the list of questions I had for him in my head.

"Gang-related activity. Weapons charge, assault, domestic violence bullshit," he said, voice getting hard.

"What do you mean, domestic violence?" I pressed, glancing at him.

"My mama called the cops on me when I tried protecting her from my pops," he spat hatefully. "Fuck that bitch. Haven't spoken to her since. Never will I speak to her again. Don't ever ask me about her or my dad again."

I nodded, hearing that it was a definite sore spot for him.

"Do you have any kids?"

"None that I know of," he said, shrugging as he rubbed his chin smoothly.

"Do you want any?"

"Two girls, one boy," he said, and I smiled. I wanted two boys and one girl.

"Have you ever been in love before?" I asked.

He became completely still, body stiff as the emotions went across his face. His eyes were searching, like he was remembering something, before his face became blank.

"One time."

Another sore spot. I wondered who the girl was that caught the hard heart of Shiloh, and how she did it.

"Have you ever . . . killed someone? Or shot somebody?" I asked hesitantly.

He just looked at me as we locked eyes. His red, low-lit eyes stared expressionlessly back at me. I took a deep swallow, knowing that was a yes. He didn't have to answer it, and I didn't think he was going to ever answer it. The look in his eyes that day said he didn't value human life once he was crossed.

I looked at the road, thinking about my next question.

"Have you ever hit a girl?"

"No."

"Have you ever cheated while in a relationship?"

"Never been in a real relationship before," he stated.

I glanced at him. So, who was the girl he was in love with before?

"I'm your first girlfriend at twenty-eight, Shiloh?" I teased.

"I don't commit myself to someone or something unless it's worth my time."

I smiled, glancing over at him again before looking back at the road, getting off the main highway. The streets were so empty, so peaceful and quiet. There was nothing out there for miles, except fields of whatever was being grown.

"Can I ask my questions now?"

"Oh? You have questions you want to ask me? I'm not as crazy as you are." I laughed before shrugging cutely. "Ask anyway."

He fell silent as I pulled up to a gas station with only two pumps working. It was barely lit, as the lights flickered, and the small store looked full of inventory with nobody inside. He leaned in close as his eyes fell to my body slowly, lip tucked in as his attention went to my thighs. He tapped gently on my right thigh, tugging at his lower lip as he looked up at me again.

Oh, shit . . .

"When you gon' let a nigga have you?" he asked in a low voice.

I felt my mouth go dry as I looked at him. Looking down at his hand still tapping my thigh, I could feel my body respond strongly, just from that basic touch.

"I . . . I don't know, Shiloh," I fumbled, looking at his mouth.

He stared at me before slowly leaning in and kissing me gently on the lips. My hands gripped the steering wheel hard as he moved his head to push deeper against my mouth, tongues naturally playing. Right when his hand was about to slide in between, there was a hard knock on the window, causing me to jump with a shriek. We both looked up to see this short white man standing there with a bat in his hand.

"You here getting gas or playing around?" he spat, pushing his glasses up as he stared at us through the window, bent down so he was eye level. There was no way he could see us through the tinted window, but we certainly saw him.

I looked at Shiloh, who was still leaned in close to me.

"You still homesick, shawty?" he asked.

I rolled my eyes, watching him throw on his coat before hopping out, gun tucked behind him. He towered over the man, and the white guy backed up a little, looking up at Shiloh, who was barely five foot ten.

"Is there a problem?" Shiloh asked blatantly at the man, who shook his head.

"I get a lot of whack jobs coming by here messing up my store, stealing my shit, so I'm always careful about who comes by here in the middle of the morning," the man said, trying to explain himself. "How much you want on gas?"

Soon as we left the gas station, we decided to find the nearest hotel and rest there for the night, not wanting to drive back to Atlanta until we woke up. Unfortunately, it was a ratty motel with the neon flashing one letter, the O. Not seeing anything for miles, phones barely charged, we decided to just rest there for the night.

He got the room key, and the moment we stepped inside, I nearly fainted. The red carpet was stained with thick dirt and mold. Walls were a funky floral print wallpaper, matching the small bed. An old TV sat on the dresser, and the nightstand lamp had a red lightbulb. Shiloh wasted no time going to the bathroom to pee like he was home, but I could barely allow myself to sit on the bed without being disgusted. There was a small mirror up against the wall where the bathroom sink was, just outside the bathroom door, and an ironing board up against the wall. You could hear the sounds of people next door to us laughing, or maybe it was their TV. Either way, I didn't know how I was going to get any sleep that night.

"Aye," Shiloh said as he walked out of the bathroom, completely shirtless and pantless. His hand was in his boxer briefs as I looked his body over. Tattoos were perfectly placed against his light complexion. "You hungry or nah?"

"Not really. I just want to get some sleep and leave this place," I said, looking around before standing up. "How does the bathroom look?"

"It's straight, Noe." He smiled with a shake of his head. "Quit being a baby. This shit could be worse."

"I don't live in filth, Shiloh. Sorry, but I don't," I retorted as I walked past him to get to the bathroom.

It was the quickest shower I ever took in my life. I ended up washing my panties since there was no clean pair for me to change into. Because I didn't want my feet touching the carpet, I kept my heels on until I got to the bed, wearing my dress, body soaking through the thin material. Shiloh was sitting on the edge of the bed with his back toward me, talking on his phone as I grabbed his shirt to put on instead. Fuck it. With no bra, wet panties hanging to dry, and no socks or regular shoes in this dirty-ass motel room, I was irritated, but I wasn't going to let it show.

"Yeah, a'ight bet, bruh," he said, hanging up.

He looked back at me and stared, eyes wide.

"I know what it looks like," I mumbled with a roll of my eyes. I didn't use the towels to dry my body off, and once I put on his white shirt, my body pretty much seeped through that too. He could see an outline of dark skin pressing against the white material, my nipples staying on hard. "I don't want to touch their towels."

"So, you put my shirt on instead?" he questioned as I smiled.

"You sleep naked anyway."

"Mannn." He sighed, dragging a hand over his face slowly with a frustrated groan. "You don't know how bad I want you right now. I don't know how the fuck I'm going to get some sleep with you looking like that."

"We can put pillows between us," I suggested with a laugh as he shook his head.

He got up and cut the main light off, keeping on the red light from the lamp as he lay down next to me.

"Yo, you want some music to sleep to?" he asked, glancing at me. "Drown out the sounds of people next door and shit?"

I nodded, and he grabbed his phone off the nightstand, putting it on Pandora. The moment I heard "Bump & Grind," I immediately hit him hard in the arm.

"What I do?" He laughed.

"You're trying to set the mood, Shiloh."

"Baby, if you not ready for sex, you not ready. You see me trying you?" he pressed. "I haven't even touched you, and I don't plan on it."

"Yeah, right," I mumbled, suddenly wanting him to try to touch me. Funny how that works. I inched closer to him, resting my head against his shoulder. R. Kelly was singing the hell out of this song. When he didn't react to my physical advances toward his body, I sighed.

"Shiloh?" I asked, looking up at him, red light bouncing low off of us as he looked at me. "I'm ready."

He slowly closed his eyes, licking his lips, almost like he had been anticipating something happening. "Ready for what, Noe?"

"You." He stayed quiet. "To have me." It became so quiet that even R. Kelly almost sounded like he toned it down a little bit.

He got up from the bed and disappeared around the small corner before appearing back at the edge of the bed. I lay flat on my back as he grabbed my ankles to gently pull me closer to him. My heart was beating so fast I didn't know what to expect. I'd never had any type of sexual experience, not even oral. I was so nervous I could barely hold it in.

"I'm not going to know what to do," I spat out quickly as he leaned down on the bed, slipping the shirt over my head, exposing my naked frame. "I don't know how to—"

"Chill, Noe," he mumbled, eyes roaming hard.

My heart . . . I could barely breathe. There was no way in hell I was ready for this. I wasn't ready.

When his eyes landed on my face, we just stared at each other before he dropped his head with a big sigh. "You not ready for me. I can tell."

"I just imagined me getting married before doing this," I argued with a small whine, hearing him sigh once again.

The music played softly in the background as he leaned down, delicately kissing my breasts before laying down beside me, tossing the condom wrapper on the floor as he closed his eyes. I hated that I did this to him. I knew there were girls that were probably throwing themselves at him every chance they got, while he was stuck waiting on me.

"Shiloh, if you want to have sex, I won't care if you sleep with someone else. I know men have—"

He turned around to look at me with his brows furrowed deep in confusion. "What the fuck is that supposed to mean, Noelle?" he snapped as my mouth dropped.

"I just don't like feeling like you have to wai—"

"So, you want me to fuck other bitches? While I'm with you?"

I said nothing. He just rolled his eyes, cutting the music and lamp off before turning over in the bed with his back facing me.

"Shiloh?" I called out softly, realizing how that must have sounded. I really didn't know what else to say. "Shi—"

"Don't talk, shawty. Sit there and think about that stupid-ass shit you just said to me," he retorted angrily. "I told you I would wait on you. I don't have a fucking issue waiting on you to be ready, because if I think it's worth my time, then I'll commit to that shit. Didn't I say that?"

I said nothing. Just lay there in silence.

"Fuck outta here with that 'sleep with another bitch' bullshit," he mumbled. "Don't ever try me like that again. In yo' life."

That entire night, I didn't sleep one bit. You know how you close your eyes, but your mind is so wide awake with thoughts that it's impossible to sleep? Mentally, you're up and about. I thought about everything that had happened between us; how through it all, I was still with him, even though I had the chance to back away. I was curious to see where Shiloh and I would end up. It hadn't been that long, but I knew God put him in my life for a reason, and my daddy always told me I would know it when I found the right man for me.

So, the next time we woke up, he was obviously still upset. He refused to speak to me while we got ready, so when we got back in the car, stopping at a local corner store to grab something to eat, he stood outside his car on the phone, talking business while I stepped in the store, wearing some of his sweats that he had in the trunk of his car, along with a hoodie. I was looking like a pure stud, with my ponytail bouncing with every step, clothes literally draped on me. When I walked back out, he was leaning against the car with his jeans and shoes on, thermal shirt, and thick Nike hoodie. Neither one of us dressed to impress, because this was a random road trip we took. So, with the small black bag in hand, I stepped toward him, making sure I stood directly in front of him as he glanced down at me.

"Nah, I'll probably be back tomorrow," he said, looking me over. "Yeah, tell them mothafuckas to hold off on that shit. Tell Tana to stand down."

"Shiloh?" I pressed. He ignored me, hand placed on my side to move me out the way, but I wasn't going anywhere.

"Yeah, we can do that. Move all of it out of Atlanta by tonight. I don't want to see no trace of it," he continued with me stepping closer.

"Shiloh?"

"Hold up, bruh," he said before staring hard at me. "Noelle, what the fuck you want?" I ignored the attitude and smiled sweetly, overlooking the fact that he was still irritated with me.

"I just wanted to say I apologize for what I said last night. I want to thank you for not pressuring me into sex," I continued, reaching up to kiss his cheek gently. "And that I am in love with you. That's all," I said before quickly turning to walk to the other side of the car, leaving him speechless.

Tia

"What!" I flipped at my roommate as I stood outside her room door, arms crossed, watching her put on her shoes. "You want me to do what, Jade?"

"We are going to Jordyn's house to apologize," she said.

I just stared at my roommate, who looked at herself in the mirror, checking her face. She had finally changed her hair color back to natural black, letting that blond shit go, because it did nothing for her complexion. Her thick locs, barely hitting her shoulders, were a natural dark brown, complementing her skin tone and somehow making her pretty. Shit, maybe she'd gotten her eyebrows done. I don't know, but there was definitely something different about her. With cute silver beads on some of the locs, she grabbed her room keys and walked out with her coat in hand, expecting me to follow.

"I'm sorry, but I don't want to have to apologize to the girl's face," I retorted as Jade looked back at me, slipping on her white coat with a flip of her dreads. "I'm not going."

"Fine, but I'm apologizing, because turns out, Trent is a fuck-ass nigga after all, and we fucked with Jordyn for no reason. You were jealous because she got Elijah, and I thought I was defending my man." She shrugged. "We all dating brothers at the end of the day, and you're going to eventually run into her one of these days. If Elijah finds out it was you that fucked with her, do you honestly think Jahiem is going to fuck with you afterwards? Or the fact that you slept with Trent the night before Jahiem, and

the only person who knows that outside of me is Jordyn?"
she stated as I dropped my head in shame.

Shit. Even I couldn't deny the fact that Jordyn was the
key to the Carters. Of all the girls I couldn't stand, Jordyn
was the one bitch I needed on my side more than ever
now. She could make or break me at this point. She was
in good with the brothers, who treated her like their own
sister. At least that was how Jahiem put it.

"Let me get dressed," I mumbled, walking back to
my room to throw on some cute skinny sweats and a
matching hoodie. My ass was poking out as I put on some
makeup. My hair was wrapped up neatly in the fresh
weave I'd sewed in the night before, and my nails had a
fresh coat of polish. I was supposed to be spending the
night with Jahiem, but he and his brothers were shooting
a music video over on the south side. Saturday in Atlanta,
everyone was out at some event, despite it being cold
as fuck. People were out doing something, getting it in
before Thanksgiving hit. Walking out of the room, I followed Jade out of the apartment as we walked in silence.

"You think she's going to forgive me?" I asked, and
Jade shrugged.

"As long as you get that shit off yo' chest, do it matter?
It's on her, but it was too easy fucking her ass up that day."

"It was." I laughed, feeling my phone vibrate. I looked
at the incoming text from Jahiem. It was a picture of a
crib he saw in a magazine.

He was asking me, What about this one?

Zooming in, the moment I saw the wheels on it, I was
done.

I texted him, No to the wheels, nigga.

"Where she stay at?"

"Over there in the woods where all the Greek houses
are at. Her and that girl she stay hanging with. What's
her name? Rita or some shit?"

"I don't know," I said, waving her off as we stepped out into the parking lot of our building, that cold air whipping us hard. "Ooooh, shit! It's cold!" I shrieked. "We walking to her place?"

"Well, neither one of us got a car, so . . ."

"Shit!" I flipped again, stuffing my hands in my pockets as we walked across the yard to the back woods of the school. Nobody was out that night. The yard was completely dead. It was too cold, and it was a Saturday night too. Nobody was trying to hang outside in the middle of November like that in Atlanta. We turn up indoors, bruh.

"You think she'll give us a ride back?" I joked, and we laughed, trudging our way to cross the street, officially stepping off the yard. I couldn't believe I was going to apologize to this girl. I never apologized to no bitch. I mean, I was sorry, but I didn't think I had to speak on that shit.

Walking up alongside the dark street, we came up to a small house with the porch light lit.

"This is it?" I asked, blowing hot air into my hands.

Jade nodded as we walked up on the grass, making our way to the front door to knock. As soon as the door pulled back to open, Jordyn stood in shorts and shirt, with those infamous thick socks. Her black curly hair was all over the place, with those thick-rimmed glasses on. Whatever Elijah was doing to her, bitch was getting thick in the hips.

"Yo, can we come in?" Jade asked, and Jordyn stepped aside, allowing us to walk in.

I looked her directly in the eye, and for the first time, she didn't look away. She just stared back.

Oh, okay, bitch. You bold, I see. Got some of that brave dick hitting you every night, you think you about it. Don't get stupid, though. Pregnant or not, I will still tap that ass.

Stepping into her house, I looked around, seeing she had her basic shit: couch, chair, TV, and dining room set. Nothing fancy. I sat down on the first spot available, and Jade took the seat next to me, while Jordyn sat on the chair, tying up her hair in a bun.

"So, look." Jade sighed as she dropped her head. "I'm sorry for how I treated you this semester, Jo. I know it's not a possibility of us being friends, but I do want you to know I am truly sorry for the fucked-up shit I did. For the fight. And if Elijah was here, I would apologize to him, too. So, on your behalf, I am sorry to him, too, for how I came at him. I just—" She stopped as she stared at her hands. I nearly had to do a double take, seeing tears forming in her eyes. "Trent has been cheating on me this whole time, and I just . . . before I go off on this nigga and break it off, I wanted to clear the air with everyone. All three of us are dating brothers, and none of us are cool like that."

Jordyn pushed her glasses up as she looked at me like she was waiting for me to say something.

"I'm sorry I don't have a long-ass speech like that," I started, patting the side of my head to scratch my weave. "But what I did was fucked—"

"You treated me like shit from the moment you met me, Tia," Jordyn started as I cocked my head back.

Oh, okay, bitch! So we really doing this.

"Okay, first of all," I started, finger already pointing. "You were acting weird as fuck when we met. Did I like you on sight? Fuck no, I didn't. You tried waaay too hard, Jordyn. You tried so hard to be cool like—"

"I didn't give a fuck about being cool and being cute, and whatever the fuck else you want to say. You did! All of y'all are so focused on fucking image and looking a certain way that because I was the one girl who stood out, who didn't care, y'all treated me like an outcast. I tried telling you

Trent made a pass at me," she said, pointing at Jade before turning her attention to me. "I don't even . . ." She stopped, shaking her head with a laugh as she got up. "You and I will never be anything other than two people sitting across from each other right now."

"Bitch, I didn't come here to be friends with you!" I snapped, standing up. "You really think I'm the type of bitch to beg for friends? I whooped yo' ass, and I will do it again if—"

"Tia!" Jade snapped, pulling me back down on the couch. "Both of y'all need to stop it! We didn't come here to argue."

I took deep breaths, gripping my stomach to remind myself I was pregnant with a child. I almost forgot I was carrying a baby, because I would have surely crossed this table to get at Jordyn and fucked that face up once more.

I'm a mother now. Mothers don't fight basic bitches. Gotta keep telling myself that.

"Why are you here, Tia?" Jordyn asked, standing up with her hands on her hips.

"To apologize for fighting you that day."

"Why did you even hit me? It still doesn't make sense why you don't like me, because whatever you just told me wasn't a valid—"

"She was jealous of you," Jade snapped as I looked hard at her. "Look, keep that shit one hundred, ma. You've always been jealous of Jordyn from day one. Now she got the nigga you wanted, and that made it worse. Jordyn, when a girl don't like you for no reason, that shit is jealousy and hate. Tia came over here to apologize for that jealousy and hate, because now that's she's a part of the family with this baby, she wants to make amends. Right, Tia?" Jade pressed as she gave me a hard look.

I bit the bullet on this one as I looked at Jordyn. *Stupid bitch.*

"That's right," I answered instead with a fake smile.

"What's done is done," was all Jordyn said with a wave of her hand as she walked to her room before coming back out with sweats and hoodie on. "We will never be anything other than what it is now. You don't have to talk to me, and I don't have to respond to you."

"Fine with me, bitch," I mumbled, and Jade hit my arm.

"You can apologize to Elijah yourself if you want to, Jade. I'm going to their video shoot right now if you want to come," Jordyn suggested, slipping on her coat.

"Trent's not there, right?" she asked hesitantly.

Jordyn shook her head as Jade and I stood up, making our way out the front door. Jade looked at me with a knowing look, and I shoved my hands in my pockets. I wasn't walking back to the apartment. *I'll be damned.*

"Aye, can Tia come too?" Jade asked.

Jordyn didn't even respond as she opened the car door to get in. Shit, we took it as a yes. I sat in the cramped back seat, holding onto my stomach as I texted Porscha. I knew she wasn't going to ever believe what the fuck I was doing.

The ride to the shoot was uncomfortable to say the least. Jade and Jordyn were barely making light conversation. Hooking her phone up to the radio, Jordyn dialed a number that rang through the car speakers.

"Yo," Elijah answered, and I heard all the commotion in the background. "Where you at, baby?" I almost cringed at the thought of him calling her that.

"I'm on my way now. What am I supposed to be doing, Elijah?"

"You're the leading lady, shawty. Mannn, wait until you see the bitch they got to play my girl for this video, Jordyn. They had to have picked her ass up from the streets. Bitch looked like she was cracked out. Aye!" he called out to someone as I smiled. "Bring it closer this way, Mike!"

"Was she at least pretty?" Jordyn continued, and Elijah laughed.

"Nah, we got the same taste in women, baby. I'ma show you her when you get here. Body was banging, though, but you know me. Weave was fucked up, no edges and shit. You know how a nigga be about that hair," he stated, and I tried so hard not to laugh. He sounded so much like Jahiem just then, it was uncanny. "What you doing afterwards? You staying with me tonight?"

"I don't know yet. I had someone coming over," she said softly, almost like she wasn't trying to say it.

What the fuck kind of relationship do they have? Same taste in women? Niggas coming over? But y'all together?

"We'll see when you get here," was all he said, and Jordyn sighed. "Yo, hurry up." With that, he hung up.

Jade looked at Jordyn. "What's up with these Carter boys being pretty boys?" Jade started as Jordyn and I laughed. "I thought it was just Trent, but apparently not."

"Nooo! Elijah stays looking in a mirror," Jordyn stated with a shake of her head. "If my hair isn't right, he will fix it to his liking before we step out."

"That's nothing," I mumbled with a smile. "Jahiem will damn near cuss me out if I don't look a certain way. What the fuck you got on, Tiana?" I said, mocking his voice, and we all laughed. "When the nigga be bumming it out all the damn time. I can't even wear makeup around him."

"Shit, I wish I could go without makeup for a day without Trent saying something," Jade chimed in. "Do they snore in their sleep?"

"Ohhhhh! Gurl!" I flipped, hands in the air like I was praising the Lord. "Yasss! Jahiem sounds like a fucking monster in the bed!"

"Can't be no worse than Trent."

"Thankfully, Elijah doesn't do that. He moves in his sleep a lot, but he doesn't snore."

"How did you even meet that nigga, Jordyn? Like, real shit. You don't go nowhere, so how did you meet Elijah?"

"At a gas station." She laughed as she thought back. "Him and his brothers pulled up so loudly and obnoxious, and you know I don't keep up with this Atlanta music. So, I didn't know who he was," she said, shrugging as she got off the highway. "He came after me so hard, and I kept turning him down until finally, I just asked him to have sex with me. Vibrators weren't doing the job no more."

"Vibrators!" Jade and I shrieked before laughing.

"You guys were so busy bashing me all the time and making fun of me. Had you actually sat down and got to know me, you would know I'm . . . probably the biggest sex whore you'll ever meet," she said sarcastically, poking fun at herself. "I love men, and I love women."

A proud ho, I see.

"That was you that night! You and Elijah! When we heard the screaming?" Jade let out, and Jordyn nodded. "Oh my God! Girl, you were giving that nigga the business, yo. You gotta teach me all the shit you know."

"I remember that night," I said, thinking back.

"After that night, Elijah really hasn't left."

"So, Elijah doesn't care that you like girls?" I asked.

She shook her head. "There have been a few times that we will go out to meet girls to bring back to his place for the night. It only becomes a problem when the girl doesn't want to leave."

"I can't believe you're like that, Jo. You look so fucking innocent," Jade said with a stunned expression.

"I have certain needs that only a woman can fulfill," she said, shrugging.

Bisexual proud ho. I knew something was off about her weird ass.

"Hey, this is weird to ask, but during sex, do y'all men always make these weird grunt-like noises and ask if you like what they're doing?" Jade asked.

I laughed, already hearing Jahiem in my head. "Girl, Jahiem is a fucking beast in the bed. And he do ask me all the time, but shoot, I be so focused on the dick that I don't even care. I'll answer whatever if you keep going, nigga. Shit," I said, and they laughed. "That's how my ass is pregnant now, fucking around with him."

"Trent likes it rough," Jade said with a slow smile. "Nigga will choke, bite, pull, slap as hard as he wanna. I be telling him to slow that shit down, because sometimes I want something more sensual, soft. Make love to a bitch, like damn, nigga," she let out, and we laughed.

"I like it rough, too. I can't handle it slow. Drives me fucking insane," Jordyn said with a shake of her head. "That's why I almost always dominate Elijah, because the moment I let him get control, it's done."

"Fuck that. Jahiem give it to me different every time, so I can't complain," I boasted with a smile. "Whatever the mood is for the night is what we doing."

"Amen," Jordyn agreed softly, and I smiled.

"So, y'all have an open relationship?" Jade pressed.

I sat up curiously, wanting to hear about this shit. This foolery.

"Yeah, but . . . it's complicated. He can go out and sleep with whoever, because of who he is, but if I do it, it's a problem," she stated, and I shook my head. "I've been talking to this guy for about a week or so, and I really like him. He's . . . the first guy I met that doesn't want sex. We hang out, go to the movies, work out together, and just do whatever."

"Elijah doesn't know?" I asked.

"Nope. I have to tell him soon, because everything him and I are doing has to stop if I want to give this relationship a chance with Desmond."

"Well, is the sex with Desmond good at least?" I asked.

"I don't know yet. We never had sex yet," she beamed, sounding so excited.

Mmmph. It's nice when a man wants to get to know a woman without sex being involved, but that shit is scary, too, because if that nigga turn out to have a li'l dick, or that stroke game is weaker than a basic bitch? Uhh . . . you got to make that life decision on whether you want to stay and train, or bounce. Shit, or hope that head game is twice as strong.

"I can't believe we're dating brothers," Jade mumbled as Jordyn turned down a street where a bunch of cars were parked alongside the curb. I could see huge stage lights flashing down and a crowd of people on the side, watching the commotion. Video girls walked by wearing their best, and I suddenly felt like a slob. Shit, had I known, I would have come better prepared.

Getting out of the car, I could already see Elijah and Jahiem talking with the director, while the other two brothers were enjoying the company of the women, chopping it up with the whole neighborhood that came out to show love. Walking slowly up to the chaos, Jordyn waved at Elijah, who immediately rushed over, all smiles, before glancing at Jade and me. His dreads were loose, and his straight-leg jeans were sagging. He wore a thick black coat with the fur on the hood. He was decorated in chains, rings, and all in all, still looked good as fuck. It's one thing to look like a street nigga; it's another to truly be a street nigga to the core. Yet, the moment his eyes landed on Jordyn, everything hard about him softened up. He looked at her like she was the reason he was alive.

Jahiem don't look at me like that.

"I brought her along because she had something to say to you," Jordyn said to Elijah, who looked at Jade.

"Look, I know we not gonna ever be cool, but I apologize for how I came at you that day, B. And I already told her I was fucked up for what I did," Jade said, accent heavy as Elijah just looked at her, eyes squinting before looking at Jordyn.

"You good with her, baby?" he said, hands cupping her face.

"I'm over it," she said, nodding her head.

I smiled, watching him kiss her before whispering something against her ear as Jordyn looked around.

"Nah, don't look around, shawty. Damn!" He laughed. "Be cool about that shit. She's over there." He pointed, and we all turned to see the girl he was talking about in the car. Yeah, she did look cracked out, like she was a retired stripper. "You see that fuck shit? That's the girl they trying to get for me? Fuck nah."

"She's pretty," Jordyn said, and Elijah rolled his eyes.

"You would hit it?"

"Not if my life depended on it," she said, and he laughed.

"Aye! E! Bring her on so we can get these scenes knocked out!" a man yelled.

The moment Jordyn left, it was just Elijah, Jade, and me, standing there as he looked at her.

"We good, son?" Jade asked.

"If my girl good with you, then I'm good with you," he cheesed, turning that boyish charm on before turning to look at me. "So, you the other bitch that fought Jordyn? Do Jahiem know you fought my girl because of me?"

"Nigga, correct yo'self. Don't call me no bitch," I snapped. His hands went up in the air in surrender with a laugh. "And no, he doesn't. Just like Jordyn doesn't know that you and I almost fucked." I hoped to leave it at that and never speak on it again.

"You got it, shawty. Jahiem is over there if you trying to talk to him." He pointed far off, and I walked away from them.

I watched them cue a scene, and the music started playing loudly. It was Jahiem's part. He leaned on a car with two girls dancing on him while he recited his lyrics to the song, wearing all black, with a thick red coat with brown fur on the hood. He had chains around him, jeans sagging, and a trimmed goatee with a fresh barber cut. My man was fine as hell, okay? The moment they were done, he cut his eyes toward me before rushing over.

"What you doing here, baby?" he said quickly as he gently hugged me like I was eight months pregnant before kissing me on the lips.

"Long story." I sighed. "You look good out there."

"I know." He smirked with a wink before kissing me hard on the cheek. "Yo, stay put. Let me finish up my shit, baby."

Watching him walk off with the director, I smiled. Other girls were eyeing me in pure jealousy. Looking back, I saw Jade nearly crying in front of Elijah, who was talking to her like he was trying to calm her down.

So, Trent really is cheating on her. Mmmph. Trent was a selfish-ass nigga, naturally. It was only a matter of time before she found out anyway.

Walking farther into the video set, I saw where they had a house open, with people walking in and out. So, I stepped in, seeing the makeup artist hard at work, stylist changing the clothes, and directors and producers talking. Assistants were running around. There was so much chaos in the small-ass house. I spotted Jordyn in the corner, already dressed in the outfit that they gave her. She was getting her makeup and hair done.

"Hey, Ontrell! Did you call your brother? We need a whole gang of Atlanta guys present within the next fifteen minutes!" someone yelled out as everyone continued to run around, making the small house so chaotic.

I looked at Ontrell, who was on the phone, and smiled. He looked like his older brother Anthony. They were both dark brown with dreads, although Ontrell had his head shaved on the sides and back, with his locs pulled in a ball on top.

These damn Carter boys. And I wasn't even talking about the rap group, just the brothers in general.

Suddenly, I heard the music go off to their new song, and I stepped back outside, with them guiding Jordyn out behind me. They were doing Jahiem's part again, with Elijah singing in the back, sitting on top of the car with a girl, while Jahiem took center stage to rap. With Jade coming to stand beside me, we ended up watching Jordyn's video debut as they told her she was the love interest of Elijah. She was the girl he was going to be singing to. I'm not even going to lie—I was almost happy for her. Damn near wanted to shout out, "That's my roommate!" In between takes, he would continue to sing to her, and I caught them kissing quietly amongst the chaos as he spoke against her mouth.

"Look, I know I didn't care for the bitch in the beginning," I started, looking at Jade. "But they are the cutest thing next to Jahiem and me."

"Jahiem look means as fuck, yo," Jade said as we looked at my nigga, seeing he was talking with some nigga sternly.

"He got a mouth on him, but he means well," I told her as the other two brothers came out of the house.

By the time it was over, we had watched the entire thing being played out. All four brothers had their love interest playing the part. The very last thing to happen was five cars pulling up to the scene, damn near blocking the road, and about five niggas from each car hopped out, looking uncivilized as hell, like all they knew was the streets, and they wouldn't know how to act around people.

"That's the other oldest brother, Shiloh." Jade pointed at the light-skin man who stepped out of his car, face instant mean-mug. *Shit.*

"He looks like a light-skin version of Elijah." I laughed as we moved closer, seeing all of the men crowding in the street with the cameras on them.

Shiloh stood in front of his small army, as the rest gave shout outs, making faces, hollering out. They were wild niggas, being wild as fuck, almost scaring some of these white people that were here. They were waving red bandanas in the air as the song played.

I watched Elijah, with Jordyn in hand, jump in the front with his brother, and I nearly gasped at the resemblance.

"So, he's related to Elijah by his mama?" I asked Jade, who nodded.

"That's Trent and Elijah's older brother on both sides. Nigga is fine as fuck, too," she said, and I smiled, eyeing Shiloh.

It looked like everyone was just having fun. Even Jordyn got into it. You know when it's a group of Atlanta niggas, somebody is going to start dancing.

"Aye, lemme give a shout out to the streets that raised me!" one guy yelled into the camera.

"East side, partna! Zone six, mothafucka!" another yelled as Elijah stepped up.

"Bruh, we doing big thangs out here! You see how we roll in the A!" Elijah said, looking back at the huge crowd. "Never forget where you came from, you feel me? This the big homie right here!" He put an arm around Shiloh's neck. "This the nigga you don't wanna fuck with! We run these streets! Every mothafucka is on payroll under this nigga right here! This woman right here," he said, taking

Jordyn's hand, kissing it affectionately. The director nearly ate this shit up, signaling for him to keep going, even with the music already stopping. "Only woman that matters in my life. Fuck every other bitch. This is the only one." It was cute until he damn near attacked the side of her neck with kisses.

Jahiem even got Jade and me in the video before it finally wrapped up. Shit was long as fuck, and it was well past midnight when everyone started to pack it up and head home. I saw all the brothers talking in a small circle as Jade and I slowly walked up to them.

"What time we gotta be there?" Elijah whined, and Shiloh cut his eyes at him. Damn, he was fine. Nothing better than a hood nigga that was fine, with pretty hair, and truly about that life.

"Nigga, just show up. Y'all owe her that. I didn't want her to see that side of me, and now she has, so bring whatever the fuck you gonna bring, and be at the house. Apologize to her," Shiloh demanded.

I felt Jahiem slip his arms around my neck, kissing me hard on the cheek.

"You ready for bed, baby? You shouldn't be up this late anyway in this freezing cold," he said, babying me as I rolled my eyes.

"Nigga, I'm good, but I do want something to eat before we get back."

"Is she going to want to see us after that incident?" Anthony asked.

"I'm still trying to convince her, but just show up, bruh. Don't fucking embarrass a nigga either, because I will call everyone out on y'all shit."

"Nigga, what?" Elijah laughed and Shiloh smirked. "Embarrass you? She must be something if you worried about us embarrassing yo' quiet ass. Trent said Mama want us at her house tomor—"

"Fuck her," Shiloh spat, and Jahiem held his hand up to Shiloh, bringing it in for a quick hug and dap. Getting ready to leave, he said, "Just be over there. I don't ask for nothing from y'all niggas, but I like this girl, so tone all that thugging shit down when you get there. She's not used to all of that."

"How she get with you, then?" Anthony joked.

"She's too good for me. That's the problem," Shiloh admitted, and I smiled.

He got himself a good girl and don't know how to act right now. Cute.

"I'll be over there tomorrow around noon, nigga. I need to get her home," he said as all eyes were officially turned to me like they'd just noticed I was there.

"This is the newest addition. I remember you," Anthony said with a laugh. "Welcome to the Carter family, baby girl."

"Thank you," I gushed, feeling him hug me before the rest brought it in.

Suddenly, all eyes fell on Jade. None of them knew who she was, but she knew who they were.

"Yo, that's Trent's girl," Elijah said, and their mouths dropped. Even Jahiem, who just now noticed she was there, was surprised.

"Ahh, you the one that got into a fight with that nigga." Ontrell laughed as Jade shrugged.

"He tried the fuck out of me. I wasn't about to take that laying down, son. Not for a second," she said easily.

Despite how she'd started off with Trent, no country nigga, especially from Atlanta, could resist a girl from up north. She could talk all the shit she wanted, but her accent was what kept them by her side. That night was no different, because each brother damn near looked infatuated with her way of speech.

"I can't believe he even got a girl like you, shawty. You fine as fuck, too, but you already know you not his type," Jahiem said, and I hit him hard in the chest.

"What I say?" he yelled.

"Nigga, just shut the fuck up," I snapped with a roll of my eyes. "We need to go."

"Aye, I'll see y'all tomorrow," Jahiem stated before we turned to walk off. "You ain't had to hit me in from of them."

"You didn't have to eye my roommate like that in front of me, nigga," I mocked back as he laughed.

"I like girls with dreads. Shit is sexy when you can pull it off. And she got tattoos, too? She look good—okay! Okay!" He laughed, and I aimed my fist at him, ready for round two. He wrapped his arm around me, kissing me hard again on the side of the face. "I love you, crazy mothafucka," he said against my ear, and I smiled. "You already know as soon as we get home, I'm coming for that pregnant pussy before you even step foot in that bed."

"Eww, Jahiem! You so nasty!" I laughed, pushing him away from me. "You ain't coming for shit."

"We'll see."

Sure enough, we didn't even make it to the house. I let it slip that I never had sex in the car before, so this nigga pulled over on the side of a major highway, pulled his dick out, and had me riding him in the driver's seat like it was nothing. He ended it with a shaky "I love you" against my lips before starting back up again—just because we could.

Noelle

"So, while y'all do that, I'm going to be in New York for a few days. I don't even want to be in Atlanta knowing he's here," Tyree said, grabbing his suitcases. It was only seven something on a Sunday morning, and instead of me going to church, I had to get ready to cook.

"You're going to have to talk to him eventually." I yawned, standing by the door as I watched him pack his stuff in the car. Shiloh and I had gotten back from our road trip late yesterday evening, and somehow, he'd convinced me to meet his brothers—the same ones I saw in the house that day. They were the same ones that felt up on me, and now they were coming over. I told Shiloh I didn't know if I was ready for this, but he wanted to clear the air, and he claimed they were going to apologize.

"Noelle, boo, do me a favor," Tyree said as he stood next to his car, hanging on the window, wrapped up in his coat and scarf from this morning cold.

"Yes?"

"Fuck yo' nigga by the time I get back," he said, and I laughed, watching him get in the car before pulling out.

I walked back in the house, closing the door, and started to clean up a bit. I took away the air mattress and sheets from Tyree's makeshift bed. Today was going to be an interesting day. Shiloh had already warned me that Sundays, when they got together, it could be hectic, as I'd witnessed last Sunday.

Hearing the house phone ring, I suddenly looked around for the cordless phone. Yes, I still had a house phone. My daddy made me put one in, just in case something were to happen. Tyree had mostly been on it, so I knew it was in the living room somewhere. As it continued to ring, I lifted up the couch cushions and found it. I answered without even looking at the caller ID.

"Hello?" I said politely, only now realizing who would be calling at 7 o'clock on a Sunday morning. *How rude.*

"Hey, Noelle, this is Michael from church," he said smoothly as my mouth dropped. I didn't even give this man my cell phone number, let alone my house number.

"What are you—"

"I know you're a little surprised. I was just seeing if I could carpool with you today for church. My car is acting up. Dang near driving me insane," he said, sounding stressed.

I sighed, walking to my room. "How did you get this number, Michael?" I opened the door, seeing Shiloh. He was lying flat on his stomach, legs wide, one eye barely open as he slowly turned over. He slept like a caveman at times.

"One of the ladies at the church gave it to me a while back. You know I wouldn't be calling unless this was serious. I know you have a boyfriend and all, but if you were going to church, I wanted to cop a ride with you."

"I, um . . ." I looked at Shiloh, who just stared at me, fully awake after hearing the male voice on the other end. "I don't know, Michael. I'm not even going today."

"Come on, beautiful angel. Help me out here," he cooed, and I smiled before quickly dropping it when I saw Shiloh's eyes squint.

"Hold on," I said, pressing the phone to my chest as I looked at Shiloh. "He wants a ride to church."

"Who the fuck is he?"

"Michael."

Shiloh just stared at me.

"His car is messed up, and he wanted to carpool with me to the church, Shiloh." I watched him yawn as he turned back over on his stomach.

"Ain't shit wrong with that nigga's car."

"Shiloh, come on now. Show some compassion," I pressed, and he looked at me, holding his hand out for the phone.

"Hold on, Michael. I can maybe have my boyfriend take you. Will that be okay?" I asked.

There was a small pause.

"Yeah, that's cool," he said, clearing his throat.

I smiled, handing the phone to Shiloh. It's an amazing feeling when you can get your boyfriend and a male friend to be cordial to one another.

Shiloh sat up on the edge of the bed as I sat on top of my dresser, watching the exchange.

"Aye, who is this again?" Shiloh said into the phone.

I could hear Michael introduce himself.

"You needed a ride to church?"

I could hear Michael explain the situation as Shiloh looked at me through tired, lazy eyes, sitting on the edge of the bed, shirtless, wearing gray boxer briefs. I definitely loved this man more and more with each passing minute we were together.

"You know what you should do?" Shiloh said into the phone, probably about to give out some mechanic-like advice. "You should pray to your God that I don't ever catch you outside that church, nigga," he said in a low, deadly voice.

I nearly hopped off the dresser in a panic.

"Ain't shit wrong with yo' fucking car, nigga. Fuck you doing, calling my girl's house this early in the morning, thinking you can get a ride? Bruh, tell Jesus to carpool with yo' stupid ass, because she's not doing it. All this transportation in Atlanta—buses and trains—and you pressing on my girl for a ride. Nah, nigga, not to-motha-fucking-day, bruh," he snapped.

I tried reaching for the phone.

"Call this number again and see what happens." With that, he hung up and politely handed me the phone as my mouth dropped in horror.

"Shiloh?" I said, trying my hardest not to laugh as he lay back down in the bed, pulling the covers over him like he didn't just go off on someone.

"Nothing was wrong with that nigga's car, Noe. He wants it. He wants you. I'm not stupid. Matter of fact, he better be glad I don't know what that nigga look like, because I would have already taken care of this shit."

"Shiloh . . ." I sighed with a slow smile. "He's the guy from the church."

"I only caught the back of his head, Noe. That's a blessing for that nigga that I don't know his face."

I shook my head, thinking. "I gotta change my number now."

"Yeah, you do that," he mumbled.

I walked out of the room, closing the door behind me. Last night when he came in, we'd already set aside some money to buy the groceries, so as I was getting dressed in and out my room, making a mental list of things I needed, I thought about Tyree. He and everyone else seemed to be pressuring me to have sex with Shiloh. With my luck in life, I would be the one that has sex for the first time and gets pregnant. I refused to have a baby out of wed-lock. It was not how I was raised, and not how I planned on raising my future children.

At the store, I started picking out the food. I stocked up on everything. I was feeding seven boys—no, men—seven men, three women, not including myself, and just to be on the safe side, I bought kiddie snacks if they were bringing kids over. By the time I made it back to my house, my driveway was already full, with cars lined up. What in the world? I wasn't even dressed yet. My hair was a wreck, and I was meeting his family for the first time looking like a bum. Smoothing my edges down, I quickly looked my face over before getting out, deciding to park at Shiloh's house since there was clearly no space in my driveway for my small car.

Shiloh stepped out, shirtless, wearing his long basketball shorts, with a beer bottle in hand. The sun was barely out, looking like it was trying its hardest not to rain, but the gray clouds were looking heavy with water.

"So, I can't park at my own house?" I asked, closing the door as I walked across the yard to my steps.

"My bad. I'll get them to move their cars," he said. "You left the car unlocked so we can get the groceries?"

"Yeah." I heard the commotion from my own living room as I stepped in. All eyes were on me. I had a flashback to the night at Aunt Alice's house, and it nearly made me faint as I stared at the same faces. I saw two girls I didn't recognize standing up against the wall, smiling at me. Then there was another woman who was pregnant, sitting down next to her guy.

"I apologize for the mess," was all I could say as they all stood up, smiling at me.

"Bruh, she's beautiful," one said, tapping Shiloh on the arm in confirmation. "We want to apologize for that day you saw us. We were just trying to protect our sister standing over there," he said, pointing at the dark-skin girl with the hazel eyes as she waved shyly.

"Aye, introduce us, Shiloh," another said as I felt his hand come to my lower back.

"A'ight, so look," Shiloh started, pointing as he introduced every sibling in the room. They even brought me two dozen roses, putting it in a vase with a red ribbon tied around it, and a "Sorry" card. It was confusing at first to learn who was related to each other under the same parents, but I knew the triplets were Shiloh's main siblings, since they shared a mom as well. Another was married with the pregnant wife, and the biggest one was the one that had all the damn kids. He was also the oldest by a few months, with Shiloh coming in as the second oldest.

Like clockwork, I watched the boys go to my car, grabbing the groceries and dropping them off in the kitchen as I prepared my stove and oven for this meal. The girls came in the back to help me. We ended up swapping college stories, and it turned out Olivia and I were sorority sisters. So, it was definitely easier talking to the girls than getting along with the boys, who were watching a football game.

"I can't believe Shiloh could even pull someone like you," Olivia said as we all sat on the countertop in different corners of the kitchen. Toni grabbed a chair to sit in, rubbing her belly, with her locs pulled up in a bun.

"Girl, Shiloh probably wouldn't know what to do with a street chick. It would be a chaotic relationship," Taylor said to Olivia before smiling at me. "How did y'all meet anyway? Besides living next door to each other," she asked, eyes squinting with a curious smile, just waiting.

There was something Olivia was giving off. I wasn't sure what it was, but I needed her approval if I was going to fit in with her brothers.

"Well, I just went over to his house one night, wanting his friends to turn down the music. That's when I first saw him. Of course, he didn't say much, but once we saw each other in a club, he came over to me, asking if he could stay by my side that night. The rest is pretty much history." I shrugged as they all "wooed."

"I can't even imagine Shiloh liking someone," Olivia said, looking at me with a particular gaze and a simple smile. "You have to be special to him. He was nervous about everyone meeting you."

"Shiloh? Nervous?" I questioned as we laughed. Shocking.

"Ohhhh! Nigga, I told you he was going to drop the ball!" Elijah yelled out as the boys started all talking at once. "Fuck-ass Falcons!"

"Do you see yourself marrying him?" Toni asked, hand on her pregnant belly.

"Yeah." I smiled.

"Oooooh, I've always wanted another sister-in-law! Toni can't be the only one, and Anthony's baby mamas are crazy as fuck," Olivia said, and they laughed.

We continued to talk, moving food around as it grew closer to the time to eat. I baked macaroni and cheese, green beans, black-eyed peas, collard greens, brown rice, and baked chicken, with Toni making steaks for some of the serious eaters. Then we had garlic bread and dressing. It was almost like a pre-Thanksgiving dinner.

Olivia baked brownies while Taylor got the plates ready. It definitely felt like everyone was a tight-knit group with a lot of respect for the elders and a lot of playfulness from the younger siblings. Talin would occasionally come in to check on his wife, Toni, while Trent and Taylor would be kissing each other in a loving way. Tyree's boyfriend, Ontrell, looked like he was trying to cover up his sadness, but I could see right through it. And with Tyree texting me, wanting me to take pictures, asking me what he had on, what was he doing or saying, I decided to cut all of this short and call him. I changed out of my hot jeans, throwing on some shorts and a tank top, with my hair bouncing in a small ponytail.

"Bitch, what are you doing?" Tyree answered with a hiss as I rolled my eyes. "I don't want him knowing you talking to me."

"Both of y'all need to talk to each other—without your friends rallying behind you. Just you and him need to talk. He looks so sad, Ty," I cooed, looking at Trell, who had his head dropped down, staring at the carpet. Everyone was so in tune with the game, but he kept quiet, to himself.

"So, what? You want me to fly back down to Atlanta and talk to that nigga?" he snapped as I walked over to the couch, tapping Ontrell on the shoulder. He had no idea I knew his ex-boyfriend, but he was about to find out. He turned to look at me, confused, but I just put the phone up to his ear.

"Hello?" he answered hesitantly.

I could hear Tyree going off just as Trell's face scrunched up in pain. He quickly got up to step outside.

"Baby, please don't hang up on me," he said, closing the front door behind him.

"Y'all, the food is almost ready," Olivia called out from the kitchen as the boys looked back.

"She talking like she made that shit," Elijah joked, and they laughed. "Olivia, yo' non-cooking ass know you ain't did shit but watch this girl do it all."

"Hey! I can make some good-ass brownies," she snapped.

"Yo, even I can make some food," Trent said as Taylor sat down on his lap and he wrapped his arms around her waist.

"Who can cook, and who can't cook in this family?" I asked, and they all started talking at once.

"Well, I can grill anything, shawty," Jahiem boasted. "Shiloh is the type of nigga who will show up with a plate in hand looking for food. He like a mothafucking stray dog, my nigga."

"Tell me about it," I mumbled, seeing Shiloh smile.

"Why I gotta know how to cook when I got family to do that shit?" he argued as I sat down next to him.

"I can throw down in the kitchen," Anthony said as I looked at him, smiling. He was the heavyset one of the bunch, so I knew he wasn't lying.

"My girl got me into eating salads lately," Elijah admitted, and they started clowning him immediately. "Aye! Aye! Ain't nothing wrong with being healthy, bruh!"

"Ahh, shut yo' ol' vegan ass up." Trent laughed while playfully hitting his brother.

Taylor looked at me with a roll of her eyes as I laughed.

"How long have you guys been dating?" I asked curiously, and the room went deadly silent. I quickly looked at Shiloh, who looked away, trying to hold a smile in as he took a swig of his drink. "Did I ask the wrong thing?"

"Nah, you good. Ain't that right, Trent? Tell her how long y'all been dating."

"Elijah, shut the fuck up," Taylor snapped.

"Yooo, we didn't even tell you yo' girl came to the video shoot last night. We met Jade last night, nigga," Jahiem said as Trent's mouth dropped. "Yeah, she's cool as fuck. I don't know what I thought of her before, but she wasn't what I expected."

"Yeah," Elijah agreed.

I was more confused than ever, but I decided to let it go as I walked back to the kitchen with Olivia smirking at me.

"Do you know if I asked something out—"

"Girl, you're fine. That's not his girlfriend. They've known each other since they were kids, but he's been cheating on his girlfriend with her," Olivia whispered as we looked back.

Oh, wow! None of my business, though. I checked the oven, seeing the chicken was just perfect.

"Tell the guys to come get it," I told Olivia, who called out to her brothers. They were almost like a herd of hungry bulls rushing to the kitchen.

"Back up!" Shiloh snapped. "My girl, her house, I'm first. Fuck is wrong with y'all?"

"Nigga, quit being greedy. This is for all of us," Anthony retorted.

Toni pushed her pregnant self in the front. "Okay, first off, y'all niggas sat on y'all asses all damn day. The women are getting their plates first, because we cooked this shit, so move," she snapped, and they all backed up.

"Talin, yo' wife mean as fuck, bruh," Jahiem complained as Toni cut her eyes at him.

"We got a problem, mothafucka?" she snapped, and Jahiem dropped his head.

I loved her. She was so quick tempered, but she could switch it up and be so nice all in one sentence.

"Nah, Mama," he mumbled, and they laughed. Talin just shrugged with a Kool-aid grin.

"Noelle, get your plate," Taylor said. I glanced at Shiloh, who looked like he was about to die at the sight of the food.

"Yo, save me a steak, Toni," Talin called out.

"Nigga, you eating. Don't worry," she said as we picked over what we wanted. "These niggas here act like they be starving, making all that money and starving."

I ended up making Shiloh's plate anyway, just as Toni made her husband's plate.

"I don't know why," Taylor chimed in as we looked back at the boys, all anxiously waiting to get in the kitchen. Like little boys, they were already eyeing what they wanted.

"Where is Ontrell at?" Olivia asked. "Can y'all go see about him?"

I watched Toni pause before dropping the empty plate, which crashed hard to the floor. She gripped her stomach, wincing in pain. Everyone immediately came to her aid, with Talin supporting her to keep her off the floor.

"Call the—"

"Nah, I'm good," she breathed, struggling to stand up as she looked at her husband with a weak smile. "Baby kicked me for the first time."

Everyone rejoiced in excitement as she let Talin feel the movement, looking like a proud daddy.

"You need to sit down and stay off yo' feet for the rest of the day," Trent suggested.

"Nah, she's good. You already know she don't want to hear no shit like that." Talin laughed, picking up the broken pieces from the plate. "You good, Mama," he said, kissing her affectionately on the head.

I smiled. I couldn't wait to be married and pregnant.

As we continued fixing plates, with the men merging into the kitchen with us, Shiloh kept close behind me, holding his plate that I fixed for him. "Where the drinks at?" he asked.

Olivia pulled out this huge punch bowl with this red liquid that she had mixed together, infusing different fruit juices with a small dose of alcohol in it. Once everyone settled down with their plates, everyone kind of sat together but separately. Toni and Talin sat at the dining room table together, with her feet propped on his lap. Trent and Taylor sat on the opposite side of the table together. Anthony, Jahiem, and Elijah sat in front of the TV, watching the game, while Shiloh and I sat on the small couch together, with Olivia grabbing a chair to sit on the side. Ontrell had left with my phone. Lord knows what he was doing, but I wasn't concerned at this point. I actually enjoyed myself with his family.

"When you throwing this graduation party, Trent? And where?" Jahiem asked, checking his phone as I looked back at Trent.

"Oh, shit, bruh. This is the semester you graduating? Why nobody told me?" Anthony asked, and they all started talking at once.

"I reserved the Spring Lounge on a Saturday night. My frat brothers and I already started promoting that shit. It's going to be fucking wild."

"College educated. What's next after that?"

"Nigga probably ain't gon' do shit with the degree," Elijah mumbled, and everyone turned to him. Jealousy was laced in every word.

"Bruh, you hating?" Trent teased. "If you wasn't so focused on running after Shiloh all the time, you could be getting like me and Olivia."

"Nigga, I'm still going to make more in a day than you will in a fucking lifetime! Just because you got a fancy-ass degree don't mean shit at the end of the day," Elijah snapped.

"Here we go." Jahiem sighed, continuing to eat.

I looked at Shiloh, who shook his head, still eating.

"Why is it always a competition between y'all two?" Taylor pressed.

"Because that nigga stay trying to compete with some-one!" Trent argued. "I'm in a league of my own. You will never be on the level that—"

"You'll never be on the level," Elijah mocked, trying to talk proper as a few of the brothers laughed. "Man, shut yo' white ass up, bruh. Fuck outta here with that bullshit. A degree ain't nothing but a piece of paper, my nigga!"

"Whatever. That's why I never fucked with you like that—you or Shiloh—because y'all stay on that street mentality bullshit," Trent mumbled as Shiloh's head popped up.

"Fuck you keep putting my name in yo' mouth for, bruh? I didn't say shit—"

"You never say shit! That's the fucking problem! You stay taking his side! When were you ever there for me, or Olivia? Let Elijah call, you drop everything for that nigga, but if it was me—"

"Aye, aye, everybody chill out!" Anthony said. "Trent, we proud of you. Elijah, why you knocking yo' own brother's accomplishments down?"

"Because he stay throwing that college shit in my face! Him and Mama always tell me I'm running behind Shiloh. I get sick of hearing that shit!"

"Y'all act like some fucking kids," Jahiem mumbled. "Talin, you ain't got no problem with me, right?"

"Nah, we cool," Talin said as they laughed.

Just like that, the conversation shifted into something else. I eyed Shiloh, who kept quiet as usual, blank expression on his face telling nothing. I remembered him telling me that he was the one that felt like he had to raise his younger siblings when his dad wasn't around. Well, now I believed it, because they fought for his attention and approval as if he was their dad. But as quickly as the fight started, it was already over, with Elijah getting up quietly to go hug Trent, slapping hands. I don't think anyone noticed but me. Interesting family.

"So, when you putting a ring on her finger, Shiloh? I like Noelle for you," Olivia said, giving me the stamp of approval as the sister of the bunch.

"Hell yeah, let me find out it's another girl like you, shawty. I would settle my ass down so quick," Anthony said as I laughed.

"If she wanna marry a nigga, I'm down with it one day soon," Shiloh said. I smiled from ear to ear.

"Ahhh, shit! Big brother talking about taking that next step!" Elijah flipped.

"Do I hear wedding bells coming soon, Noelle?" Olivia cooed. I looked at her, almost looking identical to Elijah and his excited expression.

"I'm down with it." I shrugged shyly, looking up at Shiloh. "One day soon."

Everyone started freaking out in excitement at the thought of us marrying each other, but Shiloh kept his eyes on me.

"I love you," he mouthed, and I smiled back. It was the first time he'd said it to me.

"Love you too," I mouthed in response, with no one knowing about our love exchange as they continued to celebrate the possibility of a marriage. It was still way too soon to say, but it could happen.

Suddenly, we heard a car door close. Elijah stood up to look out the window.

"Aye, Ontrell went and got that nigga." He laughed, and my eyes lit up.

So, I was right. Tyree never even left Atlanta.

Tyree

"Okay and what, Trell? Nigga, you stay talking about you're gonna do this, you're gonna do that," I snapped into the phone as I stood at the airport, waiting with my duffle bag in tow. I was on the phone with my ex because Noelle had forced me to talk to this fuck nigga. I just wanted to go back home for a minute, be with my family, and forget about the shit that had happened to me in Atlanta. It was definitely time to relocate. I was ready for a change of scenery, a change of dick, and a change of wardrobe.

"Where you at, Tyree?"

"I'm not telling you—"

"I know you at the airport. I can hear that shit in the background, but where? Because I'm on the way to get you."

"Nigga, no you not!" I shrieked, causing people to turn their attention to me. "Ontrell, you got me out here looking stupid, yelling on this phone at yo' ass. Nigga, stay the fuck where you are, and leave me alone. We don't have nothing—"

"Where are you?" he pressed again as I rolled my eyes, smacking my teeth. "Nigga, don't do that, smacking yo' teeth at me. Tell me where you are. I'm not gonna do this shit over the phone with you. I haven't seen you in over a fucking week—"

"You've been longer without me when you be fucking those broads, nigga. Don't play me, boo. Not today," I went in before sitting down on the bench, telling him where I was like a fool.

We all have that one nigga that will drive you crazy in one minute, but you still want him around you to drive you crazy. Hanging up the phone, I sat with my legs crossed, leg bouncing over the other, with my black riding boots, black skinny jeans, and hoodie with a black skull cap on. I had on a black leather motorcycle jacket like I was about that life as I waited for that phone call. I debated on whether to leave, but as soon as he called me, I met him outside where the pickups were and got in the car.

I stayed quiet, face fixed on attitude as I crossed my arms over my chest. Just being near him made my heart flutter as he smiled at me. I saw where he shaved the sides and back of his head, just leaving the dreads at the top in a ponytail. His face was still perfect with that brown complexion smooth as ice, perfect pearly white smile, and smelling good too. He was dressed like a man with money and style.

"I missed you," he started.

I rolled my eyes, snorting in the process.

He just smiled, tucking in that lower lip. "I can't get a hug or nothing?"

"Nigga, we not together no more. We will never be anything other than exes, because I'm not going to let you put me through this bullshit again. Go ahead. Say you sorry. Say you won't do it again. Tell me you love me. Lie to me that you love me, because you don't."

"I do."

"No! You don't, nigga! Because if you did, you wouldn't have even thought about half the shit you did to me!" I screamed.

He dropped his head, starting the car before pulling off. I wasn't finished, though. He didn't want to hear it over the phone, but he was going to hear it to his face.

"Oooh, you ain't shit, nigga, I swear!" I spat. "Two years of my life that I gave to you, and you disrespected everything we stood for. Fucking broads because they throwing that shit at you, and you act like you can't turn it down! Boo boo, news flash! These bitches don't think you cute. They don't want you or love you! They trying to see what the fuck it's like to fuck with a gay man! You're a fucking fetish to these nasty broads out here! Same hoes you fucking with are the same hoes that bash men like you and me!"

He stayed quiet as he got on the highway, jaw clenching because he knew I was right.

"Then! If that wasn't enough, you go and fuck niggas too! Because my dick ain't good enough for you?"

"It's not like that—"

"Oh! Did—did I say speak, nigga?" I snapped, hitting him hard upside the head as he silently cursed me out, clenching the steering wheel hard with his face tightening up. "I am so sick of you, Ontrell. I'm not . . . you not about to have me lose my voice over you. Yelling at you because you fucked up, not me. You're the reason we're not together anymore," I snapped before officially going silent.

"Can I talk, Tyree?" he asked hesitantly.

I said nothing, just stared out the window, sitting comfortably in his truck as he drove.

"I did some growing up—"

"Over a week, nigga? You grew up that fast, nigga?" I retorted. "Only thing that should have grown was that li'l-ass dick you got," I mumbled. Okay, while y'all reading this, know that my ex's dick wasn't little, never that, but you sometimes got to hit 'em where it hurts.

"Man, chill the fuck out on that and let me finish talking!" he snapped. "I did some growing, and I learned a lot about myself when you wasn't around. I don't—"

"You know what? Think about whatever you're about to say before you say it to me, Ontrell. Everything that comes out yo' mouth is a lie right now, so the next words you speak to me better be the truest shit you ever told me, nigga. Think about it," I said.

He went completely silent. Lying-ass nigga. He stayed quiet the entire way back to Noelle's place as I texted one of my clients and friends, telling her everything that was happening. As soon as we pulled up to her place, I got out the car. He closed and locked the door, still silent. See what I mean?

"You don't even know how to fucking have a conversation with me without lying," I snapped as we walked up the steps.

The door opened. Elijah smirked at us, mouth full of food.

"Aye, you missing all this good food, bruh," he said to Trell. Elijah then held his arms out to me for a hug. "You good?"

"Nigga, move. All of y'all ain't shit right now," I retorted, closing the door.

"Don't come in here bitching. Everything was peaceful until you—"

I cut my eyes hard at Anthony, who felt like he was bold.

"Don't say nothing to me, nigga, because y'all let this man treat me the way he's been doing for years!" I snapped, watching Ontrell walk in the kitchen to grab a plate.

"You let that nigga do it! Not us! A man is going to be a man at the end of the day. You chose to stay with him," Jahiem reasoned.

I looked at Noelle, who looked stuck.

"You're already here. Just sit down and eat," Olivia chimed in as Ontrell came back with his plate, setting it down on the table.

"I'm not hungry. I told you I don't even want to—"

Ontrell took both of my hands and got down on one bended knee. I gasped, seeing him reach in his coat pocket to pull out a small black box. My body became so numb, the house became so silent, and my hands started to shake as I covered my mouth with my palm, feeling tears about to fall.

"Oh, shit! Yo, get the camera out!" Elijah demanded as everyone started recording.

I only had eyes for Trell, who took a deep breath and looked me directly in my eyes.

"Oh my God!" Olivia cried out. "My baby brother is getting married!"

"Shhh!" Jahiem hissed. "Let that nigga do it first. Damn!"

"You're the only . . ." Ontrell started, voice shaking as he tried clearing his throat. His eyes started to water up, and I started shifting from one foot to another in anticipation, trying to keep from crying my damn self. "You're the only person in the world that knows me better than I know myself. I . . ." He was fighting back tears as I looked up at the ceiling, blinking hard to keep it together. "There is nothing I can do to make up for the bullshit I did in the past. You are my best friend. You make me laugh at the worst of times, and drive me fucking insane at the best of times. You held me down when I wasn't shit but a nigga on the streets, and you make everything right in my life, like . . ." He shook his head as the tears started to come. "You already know I love you, and I hate that I did that stupid shit to you. I just thought you would never leave me, and when you did . . . I never been at my lowest point in life until I realized that when I woke up, you weren't going to be next to me," he said as I wiped my eyes.

"Shit, this is some deep-ass shit, bruh," Elijah sniffed, wiping his eyes.

"Nigga, yo' gay ass crying too?" Jahiem laughed, and someone shushed them.

"What are you trying to say, Ontrell?" I pressed, voice trembling as he tightened his hand around mine.

"You told me the next words that come out my mouth better be the realest shit I ever told you, so . . ." He opened the box, exposing two wedding bands. Both were black bands, with mine having black diamonds going around it with white diamonds in between. His was three rows of black diamonds. "Will you please give me another chance? Be my lover, my best friend, my partner for life, my nigga, my ride or die, my baby, my bae, my everything. The sun, the moon, and the stars," he pleaded as I choked on my own tears. "I'm done playing around. I'm done. If all that shit means I go without you for a fucking week, I don't know how I'm going to go without you for the rest of my life."

I looked around at his family, seeing they were all waiting on my answer. I looked back at Ontrell, tears building up as he anxiously waited for my response.

"Yes," I mumbled with a small nod.

He jumped up, hugging me. Everyone was clapping, coming to congratulate us. Slipping the band on my finger, I smiled, sticking my hand out to eye the precious gems.

"You like it?" he asked, kissing me as he put his on.

I nodded with a laugh, feeling giddy.

"Yo, welcome to the family, bruh! Shit, you already been rocking with us this long. Might as well make it official," Elijah said, patting me on the back. Everyone started taking pictures, with the girls all crowding around me to eye the ring.

"When is the wedding?" Noelle asked.

Trell looked at me.

"I want a spring wedding," I cooed. "Oh my God, so much planning to do. I have to start planning now!"

"Aye, it's going to be the biggest party, bruh. We turning up at that wedding," Talin said as the boys slapped hands.

I turned to Elijah, who already knew what I was about to ask him.

"You want me to sing at that shit?" he said.

"Would you?"

"I got you," he said, and we hugged. "Yo, let's get fucked up! Where the drinks at?"

"Uh, no. Not at my house," Noelle said softly, trying to speak up as we laughed. "It's getting late anyway, and I have to work in the morning. You guys have been lovely company, but it's time to go."

"Can't believe my younger brother is getting married before my old ass," Anthony said, hugging Ontrell. "Proud of you, li'l Carter. You manning up. I wouldn't trust no other nigga for you to be with other than this crazy fool."

I smiled, knowing there had been too many nights where Anthony had called me, telling me to get Trell from somewhere.

So, on the ride back to the house with my things packed up, ready to come back home, Trell had one more surprise for me. Pulling into this fancy-ass subdivision, he stopped in front of a house that had a SOLD sign in the front. It was a pretty white house with a two-car garage. The area itself was nice. Everyone knew about Vinings, Georgia. Only fancy niggas stayed there.

"Trell, what are you doing? Who lives here?" I asked slowly as he got out. I followed him as we walked up to the door. The moment he pulled out the keys to open it, I nearly fainted.

"Nigga, no you didn't!" I shrieked as he shushed me.

"Nigga, hush. This is not one of them neighborhoods." He laughed.

"Whose house is this?" I pressed as he opened the door.

The house was brand new, with the plastic leading a trail into different areas of the house. Walls were painted with a new coat, and everything was squeaky clean. We just needed to decorate it.

"Ontrell Carter, whose house is this?" I repeated, and he smiled at me.

"You thought we was gonna get married still living in that apartment, nigga? I've been working on getting this house for us for a few months now," he said. "Closed the deal two days ago. I was trying to—"

"Baby!" I shrieked as I jumped in his arms, hugging him tight. I'm not saying a nigga would forget about him cheating on me, but a ring and a house in one day? Uh, that will make a bitch have amnesia for a minute or two.

I started looking around the house, already having ideas on how to decorate it, nights I wanted to entertain my guests and his guests, places where we could fuck. My mind was running rapid with thoughts. Looking at Ontrell again, I smiled.

"Oh, we gotta step our hustle game up, boo," I told him, arms wrapped around his neck. "I want the finest shit in here. The best of the best," I said, cheesing. "I want my wedding to be top notch, too, so we gotta put our money together. Next year, we going in, Ontrell. You understand me?"

"We finna make this money, nigga. I got you," Trell said as he kissed me. "You with me till the end?"

"I'm with you till the end, bae."

Move on to the next story, bitches, because we not finna keep writing my life in. I want my story to be a fairy tale ending, so turn the page. Be blessed, and thank you.

The Breakup

Trent

"This has been an interesting day." Taylor sighed as she relaxed in the passenger's seat. It was Sunday evening, and we were just leaving my brother's girlfriend's house on a full stomach with plates wrapped up. "I can't wait until I get married and have kids."

I glanced at her, smiling slowly as she looked at me, matching my grin.

"Nigga, you ain't cute."

"Yeah, I am," I stated, and she laughed. "You gon' have my babies, Taylor?"

"Maybe, if you treat me right."

"I'll always treat you right," I said with a laugh just as my phone rang. Looking at the caller ID, I saw Elijah's ugly face pop up. *Man, I just saw his ass. Fuck he want now?*

"Answer the phone. It's yo' own brother," Taylor said, taking the phone away as she slid to answer it, putting it on speaker. "Helloooo?"

"Aye, where Trent at?" he asked, dogs barking in the background.

"Right next to me driving. What's up?"

"Look, I wasn't about to do this shit in front of everyone at the house. Not with mothafuckas getting married and crying about love, but yo' girl knows you fucking around on her with Taylor," Elijah said.

I nearly stopped in the middle of the street, car jerking violently forward. I reached my hand out of instinct to protect Taylor before continuing to drive, body full of numbing nerves. I should have broken up with her when I said I was going to. Fuck, I should have left Taylor alone after the first night. *Shit!* I didn't know what to do!

"She what?" Taylor shrieked, adjusting herself as she looked at me with wide eyes. "I didn't . . . How does she know? You told her?"

"Nah, she came crying to me and asked me how long it's been going on. I said, 'What the fuck you talking about, shawty?' And she said . . . Trent sleeping with you. She doesn't know who you are, Tay, but she knows what the fuck you look like and where you stay."

My mind went back to a few nights ago when I caught Jade crying in the bed. *Shit!*

"Surprised she's still with yo' ass, but if you going to see her tonight, I was just trying to give you a heads up," Elijah said with a laugh. "Should have broken up with her if you and Taylor was gonna keep fucking. I personally like y'all two together but, Trent, you should have known better, bruh."

I hung up the phone on Elijah, not really trying to hear a lecture as Taylor and I sat in complete silence. The yelling, the screaming, throwing shit at me, the blows to the face, and body—Jade was going to go the fuck off on me the moment I saw her. I'm man enough to admit to y'all reading this shit now that I was scared as fuck.

"Now what?" Taylor asked quietly, looking at me with worried eyes.

"I gotta go hear her mouth now." I sighed, pulling into the driveway of her house. "She's going to go the fuck off on me. I'm not going to say shit. She'll break up with me, and then that's that. It's done," I said, shrugging as I looked at Taylor, who was putting on a smile.

"And then we're together, right, baby?" she pressed.

I nodded, leaning in to kiss her. My mind flashed to Jade. I hadn't seen her since yesterday morning. She hadn't called me, texted me, or anything, so I knew she was waiting on me to come by. She was ready to go off on me. I could feel it.

"Call me as soon as you're free, bae," she said before getting out.

I watched Taylor walk to her front door before I backed out. My heart was pounding as I got closer and closer to the yard. My girlfriend was the craziest girl I'd ever dealt with. She didn't take shit from no one, could hurt yo' feelings without realizing it, and rarely did she apologize. So not only did I sleep around on her, but she'd known about this shit for days and sat on it, mulling over the idea of me sleeping with another woman while being with her. I knew I was in for some shit.

It didn't truly hit me, though, until I made my way down the hallway of her apartment, already seeing my shit packed in a box outside the door.

"Fuck, man," I groaned, reaching down, seeing all the clothes, pictures of us, and random shit we had together. You knew going in her room that she had a boyfriend, because my shit was everywhere. Just like going in my room at the frat house, her smell-goods were in the bathroom with lotions and tampons and shit. Panties sometimes got washed with my shit.

I smiled, looking at one picture of us at a football game that she had forced me to go to. I always said she was beautiful for a dark-skin girl. I started to knock on the door before realizing it was slightly cracked open. I could hear Biggie playing from her room as I walked in, closing the door before entering farther into the dark apartment.

"Jade!" I called out, and the music stopped.

She stepped out, wearing a small white T-shirt. Bangles decorated each arm with her now chocolate locs pulled back into a ponytail with the back hanging freely. Changing her hair color did so much to improve how she looked. I almost smiled, proud to even say she was my girl. She was standing there with her tattoos on her arm, looking at me with those sexy, dark eyes. I tried to approach slowly, using the light from her room as a guide, illuminating into the living room.

"I wanted to say—"

She held her hand up. "Just get yo' shit and go, nigga," she said softly as I backed up. "I . . . I don't have the energy nor patience to argue and fight with you anymore. I know you been fucking around with shorty, and at this point? I did my crying. I did all the yelling I can do, Trent. I hope she was worth it."

"You not gonna even let me explain myself? Why I cheated on you? This whole time you have done nothing but bash a nigga from day one!" I snapped, moving closer. "You treat me like one of yo' homeboys, like I'm just a regular nigga you fuck with. So yeah, I like affection. I like attention from my woman, and since you thought that shit was gay, I found someone else that would gladly step up in your place!"

She didn't even blink. Her eyes watered up, but she refused to let one tear drop.

"Jade, I'm sorry, but you already knew this was going to happen."

"Is that it?" she asked.

I backed up in confusion. Where the fuck was Jade? Where was the girl that was quick to cuss me out? "I mean, if you don't have nothing to say—"

"I have nothing to say. We can break up, and you can let the woman take my place. I wasn't the kind of girlfriend you needed anyway," she said.

I stood there, stunned, not knowing what to do, what to think.

"You not going to even fight to get me back?" I asked, feeling myself get angry. "I stood up for you so many fucking times when people used to talk shit about you! Almost got into fights over yo' stupid ass, and you telling me it's over like you don't give a fuck?" I flipped.

She just tilted her head to the side, looking hard at me. "What's my first name, Trent?"

My mind went completely blank as I tried to think back. I heard her sister use it all the time. *Shit!*

"My favorite color, favorite thing to eat? My friend's name? Any one of them. Where do we always hang out at? My birthday? Shit, do you even know my zodiac sign? I have a tattoo of it on my arm. Do you even know how old I am?"

I stayed quiet, realizing her point. I didn't know my own girlfriend, but I made sure she spent her time knowing everything about me, my family, my fraternity brothers, and history. All those times she tried to get me to hang out with her friends or hang out at places that she wanted to go to, I always had an excuse, because I just never wanted to go. Now, all this shit was coming back up in my face, because I couldn't even figure out her first fucking name. Looking at her, I just shrugged pathetically.

"I'm not going to fight for a nigga who don't even know my first name, yo," she said softly as she turned to walk back into her room, closing the door.

I stood there, feeling like I was sick to my stomach as I went to her door, knocking on it. Trying to open it, I was feeling frantic.

"Jade!" I yelled, banging on her door. "Open the fucking door!"

She turned up her music once more, drowning me out. I dropped my head, arms falling weak to my sides.

What the fuck did I just do?

When I made my way back over to my sister's house, I sat on the couch, waiting on Taylor to get out of the shower. Olivia walked back and forth around the kitchen, running her mouth on the phone.

"Girl, I know, right?" She laughed, rubbing her nose to relieve an itch. "We can meet up with them niggas next weekend, though. . . . Uh-huh."

I watched my sister talk, wearing some short-ass shorts and a cropped shirt, with mismatched socks. Her hair was wrapped in a scarf, hazel eyes were beaming as she laughed again.

"Girl, please. He wasn't about it," she said, looking at me. Her smile dropped before letting out a sigh. "Yeah, let me call you back. Give me like fifteen minutes. Okay, bye," she said, putting her phone down as she came and plopped down on the couch next to me.

"What's wrong?"

"Jade knew about Taylor and me," I mumbled. She gasped. I was surprised Taylor hadn't told her. Maybe she had, and she was just playing like she didn't know. Fucking females.

"Well, I mean, you said you were going to break up with her anyway. So really, it's a blessing, right? So you can be with Taylor?" She sounded hopeful.

I stared at my sister, eye for eye. She knew me better than anyone from the clan, so when her face dropped, smile disappearing? She knew.

"Trent, do not do this to Taylor. That girl has been in love with you for years."

"I didn't mean to fuck with her head like that," I groaned, gripping my own head as I closed my eyes. My mind was going crazy over what had just happened. I was still trying to remember Jade's first name, still trying to grasp at the answers to her questions.

"Trent, you ain't shit. You know that?" Olivia snapped, mushing me hard in the head. "I never set you up with none of my friends, because you are almost always guaranteed to fuck it up. Why would you even start something with Taylor if you never liked her?"

"I did like her," I argued, looking up at my sister. "I just . . . I just wanted to fuck. That was it."

She rolled her eyes with a smack of her teeth like the typical black female. "So now what? What are you going to do? You're single, you—"

"Hey, baby," Taylor greeted.

We both looked up, seeing her wrapped in a towel, body wet from the shower, and her hair shrinking up into tight curls as she smiled at me. Olivia cut her eyes hard at me before getting up to walk back to her room, closing the door hard.

"What's good, Tay?" I said slowly as she came to sit on my lap, arms wrapped around my neck as she kissed me.

What is Jade's first name? What the fuck is her first name? She told me. I hear it all the time. I should know that shit.

"How did it go?" she asked, rubbing my head softly. "Did she come down hard on you? You looked drained as shit, nigga."

I looked at her, trying to put on a smile. "Nah, she let me go easy," I said, picking her up easily as she laughed. As I carried her to the room, my mind went back to thinking of Jade's first name, her age, and her friends' names.

"So, that means you're mine now," Taylor said easily, cupping my chin as I laid her down gently on the bed.

I just gave her a weak smile as I forced myself to get hard for her. My mind was on some other shit that I wasn't even in the mood for sex, but I made that shit work. Only now, I saw my biggest mistake was taking this girl's virginity, knowing she felt the way she felt about it.

Once all was said and done, I lay in the bed quietly, listening as Taylor snored lightly next to me. Sitting up in the bed, I slipped on my boxer briefs and grabbed my phone, looking to see if Jade had called or texted me. When I saw my phone was dry, I slid down to the floor, gripping my head, and closed my eyes tight. My chest was feeling heavy as fuck. I needed to talk to her, hear her voice or something. Anything. Something to let me know I had a small chance of talking to her again.

I started feeling panic, calling her back to back before trying to text her.

JADE CAN U TLK 2 ME?

IM SRRY. IM SRRY. IM SRRY. PLEASE TLK 2 ME.

I DIDN'T MEAN TO STEP OUTSIDE OF WAT WE HAD. I SHUD HAVE TREATED U BETTER. APPRECIATED U MORE.

BABY IM HURTIN SO FUCKING BAD RIGHT NOW. JUST TLK 2 ME. I CNT SLEEP.

JADE?

?

?

IM SRRY . . .

Looking at the messages I sent, I tried calling her again. Never had I gone after a girl this hard. I went from not wanting her to be my girlfriend anymore to realizing I never treated her like my woman in the first place. Everything I did was for my benefit. Even during sex, she would tell me she didn't want it rough, and I still took pleasure in dominating her, not even tending to her wants and needs. I just thought she was so fucking dominant in person that it was my one chance I could show her that I could be in control. Now that I looked back, I was in control the entire time. If I wanted her to hang out, it had to be with my friends or I wasn't going. She had to dress a certain way with me, because I didn't fuck with the tattoos and piercings. I made her cover up her own artwork. I made her work out, even though she didn't need to, just because I did and wanted her at the gym with me. All this shit was adding up to the fact that I didn't even know her first fucking name.

Feeling my phone vibrate, I saw an incoming text message from Shiloh.

TLK 2 ME WHEN EVER U FREE.

Staring at the message, I know he wanted to clear the air with me about what I'd said earlier. Right now? That shit just wasn't on my mind. I wasn't ready to talk about that, and probably never would be. Getting up, I slipped on my clothes and shoes. I slowly made my way out the of house, realizing Olivia wasn't even home. She was never home this time at night. Where the fuck did she go at night? I'd been meaning to ask her that, but I didn't want her thinking I was in her business.

Scrolling through my contacts, I dialed Shiloh's number as I let the car warm up.

"Yeah?" he answered.

"Where you at?"

"Noe's house."

"Can I come by?" I asked. If the nigga was feeling like he wanted to talk about some shit with me all of a sudden, he could help me figure out the girl situation I had.

"Uh . . . yeah," he said hesitantly before hanging up.

When I pulled up to his girlfriend's house, I stepped out, rubbing my hands together as I walked up to the open door. He stood a few inches shorter than me, wearing his boxer briefs with a joint in his hand and a broom in the other. He had Polo house slippers on, looking like he had truly settled in with this girl.

"Yo, take yo' shoes off," he demanded softly, and I popped my Jordans off in the corner.

Sitting on the couch, I watched him continue to clean up like it was his place. TV was on mute as he emptied out the ashtray into the small black trash bag. I sat on the couch, waiting and watching my brother clean another woman's house.

Lighting up an incense stick to get rid of the weed smell, he said, "Noe is going to go off on me, bruh," with a small smile. "Soon as she smell this weed, she's going in."

"She doesn't seem like the type to go off on anyone," I mumbled.

Shiloh cut his eyes at me. "Don't be fooled by that good girl shit."

"So, why you smoking in her house?" I pressed, confused.

"I got too comfortable," he said, sitting down on the couch opposite mine. With a simple scratch of his head and a pull on his joint, he blew a thick cloud of smoke out. Putting out his joint, he looked hard at me.

"What the fuck is yo' problem with me?" he asked bluntly.

I dropped my head. "I don't have a pro—"

"You do," he said, cutting me off. "You always did, Trent."

"No, y'all always had a problem with me," I snapped. "I don't do shit. I don't say shit to y'all, but y'all stay ragging on me because I'm not as hood, or whatever, like y'all. I don't give a fuck about being the biggest gangsta on the street. That was never my life, and I don't ever want it to be my life, but y'all seem to think it's funny when I talk about college, school, and—" I stopped, shaking my head as he stared at me, blank expression. It was like talking to Elijah if he had no heart, no personality, and no fucking soul. That's what it's like talking to Shiloh, if you want to know.

"No one thinks it's funny, Trent. You insecure as fuck. That's the problem. Both you and Elijah are insecure.

Olivia got more balls than y'all two combined. It's not a contest to see who's the dopest nigga on the block or the smartest nigga with the books. It should never be that. If I made you feel less of yourself, then you need to rethink that shit, nigga. I didn't make you feel like shit. You did. You got issues that only you can fix, because as far as I know"—he put a hand to his heart as he leaned in to look hard at me—"you are my flesh and blood. I don't give a fuck if you was this or that. College or streets. It doesn't matter, because we family, and you know if anyone fucks with you, or E, or Livie, it's done.

"Am I closer to E? Yeah, I am, because he chose this fuck-ass lifestyle that I chose. I can't relate to being in college and shit. You didn't see me not one time when I was locked up, but you *never* hear me throw that shit in yo' face, ever," he spat.

I dropped my head in regret. I went every chance I got to see Elijah when he was in, but not once did I see Shiloh.

"This is going to be my last time talking about this shit. You are my brother; therefore, you are a part of me," he said sternly. "Never will I make you feel less of yourself or take away from your accomplishments and goals. At the end of the day, all we got is each other. I love you as much as I love E and Livie, but keep my name out yo' fucking mouth next time you feeling insecure. You hear me?"

I nodded just as a door opened and Noelle came out, looking half asleep. I almost had to check myself, looking at her in a little shirt and panties with that sexy-ass complexion. She was gorgeous for a dark-skin girl. Her country accent was even appealing, and I'm from the fucking South. I still didn't understand how she got stuck with a stone-cold nigga like Shiloh.

"Shiloh," she said in a low, warning-like tone, arms slowly crossing over her chest as she stood in front of him. I could have seen pigs fly that night, because the nigga looked up at her like he was scared. Never had I seen my older brother show any trace of fear in his eyes until that very moment. She was his weakness. "What the fuck did I say about—"

"I know. I put it out already," he reasoned as she cocked her head back.

"Get out," she said, pointing to the door.

My mouth dropped. He tried to open his mouth to speak, but she went from zero to one hundred. "You are so fucking inconsiderate! I told you not to smoke that shit in my house! Did I not? Got my whole house smelling like this! This is new furniture, Shiloh!"

"Noe—"

"Get out!" she spat as he stood up, towering over her short frame. "So fucking sick of you. Don't even know why I still entertain your ass! Get out!"

He signaled for me to follow him as he grabbed his shoes.

She turned to me, eyes wide in horror before flipping out some more. "And you bringing people to my house knowing I'm dressed like this? Oh my God! Shiloh, it's like you—"

"We leaving, Noe. Calm all of that down!" he said, cutting her off as he threw on some clothes.

"Well, get the fuck on then," she spat, walking back to her room as she slammed the door shut, still yelling to herself within the walls.

Shiloh looked at me again as I followed him out to his house. "Told you my bitch was crazy," he mumbled. I nearly fell out from laughing so hard. Never seen anyone go off on that nigga, and he just took it.

"Yeah, but you slick like that shit," I said and laughed.

I caught him smiling to himself as he glanced at me. "I love that shit about her," he cheesed.

As we walked into his house, my mind instantly went back to Jade. "Aye," I said, sitting on the couch, already taking my shoes off. "How do you make it up to a woman after you cheated on her? What would you do if she didn't want to see you again?" I watched him move around his space.

"You want to get back with yo' girl?" he asked knowingly.

"She found out I was fucking around on her," I said in a low voice as I looked at my hands, gripping my fingers together.

"Well, shit. If she was worth it, do all you can do. Words at that point wouldn't mean shit, because you been lying to her. Once you feel like you've done everything you could do to get her back, let that shit go. If she truly wants you, she will come back to you. Never fight over no bitch, never fight for a bitch," he stated.

"You wouldn't fight for Noelle? Fight to get back in that house, in that bed with her?" I joked, watching him sit down on his chair, rolling up another joint.

"Not tonight," he said, shaking his head. "She not giving me none no way."

"Whaaaat?" I let out.

He nodded slowly, putting a lighter to his joint as he took a long drag on it before passing it to me.

"So, you okay with that? No sex, but y'all together?"

"I'm good. Nigga, when you been locked up and ain't had no pussy around for years? You learn to have patience, li'l bruh. I'm done chasing after these hood rats and dumb-ass bitches in the streets. I'm so tired of that shit. Ain't nothing but drama that I don't need. I'm too old for it," he said, and I nodded. "Now, my life is basic as fuck, and I'm good with that. I make my money, run my shit, come home to a beautiful girl who can cook better than Mama, and she treats me like she gives a fuck."

"So, you settling with her?" I asked, stunned.

He nodded slowly. "When you find the right girl, you catch yourself doing shit outside the norm for her. Just like she would for you. Noe came in the bathroom one day while I was taking a shit. Just walked in like, nigga, what the fuck?" he let out as we laughed. "She talking about she had to flat iron her hair or some shit. Or sometimes I wait at her job for her, entertaining them fuck-ass uppity mothafuckas while she finish up doing what she's doing. The little things, Trent. You heard E talking about his girl got him eating healthy now?" I nodded, remembering how we clowned his ass. "E is in love with that girl. He don't move, think, or breathe without that bitch knowing. You'll meet the girl, Trent, and when you do, you'll see what I'm preaching."

"So, she's the girl?" I smiled, happy to see Shiloh happy with someone for the first time in his life. Yet, when he didn't answer my question? I stared at him, seeing he was caught in his silent daze.

He looked at me with a blank face before shaking his head.

"Nigga!" I laughed. "You preaching all of this to me, and you telling me about the *right one*. You don't even believe that for yourself!"

"Nah," Shiloh said, shaking his head with a smile. "I said I'm settling down with Noelle. I'm happy with her and hope she's happy with me, but I'm settling because she's the closest I'ma get to the real thing. I'm going to be her first, her only, and last, bruh. Believe that," he stated firmly.

I squinted my eyes, wondering who could possibly have him putting Noelle in second place.

His phone suddenly vibrated hard against the table. He sighed.

"This nigga here. Fuck is going on tonight?" He answered the call. "Hello?"

I could hear someone damn near screaming into the phone as Shiloh dropped his head, eyes closing hard.

"Where he at?"

Looking around as he spoke on the phone, I realized I'd never really been to my own brother's house. He was constantly switching houses and moving around, so I wasn't going to take the fault on this one, though. But as I looked around, I noticed he read a lot. Books were everywhere, stacked up on tables and counters. Some were open, the ones close by had lines that were highlighted. The books were as thick as the law books I read for class.

"Yeah, I'm on the way," he said, hanging up. "We gotta pick up Elijah. He's over at Jahiem's crib right now."

"What happened?"

"Ain't no telling with that dumb nigga," he mumbled.

When we hopped in his black Mustang, I smiled as I looked around the interior. Shit was clean.

"You paid for this in cash?" I asked, looking around, feeling the seats.

"Yeah, paid it off in a year so they wouldn't suspect shit." He shrugged, watching me eye the car.

"This shit is too clean," I mumbled, feeling him pick up speed.

He grabbed the clutch as he switched lanes with ease. No one was out tonight. Shit, it was going on 2 a.m., Monday morning.

"You know how to drive stick?" he asked, glancing at me.

"Nah."

"I'll teach you before the end of the year. I'm about to buy another car and don't have no use for this one, so you can have it," he said easily.

My mouth dropped. I looked at Shiloh with the biggest, gayest grin I could form.

"Graduation gift, nigga. Don't tear my shit up now."

"I won't." I smiled. The one person I wanted to tell was the one person who wasn't speaking to me right now.

Shit, I hated fucking Sundays.

Let The Drama Begin

Tia

"Jahiem," I let out in a groggy voice, body sore from the sex we'd had just a few hours ago. Nigga was snoring like his life depended on how loud he could be, and if he could get louder. The banging on the front door was getting louder. "Ugh! Jahiem!" I snapped angrily, pushing him hard in the arm.

"Hit me again," he threatened in his sleep, and I did just that. I hit him right in the ribcage, but the nigga didn't do shit but turn over and continue to sleep. The banging on the door persisted.

"Jahiem, answer the fucking door!"

"The fuck? You go answer that shit!" he snapped at me.

I swung the covers back, dragging my pregnant ass out the bed because someone wanna be a bitch and not open his own door. I threw on his shirt, barely covering myself as I walked out to the living room. The knocking on the door was becoming more rapid.

"Yooo, open up!" I heard Elijah let out slowly.

I rolled my eyes. I was sick of these fucking brothers, I swear. Checking my weave to make sure it was still straight underneath my scarf, with the long braid coming down my shoulder, I opened up the door to a drunk-as-hell Elijah Carter. He fell face first into the apartment, and I barely caught him, almost dropping to the floor myself because of his weight.

"Where is Jahiem at?" he slurred, dreads all over the place, smelling like straight rubbing alcohol, face fucked up like he got into a fight. He was still fine, though. I had to throw that in there.

"He's in the room, 'sleep. What the fuck is yo' problem, turning up late in the middle of the night, drunk?" I snapped.

He just looked at me, low eyes glossy as he licked his lips hard at me. I felt his arms come around my body.

"You still want me?"

"Nigga, move!" I flipped, trying to push him off me. He was so fucking gross. I don't even know what I was thinking when I first saw him. I didn't know how Jordyn could even fuck him. "You need to be at Jordyn's house with all this foolishness!"

"She don't wanna fuck with a nigga no more. She got a boyfriend now." He laughed sarcastically before his facial expression immediately changed to rage. It was like night and day, almost scary to even be around him. His jaw was working slowly as he stared mindlessly at the floor.

I pulled myself away from his weight, backing up just as Jahiem stepped out of his room, wearing his Batman boxers that I'd bought him.

Nigga, you better come save my ass if you trying to wear those, because this right here? This shit right here, nigga? This is on some whole 'nother shit I don't want to deal with.

Rubbing his eyes, he looked at Elijah. "Bruh," Jahiem started slowly. "This better be—"

"She got a boyfriend," Elijah mumbled, fists tightening. "I told her to give me that nigga's name and address. She won't do it. Asked her, what the fuck you need a nigga for when you got me? Everybody loves mothafucking Jodie Carter. I'm the nigga every bitch wants!" he snapped, getting up, trying to steady himself. "I'm that nigga!" he screamed before randomly punching the nearest wall, putting a decent-sized hole in it.

"Bruh! What the—nigga!" Jahiem cried out, hands in the air, trying to control a wild Elijah. "Not my fucking walls, man! Damn!"

"She said she don't love me no more," he mumbled suddenly.

My heart dropped, feeling for Elijah. So, Jordyn broke it off with him. Damn, she was a coldhearted bitch like I knew her to be.

"Do you love her?" I asked.

He looked at me, eyes struggling to stay open. He was on something more, something other than alcohol. Had to be. Licking his lips in a sloppy fashion, he slowly smiled, leaning against the wall.

"You told Jahiem you fucked Trent the night before you fucked him?" he asked with a sick laugh.

I gripped my chest, feeling my breath leave me. Jahiem turned to look at me, mouth agape.

"Nah? Jordyn used to laugh at yo' dumb ass, talking about you don't know who the baby's daddy—"

"Elijah," I started, but the look on Jahiem's face could have killed me on the spot.

"He's lying?" he questioned, looking hard at me. "Tell me that nigga is lying, Tiana. After I fucking asked you was there any chance this baby wouldn't be mine? I asked you!" he screamed.

The tears started to come down. "I'm sorry," I struggled to say, voice shaking.

"Nah, there's more!" Elijah laughed. "My bitch Jordyn ran her mouth like water. Ahhh, get it! Water? Jordyn?"

"Nigga, shut the fuck up!" Jahiem snapped at him.

"Nah, nah, she told me Trent and Tia been fucking around for a minute! Tell yo' option-number-two nigga everything. He the backup baby daddy, because you

already know Trent ain't claiming that shit. Fucking ho,"
Elijah spat just as Jahiem hauled off and punched him
dead in his face.

"Jahiem!" I cried out, trying to keep him off Elijah, who
probably felt no pain at this point.

He snatched his arm away from my grip, looking hard
at me. "Get out. Get the fuck out. I don't care where the
fuck you go, but you getting out of here, out my shit," he
said in a low voice, grabbing his phone. "Both of y'all get
the fuck on."

"Trent and I only happened—"

He held his hand up as he put the phone to his ear. "Yo,
come get yo' fuck-ass brother out my house before I fuck
him up some more! Now!"

"You ain't finna do shit," Elijah mumbled.

Jahiem turned around and stomped so hard on his
chest, causing him to cry out in pain. "Nigga, you a half-
brother! We ain't all the way related, which means I can
halfway beat yo' bitch ass and halfway not give a fuck!"
Jahiem spat, stomping hard on him again. "Fuck outta
here! Nigga, come pick up yo' brother!" he snapped into
the phone before hanging up.

He stormed back to the room as I watched in a panic.
He was grabbing my things, throwing them all out on the
floor.

"Jah—"

"Tiana, baby." He laughed slowly. "Get the fuck on
before I beat that baby out of ya. I'm not playing with
you."

I quickly tried grabbing my things, but he pushed them
aside with his foot.

"Nah, fuck that. You going out on the street how we
found yo' ho ass! Go! You ain't had shit then, so you not
gonna have shit now."

"I'm not—"

He scooped me up, and I started screaming, trying to fight to get down, telling him I loved him more than anything. He opened the front door, putting me out into the cold, concrete hallway, nearly dropping me before slamming the door shut. I lay there, tears pouring down, with no shoes or socks on. As I tried to get back in, I had to keep the flimsy T-shirt from rising up, because I had nothing underneath.

"Jahiem, I'm sorry! I still love you! You—"

The door swung open, and he tossed Elijah out in front of me, causing us both to fall back hard to the ground.

"Should have never took a ho's word to heart," I could hear him say as he closed the door. "You ain't shit but a ho, Tia! Legs stay open for any nigga!"

"Fuck!" Elijah coughed, spitting up blood on my leg as I tried moving out of the way. It was freezing cold, and I didn't have on shit but a shirt, with a nigga coughing up blood on me. Still, my mind was on Jahiem, hoping he would hear me out. I wasn't the type to beg no nigga for anything, but he was the only man I'd ever truly fallen in love with. If this nigga had any love for me, he would hear me out just the same.

I was about to start trying again when Elijah coughed up more blood, going in and out of consciousness.

"Jahiem!" I screamed, banging hard on the door as I looked back at Elijah, who looked like death, covered in his own blood.

"Aye!" I heard someone yell out. I looked down the hallway, seeing Trent and Shiloh rushing toward us.

"What happened?" Trent panicked, coming to his brother, trying to hold his head up. "What the fuck are you even doing here, Tia?" he questioned, confused.

He has no idea.

"Ahh, fuck nah," Shiloh muttered, looking at Elijah before banging hard on the door. As soon as the door swung open, Jahiem's eyes went to Trent, who had no clue what was going on. Jahiem went the fuck in. Bypassing Shiloh, he started hitting Trent.

Shiloh came in between them, trying to hold Jahiem back as he slammed him hard against the wall of the apartment. Neighbors were peeking through cracked doors, trying to see what was going on.

"Nigga! What the fuck is the problem? You think I'ma let you beat on my brothers like that?" Shiloh snapped, pulling his sweats up. "Leh-go! Fight me if you feeling like you 'bout it, nigga!"

Jahiem was twice Shiloh's size, but even he wasn't trying to go there. He kept still against the wall, mouth tightening up.

"Take yo' drunk-ass bitch nigga of a brother Elijah, and yo' fucking punk-ass, sleep-with-everybody bitch of a brother Trent away from here," Jahiem said in a low voice as his eyes cut to me.

Without warning, Trent, who was in his feelings, getting caught in the moment, caught Jahiem on the side of his jaw, starting another series of fights between all three brothers. I tried to intervene, screaming, grabbing at Jahiem to get him to chill. Everything came to a stop when Shiloh suddenly reached behind him, pulling out his gun, and aimed it at Jahiem's head with no mercy, causing everyone to go completely still. I, like an idiot, ran to stand in front of Jahiem, crying and pleading for him not to do anything, but Shiloh didn't see me. His dark, empty eyes were cold as ice.

"What you tryna do, Jahiem?" he questioned. "Move yo' bitch out the way and tell me what the fuck is going on. Why you got my brother on the ground covered in blood, and then come at the other one? You got a problem with them, you come to me, my nigga!"

"Ask Trent," Jahiem spat, gun still aimed at his head.

"I don't know what the fuck you talking about!" Trent argued, jaw fucked up, with a bruise right under his eye.

"You fucked Tia?" Jahiem pressed, and Trent's eyes grew wide.

"One time, nigga. I didn't even—"

Shiloh dropped the gun as he looked at Trent, Jahiem, and then stayed focused on me. "All this shit over a bitch?" Shiloh questioned before grabbing Elijah's limp body off the ground, slinging him over his shoulder. "Over a mothafucking ho!" he snapped. "Got me out the fucking house over a fucking ho! All of this is some dumb-ass shit! I'm too old for it!"

I felt my body jerk forward as Jahiem pushed me away before going back in the house, slamming the door shut. Trent stared at me, still confused.

"You been fucking with him this whole time? Before or after—"

"Nigga, after!" I snapped. "I don't, nor will I ever, want yo' ass like that! Jahiem, please open the door, baby!" I was banging hard on the door with my other hand on my stomach.

"He thinks you're pregnant by me?" Trent asked, suddenly connecting the dots. "I didn't even nut in you."

"Well, tell him that!" I snapped.

Shiloh called out to him. "Trent! Leave her the fuck alone, nigga. We leaving! I need to get him to the hospital!"

He rushed off. I stayed against the door, calling Jahiem, praying he would open the door. I was cold, nose running, and my feet felt numb from the freezing concrete. I didn't have a cell phone to call anyone to come get me, nor did I have money to take the train back. I continued to knock on the door hard until I heard music being played.

Fuck it, nigga. If it takes me spending the night out here in the cold for you to see how serious I am about us, and how I knew in my heart you're the daddy of my baby, then I'll stay my ass right here. Love will make you do some crazy-ass shit. I swear. I went to jail with yo' ass. Staying out like this is nothing.

The next time that door opened, he walked out completely dressed. I stood up, trembling in defeat, face filled with dried tears.

"Jahiem?" I called out, watching him lock the door, duffle bag on his shoulders as he slipped his hands in his coat. "Baby, can you—"

"Who the fuck are you?" he asked in a dull voice as he looked me dead in the eyes. "I don't know who you are, but I tell you what—you got five minutes to get the fuck on from my door, or I'm calling the cops on you, shawty. Real talk. When I come back, you better be gone." With that, he walked down the hallway, getting on the phone as he cut the corner.

I felt myself about to cry once more when a door just across the hall opened. An older black man stuck his head out and looked at me with pity. "Come here, young lady. You need to call someone to pick you up," he said, walking back into his place, leaving the door open.

I was hesitant at first, but if the nigga was going to try something, now was not the time to do it, because I don't fight fair. Young or old, you touched a bitch, you're going down. Period. I walked to his place, seeing a set of basketball sweats on the table, folded neatly.

"My son got those for me. Never had no use for them," he said softly, handing me the house phone. His was the only number I knew by heart. We rarely spoke to each other since we didn't get along, but right now, he was all I had. My parents still, even after knowing I was pregnant, didn't want shit to do with me—especially my daddy.

"Hello?" he answered, sounding like he was asleep.

I immediately started crying, telling him everything that had happened. "Can you just come get me and take me to Mama and Daddy's house?"

"Where you at, T?" He groaned with a frustrated sigh.

A Night with the Gays

Taylor

"Have you spoken to him?" I asked Olivia, pressing for information on where Trent could possibly be. She sighed with a roll of her eyes. I knew I was annoying her about her brother, but the nigga wasn't picking up his phone. It had been a whole damn two weeks since he broke up with his girlfriend, and not one call or text from him since.

"I don't know. It's a lot going on with the boys right now." Olivia sighed, going through a magazine as she sat on the bed, with me sitting on the edge. "Ain't nobody really talking to nobody at this point. I'm just trying to figure out how to squash all of this."

"That doesn't mean he can't call me," I mumbled, getting up to walk to my room.

It was a quiet Wednesday evening. Both of us had gotten off work early since Thanksgiving was the next day. Schools were out, places were closed, and we were attempting to have dinner here, but nobody was coming. Whatever the fuck happened, it had divided the entire tight-knit group of boys. Even though the Carter Boys as a music group still had work they needed to do, behind the face, nobody was speaking to no one.

Sitting on my bed, tucking my feet underneath me, I tried calling him again. I must have called Trent at least fifty times in the span of two weeks.

Am I crazy? Fuck no. He would tell me during sex we were meant to be together, and that sex with me is better than with his girlfriend. He said he felt more connected to me, and I feel it too. Everyone likes us together, so why igno—

"Hello?" Trent answered. My eyes nearly popped out of my head at the sound of his voice.

"Nigga, I've been trying to call you for—"

"I know." He sighed. "It's a lot of shit going on right now, Taylor. You know I got my exams coming up, and the whole fuck shit with Jahiem—"

"What happened?" I asked, sitting back on the bed, eyeing my toes. I needed a fresh coat of polish.

"Just a lot. Too much to explain." I heard a few of his fraternity brothers in the background, laughing it up. "Just do me a favor and leave me alone for a minute. I need space and time to think some shit over."

"I thought we were—"

"Nah, Taylor, we not nothing right now," he said in a low voice before hanging up. My body went completely numb, with my heart nearly hurting to beat. I went completely still, frozen in sadness and rejection. How did we go from the best time of our lives to him suddenly cutting me off?

"Helloooooo!" Someone called out as the door opened and closed. I quickly wiped my eyes, trying to get Trent's rejection out of my head: *We not nothing right now.* If he was going to fucking dump me, the nigga could have at least used basic correct English.

"Trelly!" Olivia called out in excitement.

I watched her run up to her younger brother, who smiled, hugging her. His boyfriend, Tyree, poked his head in my room, looking at me with squinting eyes.

"What's the matter, boo?" he asked, coming into my room, looking around. He stood tall, built like a slim, muscular man, with a Polo skull cap on, long gray scarf, black trenchcoat, and cute, random red rain boots. New Yorkers do shit like that.

"Nothing." I smiled, watching the rest come in.

Ontrell always dressed almost identical to his brother Elijah, wearing a flashy color sweatshirt with FCUK U on the front, Rolex on the wrist, dark blue straight-leg jeans, and high-top sneakers that were probably hella expensive. Chains decorated his neck, with his top locs pulled back in a ball, with his sides and the back of his head in a low fade. Nigga was straight looking like Young Thug right now. Him and Tyree were so different. I didn't even know how they made it work this long. Tyree was so sophisticated; Trell was just . . . wild. No other way to describe him.

"What's good with you, Tay Tay?" Trell teased as he came in for a hug. "You rolling with us tonight?"

"Where are y'all going?" I asked, wiping my eyes, trying to conceal the fact that I was about to start crying over a fuck-ass nigga.

"We stepping out, shawty," he said, trying to dance with Olivia, who playfully pushed him away.

"Nigga, ain't nothing open," I retorted.

He smiled, looking at Tyree.

"Gurl, look, I told him the same shit, but he claims he knows a few people, so we just gotta mind what the nigga says and go with it," Tyree let out with a roll of his eyes.

"Man, just get dressed and come on. Wear whatever the fuck you want," Trell cut in. "I'm trying to turn up before I go up north with this nigga in the morning. You know New Yorkers don't know how to fucking party like Georgia boys," he boasted, tongue sticking out as Tyree rolled his eyes again.

"That's why y'all got all these mothafucking AIDS down here," Tyree mumbled, walking out the room as I laughed. "Turn up in that mothafucking death bed, nigga."

"He a hater," Trell mumbled before looking around. "Come on, Tay. Get dressed. You too, Livie."

"Oh, you already know I'm sooo coming," she stated as they walked out of my room.

I sighed. I needed to take my mind off Trent anyway, so throwing on something cute, letting my hair be wild and kinky-curly free, I slipped on my riding boots, leggings, cute long-sleeve shirt that covered just enough ass, and a cute jacket. Bangles, a few rings, and a necklace topped it off with light makeup. Never go nowhere without looking like you trying to impress.

So, when we all piled in Ontrell's Hummer H2, Olivia and I sat in the back, eyeing the interior like we'd never been inside a car this nice before.

"Uh, how much was this, and how can you afford this if you just bought a house?" I pressed. Tyree looked back at me, lips turned up like he was ready to cop an attitude.

"We just renting it for tonight, ma'am, but uh, thank you for worrying about our finances, boo," he snapped, and I laughed. "We straight on this end. Don't worry."

"Aye, you heard our song is already number two on iTunes?" Ontrell beamed excitedly, trying to look for a radio station while letting the truck warm up. "They talking about wanting us to go overseas next month."

"Overseas where?"

"UK," he said excitedly. "I already got my passport and everything. I'm just waiting on them to say go. Like, nigga, leh go! We can do this shit!" he said with a laugh. "Y'all ready for a night of foolishness and fuckery?"

"I'm ready!" Olivia shouted.

"Me too!" I chimed in. "I wanna see how y'all get down when nobody's watching."

"You'll be okay being around a bunch of gay niggas and women?" Ontrell asked, looking back at me as he backed out the driveway, hand on the back of Tyree's seat, trying to whip the truck like it was a small car.

"I'll be okay. It will be nice to be surrounded by niggas who will give you attention but still want dick," I joked.

"A'ight then, we in business." He smiled, stepping on the gas, trying to speed off down the dark street.

Let me tell y'all, when I say I haven't laughed so hard at a couple as much as I had at Trell and Tyree? They were the entertainment for the night. Our first stop was this shady-looking house over on the east side of Atlanta. Took us an hour just to get there because we stopped to grab drinks. That almost resulted in a damn fight in itself, because while Trell was pumping the gas, Tyree, myself, and Olivia went to grab the drinks. One high-school nigga thought it was funny to poke fun at Tyree because he was gay, and an obvious gay at that. Shit, he was just being himself.

Walking to the back of the store where the good shit was known to be, the teenager and his girlfriend started snickering behind us. "Aye," he called out, and we all looked back. Dude had the nerve to have jeans tighter than mine, hair dyed blond, and a sweater with Pokemon on it, like that shit was cool. What the fuck was up with the fashion these days? The girl was trying to pull him along, but even she was laughing.

"Why y'all niggas be thinking you can be girls?" he started, and Tyree's eyes grew wide.

"Don't pay him any attention, Ty. Just keep going," I said, pushing him farther back.

"I mean, I swear niggas be thinking they can try me, and think I won't say nothing, though." He laughed. "Little boy, don't get hurt with that cute Pokemon shirt on."

"Just ignore it," Olivia said before turning her attention to the boy. "Nigga, you think that shit is funny? You must be gay yourself if you notice my brother before you notice yo' own bitch. Keep yo' eyes on her, bruh."

"Excuse me?" the girlfriend snapped as I laughed. Olivia was probably the biggest stuck-up, prudest girl I knew, but her last name was still Carter, and she was raised with seven boys. My girl knew how to turn it on and turn up if she had to.

"Nah, hold up, hold up," the boy started. "Who the fuck is you? Ain't nobody in here gay but that tall mothafucka."

"And what, son? Okay, so I'm gay! And what?" Tyree snapped with a clap of his hands as he pushed past us to stand in front of him, New York coming out heavy. "Nigga, look at you! You half my size, son. I eat bitches like you fo' breakfast. Don't come for me or my girls. My nigga is at the car right now, and if he finds out you fucking around with me or them, it's going to be a problem. Yo, let's go," he said, grabbing Olivia and me. "Get these drinks and go. I don't have time for y'all country shit tonight. The gayest city in the world, but the dumbest niggas, like fo' real."

"He's young, so he don't know any better," I said as we grabbed a bottle, paid for it, and walked out.

Trell stood leaning against the Hummer, still filling up the tank. He started dancing at the sight of the brown paper bag in my hand.

"We turning up!" he yelled excitedly.

"While yo' alcoholic ass out here desperate for a drink," Tyree snapped as I laughed, "we dealing with reckless niggas in the store!"

"We handled it, though," Olivia said, taking the bottle, already popping it open.

The bells chimed. I turned around, seeing the boy and the girl walking out, still talking shit.

"What the fuck yo' big-mama ass looking at?" the girl snapped.

My head cocked back. *Nooo, bitch. And I just got dumped tonight too? You got the right one today.*

"Who the fuck you calling—" I tried to reach for her hair when Tyree grabbed me, arms around my waist, and easily pulling me away. "Let me go! She wanna talk big shit! Let me go! No problem beating somebody's kid tonight!"

"Girl, it ain't worth it!" Ty screamed as the girl walked off with a flip of her hair, bouncing her bony ass back to the car, thinking she was cute. The boy just stood there, smirking hard at Tyree.

"Bruh, I don't get how you can sleep with another nigga."

"You obviously must wanna find out with yo' curious ass!" Ty snapped, grabbing me by the arm. "Let's go before I really get heated."

We started walking back, with Olivia at the car, telling Ontrell what happened.

"Nah, but I bet you wanna suck this dick, though!" he yelled out.

Before Tyree could say anything, Ontrell rushed up, pulling his jeans up, strutting like he was ready to try something. The teenager, still smirking at Tyree, had a rude awakening when Trell got in his face instead.

"You hitting on my nigga?" Trell snapped, invading all types of personal space. The kid nearly fell back as his eyes grew wide in fear, looking up at Trell with a shake of his head. Olivia used to always tell me when I was in California about how Ontrell caught people off guard because no one would suspect that he was gay. He didn't flaunt it around, but he didn't hide it either, and he still hit on girls just because he could pull them too.

"Nah, fuck nah, I wasn't—"

"You sure? Because from what I heard, you just came at my dude like you wanted him, bruh," Trell pressed.

Ty rolled his eyes with a smack of his teeth, trying to pull him back. "Baby, this li'l boy ain't ready tonight. Come on. We're going to be late," Tyree pressed, trying to pull Trell away, but Trell only had eyes for the teen.

"I didn't—I didn't mean to—to come at him like that," he stuttered, scared out of his mind because Trell was not letting up, even though I could see he was just fucking with the boy at this point.

"Next time you feeling like you wanna run yo' mouth," Trell said, lifting his sweatshirt up to reveal his gun, "you can run yo' mouth on this dick."

Soon as the boy looked down, he backed up some more before taking off. Trell turned around all smiles, like nothing had happened.

"It's fun fucking with straight niggas," he said, and we all laughed. "Never see that shit coming. Now that the foolishness has begun, can we drink and turn up once more?"

The next stop was a house party that we were just swinging through, picking up weed and leaving, but we stayed for a bit, enjoying the good vibes. I thought it was going to be gay niggas, but apparently, it was just some hood nigga connect. Everyone knew Ontrell, either from the music group or just locally, so when he stepped in, everyone started to get excited. Music was bumping, and niggas was looking especially cute now that I was on the rebound. And shit, I was horny. I'm not going to even lie to you. I went from getting some on the regular to none at all.

Oddly enough, nobody really bothered Tyree like I thought. He went off doing his own thing with a few girls that he knew, and he even was cool with some of the guys. I collected a few numbers here and there, but I was ready to move on to the next once we got the weed.

"Yo, y'all ready to go?" Ontrell asked as he came to Olivia and me standing near the front door. "We got at least two more spots to hit up. I'm tryna roll up in the car, too."

"Nigga, you already high." I laughed, looking at his bright red eyes.

"Y'all ready?" Tyree said, coming up, already trying to steady his balance as he grabbed Trell's shoulder. "Shit, let me go before I pass out in this bitch and y'all slick niggas take advantage of a cute bitch like me. Come on, Tay Tay," he slurred, and I laughed.

"Ain't nobody gon' take advantage of yo' big ass," Trell retorted as we piled out of the packed house, back into the cold night. On to the next party!

We rolled up in the car with these two cracking Olivia and me up to no end. The next stop was another house, this time a lot bigger, like someone with money. Cars were lined up, and people were outside in the cold waiting like it was a club. Shit, we just walked right on in, and whooo! The house was damn near about to collapse the bass was bumping so loud. You couldn't look nowhere without seeing someone fucking, making out, or dancing a little too hard on each other. The lights were low, but the few lights that did shine showed a lot of people who were out-of-their-minds high. This was more of a gay crowd, with a few white people sprinkled in the mix. Shit, Olivia and I just took whatever was the drink of the hour and had fun—maybe a little too much fun. Maybe I was high or drunk as fuck; I don't know.

My body was numb, but I spotted Olivia on a man's lap, scraping up a line of white powder before sniffing it up in one breath. My mouth dropped as I looked around for her brother, wondering if he had seen that shit. Looking back, I saw her laughing with another girl, high out of her mind.

What the fuck? Maybe it ain't her. Nah. Fuck nah. I was high my damn self, so I could be seeing shit. Let me focus on me and my good time.

Moving farther into the crowd, I started to get into the music, dancing with different guys. Some were so gay it was like dancing with a woman. Others, like this one nigga who thought he was sexy, tried it with me. I felt his hands coming up in between my legs, and I quickly turned around, looking up at him.

"Nah, you already know ain't no dick down there. What you looking for?" I laughed as he leaned in close, hand on my waist.

"I'm straighter than an arrow, baby. I'm just selling products to these fruity niggas in here. I make the most money off their kind," he said as I looked at him, smiling. Before I could even protest, he cupped my face, kissing me on the lips, dropping one hand to get in between my legs, pressing against the leggings. Shit, the touch was so unfamiliar, so not Trent, that it turned me on even more. It was different. He backed me into a corner, and we continued to kiss and rub up on each other before he ripped a hole in my leggings, breathing heavy against my ear. I was so out of it that all I could think about was, *Fuck Trent. This is why I'm fucking other niggas now. I'm moving on from yo' lying dog ass.*

"Oh, shit. You feel good," he breathed, bending down slightly.

Somehow, we did that shit standing straight up. Maybe we weren't . . . I don't know. As soon as I felt him slide in me, I let out a sigh of pleasure. I couldn't believe I was having sex in the middle of the night at a party in a freak-ass house full of gays. Usher's song "I Don't Mind" with Juicy J was playing throughout the house as I started to get into it, trying to throw it back at him. Yet, as soon as I was getting into it, he pulled out quickly, with white shit spitting out in small waves.

Fucking waste of my time. Clearly. I mean, I got nothing out of that.

"You good?" he asked, and I laughed, pulling my shirt down before walking off.

I started navigating throughout the dark crowd, feeling a hand come to my back. I quickly turned around, eyes barely open.

"Yo, we going to the next spot. Go find Livie," Trell said as he moved past me with Tyree close behind.

As soon as we all got in the car, we were fucked up to the point where we were having conversations with each other, but none of us knew what we were talking about, or who we were talking to. How Ontrell drove was a mystery.

The next spot was just the same, only it was an under-ground basement–like place with the gayest of the gays in Atlanta. They were mostly men, with a few dressed as women. When I say the moment Trell stepped in and the DJ announced his arrival? These niggas went nuts. He got on stage, spitting a few bars from their latest song, with Tyree standing close by, blending in with the groupies. Olivia and I kept to ourselves, snickering at some of these men dressing like women, doing the most.

"Girl, I love me some Ontrell," one guy said as he walked by with another. "Mmmph, only reason I listen to the Carter Boys, just to hear his fine ass."

"Who you telling?" the other guy responded as we watched them. Both were wearing tight-ass dresses and heels with weave halfway down their backs.

I looked at Olivia, and we both burst out laughing against this wall. I couldn't take niggas like that seriously.

"What y'all laughing at?" Tyree said, walking over. He started dancing on me, poking his booty out, with me slapping it.

"These niggas in here fanning over yo' man," I said, letting him twerk.

He rolled his eyes with a wave of his hand. "I'm not worried, baby. I got a ring and a house," he stated, flashing his black band. "Honey boo, these niggas in here think they can snatch him from me. I am truly not bothered."

"I know that's right," Olivia said as we laughed, hands coming together in agreement.

Suddenly, out of nowhere, someone yelled out Tyree's name so loud over the music that nearly everyone looked around to see where it came from. Tyree immediately took off, moving through the crowd with ease. We tried following, and saw a growing circle form, with two men in the middle trying to fight Ontrell.

What the fuck? I swear I was too high for this.

"Aye, yo! We not doing that in here! We just trying to party!" the DJ yelled over the mic as the lights cut on.

"Take that shit outside!" someone yelled.

"Boy, wassup?" Ontrell snapped, gripping his jeans from the knees, eyes red and filled with rage. He must didn't have his gun on him, because if he did, he would have already settled that shit by now. The two guys were steady talking shit, but when Tyree stepped in, it was like a transformation. I hadn't seen this side of him. Roles switched almost immediately. Tyree and Trell were equally dominant at this moment.

"Yo, we got a problem?" Tyree asked, voice deep as hell, New York accent thicker than usual as he stood by Ontrell, who was ready, waiting.

"So, you had to call yo' li'l boyfriend to come fight."

"Son! Don't do that, B. Address me when you talking to me, mothafucka!" Tyree snapped, stepping closer. "Don't worry about what my nigga doing!"

"Call security! Someone call—"

Tyree wasted no time swinging first on the guy, while Trell took aim at the other dude. Soon, someone else tried to jump in, and I had to damn near keep Olivia from jumping in. These niggas here were too big and too grown for us females to be jumping in that shit. She slapped my hand out the way and came at whoever was going for Ontrell.

"Olivia!" I called out, trying to grab her as two more niggas jumped in, trying to grab us.

"Y'all need to back up!" one yelled. "Y'all shouldn't even be—"

"Don't touch!" Olivia yelled, pounding one man in the face who had his arm around Ontrell's neck. "My brother! Get yo' fucking hands off him!" she screamed, going in.

The moment he loosened up a little on his neck, Trell broke free. At the same Tyree handled one nigga, they both went in on the guy that Olivia had. All three of them were trying to hit him as I tried stopping it like a fucking wimp. I was just too high for that shit. They were doing the most right now, and I hadn't even eaten a damn thing all night! All of this before Thanksgiving, at that.

After all the bullshit, through everything we'd been through that night, I could honestly say as we made our way to the nearest Waffle House that I would never hang with another gay mothafucka for as long as I lived. Fight at the gas station, fucking dudes at parties, drinking, and popping Lord knows what kind of pills, and more fights—it wasn't even a gay thing; shit, it was a Carter boy thing. Only Ontrell got into these situations.

We grabbed a table toward the back, sliding into the booths, bodies bruised up. Ontrell's hands were bloodied up pretty bad. Tyree's knuckles looked worse, with a small cut underneath his eye. Olivia had a scratch, and I had a hole in my leggings. *What the fuck?*

It was quiet in the restaurant, with barely anyone there. We sat in the booth with me and Trell getting window seats across from each other. A black woman walked up to us with the biggest attitude on her face, until she looked at Ontrell, all smiles.

"What can I get y'all?" she asked, eyes on for Trell. "Ain't you from the Carter Boys?"

"Yeah." He smiled, licking his lips at her, trying to be cute.

Tyree slammed his hand down on the table, looking at the woman as I laughed. "Uh, ain't you the waitress that supposed to ask what the fuck we want to eat?"

"Bruh, come on—"

"No! You got me out here, blowing my high because we fighting niggas in the club. Like, what the fuck, Trell?" Tyree snapped.

"Um, can I get . . ." Olivia cut in, trying to sound cute. Her eyes were bloodshot red. "Lemme get an all-star special."

"Get four of those, and four Southern classics, three sweet teas, and one hot tea," Trell ordered, handing her our menus. As soon as she left, we kind of took a moment of silence, just to rethink everything that had happened.

"Yo, this was a crazy night. Least I made some money off it."

"Shut up, Ontrell," Tyree snapped, mushing him in the head.

I smiled. "How in the world did y'all meet, anyway?" I pressed.

They looked at each other at the same time, laughing as Tyree sat up, ready to tell the story.

"Okay, sooo," he started, looking up as he thought back. "Damn, baby, we getting old, boo."

"I know it," Trell said, leaning back as he stretched.

"We both had some mutual friends in common, right? So, one night at the club that all the fine niggas go to, I was with my friend, and he was like, I want you to meet someone. I'm like, bitch, I know you did not bring me here to set me up on no blind date in a damn club. Like, how tacky," Tyree said, and we laughed. "Anyway," he said, smacking his teeth, "I was like, who is he? What does he look like? What's the nigga zodiac sign? So, he was like, his name is Trell. He's a year younger than us, but blah blah. Whatever. So, we dancing, I'm talking to dudes, when my friend was walks up with this tall, dark-skin nigga with dreads all over the place, walking like he was ready to shoot someone for staring at him the wrong way. I'm like, uhhh! I'm not dating no fucking hood nigga. I'm not into thugs. Never will I—"

"Lies," Trell cut in.

"Whatever," Tyree retorted, eyes focused on me. "So, he was trying to talk his little game. I gave him the curve because yeah, he was cute, but I don't find thug niggas appealing. Plus, I'm thinking someone like him has to be on the down low. But I gave him my number anyway, and he was steady calling me, texting me, trying to link up. I'm like, son, I don't like you. I'm not interested. I don't have the time."

"But you did what?" Trell cut in, smiling hard.

"I . . ." He rolled his eyes with a sigh. "I agreed to one movie date because I wanted to see if he was openly gay like me. Turns out, the country bumpkin showed me a good time, and he wasn't shy about affection in public. So, after that, I told him I don't sleep with niggas on the first date," Tyree stated proudly.

Trell sat up, looking at him. "But you did what, nigga?"

"I . . ." He sighed with another roll of his eyes. "Slept with him."

"Ahhh!" I laughed.

"Aye, real talk, though. It was just supposed to be casual shit," Trell said as the food was brought to our table. "Hit it and move on. If I was nearby, I would see him and chill, but that was it. But this nigga caught me way off guard when we was out one night and some dude was trying to fuck with him. I was going to handle it, but nigga turned into the Hulk on my ass. Son, you doing all that talking, B," he mocked as Tyree smiled. "You talking, son. Yo,

I'm from New York, and this how we do shit up there, B. Then! He fought the nigga, throwing jab for jab, boxing like a fucking professional and shit. After that night? I told myself, if I don't lock this nigga down? I won't find another one like him," he said as Olivia and I cooed.

"You just like me because of my accent, nigga." Tyree smirked.

"Y'all are so cute," I cheesed, watching Trell playfully tug at Tyree's ear lobe.

"Did you enjoy yourself tonight? See what we be getting into on a regular? Olivia already know how we get down," Trell said as we looked at her. She was so zoned out it was unbelievable. Looking at us, she smiled sweetly, biting her lip.

"Shit, she look like Elijah," Tyree muttered, and I laughed.

"Nigga, shut up. I look like Olivia," she clapped back, taking a sip of her tea. "I had fun, met some new people."

"Yeah, I saw you upstairs fucking with that girl," Tyree said.

My mouth dropped, looking at my best friend for years. I had no idea she even got down like that. "You what?" I shrieked, shoving her playfully as she giggled.

"I was horny," she pouted.

Trell laughed. "Man, Taylor, you of all people should know how Olivia is."

"Uh, the bitch just lost her virginity not too long ago," I let out, and they all looked at me, bursting out into laughter at the same time.

What the fuck am I missing?

"Bruh, you have no idea. Do Taylor even know about Montana?" Ontrell asked.

I stared at Olivia, who was so far gone I didn't think she would make it past the meal. Instead, she sniffed, hand running up her coke-filled nose before throwing her head back with a groan.

"Ughh! All right, I'll come clean, but you better not say shit, Taylor," Olivia said, looking at me with those red, glossy eyes. I nodded, ready to hear this fuckery. "I lied," she stated simply, with a cute shrug like the spoiled girl she was known to be. "I just said it because you were still one."

"Well, clearly you lied," I retorted as Tyree laughed.

"You think partying with us is some mad shit?" Tyree said, hand on his chest to signify Trell and him. "Party with Olivia and her crew. One night in Atlanta, you will never be the same."

"Damn right," she stated as she and Trell pounded fists.

"Well, who is Montana?" I questioned.

She slid her hazel eyes at me with a low, sneaky smile. Pulling at her nails, she kept a drunken gaze on me. "A nigguh," she popped softly with Ontrell laughing.

The more I questioned shit, the more other things stopped making sense, like flashing back to see her at the party doing a line of coke on a man's thigh. So, that was her. I wasn't even going to begin to question how and what happened with her boyfriend thinking she was a virgin too. Olivia, I was starting to realize, was not this innocent girl she portrayed herself to be. I was still high, though, and at this point, I just wanted to say fuck it and go home.

"Well! I had fun," I said, shrugging, switching the attention back to me. "I did some shit I wouldn't normally do, tried some things, and I don't regret it. I ended up fucking a nigga at that house party, the second one we went to."

"Who?" Tyree shrieked. "Bitch, no you didn't!"

"I have a hole in my leggings as we speak, nigga," I stated.

His mouth dropped, and he looked at Trell, who was reaching over to grab some food from Olivia's plate.

The table was filled with plates, with us grabbing from different places, taking what we wanted.

"Baby, did you hear this girl say she got a hole in her leggings?" Tyree said to Trell, trying not to laugh.

"That's some ho shit, shawty," Trell said as they laughed, making me roll my eyes.

"So, who was the guy?" Tyree asked. "Because there was not a straight nigga in that house tonight, boo."

"He said he was straight!"

"Nah, I tell females that if I wanna fuck some, but I'm not straight, sooo," Trell said, looking at me with a slow smile. "You don't even know what he looked like?"

"I mean, he said he was just there to sell to the gays. He said he makes most his money off of y'all."

They both looked at each other as they burst out laughing.

Oh, shit. Please don't tell me I had sex with a gay man.

"Do y'all know him?"

"Honey, you talking about Aaron, selling weed and pills?" Tyree questioned. "He's gay, boo."

"How you know?" I shrieked, almost spitting my food out.

Trell handed Tyree his phone. He quickly started moving the screen, scrolling through before showing me a Facebook status.

I CNT BELIEVE I CONVINCED A GURL TO HAVE SEX WITH MY GAY ASS. FIRST TIME HAVING SEX WIT A GIRL AT 32. BEST BELIEVE IT WASN'T ALL WHAT STRAIGHT MEN HYPE IT UP TO BE.
53 likes. 22 Comments.

My mouth dropped as they started laughing, with Olivia shaking her head, still feeling her high even after the fight.

"Go get tested, boo," Tyree suggested, sipping his hot tea. "He's known to fuck with basic niggas in the A."

I sat back in the chair, stunned. *This is the absolute last time I party with gay niggas in Atlanta.*

Jordyn

"Let's go! You need to hurry up!" a mother yelled out as I watched her gather up her kids, trying to rush to their designated area in the airport.

My flight wasn't for another thirty minutes, but I was just so anxious to get home and see my family again. I missed the big dinners, the stories, the laughter. I was an only child, but I had too many cousins and uncles to count on both sides. My yaya was in good spirits, so I was definitely looking forward to spending some time with her. It was Wednesday night, and the airport was packed with travelers trying to rush everywhere, while I stood there with my duffle bag, waiting. I was wearing simple jeans, boots, and a waist-length coat. I had glasses on, with my hair hanging freely.

It has been a while since I contributed to this story, but I had a lot going on. Still do.

Elijah pretty much lost his mind. I mean, he went off the deep end this time. Two weeks ago, I broke it off with him. No more sex, no more calling, none of that could happen between us, and he went off. Sitting in my living room, I remember telling him calmly I was sorry, but he wasn't hearing it.

"So, where the fuck is all this coming from?" he asked, eyes hard on me as he pulled his dreads back, like he was ready to jump up and fight. "Real shit, Jordyn. Keep it one hundred. Who you been fucking with that's suddenly telling you to stop fucking with me? I've been with yo' ass since day one!"

"Elijah, nobody's telling me anything!" I argued, pushing my glasses up. I was trying to keep from saying I had a boyfriend, because he made it clear he didn't want to know anything about me and another man—or woman, at this point. He'd rather not know.

"So, why you trying to stop this shit?"

"It's time! I can't keep doing this with you, Elijah! We had our fun, but we need to stop and let it go before one of us gets hurt!"

His eyes grew wide as he stood up. "You already said you loved me, Jordyn. Either you lied, or you don't love a nigga no more, and that's why you really trying to—"

"Do not throw that back in my face!" I snapped angrily, hating that I fell in love with someone who didn't feel the same way, and now he thought he could throw it back in my face against me. *Fuck no.*

"So, you don't love me?" He laughed, shaking his head. "You don't love a nigga no more, or you giving up on me because I don't love you back? Man, fuck outta here. I ain't going no-fucking-where," he said, sitting back down with another laugh. "The pussy is too good, shawty. I ain't going nowhere, and neither are you, because as soon as you wake up the next fucking morning, you gon' hit me up, talking about you want this dick, you want me to come over. Take you out to eat, help you with yo' fucking bills to this raggedy-ass place you call a house, and come scoop you up from wherever the fuck you be at, and"—he laughed—"all that shit comes with a price! You trying to stop all of that, shawty? Really? Everything you got in here is because of me! Reason people know you, fuck with you now is because of me!" he stated, pointing at himself.

I slowly cocked my head back, taking a few steps back as I looked at the man I once fell in love with. He was sitting there with his arms stretched out on the couch, legs wide, with his thick Gucci boots, flashy chains, and fancy Rolex, locs crinkled to perfection. Those infamous tattoos on his face that I grew to love . . . mmm. Elijah Jodie Carter, the only man I let eat me out, and I pretended to like that shit for the sake of his ego that I was just now realizing was bigger than I thought. Pushing my glasses up, I smiled again.

"Yeah, you go ahead and rethink that shit, Jordyn, if you want us to stop, because as soon as that shit comes to a stop, shawty, everything I own is going back. Yo' li'l phone that I gave you?"

"Yeah?" I baited. "You taking that with you too?"

"When it's over, it's over, shawty. I'm not rescuing you from no bitch that fucked yo' ass up over dumb shit. I'm not entertaining yo' wack-ass conversations about politics and bullshit. I'm done! You hear me?" he stated.

I barely even blinked. *Watch how I end all of this with one sentence.*

"I have a boyfriend, Elijah," I said simply.

He froze, mouth ajar, low eyes open wide as he stared hard at me, searching my face to see if I was lying. "You what?" he let out in a low voice.

"I have a boyfriend," I said, shrugging. "I've been talking to him for a while. He's been taking me places. We talk, hang out. I've been to football and basketball games. He doesn't smoke or party as much, and would you believe it? We never even had sex," I said sarcastically.

I thought I would feel better about telling him, since he decided to go off on me like that, but the look on his face made me wish I could start this all over again. I wished I'd never said a word about Desmond.

"What's his name? I know him?" he asked, standing up, fists clenched.

"I'm not telling you—"

"Where he stay at? Fuck does he do, so I can go find him?" he snapped.

I remained quiet, and I guess that was when shit really broke loose. Next thing I knew, we were damn near fighting each other, with me trying to keep him away from my room. He wanted to get my phone that was sitting on the bed, while I just wanted him out of the house altogether. I couldn't handle him anymore. I was tired of it. It was always something when I was with him, and for once, I just wanted to be with someone normal.

"Elijah, get out of my house!" I screamed, pushing him back one last time.

"So, you don't love me no more?" he pressed, having the nerve, the audacity, to look hurt with his lying ass. "You don't—"

"I don't love you!" I snapped. "Get out!"

Three days later, I got a call from my boyfriend in the middle of the night, sounding scared out of his mind. I quickly sat up in the bed, rubbing my eyes as I glanced at the time on my phone: 2:11 a.m.

"Desmond, what's wrong?" I yawned, trying to hide my irritation.

"Aye, look, I don't know what's going on, but I . . . we can't be together any—"

"What?"

"Look, I just got a lot going on right now, and it's just not a good time for me to be in anything seriously," he said. "Don't call me again."

With that, he hung up, and my mind immediately went to Elijah. So, I called him, but he wouldn't answer. I called again and again, knowing he had something to do with it. He wouldn't answer, but he did send me a text message.

NXT NIGGA U PICK 2 B YO BF BETTER NOT BE NO WACK ASS NIGGA WORKING AT WALMART LIKE HOMIE DID. YO PHNE GETTING CUT OFF TOMORROW MORNING SHAWTY. IM OUT.

I slammed the iPhone so hard against the wall it broke, shattering the screen into pieces. I was done. Elijah was so pathetic to stoop that low, scaring someone into breaking up with me. I just . . . Shaking my head, I lay back down, using the pillow to mute my screams. *Fucking over him!*

A day later, I came home from a late night of rehearsal, and Rita was flipping out, rushing me to get inside the house. I was so tired, fingers were hurting from playing my violin so hard that I just wanted to soak my hands in some hot water. Yet, the moment I walked in, I saw we had absolutely no furniture.

"Bitch, I swear I will call the cops on Elijah's trifling ass! Did he do this, or did we truly get robbed?" Rita screamed as I rushed to my room, seeing just about more than half of my stuff was gone or destroyed. I couldn't even call—

"Jordyn!" Rita yelled, coming into my room. "Girl, he took our pots and pans! Oh, Lord God, noo!"

I sat on my bed, closing my eyes, trying to keep the tears from coming down. He wasn't going to break or scare me into getting back with him.

Rita came in the doorway, still ranting on and on, while I sat in silence.

"You need to talk to him, make it up to his crazy ass or something. The nigga didn't touch my shit. Still, you need to talk to him!"

"How can I talk to someone, be with someone who doesn't love me like—"

"Are you blind?" she snapped, arms thrown in the air. "That nigga is obsessed with you! Can't you tell by how he stole all yo' shit, made yo' boyfriend break up with you? Elijah has been head over heels in love with you since you put it down on him. I told you, yo' sex game is too strong for these basic niggas down here. Make 'em go crazy. Remember what happened with the last guy?"

"He said he doesn't—"

"A man's words don't mean nothing, girl. Like, really." She laughed sarcastically while walking out, still flipping out over the stolen goods.

I was not playing into Elijah's I-want-attention bullshit right now. I refused.

Now that all of that had happened, here I was, two weeks later, standing at the airport, the day before Thanksgiving, waiting on my flight to start boarding. I ended up getting a basic Metro phone with a different number and continued to use that to keep in contact with my family, music professor, and work-related issues.

"Aye, we may have to stop in Boston on our way back," Elijah said. I turned around, seeing him come back from the bathroom, looking at his phone.

So, yeah . . . here we are. I really can't even explain why I was still with this maniac. He called me the night before through Rita, trying to apologize. I didn't want to hear it. Not this close to Thanksgiving. All I wanted to think about was family time. I told her I really didn't want to speak on everything until I got back. Once Rita told him where I was going, he asked if he could come, and I just . . . gave in. He was about to meet my family. We hadn't even begun to address the list of issues we had, but here he was with me at the airport, locs underneath a skull cap, red sweats, and matching hoodie and coat. He knew I was upset, but he was trying to act like everything was okay.

"What's in Boston?" I asked softly as he grabbed his things, standing close to me as we started walking to our gate.

"I got some family up there on my mama's side I want to see. You good?" He looked at me, waiting for a response, but I just stayed quiet. He knew he was in some deep shit with me.

You know when a man knows he's in the wrong? They play like little puppies that just got a spanking. They try to warm up to you, being nice and on their best behavior, until the next time they act out. Elijah was no different. Wasn't loud, being rude or obnoxious. He was being overly polite with the doors, making sure I was comfortable in the seat. The entire ride there was quiet and smooth-going. It wasn't until after picking up the rental car and driving to my place that he began to show some nerves.

"Yo' family knows about me?" he asked.

I glanced at him before focusing back on the road. "My parents know you're coming," I said, turning down a street. I missed home. It wasn't as vibrant as Atlanta, especially where I lived, but it was still home.

As soon as we pulled up to a small house on the corner, I sighed, seeing all the cars parked sloppily in front. It was going to be a long night. I blew the horn as the porch light came on, with my little cousins running out.

"Jordyn, before we go in, I just wanted to say—"

"Not now, Elijah. Wait until I'm back in Atlanta," I cut in, getting out.

"I'd rather talk about this shit now before we get in front of yo' family looking like we can't stand each other."

"You should have never come if that was—"

"But I'm fucking here," he snapped.

I looked at him, watching him get out of the car. It was pitch black out here as the rest of my family came piling out. My mom, who is this heavyset, chubby-cheeks woman with a sharp tongue who passed for white most of the time, went straight to me, hugging me hard.

"Oooh, I missed you, baby girl!" she let out as I hugged her, feeling her smooth my hair down. My daddy kept his eyes hard on Elijah, who was talking to my cousins. He was your typical Spanish man from the South—cowboy hat, boots, and jet black hair slicked back, with a thick mustache.

"You're Jodie from the Carter Boys! Oh my God! Jodie is at my house!" Amber screamed excitedly, quickly pulling out her phone. "Wait until I tell everybody—"

"Get back in the house, Amber," my dad snapped as he stepped up to Elijah, hand out for a shake. "First boyfriend to come to the house, I see."

"The last boyfriend," Elijah corrected, and my dad smiled.

"We'll see," he retorted.

I looked at my mom, who smiled sneakily at me.

"What, Mom?" I laughed.

"We need to talk about this, chi chi," she said, patting my stomach gently as I looked down.

"I know I put on some weight, but—"

"You're pregnant," she whispered, and my mouth dropped. "I can see it in your face. You haven't had any signs? No sickness?"

"Uh, no, because I'm not." I laughed nervously.

She just smiled with a shrug. "Okay, you're not. Come on, let's go in. Yaya has been nonstop about you, baby."

Let the crazy holiday begin. That entire night was nothing but my girl cousins and aunts swarming Elijah, wanting to take pictures, take him upstairs. Some wanted him to play Barbies with them; others wanted him to talk to their friends on the phone. Once word got out that I brought a man home, it was only a matter of time before my older cousins came through. They were all full-blown Mexican, raising hell as they came at him, speaking Spanish, trying to scare him, but he wasn't moved. Not one bit. It became an event with my mom's sisters and their kids coming, wanting to see. So, a three-bedroom house turned into almost thirty people running around in it. By the time anyone got any sleep, it was going on three in the morning. Food was already on the stove being cooked and prepared.

Elijah slept downstairs with the male cousins, while I stayed in my room with my little ones, constantly asking me questions like, "What are his brothers like? Can he really sing? Does he have a lot of money?" To get my point across that I wanted my sleep, I had to cuss them out in Spanish so they knew I wasn't playing.

Yet, the thing that stood out in my mind that night was the fact that I could be pregnant. I didn't think I was, because I was still getting periods and I was on birth control. I couldn't be. I knew I had put on some weight, but that was because Elijah was always constantly taking me out to eat somewhere. Nah, I couldn't be pregnant. There would have been some sign by now.

The next morning, Thanksgiving Day, it felt like a rush trying to eat, because everyone was preparing to do Black

Friday shopping. We had people with plates sitting on staircases, and on floors in the living room, kitchen, and dining room, because there weren't enough seats. Mom said she didn't plan to have this many people over, but ever since Elijah showed up, everyone was curious. I had to keep reminding them not to speak Spanish so much, because he and my mom's side of the family didn't understand it. Ugh. It was just chaos, but I enjoyed it.

"Okay, let's go, let's go! We need to get moving!" my mom called out, holding the door open. "Everybody needs to be ready and in cars in minutes. I want me a smart TV. Now, let's go!"

"When Mama says go, we need to go!" Dad chimed in, pushing the little ones out as Elijah came up behind me, hand on my lower back. "You guys are not staying in this house by yourself."

"Daddy!" I gasped, horrified he would even say that out loud.

"I'm just saying. Better be out this house fifteen minutes after us. Yaya will tell me if y'all still here," he warned, eyes hard on Elijah. "We're not violating my daughter in this house."

"Mom!" I let out.

She grabbed her husband, smacking him hard upside the head.

"You were just saying last night you wanted some, and I told you no because Yaya and my nana was here."

"Ahh, ah ah, okay." He laughed. "Just be out the house."

"No problem." Elijah smirked. Once the last of the relatives were out, Elijah and I headed upstairs quietly, careful not to wake up the two sleeping grandmothers.

"I haven't really had the chance to check on you to see if you're okay with all of this craziness." I sighed, sitting on the edge of the bed as he closed the door behind him. My room was not the typical teenager room. It was straight to the point with a desk, full-size bed, yellow curtains for the window, books everywhere, music sheets stacked on the desk, and a tiny picture of me as a baby stuck to the corner of my mirror. Nothing fancy.

"I'm good. It's no different from my family, baby," he said, sitting down on the floor against the door. "That food did me in, though. Shit, a nigga ready to sleep like a baby. Why you don't be cooking like that?"

"I want to eat healthy," I said simply, pushing my hair back off my shoulders. I took my glasses off, setting them on the desk as Elijah looked lazily at me. He watched me get up as I slipped my jeans and shirt off, leaving just the bra and panties on as I looked in my closet for something to wear. My stomach was poked out like I just ate a full meal, and jeans right now? They were not doing it for me.

"Aye."

I turned around, seeing Elijah standing there, already stripped to his boxer briefs, locs hanging freely as he grabbed himself.

"What are you doing?" I laughed as he pulled me to the bed. "Not with my—"

"Yaya already know how a nigga gets down. She was young once," he said smoothly, grinning like a kid as he pulled me in front of him. We stared at each other before he leaned down and kissed me. "I missed you, baby, and I'm sorry."

I gripped his neck, bringing him closer as he picked me up, laying me back on the bed in one easy move. We were like two teenagers fumbling to get our underwear and my bra off before coming back together, naked, mouths never leaving each other.

"We shouldn't be having sex, Elij—"

"Why not?" he whispered, spreading my legs wide and sliding into me ever so slowly. "Ohhhh, shit," he hissed. I bit down hard on my lip to keep from moaning, but damn, I missed him too. He sat up, looking down at himself before watching me as those hips started to grind slowly in different angles. The headboard was hitting back every two seconds as he pushed harder. I cried out as he smirked. "Got that ass, baby. That's it. That's my spot," he muttered, hitting it again as I gripped the sheets, trying to keep quiet.

He had gotten so good at fucking me that if I was faking it, he would know. I could moan all damn day, but he waited for a facial expression to appear, and as soon as he saw it, he knew he had the right spot, making me cum instantly, which I did. I never lasted more than five minutes. That's how much we had sex. He mastered having sex with the master of sex. Unbelievable. I had trained him well, but damn. Leaning down against my body, he continued, dismissing my orgasms as irrelevance while I gripped his back, legs wrapped tight around him, enjoying the ride.

"Fuuck, Jordyn, you feel like you were made for a nigga, shawty," he breathed, going faster. He looked at me, eyes halfway closed, before kissing me, hips still moving as he slowed down.

"Elijah," I moaned, closing my eyes as he kissed the side of my face gently, dreads coming down on me. "I'm sorry, baby." I could feel myself about to get emotional as I buried my face in his shoulder, tears trying to come down. I was still in love with him. Even after all of that, hearing him say he didn't love me, I still felt like he was the only person for me.

He wiped my cheeks before kissing my eyes so gently. "I told you I'm not going nowhere," he said against my mouth as we kissed again. "Fuck everybody else. Just you and me."

I looked at him through blurry eyes, still feeling him slowly stroke in me, just out of comfort, because I already knew he came at least twice in me. Sex was the only way we could effectively communicate with each other.

"Do you still not love me?" I asked softly.

He looked me in the eyes before turning away, just kissing me on the chest instead. He couldn't even say it. How could I follow a man's actions instead of his words, when something as powerful as "I love you" didn't need any action behind it? *Just fucking say it.*

"You know how I feel about this, Jordyn. About us," he mumbled. I nodded. "But, I'm not messing with no other chick. I . . ." He looked at me, kissing me on the side of the jaw as I closed my eyes. "I do—"

We heard a car door slam shut as voices rang throughout the yard. He quickly got up, looking out the window. "Yo, it's yo' pops."

"Oh my God!" I shrieked, jumping up, trying to frantically grab some clothes. "Get dressed! Hurry up before he finds you in here. This whole room smells like sex. Open a window!"

"It ain't that serious, shawty." Elijah laughed, taking his time as I heard the front door open.

I quickly grabbed some clothes from the closet and ran to the bathroom, closing myself in it.

"Jordyn Maria!" my dad yelled, Spanish accent thicker than usual.

"Would you stop embarrassing them like that? Move," I could hear my mom say as I turned the sink on, throwing on some sweats, a bra, and a T-shirt. "Go wait downstairs, Victor. Now!" she snapped.

"She's my daught—"

"Now!" my mom repeated. "Did you have her, or just lay on your back and make her? Get downstairs now!" I told you my mom was no joke. The attitude was the black side of her; the stubbornness was both black and white.

I heard the door open and close as I poked my head out, seeing my mom walk in with a small black bag. Elijah sat on the bed, shirtless and cool, like it was all good.

"Hey, baby," she greeted him before handing me the bag, giving me a cold look. "You better tell me as soon as you know." With that, she walked out, closing the door, with Elijah looking at me, confused.

"What is she talking about?"

I felt the long box and nearly sighed. A pregnancy test.

"Nothing. Go smooth things over with my dad, please," I told him.

"Why I gotta—"

"Go!" I snapped.

He stood up with a smack of his teeth, throwing on a shirt, and walked out. I took the box out, keeping the sink running as I read the directions. I wasn't even worried, because knowing my body, there would have been some type of sign that I was pregnant. Anything. So, as I waited for the results, I looked at my stomach in the mirror. It looked ordinary to me, nothing significant besides the extra weight gain. I just needed to get back in the gym. Holidays were always a rough time for me.

Hearing a knock on the door, I opened it a little, seeing my anxious mom waiting outside.

"Oh my God, Mommy, I'm not pregnant."

"Baby girl, your body is spreading so badly, I don't know how Elijah didn't notice it."

"We eat out a lot."

"No!" She laughed, pushing her way in as I sighed. "Body-is-preparing-to-have-a-baby type of spread. Look at your hips. And your stomach is sitting low."

"We just ate a full on—"

I watched her grab the stick, eyes nearly popping out of her head. "Ahhhh! Jordyn Maria! You're pregnant! I told you!"

My body went numb as she showed me the results on the tiny screen.

"Oh my God! I'm a grandma! I've been wanting some grandbabies for the longest! I want to know how far along you—"

"I'm not pregnant," I said, mumbling to myself as I sat down on the toilet in utter shock. I didn't even graduate college yet. I didn't . . . I'd been so careful with the pills. I'd been drinking so much, and . . . I was pregnant by a man who didn't even love me the way I loved him. If this test came out to be true—and I would be going to the doctor to confirm this for sure—I was getting an abortion, no hesitation. I had already made the decision to not tell Elijah a thing about it. The less he knew, the better.

PART 2:

The Finale

Noelle

"I have to volunteer at a women's clinic today for my church," I said to Layla as I finished up my work. I was putting together models' portfolios and designers' look books.

"So, you not doing nothing for your birthday? You getting old, Ms. Twenty-six," she teased. "I'm shocked Shiloh isn't doing anything for it."

"How was your Thanksgiving?" I said, changing the subject as I fixed my hair, looking in the compact mirror. It becomes annoying when your friend talks more about your boyfriend than you do. Really, annoying.

"Well, I ain't really do nothing. Ate with the family, you know," she said, shrugging with a smile as I looked at her curiously. "What?" she retorted, moving her braids back as her bangles jingled with the movement.

"You slept with that guy we met at the club again, didn't you?" I pressed before laughing hard. "What's his name? The one you poured a drink on."

"Ronny," she gushed. "He got good head game. What can I say?" She laughed. "We still argue and hate each other to no end, but . . ." She shrugged, and we both laughed. "Girl, speaking of which, he's here to pick me up. Come out and say hello."

"I can't. I have to finish up with this stuff," I told her regrettably. Did that stop her? No, she just grabbed my coat for me.

"Girl, come on before he cuss me out. I want you to say hello," she said quickly as I tried to adjust my coat. As you know, I always dress to a T. No imperfection over here. I kept it simple this time, wearing black skinny pants, black-and-gray Michael Kors riding boots, black sweater, with my hair having the side-swoop bang, gently falling to my shoulders, and my MK coat. Makeup was light, with red lipstick, and eyebrows perfectly arched after my waxing session. I was completely hair free all over.

Walking out with Layla, we saw Ronny's Honda parked out front, smoke coming hard out the back pipe.

"Girl, look at my man and this beat-up car," she joked. "Nothing fancy like Shiloh's car I'm sure, but shit, he's driving. Nigga, get out the car and speak!" she snapped as he rolled the window down, thick cloud of smoke pouring out. "Quit being rude!"

I just waved awkwardly as she turned to look at me, smacking her teeth with a smile.

"So, anyway, is Shiloh getting you or nah?"

"Umm, I drove," I said with a shrug. "I actually have no clue where he is. Haven't spoken to him all day."

"Hmm," she said, eyeing me. "Interesting. Ronny better not pull no shit like that. I'll see you later, girl! Oh! Did you need a ride? Ronny can drive you."

"Shawty, what?" He coughed.

I looked at Layla. What was her deal? "I said I drove today. I'm parked right—"

"Oh! Okay, see ya, girly! Happy birthday!" She waved, hopping in the car, fussing at him as they pulled off.

Wow. I almost wanted to laugh, but then I realized I didn't care. She was in a competition with someone who didn't even realize there was one. Please. She didn't even get me a birthday card, at that.

Walking to my car with my bag in hand, I felt my phone vibrate. I looked at the unknown number. I had no

clue who this was, and it was past 6 o'clock. Who would
be calling me this late on a Thursday night?

"Hello?" I answered. Getting inside my car, I turned it
on to warm it up.

"Hey, this is Michael. I was just—"

My mouth dropped with a gasp. "How in the world did
you get this number, Michael?" I laughed. *Oh my God,
really?*

"One of the ladies gave it to me a while back. I just—"

"No one has my number at that church, Michael."

"Well, when you changed your house number on me, I
figured if I wanted to talk to you, just to call your—"

"So, you tried calling my house again? Oh Jesus." I
sighed with a shake of my head. *Let go and let God,
Noelle.* "What's up?"

"I was calling to say happy birthday," he said sweetly,
and I smiled. "I actually got something for you. I was
gonna hand it to you at the women's clinic, but they
cancelled it."

"Oh, I didn't even know. Nobody told me about it," I
said, confused. I should have gotten a call or something.

"Yeah, I just got word, so you should be hearing from
someone shortly. Anyway, I was wondering, could I just
drop it off at your house, if you don't mind?"

"I, um . . ." I started, looking around as if someone was
watching me. "I don't know if that's a good idea, Michael."

"Your boyfriend won't mind—"

"Actually, he would. He's a little crazy." I laughed nervously. "I'm almost scared to even be talking to you on
this phone for this long. But . . . I do love a good birthday
gift. What did you get me?"

"Let me come over and you'll find out," he said seduc-
tively with a low laugh.

"Oh my God, Michael." I laughed, slightly turned off.
"Settle down with the voice and flirty undertones. If I let

you come by, you have to promise to leave immediately once I get it. Okay? You're gonna get us both in trouble."

"You shouldn't be scared of him, No—"

"I'm not," I said, cutting him off. I was more scared for Michael than myself, but I wouldn't tell him that. "Just come by, drop it off, and go."

"A'ight," he beamed before hanging up.

It didn't hit me until a few seconds later. How in the world did he know where I stayed in the first place? The moment I pulled up to my house, I could see his car was parked in the driveway, waiting. Looking around, I saw no Mustang in sight, so I parked on the side of the street and slowly got out. I felt like I was cheating, with my heart beating so fast, constantly looking out for Shiloh or any of his friends. They tracked and reported almost everything I did to him if they saw me. He claimed he didn't ask for them to do it, but I believed he was lying.

Michael stepped out with a thing of pink balloons, some with *December 4th* on them, and a small black box in his hand. He stood tall, looking like a Calvin Klein model, with a pearly white smile and handsome chocolate face.

"Hey, beautiful," he cheesed as I continued to glance at Shiloh's house.

"Michael, you know this is the last time you can come up here," I warned, taking the balloons and box. "What in the world did you get me, fool? What's in here?"

"Open it. I know what a girl's best friend is," he said simply.

My mouth dropped. I quickly opened the box and saw the stunning diamond necklace sitting so smoothly against the velvet interior.

"Oh my God! No, you didn't!" I freaked, jumping up to hug him. "Why would you do this? We've only been friends for—"

"I want you," he said slowly, licking his lips. "If I have to wait for you to go through this bad boy phase with your boyfriend, I'll wait, but I know you and I are meant to be together."

I looked up at him, smile slowly dropping as we locked eyes. He was serious. He was actually serious. "Michael, you know I can't—"

"I know," he said, stepping closer. He tried to place his hand on my waist, but I backed up with a shake of my head. "You feel it as much as I do that we are meant for each other."

"I am meant for my boyfriend," I said, almost having to remind myself I had one. This necklace was no joke.

"You say that now." He smiled, licking his lips as he backed up. "Watch," he said, walking back to his car. "I'ma show you how much you mean to me."

"Michael, don't—"

"I'ma show you," was all he kept saying.

I knew I had hurt his feelings, but he needed to know the truth. There was no way I could possibly be with him. Even if Shiloh and I broke up, I still wouldn't be with someone like Michael.

Watching him back out, I headed to the house, setting my things down, and slipped into something more comfortable. It was my birthday, and Shiloh was nowhere to be found, not even a call or a text, yet Michael dropped by and freely handed me a diamond necklace. I smiled at the irony.

Grabbing my phone, I called Tyree, knowing he would have the best, funniest advice I could ever ask for.

"Hey, booski," he greeted. I could hear the commotion of a photo shoot going on in the background. "What's up, birthday girl?"

"So, you remember the guy at the church, the one I was telling you about?"

"Mm-hmm."

"So, he gave me a diamond necklace for my birthday," I said.

He gasped. "Bitch! Are you serious? You been sucking his dick on the side, or what? What was the purpose of just randomly giving out—what does he do for a living?"

"He's a personal trainer." I sighed.

"No, he's not." He laughed. "Ah, Harlem, you hear this shit? Nigga just drops by, hands her a diamond necklace, and says here: no sex, no kiss, not even a date. Girl, I wish I could bag 'em like you."

"So, then he confesses that he wants me and that he's willing to wait until Shiloh and me break up."

"Ohhh! Gurl!" he screamed again. "Did you tell Shy-Shy?"

"No, and I don't know if I should."

"Mmmmph. Have you seen Shiloh at all?"

"Not even a fucking text message," I muttered, looking at the balloons floating in the corner as I paced the floor.

"Did you see my birthday gift that I left in yo' room?"

"What?" I laughed. "You still got the key?"

"I was just dropping off your little gift from me and mine to you and yours. Hope you use it wisely, trick," he said sneakily.

I groaned. Knowing him, it was something I wouldn't even know what to do with.

"What do I do about Michael?" I asked.

"Gurrrrl," he sang. "Tell that nigga he don't want it with my man Shiloh, honey. Personal trainer my ass. Please. Nigga selling dope and passing out bootleg mixtapes like every other bum nigga in Atlanta. Check and see if that necklace is even real, boo, before you get all wet in the panties over that nigga," he said.

I smiled. *Why did I call him?*

"You know what you need to do?"

"What, Tyree?" I pressed as I heard a loud engine sound outside of my house. I quickly glanced out the window, seeing Shiloh step out of his truck, wearing a suit.

Hold up. Huh?

"Tyree, let me call you back. Shiloh just came by."

"Tell him I said heeeyyy!" he sang.

I heard girls in the background laughing as I hung up on the fool. Opening the door, I watched him walk up looking like . . . damn. He had cut his hair to a low fade, no more curly hair. He had a diamond stud in each ear, and he was wearing all black—pants, dress shoes, tie, and blazer buttoned up in the middle, with a black Rolex. Those low eyes, dark as coal, with the teardrop tattoos underneath his eye, stood out against all the black.

"What's good, birthday girl?" he said in a low voice as I wrapped my arms around his neck, cheesing like a spoiled child. He walked us both into the house, closing the door behind him as I kissed him.

"You look amazing," I said, stunned, touching his hair. "I thought you forgot about me."

"Go get dressed. Put on something sexy and pack an overnight bag. We stepping out tonight," he said.

I quickly let go, already trying to think about the outfits in my head. *Sexy, sexy.* I took a shower, still trying to think of an outfit. Red was best on my complexion, and it was his favorite color by association. Soon, going through my closet, I decided on a cute wine-colored, body-con long-sleeve dress that dipped low enough to show the right amount of cleavage. My hair just needed to be retouched, rebounced a little. I put on smoky eye makeup with the right amount of accessories.

As I packed my overnight bag, I caught the small Victoria's Secret bag beside my bed with another bag inside of it. Grabbing it, I looked at the birthday card inside.

*Word on the Carter Street is that Shiloh said ur
the one. One. Well, if that's the case, I bought some
goodies for u. Use them wisely. Let that nigga dick
u down, and then call me and tell me all about it.
Kisses!*
    XOXO
    Ontrell & Tyree

I looked in the bag, seeing a full-blown red lace lingerie
ensemble, red vibrator, and condoms decorating the
bottom of the bag. I was so going to kill Tyree when I saw
him. I ended up taking the vibrator and lingerie, putting
it inside my bag. When I walked out, Shiloh looked up at
me, and his eyes explored. A slow smile spread across his
face.

"You like?" I asked.

"Turn around so I can see the back," he demanded
softly.

I did a slow turn, hand on my hip, before facing him
once more. He said nothing. He didn't need to.

"You ready?" I asked, grabbing my coat as he stood up,
almost eye level with my heels on.

Just when we were about to walk out—I mean we were
sooo close to the door—he stood behind me, hand on my
lower back, grabbing the balloons.

"Who got you this?" he asked before looking at the
small box sitting on the table next to the door. He opened
it up, and I sighed.

Fuck it. It was going to come out anyway.

"Michael did," I mumbled, looking up at him. He eyed
the necklace, confused. "I didn't know he was getting me
a gift. He just dropped it off not too long ago."

"He came by here?" he asked, still eyeing the necklace.

I just wanted to walk the hell on out already. "I didn't
let him in the house," I said quickly. "Just stopped by,

handed me the gift, and that was that. Small gesture of kindness. I hope you're not upset."

He looked at me, no expression as usual, before cutting the light off, gently pushing me out the door. "I'm not threatened by a nigga who gives a girl jewelry made in China," he said simply as he locked the door. "How he know where you stay?"

"I honestly have yet to figure that out," I told him as we walked to his brand new, all-black Escalade.

He glanced at me as he opened my door. I already knew that blank look.

"I don't know, Shiloh! I'm telling the truth!"

"Let me find out you talking to that nigga on the low, shawty," he threatened as my mouth dropped. "How did he get in contact with you? I thought you changed your house number."

"He called my cell," I admitted quietly.

He smirked, closing the door as he went to the driver's side.

Fucking Michael. Ruining my birthday, and he ain't even here!

"Shiloh, I put this on everything I love, including you," I said, staring hard at him. "I shouldn't even have to explain myself, but out of respect for us, I will. I don't know how he has any access to me outside of the church. I have never given my number out to anyone, nor my address, so I'm a bit freaked out about it, to be honest."

Just as soon as I said it, my phone started to ring. UNKNOWN flashed on the screen. Shiloh looked at it before snatching it out of my hand to answer.

"Are you serious—"

"Who is this?" he answered.

"Who the hell is this?" I heard my daddy snap back.

I tried reaching for the phone.

"Why the fuck is you calling my girl's phone if—"

"Daddy!" I called out, snatching the phone away from a shocked Shiloh. "Hello?"

"Who is that talking like they fucking crazy on the goddamn phone, Noelle?" he screamed as I sighed, trying to apologize on Shiloh's behalf.

As soon as I smoothed it over with my dad, I hung up.

Wonderful fucking birthday so far. Awesome to turn twenty-six. Feels great.

As Shiloh drove, he glanced at me. "Aye, I'm—"

"Shut the fuck up," I snapped, and he immediately went silent. "Don't say shit. Just drive."

I couldn't and wouldn't allow myself to be mad at him for too long, but he needed the silent treatment from me. Me being quiet made him uncomfortable, so it was effective.

He took me to this nice, fancy restaurant in Buckhead. We were served personally by the head chef, who let us try a little bit of everything from the menu. The wine was amazing, and the atmosphere was rich in every sense of the word.

Once we left the restaurant, he drove into downtown Atlanta, letting a valet take care of his truck as we entered the Hyatt Regency hotel. The view was amazing as the elevators carried people up and down the floors. There were bright lights with beautiful decorations all throughout the hotel.

Waiting on the side as I looked around, I felt a hand on my back.

"You ready, baby?" he said, taking my bag in his hand.

I nodded, and we got on the elevator, going all the way to the top floor. As soon as we entered our room, I nearly fainted at the sight of it. It was certainly bigger than your average apartment. There was a living room, with floor-to-ceiling windows showing the view of downtown. There was a flat screen TV, king-size plush bed, and a garden-size Jacuzzi tub that was already waiting and ready for me to get in. Rose petals floated on top, with two glasses of champagne on the side.

I looked at him, watching him take his jacket off. "Shiloh," I said slowly, feeling myself get excited. "How long do we have this room for?"

"Two nights."

"Oh, I am so calling off work tomorrow," I shrieked, hugging him hard as I kissed him. "I can get in? I can get in the tub?" I asked, pointing.

He nodded, smiling. I'd never had anything this fancy, or been around anything this nice before. Stripping down in the bathroom, I stepped foot in the tub, feeling the heat numb with each rising on the skin. Oh my God . . . Sinking my body completely in, I sighed, head resting on the towel propped for me as he walked in.

"You good?" he asked, sitting up against the wall on the floor, watching me.

"Aren't you getting in?" I questioned.

"I'd rather sit and just talk to you," he said as I smiled.

Taking the two glasses, we clinked them together, added a simple kiss, and relaxed. We talked about everything—stuff at my job, the future, his family, and my family. Everything.

"How can you afford all of this?" I asked.

He smiled. "How you think?"

"You sell drugs, I know, but it can't be this profitable," I reasoned.

He just smiled, licking his lips. "I own a couple of clubs here in Atlanta and New York," he said simply, and my mouth dropped. "A couple of properties in Miami, too."

"Legally?"

"Yeah. My pops, when I was about seventeen, told me to start investing into some shit early while I had the money. I still didn't fuck with him after they had me put in juvie, but he told me some real shit back then. So, I got into it. Sold everything you can think of. Money was either saved up or put somewhere else. So, even while I was in prison, I was still making money. I got a couple of things in the triplets' names just in case something was to ever happen, but I don't sell drugs no more," he said simply. "People think I do, but I got tons of young niggas that will do that shit for me without hesitation. It's a small fee to sell, move product of any kind in my territory. I got cops on payroll to watch out for the niggas selling in their area, and I got the top-of-the-line lawyers ready and waiting if some shit were to go down."

"So, why do you live in that house if you make all this money?" I asked, stretching my legs up as he watched the movement.

"I don't live there all the time. I got other places I could stay, but I like to keep close to you, so that's where I stay," he said softly.

I smiled. He was so damn bashful and shy it was almost cute.

"What time is it?" I asked.

He looked at his phone. "Going on eleven o'clock at night."

I smiled, sitting up as I let the water out, careful to get the soapy suds off of me. Tonight was the night. I wanted to lose it before my birthday was over.

"You'll get me a towel, babe?" I asked, slowly stepping out as he eyed me, standing up against the wall. He handed me a towel and looked away as I dried myself. The ends of my hair were wet, so I pressed the towel against the strands, trying to dry it.

"Babe?" I started, his back still toward me.

"What's up?" he asked, clearing his throat.

"You have less than an hour to take away my virginity. I want to give it up before midnight," I said softly.

"Man, Noelle, don't play with a nigga like—"

"I am so serious," I said, stepping in front of him, knowing he was trying his hardest not to look at me. "It has to be perfect. Music, rose petals, beautiful view. This is as romantic as it gets."

"You playing," he said with a roll of his eyes. "I can't keep having blue balls fucking around with you."

I just shrugged, turned, and walked out, making my way to the bed. I cut off all the lights, so the only thing brightening the room were the city lights from other buildings. I lay back on the bed, slowly opening my legs wide, coaxing him with my finger.

"Nah, fuck nah," he said, and I laughed. "You not getting me caught up with yo' sexy ass. Hell no."

"Shiloh? Baby, come here," I let out.

He would not move from that bathroom; just stared at me. "Aye, I'm going the fuck off on you, shawty, if you tell me no right before. All this shit will get shut down. You feel me?"

I just smiled and nodded. I was so anxious now, because it was really happening. I was going to have sex for the first time!

Walking to the bed, he slowly stripped down to his boxer briefs while reaching in his bag, pulling out condoms. Several.

"Now is the time to tell me to stop, Noe," he pressed, pulling his phone out as he set it to a playlist.

"I promise I won't." I smiled as I watched him move about the room. "What are you doing?"

"Giving you time to change yo' mind," he mumbled, sitting on the chair across from the bed, looking at me, waiting.

I scooted to the front of the bed where the pillows were, and lay back gently, closing my eyes as the music started. Silk's "Freak Me" came on. I opened my eyes, seeing Shiloh walking toward the edge of the bed, licking his lips. His body was rough with marks, tattoos, bruises, and ripped with toned muscles lining up his stomach.

He grabbed my ankle, pulling me down closer to the end. There was no turning back now. I was ready for this. I wasn't the type of girl to want to have sex with different men. It had to be one man, same man, every time.

There was no body part left untouched by the time he lay completely on the bed on top of me. I was licked, kissed, bit in so many places, with my thighs being the most sensitive. He came up to my neck as I gripped his sides, feeling his right hand hold onto my left thigh, keeping it up against him.

"Anywhere" by 112 dropped in, and I smiled. I loved this song. I'd never imagined myself making love to it. I hissed hard before replacing it with a moan as he bit down on my neck once more.

"Again," I breathed as he lifted my chin up, biting underneath before kissing the same spot. Feeling him move lower, I kept my hands on his shoulders as he played with each nipple in such slow, dramatic form that I nearly starting whining. I couldn't handle that kind of torture, not on my first try.

"Mmm," he groaned, head looking at the thigh he had so close to him. "Sexy chocolate thigh right here," he teased before biting down on my inner thigh, causing me to moan. Leading a trail with this thick tongue, he came to the center, clamping down on everything, hitting every sensitive nerve as I gripped his head, looking down at him with my mouth dropped.

"What are you . . . doing to me, Shi," I groaned, head falling back.

He lifted his head up, gripped both thighs, spreading them wider, lifting them higher as he dove back in. I felt his tongue slide inside of me like he was searching for something. I didn't have it. I swear, whatever he was looking for, I didn't have it. My God, I couldn't handle this!

"Please!" I cried, gripping the sheets.

He lifted once more, spread my legs as wide as they could go, before taking his tongue farther back, until he reached a spot I never knew could be licked in the first place. My body started jerking violently as he let my thighs rest on his shoulders.

He came back up, wiping his face as my body continued to tremble. I realized I just came so much on his nose, mouth, and chin. I was embarrassed.

"I'm so sorry," I breathed, trying to wipe his face. He smiled as he got up, taking my hand to get me to stand up. "What are we doing?"

He stepped out of his briefs. His dick stood long, thick, and proud in the city life, almost at an upward angle. Coming to me again, he moved my hair out of the way as he went for my neck, hands grabbing my ass as I wrapped my arms around him.

"No other nigga better not have what I'm about to take," he breathed hard against my ear. I nodded, and in one swoop, he picked me up.

I gripped his face, looking him directly in the eyes.

"You love me?" he asked, trying to playfully bite my finger.

"I love you, Shiloh," I stated, kissing him.

He lifted me higher to adjust my weight on his arms, then walked us to the window with his back against the glass.

"Damn, you dripping on my chest, baby," he breathed anxiously as I held onto him tighter, looking out at the view of Atlanta.

The song switched to ScHoolboy Q's "Studio." *He would have this on his playlist for sex.*

"Don't let go," he demanded as my eyes lit up.

"You're not about to—I can't lose it like this!" I shrieked, seeing him smile, hearing the intro of the song start to build up. "Shiloh, I'm so serious. I'm not—"

He slowly lowered me down, eyes never leaving mine, and just as I felt his tip at the entrance, I started to freak.

"Shiloh, I'm not ready. I'm not—"

Soon as the beat hit, he dropped me down on him in one swift move, and everything came to a complete standstill. Our bodies were as one, as I stared at him in awe and pure ecstasy

"Baaee," I breathed in a low voice, taking in the feeling of him inside of me. It was slight pain, but nothing I couldn't handle. Shit, this wasn't what I'd been expecting at all. He lifted me up and started to slowly pump as my head went back, mouth wide. No words. He was thrusting in and out with his hips, pushing and pulling into me, low eyes at the lowest I'd ever seen.

He bit his lower lip in concentration as he stroked. My nails gripped his shoulders before I took a hand to his curly scalp, fingers dipping between the black curls, mouth hung open unintelligibly.

"Fuucck!" he let out. "You feel good, baby. I've been waiting on this." He breathed heavily, moving back toward the bed. He laid me back on the edge. Gripping my thighs, he came down on me, and I went straight for his mouth, wrapping my legs tight around him to pull him deeper.

My hands gripped the back of his head as we pulled away from each other's mouths. Breathing hard into each other, our eyes never left each other for a second. I couldn't explain it. Lord knows I couldn't explain how good this felt, but he was into the song, and so was I. All we knew was each other at that moment. Nothing else mattered.

He sat up, moving my legs to place on his shoulders as he slid back inside, causing a whole different feeling from the first two positions. Leaning forward, he held onto my legs as I gripped the sheets, dragging them down toward me with every stroke.

"Oh my God," I called out as he slapped my ass.

"Don't call that nigga name. What's my name?" he demanded, going faster as my head went back.

"God, I don't know!" I moaned, feeling him slap my ass again.

"I'm not mothafucking God. What's my name?" Shiloh repeated, spreading my thighs as he pulled me to the edge of the bed, causing me to hang off of it. As he slid in once again, I damn near screamed out Shiloh's name.

"Who's fucking you?" he started.

I felt his tip rub hard against a certain spot, causing my body to tremble.

"Nah, nah," he said, pulling out quickly. "Not yet, baby."

"Shiloh!" I whined, and he backed up, smiling. Why the fuck would he do that?

"Turn over," he demanded.

I did as I was told, feeling him slide my body forward as he picked my ass up in the air before slipping back in. I came instantly. I . . . I have no words for this sudden release other than the back was my new favorite position, hands down.

He pulled out so fast, shooting out everywhere. I hadn't even realized he didn't have on a condom until now. We lay limp on the bed, with him on top of my back, kissing my shoulder, resting his head on me.

"We not done, baby," he said in a low voice.

"You put me in a million positions already."

"I was just trying to see which you respond to, so I know what you like and don't like."

"What have you found out?" I asked, turning my head to the other side, feeling him kiss my back before slowly laying down next to me.

We were sweating so bad, the sheets were soaked, bodies soaked, and hair wet. I was still shaking a little, but I felt like a new woman. Everything was different now that I'd had sex.

"You take direction well," he teased, and I playfully hit him.

"Did I feel okay for the first time?" I asked, and his eyes grew wide. "I mean, I know you are used to girls—"

"Everything I imagined and more," he said, cutting me off.

I kissed him on the cheek before making my way on top of him.

"You ready to ride a nigga now?"

I smiled, whipping my hair back as I sat up, dropping my head back before lowering down on him ever so slowly. That angle caused me to lean forward as his hands gripped my hips.

"Shit, that was sexy as fuck what you just did," he moaned in a shaky voice. "Fuuck, Noe!"

Covering his mouth with my hand, I smirked. It was my turn. One thing I can say is that I learn quicker than most. It was definitely going to be a long night.

Next time we woke up, it was going on one in the afternoon. We'd had sex four times last night, not including waking up at eight for a small quickie in the living room, trying to get some breakfast brought to us. I couldn't get enough. Stretching, I yawned as I opened my eyes. My body was hurting so good. We even put the vibrator to use, which he enjoyed watching me react to.

Sitting up, I looked down at his sleeping body before grabbing my phone off the nightstand, seeing I had several missed calls. One was a call from the women's clinic I was supposed to help with yesterday before they canceled. So, I decided to call them back first.

"Hello?" a lady answered.

"Hi, this is Noelle from—"

"From Primary Baptist, right? Yeah, we missed you yesterday. We could have used your help a great deal," she said.

I scrunched my face up in confusion. "I was told it was canceled."

"Uhh . . ." She laughed slowly. "No way to cancel a women's clinic. We just needed a few volunteers. Don't worry, though. Next time we will definitely need some more help."

"Yeah," I mumbled, feeling Shiloh move about in his sleep. I hung up and just stared at my phone.

"What, baby?" he said in a low voice.

I looked at him, seeing his eyes were barely open before he let out a deep yawn. "What's the matter?"

"I was supposed to be at the women's clinic yesterday after work," I told him.

"Oh, yeah? So, what's the problem?"

"They asked where I was, and I thought . . . Michael told me it was canceled," I said, looking at him. "But she was just telling me they were calling and looking for me. Why would he even lie like that?"

"To give you that kiddie necklace he got from the bubblegum machine." He yawned again as I hit him on the side. "Shawty, what?" He groaned. "I don't know why that nigga lied. Don't even know why you still fucking with him."

"I'm not. Now isn't the time to be sarcastic, Shiloh. What if he's, like, crazy or something? I didn't even tell you what all he said to me yesterday."

"What he say, since you wanna spend the next morning after we fucked to talk about this fuck-ass nigga?" he snapped. "If you feel threatened by ol' boy, let me know now and he will be gone by the end of the night. If not, I'm not trying to hear that shit."

I remained quiet as I watched him check his phone, rubbing his eyes, sniffing his nose while glancing at me.

"What, Noe?"

I just shook my head, laying back down next to him as we both went through our phones in silence. Hearing the phone ring on speaker, I looked over, seeing he placed the phone on his chest, eyes closed.

"Hello?" someone answered.

"What's good, Ant?"

"Mannn, we gotta have some type of family meeting or something. Everybody needs to come together to figure out what the fuck the problem is. Elijah, Trent, and Jahiem still not fucking with each other. Talin siding with Jahiem, and the shit is about to get out of control. You need to fix the shit you created," Anthony snapped.

"I'm good on it," Shiloh said easily as I looked at him.

"Nigga, fuck you mean you good? You the one threatening to kill yo' own bro—"

"Listen," Shiloh started, sitting up as he put the phone close to his mouth. "At the end of the day, we all family, we all related, right? My responsibility will always be the triplets. Nobody else but them. Jahiem had Elijah coughing up blood on the fucking ground over a bitch! Came at Trent, who didn't even know what the fuck was going on, over a bitch's mistake! Nigga, what's done is done. I'm over the shit. If they want to continue to bitch and ignore each other, that's them. I don't give a fuck, but I know nobody better not lay a mothafucking hand on Eli and Trent. I know that," he threatened.

"You supposed to set the fucking example! How you—"

Shiloh hung up. I watched him get up from the bed, naked, wondering if I should put in my two cents. Going into the bathroom, he turned the shower on. I felt his phone vibrate against the sheets on the bed. Looking at the screen, I saw it was his brother calling back.

Well, I'm just going to have to get cussed out if what I'm doing is wrong. I'll take the risk.

"Hello?" I answered softly.

"Oh, Noelle? Where did he go, sweetheart?" Anthony asked, Southern drawl laced in every word.

"He's in the shower at the moment."

"Do me a favor. Convince my brother to talk to Jahiem—"

"I don't really want to get involved in the family issue. I don't think it's my place."

"I know, and if he say something, blame it on me. I'm the one nigga he won't step to like that. You're his woman, so you have a certain hold on him that nobody else has. Just convince him to have a talk with Jahiem about what happened that night. I want this shit cleared up before Trent's graduation party next weekend."

"What do I say to him? Just—"

"Baby girl, whatever you gotta say to convince him. Nigga is stubborn as fuck." I could hear his kids in the background, crying out as he sighed. "Shit, I gotta go. Yo, take down my number in yo' phone and text me when he agrees to a talk." He hung up, and I immediately did as told before thinking.

I'm his woman, so I have a certain hold on him.

I watched him walk out of the bathroom, drenched in water, with a small towel for his face. He walked around to the other side of the bed, pulling out clothes.

Looking his naked body over, I smiled. "I think you should talk to Jahiem," I stated simply.

"I think with all due respect," he said, looking at me, "you should mind yo' business."

I smiled, not even the slightest bit moved by the sarcasm and attitude.

"Maybe I should, but being childish isn't like you, Shiloh. It's not in your nature, doesn't suit you very well," I said as he glared hard at me. "You're usually so mature, and so ahead of your time in terms of thinking, that it's almost shocking to see you stoop so low like this. Hmm," I said, getting up with a shrug. "Almost kind of glad to see this side of you, really. Kind of lets me know you're not as perfect as I thought."

With that, I went into the bathroom to take my shower. As soon as I walked out, he was sitting on the edge of the bed with the phone to his ear.

"Yeah," he mumbled. "We can all sit down and talk, but I won't have shit to say, Anthony. Ain't nothing left to say, but I'll do that shit."

I smiled, leaning on the doorway as he glanced back at me.

"Yeah, let me go. A'ight, bye." He stood up, gray slacks unbuttoned, with the belt hanging loose, showing off his white boxer briefs. His body was dried and smoothed over with lotion as he stood in front of me, with my towel clinging to my body.

"Good afternoon, baby," I said as he leaned down to kiss me gently. I was going to gloat in his face about him agreeing to it, but I decided just to leave it as is. I knew the hold I had over my man.

"Good afternoon, beautiful," he said against my mouth.

Now, the moment Shiloh told me he had to step out to take care of business, of course, the first person I called was Tyree and Layla, who weren't far from where I was staying. Instead of talking on the phone, giving them detail for detail, I told them to come over.

They made their way over in less than fifteen minutes. The banging on the door almost scared me half to death as I rushed to open it. There they stood, with shades on, coats in hand, high fashion boots, and designer labels, fresh from a photo shoot where a stylist probably let them keep the clothes.

"Girl, look at this room!" Tyree shrieked. He walked in, hands out, taking his shades off as he looked around. His bald head was shining in the sunlight from the window as he smiled at me. "I'm so jealous. I swear sometimes I can't stand you, bitch."

"What did I do?" I laughed as Layla walked around, eyeing the place, nose turned up in her usual fashion.

"I mean, it's probably bigger rooms than this," she started.

Tyree rolled his eyes at me before making for the bed, jumping body first into the center. "Ooo wee! Y'all had mad sex in this bed, I can tell! Gurl, I can smell it!" He laughed as my mouth dropped.

"Oh my God, get up!" I shrieked, embarrassed, before we all made our way onto the bed, kicking our shoes off. I wore a simple T-shirt with a pair of Shiloh's boxers as I let my hair air dry. I was keeping it simple because I didn't plan on leaving this room until it was time for me to go. I still had another night.

"So, how was it?" Layla asked.

"It was . . . amazing."

"Ahhhhhh! She did it! She's a woman now!" Tyree screamed, hugging me hard. "How was that stroke game? Girl, please let a nigga know if my dreams are true about Shiloh's fine ass."

I ended up telling them everything from start to finish—from how I sat in the tub to losing my virginity in the air, to waking up to eat and have more sex. They knew everything. By the time I was done, Tyree shook his head, eyes closed.

"Girl, I'm hard as fuck right now. I'm not going to even lie to you," he stated as Layla and I laughed. "So, he ate the booty too. I had to turn Trell on to that about a year ago, because the nigga was not having it."

"Well, Ronny don't have a problem doing it," Layla boasted, whipping her braids back.

"Well, Ronny is a no-name nigga," Tyree retorted. "He ain't got no choice but to do it to make up for lack of status. Now, back to Shiloh. Did you like it?"

"I loved it," I cheesed, ignoring the fact that he just made Layla feel like shit.

"Mmm, just like Shiloh to fuck a bitch in the air. Hold up! Let me call my man and ask why he not doing me like that," he said, grabbing his phone as I laughed. "Listen to this fool's answer. I know he's gon' have something stupid to say."

"Y'all are a mess." Layla laughed as the phone rang on speaker.

"Yeah, bae?" Ontrell answered.

"What you doing?" Tyree asked, signaling for us to keep quiet.

"About to walk in this studio to start recording."

Hearing a door chime, I could hear Elijah yelling in the background. Then I heard Ontell address someone: "You good, folk?"

"Yeah, man, everything is everything, cuz," the other guy said.

"Bae, I'm about to hop in this studio. What did you need?"

"Why my friend getting fucked in the air, but I can't?" Tyree complained.

I nearly fell off the bed from laughing.

"Nigga, *whet*, bruh?" Ontrell retorted. "Fuck is you talking about?"

"Why my girl having sex in the air, standing up, but I can't get that?"

"'Cause ain't nobody picking yo' big ass up like that. Nigga, get off my phone playing," he snapped as we all laughed before hanging up.

Tia

Sitting at the MARTA Westlake train station, I waited for my train to arrive. I'd been waiting for damn near three hours. It was not because my train didn't come. That shit ran like clockwork on a good day. I just didn't have no place to go. It was almost the last week of school, but I had already finished up my exams, and they wanted everyone out of the dorms and apartments on the yard by Friday afternoon. It was now Saturday. I packed everything I could possibly pack into two suitcases and dipped. I spent Thanksgiving with Porscha and her family, because like I said, my parents weren't fucking with me like that no more. My brother and I never got along, and I told Jahiem that shit. I fucking told him the issue with my family, and yet still . . .

Shaking my head, I watched another train pull up as people stepped up to the platform, ready to board. I had my last bundle of weave in my hair that had I put in a few days ago, and I was wrapped up in my thick coat, leggings, and UGG boots, with no makeup. My Chanel shades concealed the bullshit in my eyes that I'd had to go through these past couple of weeks. I went from shopping in the best stores, looking for shit to decorate a baby's room with, being in love with the funniest, craziest man I will ever know, to this—waiting at a train station with one last trip to my card, ten dollars in cash, and a suitcase full of clothes I couldn't fit. I had missed my doctor's appointment last week because who the fuck was going to pay for that shit? Jahiem had all of that taken care of, not me.

I just wanted my first ultrasound. I was almost fourteen weeks pregnant. I had so many fucking questions. Why was I so big this early? I constantly prayed I wasn't pregnant with more than one, because that was a definite possibility between Jahiem's family and mine. He had triplets and twins in his family, while I had twins on my side. We always talked about that, and he said just to prepare. He was going to stock up and buy two of everything. My stomach was to the point now where people looked at it before they noticed me or my face. Why the fuck did my breasts hurt? My body was going through so many changes, and I could barely handle them with Jahiem by my side. Now that I had no one?

I looked around the station, feeling the wind whip as I kept my scarf closely wrapped. I watched a few ladies hand out flyers to women, talking to them about whatever. Oh, shit. I couldn't stand people who do that shit while I was on the train. *Don't ask me for no money, don't ask me about God, and don't ask me about what the fuck am I getting into tonight. Mind yo' fucking business.*

I spotted one girl, who stopped a few feet in front of me. She smiled slowly at me. I continued to stare at her weird ass through the shades as I kept a tight grip on my belongings. She wore jeans with some riding boots with a cute gold buckle on the sides, a hoodie with a cute, long trench coat over it. She had dark skin with a pretty face, and dark brown hair straightened to perfection as it hung loosely just above the shoulders with the side swoop.

"Hi," she greeted softly as she walked up to me, handing me a flyer.

I just stared at her; didn't even glance at the paper. She just smiled sweetly, and without so much as a hello from me, the bitch took it as an invitation to sit down next to me.

"Whoo, Lord Jesus, it's cold. I've been watching you for at least twenty minutes now, and not once have you gotten on a train. You must be waiting on someone."

"And you must be nosy as fuck," I retorted, scooting down on the bench.

She just smiled, shook it off as if she didn't recognize when someone was being rude to her. "My name is Noelle," she said with her hand out.

I continued to mind my fucking business. *Fuck is this bitch's problem? Ain't that much Southern hospitality in Atlanta. We don't do that here, boo.*

"Anyway," she continued, "a couple of us ladies are out here trying to get women to come out to our free clinic," she said, showing me the paper.

The moment I saw First Primary Baptist Church on it, I cringed, quickly getting up. "I don't fuck with nobody from that church," I stated, trying to redo my zipper on my coat, which I realized was broken.

She glanced at my stomach before a flash of concern hit her face. "Oh, wow, how far—"

"Don't worry about it," I snapped. Where the fuck was Jahiem at? I didn't want to be out here on MARTA talking to random strangers. I couldn't do this. *You got me pregnant, and you promised you would help me even after I agreed to a DNA test, but you still got me out here—*

"Are you okay?" she asked, hand on my shoulder as I sniffed, wiping my wet cheek before flipping her hand off me. Everything sweet and nice about her changed instantly in that moment. "Look," she started, voice dropping as she looked around. "I'm tired as fuck. I just woke up not too long ago, and I really don't want to be out here longer than I have to. Okay? If you don't need any fucking help, say that shit, but you don't have to be rude about it."

I cocked my head back, looking at this girl. *Oh, okay, bitch. I see ya.*

"I don't fuck with your church."

"Why not? This has nothing to do with going to a women's clinic. Clearly you need some type of help. You're pregnant and obviously have no place to go, unless you're waiting on someone."

Fuck it.

"A man who I called father molested me when I was eleven. I told my mama this, and she said I was lying. I told everyone, and they said I was lying, said I was being a fast ass. He's not my real dad, but because he raised me as his own, I was supposed to be grateful, even though he snuck into my room and did what the fuck he did that night," I said as her eyes widened in horror. "I decided to let that shit go, but everyone said I was trying to break up the family. My brother doesn't fuck with me like that, because that's his dad. Barely talks to my mom because of me, and I was the one that was put to shame when this nigga shoved his dick in me—over and over again.

"So, why I don't fuck with that church? I don't believe in churches making money off dumb bitches like you. I don't believe in paying to pray for God, and that same nigga that is your pastor is the same nigga I'm supposed to call my dad," I let out as her mouth dropped. "Now, I have no place to go. My baby daddy doesn't want shit to do with me. My so-called family been stopped fucking with me after that, and I'm hungry, tired, and I want to check on the health of my baby, but for what when I can't even take care of myself at this point?" I let out, hands in the air as I felt the tears coming down. All I wanted was Jahiem. I just wanted to be at home with my man, in his arms, hearing him tell me stories about his childhood. I loved it when we would lay in the bed and just talk.

"Come on," she said, taking my things as she looked around.

"*Whet*?" I flipped as she started walking.

"Let's go. I'm taking you to the doctor. I'll pay for it," she said.

I quickly followed her, shocked. Now, if I was lying, this bitch would have been got, but damn. There are people out there that will do things like that for a complete stranger? In Atlanta?

I followed her to the gate with her tapping her card, and me following quickly behind her. As soon as we got in her car, she cut it on to warm it up just as her phone rang.

"Hello?" she answered, putting it on speaker.

I looked around her car, seeing the wooden cross necklace hanging down her rearview mirror. Pink small pillows with her sorority letters embedded in them sat in the back seat.

Of course she's a sorority girl. They live off this community service shit.

"Just wanted to call you and say I love you," the man said softly as she smiled, looking at her phone. I wished a nigga would even think about doing some shit like that for me.

"I love you too, babe," she beamed before they said their goodbyes and hung up. She let out a contented sigh before looking at me, smile dropping. "Do you know what you're having?"

"I think it's a boy," I said, looking down at my stomach through my coat. "I'm not sure, but I feel like it's a boy. That's what I want, at least. I just pray I'm not having more than one. The father comes from a family of triplets and twins. His dad's granddad was a twin. My real dad is a twin, grandmother was a twin, and so many cousins between the two of us that are twins."

"Oh! That's exciting!" she freaked.

I stared at her dully. *No, bitch, that's not exciting! I'm by myself taking care of multiple children? What the fuck? My first time having a baby and I deliver a basketball team. That's not exciting at all.*

"I can't wait until I have kids," she continued. "I went to the doctor's last week to make sure everything about me was healthy and ready to have kids, so today I'm going back to see my results. While I'm there, you can find out everything you need to know."

"How many do you want?" I asked as she pulled out of the parking lot.

She shrugged with an easy smile. "My boyfriend and I say we both want three, but he wants two girls and a boy. I want two boys and a girl. I just think boys are easier to raise," she said as I nodded. "I can't have another girl like me, same attitude, and nasty mouth? Ugh, drive me insane. But maybe one day, I'll pop out triplets, since he comes from a family of them too."

"Tell me about it," I mumbled.

We drove in silence through the back ways of MLK, with her occasionally glancing at me.

"If I could get you a place to stay, would you be willing to leave Atlanta?" she asked.

I looked at her, eyes wide.

"I mean, it's not much, but I have family in Albany that will gladly take you in, in your condition. My grandmama loves babies." She laughed.

"I don't know what to say," I mumbled, staring at her. "You would do that?"

"It's no biggie," she said, waving me off. "You're catching me on a good day. Just had a birthday that passed. Spent it with my man in a wonderful hotel for two nights. I'm at my happiest right now."

I didn't even have time to be jealous. I just reached over and hugged the fuck out of her.

"You have to promise me that you will be the best mother you can be to that little one. Raise him or her, love him or her, and—"

"Never rely on a nigga for shit," I cut in. She looked at me. "It's just me and this baby. Fuck him, fuck him!"

"Fuck him, whoever he is," she agreed. "You don't need him."

"Damn right I don't."

The moment we got to the doctor's office, because it was a Saturday, she had to do some begging to squeeze me in with her appointment time, since hers was just a consultation. So, while she was doing her thing, I was in the room, laid back on the bed, with the cold gel being spread on my stomach by the technician.

"You excited?" she asked, popping on her gum as I eyed her weave. Shit was stiffer than a cold bitch. She needed to do something about that.

When she glanced at me, I smiled sweetly. "I just want to know if the baby is okay, healthy and whatnot," I said as she looked at the screen. Shit just looked like nothing to me. I didn't even know what the fuck I was looking at.

"Mm-hmm," she said, nodding her head as she continued to look. "You see that right there? You see the head?" She pointed.

Got me up here squinting hard, looking at the screen. Didn't know what the fuck I was looking at, but when I finally caught on, boy, did I catch the fuck up. More than one. My mouth dropped, along with my heart, my soul, and my life. I saw them a second before she did, and this was her fucking job.

"Ooooh, look," she said, pointing at another one, and another one. I felt myself about to faint. "So, you're having three babies," she said, trying to sound excited. "This is my first live ultrasound I did on my own with triplets. You see how they're together?"

I nodded, tears sliding down the side of my face. All I could think about was Trent. Even though Jahiem said on his mama's, and clearly his daddy's side there was a history of multiples, my mind just went to Trent. I knew in my heart it was Jahiem's, but it would always be that moment of thinking they could be Trent's kids.

"Hey, are you okay?" she asked, waving her hand in front of me. "I was asking if you wanted to know the sex of your babies."

My eyes lit up as I looked at the screen.

"It's still early, but from what I can see, I'm almost a hundred percent sure you're having all girls."

Bruh...

"Cut the machine off," I mumbled. She looked at me. "Cut that shit off. I don't want to it see anymore," I said, moving her hand away. "Let me a get a napkin so I can wipe this shit off me." I couldn't even have a fucking boy. Not even one.

As soon as I walked out without so much as a thank you, I met up with Noelle, who sat in the waiting room, eyes red from crying. When she looked up at me, she smiled, quickly trying to cover it up as she stood up.

"You ready?" she asked, sniffing.

"What's wrong?" I asked, walking out of the building to her car. She just waved me off.

"They just told me a bunch of stuff, technical terms I don't really understand, but to put it bluntly, I won't ever be able to have children."

My mouth dropped as she continued walking to her car, fingers struggling to dial a number on her phone.

Damn . . . and I'm bitching about not having a boy when I was blessed with three girls. She can't even have one.

Sitting in the car, I watched her cry as the phone continued to ring with no one answering it.

"Well, if it makes you feel any better, I know we don't know each other. Just met at a fucking train station a few hours ago." I laughed as she looked at me. "You can be the godmother of my load," I said, rubbing my stomach. "Three girls."

Her mouth dropped. The title was going to go to Porscha, but this girl and her damn random act of kindness did it for me.

"Yeah," I continued, looking at my stomach. "Don't get all excited now. If I'm staying with your family, best believe you will be getting calls when I need a fucking babysitter. Christmas and birthdays will be an event every time, and I mean it," I said, shaking my head with a roll of my eyes and a smack of my teeth. "Shit, you can even name one of them."

"Are you serious?" she damn near stopped breathing as I nodded slowly. "Ahhh! Oh my God! Okay, let's think of a name. What's the last name?"

"Car—"

"What about—oh my God, let me think," she said quickly.

I smiled, watching her take on this big-ass responsibility.

"I love April, but Christina is—"

"Both ugly," I said, cutting her off, and she laughed. "Think of something else."

She sat quietly, thinking. The car was heating up, and I got comfortable. I was starving like hell.

"Well, my name starts with a N," she muttered as she backed out of the parking space. We rode around, grabbing a bite to eat, and in between that, she shot names out at me before disregarding them herself. She got on the phone with her parents, and they gladly accepted me in, on the condition that I finish up school down there and not cause any foolishness.

Fuck I'm gonna turn up for with three bitches in my stomach? Fuck I look like? Please. I'm looking for a job. They lucky I agreed to finish school, because my ass was already looking up places on my phone that were hiring in Albany. I needed a car, and to start preparing for these kids. There was so much I had to do, the last thing I was worried about was naming them, so she didn't know it, but she was going to name two of the three, and one of them was taking her first name.

"Okay," she said, sipping on her drink as we sat at Zaxbys, eating courtesy of her, once again. She told me to keep my little ten bucks.

"How about . . ." she started, moving her hair out of her face as she smiled at me. "London is my middle name, so let's go with that."

"I like that," I said with a nod, but the bitch continued.

"But my mama said she wanted to name me Peyton after my grandma," she said as I smiled. Peyton was pretty too. "Which one do you like? You're the mama."

"Their names are London, Noelle, and Peyton, in whichever order they come at, I guess. You want to do middle names too?" I asked as her eyes watered up.

She got up so quick, wrapping her arms tight around me as she hugged me hard. "You better call me as soon as you get in labor! I will be coming down there every chance I get to check on you. Do you hear me?" She flipped.

I looked around, seeing people looking at us. "Girl, if you don't sit yo' overemotional ass down." I laughed, nearly having to pry her hands off me. "Come on. I need middle names. Think."

Later that evening, with a Greyhound ticket in my hand at the station, we said our last, but not final, good-byes as the bus pulled up. I tried calling Jahiem one last time before giving up. He was done with me, and you know what? I was done with him too. I didn't have the luxury to worry about a nigga right now, chasing behind him. My priority right now was these girls and myself. Noelle Tierra Carter, London Jasmine Carter, and Peyton Makayla Carter were my main and only concern at this point. Fuck everyone else.

Jordyn

I sat across from Trent in my living room, staring at him as he looked around awkwardly at my place. Elijah had my furniture put back in, but it didn't matter, because I was beyond upset right now. He was supposed to be there with me. I told him the moment after we landed in Atlanta from Thanksgiving with my family that I was pregnant. We talked about it, and he agreed that it was best we abort it. He was a little upset about it and upset that I wasn't taking it as seriously as he was when it was my fucking body in the first place.

I set up the appointment for Saturday at 11 p.m., trying to time it right against his schedule. I was supposed to have it in an hour, but he had missed his flight because why? The man overslept and had to wait. He was all the way in California right now, recording music. I told him I didn't want to do this by myself, and now I had no choice.

I was nine weeks pregnant and decided to get the surgical abortion. I told my mom about it, and that didn't go over too well. She wouldn't speak to me, but my dad continued to check on me.

Looking at my phone, watching the screen light up with Elijah's name blaring, I pressed IGNORE once more as I looked at Trent. He sat on the couch, keys in hand, waiting, dressed in his fraternity letterman's jacket with jeans and Timberland boots, and a fresh fade with diamond studs in his ear.

He cleared his throat. "So, how you gonna get there if you don't want me to take you?" he asked blatantly. "No bus goes out that way, Jordyn. We don't have to talk in the car, but I'm doing this as a favor to E. I don't—"

"Why are you talking?" I cut in, looking at him as he rolled his eyes, shaking his head.

"Fuck it. I'll be in the car waiting," he said, pulling out his phone, no doubt to call Elijah.

Why would Elijah send him over here? I could have made other arrangements had I known Trent would be the one to take me while my car was in the shop. I watched him through the screen door on the phone with Elijah, hand thrown in the air as if he didn't know what else to do.

I'm not the type of person to forgive easily. Well, when it comes to certain people, obviously. I am stubborn and can hold a grudge for as long as I feel like it's necessary. Just because he was the brother of the one I was with did not mean I had to like him or get along with him.

Trent turned back around. He opened the door and stepped in, letting the cool air in. "Aye, he wants to talk to you. He said pick up yo' phone," Trent said in a dull voice.

I could hear Elijah's tiny voice screaming as Trent put it on speaker.

"Jordyn, what the fuck, shawty? Just get in the car and go! I'm not going to be there until later on tonight!"

"Why would you send him of all people? I could have arranged for someone else to come get me if—"

"He's my brother! Why wouldn't he go in my place? Whatever the fuck y'all got going on, squash that shit now, because I'm sick of it!"

"You two being related has nothing to do with me wanting to be with you, Elijah," I said as Trent's eyes grew wide. "I don't care who the fuck he is. I'm not—"

"Aye, Jordyn," he said slowly with a sarcastic laugh. "Check that mouth and watch what the fuck you saying, shawty. You my girl, but I'll have yo' ass out that fucking house with yo' shit packed on the corner, waiting for dick like a basic bitch, you hear me?" he threatened as I rolled my eyes. "He ain't just a nobody; that's my brother. Get the fuck up and get in that car. I'm not with this childish shit. Nigga apologized already, so be respectful, handle yo' business, and act like a fucking woman!" With that, he hung up.

I looked at Trent.

"So, can we just go? I won't say shit to you in the car," he said, pointing to the door. I got up, grabbing my coat, and followed him out to his nice black Mustang.

Once inside the car, he cut the music on, and to my amusement, classical music started to play.

"I know he said you like to listen to classical shit when you stressed out," he said as I stared out the window, watching the cars go by.

"I do," I mumbled, glancing at him. He was leaned back comfortably in the seat, one hand on the wheel as he licked his lips.

We remained silent until his phone started to ring. Of course, it was Elijah, checking to see if I even got in the car. So, Trent had him on speaker, propped up on the dashboard.

"Yeah, E," Trent answered.

"She got in the car with you, bruh?"

"Yeah, she right here next to me. What time you getting back? I got a date tonight."

"Taylor or New York bitch?"

"Neither. I met this girl at the store, fine as fuck too. I'm done with both Taylor and Jade. I tried with Jade, but she not trying to hear me out, so . . ." He shrugged.

"Ahhh, you ain't tried shit. Now that you got that car, you thinking you finna bang all the bitches in Atlanta." Elijah laughed, and I smiled at his stupid, boyish laugh. "Whatever you do, don't get a bisexual ho."

My head popped up as Trent looked at me. I guess he didn't know he was on speaker.

"Why not?" Trent asked, signaling for me to be quiet.

"Because, man, they will drive you crazy. Good thing about it is, when you be checking girls out, they'll be right there with you, doing the same shit. But, bruh?" he let out with a huff of his breath. "You see how Jordyn got me doing shit I would never do. Bitch drove me crazy in a matter of months. I told you I went to her boyfriend's job. I found that nigga, and me and Rob hit that nigga up something serious."

"What you say to him?"

"We caught him outside, walking to his car after some-one pointed him out to me. I walked up to him like, you know how I be. I don't waste no time. I said, 'Aye, man. Aye, sir. You Desmond? He was like, 'Uhhh, yeah?' I said, 'You know Jordyn?' He said, 'Yeah, I know her. That's my gir—' WOP!" Elijah made a popping noise. "Bruh, I didn't even let that nigga finish. We grabbed him, forced him inside the car, and I threatened that man's life. I told him, 'As soon as I leave, call her and say you can't fuck with her no more. If I catch you talking to her, looking at her, talking about her, think-ing about her, nigga, we gon' have a problem. You hear me?' So, he started stuttering like, 'I didn't know she—' WOP!" He made another popping noise as my mouth dropped.

"Why did you hit the man again?"

"Shit, I was high off everything that night. She did that shit, man. I can't even think about her fucking somebody else. So, when she said she had a boyfriend, I lost it. Bitch drove me insane in one night." He laughed.

Trent shook his head, glancing at me. "Yeah, but you love her, though."

"Yeah, bruh, she got my heart," he mumbled as I closed my eyes, shaking my head with a soft smile. I knew it. "I don't tell her that, though, because you know how females get. They act funny as fuck after they find out a nigga love you. I just want it to be her and me, nobody else, without all that lovey-dovey shit. Kills me when she say she loves me, and I'm trying to keep it together, because you know how I am. I rather show her than constantly tell her, because that shit ain't nothing but a word at the end of the day."

"True," Trent agreed, turning down a street as he followed his GPS. "You did good, bruh. I know she don't fuck with me like that, but the other day, I caught yo' ass reading a big book. No pictures in it, too?"

"Ahhh, shut yo' lame ass up!" Elijah let out as they both laughed. They had the exact same laugh. "Yeah, she got me reading. She be talking about a lot of shit that I never understand, so I'm trying to get on her level, you know. Trying to spruce up the mind a bit, my nigga. You might not be the only one with that degree."

"I hope not. Aye, look," he said, pulling up to the center. "We just got here, so I'ma call you when it's done."

"Aye, I might be on the plane afterwards. I'm on my way to the airport. I'll hit you up as soon as I touch down in Atlanta," he said. "Put J on the phone real quick. Let me talk to her."

"A'ight," Trent said, handing me the phone, taking it off speaker.

"Hello?" I answered weakly, chewing on my thumbnail as I looked at the place, PLANNED PARENTHOOD in bright letters.

"You good? We not going back on our word, are we?"

"No, I'm not ready for a baby, and neither are you."

"Shit." He sighed. "Ask them mothafuckas before you do it if it fucks up yo' chances of having babies in the future. Make sure whoever is there that they know what they doing. If they look like—"

"Elijah, I know," I said, trying to calm him down. He was freaking out more than I was.

"Nah, just check them. You read the reviews on this place, and if they cleanliness is straight? If you feel uncomfortable about any of them niggas in there, leave. You hear me, shawty?"

"I know, Elijah." I sighed, looking at Trent. "It's going to be okay. Just calm down and stop worrying."

"Man, put Trent on the phone," he snapped.

I handed Trent the phone. They exchanged a few words before Trent hung up, getting out of the car. Walking up to the place, I felt Trent put his hand on my mid back, keeping me close as we walked inside. He went up to the desk, asking all the questions I was sure Elijah wanted to know. Going straight into business mode, he turned on the proper voice.

"If you want to talk with the doctor before she goes in, you can do that as well," the nurse said with a nod.

"If it's not too much trouble, I'm just trying to make sure my sister is straight and in good hands," Trent said as I smiled.

"Certainly. I'll have you sit down with him, so he can go over the process," she said, getting up from her chair.

Trent looked down at me and smiled.

"Thank you, Trent," was all I could manage to say as he wrapped his arms around me, hugging me gently.

"No problem, sis," he said.

Trent

It had been a crazy-ass day. I had one more final to go next week, and then it was time to party. Next Friday was my graduation party at the Spring Lounge. I was preparing for that, constantly adding people to the guest list and looking for the hottest girls to pass out flyers and to stand there at the party just to look good. I told Elijah if Jordyn was up for it, she could be one of the girls to somewhat model at my party. He said no, but I was going to convince her to do it anyway. Nigga would be a'ight for a night.

Taylor had been blowing my phone up for the longest, even after I told her to leave me alone. I hadn't been to my sister's house since, because of Taylor's stalking ass. She needed to move the fuck on, because I already had, a couple of times. Once I got this Mustang from Shiloh, I was A-1. I was straight, nigga, picking up girls night after night, feeling like I was back to my old self. I wanted Jade back. Really, I did, but the car had me feeling like I could do better than that. Besides, she went back to New York and changed her number on me. She wasn't fucking with me, so fuck it. I don't chase after no bitch.

Looking up from the waiting room, I saw the nurses escorting Jordyn out of the room, with her barely able to stand. I quickly got up. I mean, you should know what the fuck is going on by now, but for the sake of the story, I'll repeat that shit. She just got an abortion. Elijah couldn't be there, so I stepped in on his behalf.

"She did wonderful," the nurse said as I looked at Jordyn. Her eyes were barely open as she looked at me. "Make sure she gets plenty of rest. The list of things she shouldn't do are in her papers, and to make the payment, you do it right here," she said, pointing to the desk.

Shit, okay. Couldn't wait to get that money, huh?

When I got her in the car, she stayed quiet, leaned against the door with her eyes closed. I didn't know whether to speak, but seeing my phone ring, I was just about to answer it automatically, until I saw the name.

Taylor. What the fuck, man? I don't have shit else to say. Fuck it.

"Hello?" I answered, backing out of the space.

"So, how long you gon' keep this shit up, nigga?" she snapped angrily. "I mean, I still feel like you owe me some type of explanation as to why you went back on yo' word."

"Taylor, come on." I sighed, glancing at Jordyn, who winced in pain, gripping her stomach and causing me to panic.

"You good? What's the matter?" I asked quickly, and Taylor went off.

"Nah, nigga, I'm not good! I went through hell these past few weeks, wondering if you will ever come back around—"

"I'm just cramping really badly," Jordyn let out, grabbing my arm tight.

"Who the fuck is that?" Taylor flipped. "You are talking to another bitch, aren't you?"

"No, I—"

"Why would you do me like that, Trent?" she cried.

I groaned.

"When is Elijah coming home?" Jordyn let out as Taylor continued to go off.

I couldn't handle this shit. First thing I could think of to calm a woman down was lie. "Taylor, baby," I said, holding Jordyn's hand, letting her squeeze mine. "We can talk later on this evening. I will explain everything, I'm going to apologize, and we can talk about our next step. I just needed some space. I just broke up with my girlfriend, and you expected me to hop right on to you?"

"Nigga, that's what you said you would do!"

"I'm sorry, but now I'm ready to talk if you are. Just give me until about seven. I'm handling something for my brother right now. I'll call you back."

"Okay, you better do it, too," she threatened as she hung up.

Fuck! I grabbed my phone and cut that bitch off. Shut it down. I looked at Jordyn, making sure she was okay.

"You straight?"

"I'm fine," she muttered, eyes closed. "Just want to lay down. Never want to do anything like that ever again."

When I got her back to her place, I helped her to the bed, keeping my back turned as she changed. Even though she was pregnant, she put on her weight in all the right places, and I hoped that shit stayed, too.

When she was ready, I helped her in the bed as she started to cry.

Fuuck no. Come on, now. Where the fuck is Elijah at? I don't want to deal with this shit.

"Are you staying until he gets here?" she asked, eyes watered down. I nodded. "I regret doing it. I wish I hadn't done it."

"Don't tell Elijah that," I warned, wondering why he hadn't called me yet.

Just as I was about to step out, she turned over on the side of the bed and threw up.

Ahhh, man . . . I can't do this shit. Fuck no.

It was just a little bit, but it was enough to keep my ass out the room. It wasn't until I saw her trying to clean it up herself that I let out a groan. "Hold up, Jordyn. Just lay down. I got it," I muttered, going in the kitchen, looking for a rag. Where the fuck was her roommate? Her friends, family? Anyone?

I came back in with a chair and a wet rag, trying to clean it up and keeping myself from throwing up in the process. Once that was done, to get the smell out, I sprayed some shit and sat near the door, watching her.

"Where yo' people at, Jordyn? Friends? Roommate? Somebody? Family? We can't be all you have," I said.

"Rita moved out because she wanted to stay back on the yard next semester without paying, and I don't have any other friends. Never did," she muttered, half asleep.

Shit, I would move in if Elijah let me. I'm ready to have my own place and get the fuck up out the frat house. I might just make that happen.

Waiting some more, I looked around her room. It looked like your typical female room. As she slept, I took a look in her drawers, seeing she had every type of panty you could think of. I know I'm a creep nigga for this, but I was curious, and Elijah wasn't calling me, so shit. Looking through some more stuff, I saw where she kept all her sex devices. She had a box full of toys—vibrators, cream, gel. Everything you can think of, she had it. Fuck is anal beads? She definitely was a freak.

I smirked, seeing photos of her as a teenager in another shoebox. She looked like an awkward nerd. She still did, but I could see what Elijah saw in her.

Damn, where the fuck is this nigga?

It was getting dark, and I had shit to do. Looking back at Jordyn, I could see tears dried up on her face as she slept. She would occasionally wake up and cry herself back to sleep, but for the most part, she was good. I grabbed my phone and looked at it, realizing I'd turned it off. Shit. I knew this nigga was about to flip. Soon as I cut it on, sure enough, he was calling me.

"Hello?"

"Bruh!" Elijah went in. "I've been—"

"Aye, I know, I know. I cut it off because of Taylor's crazy ass. Are you here or nah?"

"I'm right around the corner. How is she?"

"She's good, man. She crying a lot, but she's good," I said, looking at her as she slept soundly.

"What happened with Taylor?"

"Bruh," I let out as I walked out of the room. "I don't even want to get into it right now. Just bring yo' ass on."

"I'm here, right here," he said, hanging up.

I saw some headlights flash outside. I went to the door, watching him hop out with his chains jingling, dreads wild, with a thin red Polo jacket and jeans sagging as he walked up. We slapped hands as we came in for a quick hug. We were nothing alike, but more similar than most.

His low eyes immediately went to a sleepy Jordyn, who stepped out of her room looking like a little girl with the sheets wrapped around her.

"Jordyn, when you get better, let's talk about me moving in this place with you. I need a place to stay," I told her, and she nodded.

"Oh, so you ain't gon' ask me?" Elijah cut in. I shook my head no with a laugh. "Fuck you too then, nigga. Shit. You good, baby?" he cooed as he wrapped his arms around her neck, telling her something only she could hear against her ear.

Her hands came to his waist as she started shaking her head, crying. It made me think of Jade, wishing for a split second I still had her. It was only for a second, though. I smiled, watching the two interact. My brother—never thought I would see this day—but he was in love. She started telling him the process as they went in the room, closing the door with a lock. Well, damn, I couldn't even get a thanks.

Grabbing my letterman jacket, I started to walk out, then the door opened, with Jordyn walking out, pushing her glasses up.

"Thank you, Trent," she said in a soft voice before holding out her hand. Her eyes were red from crying.

"What?" I smiled, guilt all over my face.

"Give it here," she demanded with a smirk.

I dropped my head as Elijah walked out shirtless, watching me give his girl her own handcuffs back.

"Thank you. I use these regularly on my girls and him, so I know instantly when they've been taken."

Elijah's mouth dropped as he looked at me.

Shit, let me back up before he—

"Bruh, I oughta bust you—" he said, trying to hit me as I laughed. "Get yo' nasty ass out of here, nigga! Fuck is wrong with you?" Elijah flipped.

I continued to laugh while walking out with a wave. "Later, fam!" I called out to them both as I hopped in the car.

Next stop, on to see a pretty girl named Cassie. She was a gorgeous, light-skin girl with a phat ass. I'm talking beautiful face, sweet-sounding voice, and an ass I was ready to slam into that night if everything went well. Checking my phone, I saw where she was texting me too, sending me pictures of her getting out of the shower.

Hoes, man. They know how to fuck with a nigga's head if you let them. Can't say I wasn't jealous of the stability Elijah had with Jordyn, but I would say he was missing out on meeting different women and having fun with no thoughts of feelings and no strings being attached. I was a free man! No crazy-ass Taylor stalking me no more, because I was going to end that shit tonight as well! No

Jade, because she wasn't trying to fuck with me no more. Still, every time I thought about her, I felt a little pain in my chest, because it wasn't her that fucked up, it was me, and I had to live with that shit every time I thought of her. But! A mothafucka was still single at the end of the day, and I planned on staying that way all throughout the up and coming year. No time for girlfriends, and no time for drama. Like Shiloh said, *I'm too old for it.* I just wanted to fuck around and be happy—which was exactly what I did. I swung by my place, changed clothes, because you know I gotta keep it looking fresh.

On my way to pick up my girl of the night, Shiloh called me, so I had him on speaker phone throughout my car. I decided to call the Mustang Victoria. Yeah, my bad bitch Victoria. I was in love with this fucking car. The moment Shiloh taught me how to drive stick and I got the hang of it? Boy! You ain't seen a nigga go out so much until you met me. Shit, I was never home.

But back to this phone call. Got me all off track, talking about my new car.

"Hello?" I answered, hearing him talk to someone in the background.

"Yeah, what up, Trent?" he greeted in his usual dull voice. "You coming by tomorrow still, so we can all talk about this stupid-ass shit?"

"I don't have nothing to say to Jahiem," I said with a shrug. I hadn't spoken to that nigga since that early morning he caught me off guard with a hit to the face and had my brother on the ground coughing up blood. *Fuck that and fuck him.*

"I know, but they want to squash this shit and move on before yo' party. Is Elijah with you?"

"Nah, you know his girl had the abortion today," I told him, stopping at a red light as I looked around me at the people in their cars, being nosy as fuck as I waited.

"Ohhh, I didn't know," he said in a low voice. "Is she good?"

"She's good. I had to take her, since Elijah wasn't even in Atlanta until later on. I hope I never put a girl through nothing like that."

"Aye, what's this beef between you and Jahiem again? What's the real issue?"

"Man!" I started as the light turned green. "The girl he was messing with turns out to be a girl I only fucked one time when school was in. I didn't even fucking nut in her, and he acting like I slept with his girl while she was with him. Had I known that was the girl he was with all along, I would have told him in the first place she was a fucking ho. But me and him ain't never been close like that. He's closer to Elijah than me, which is cool. But now that I saw how he had my brother on the ground like that? Bruh, ain't shit else to say to you, dawg," I said, shaking my head.

"I know. I feel you," Shiloh agreed. "Just do me a favor and show up. Try and bring Elijah too, if you can. Entertain what these niggas got to say, and then dip. They—"

"Is that Trent?" I heard Noelle faintly ask in the background. I smiled. "Tell him I said hiii!"

"You hear her?" Shiloh asked, a smile in his voice.

"What up, queen?" I greeted, using the nickname I heard Shiloh usually call her. I could hear her saying something to Shiloh, who started to laugh.

"Aye, she said yo' girl has been blowing up her phone, asking about you."

"Who's my girl?"

"Tay."

"Ahhh, what the fuck," I groaned with a shake of my head as I turned into some apartment complex over on the east side near Stone Mountain. I'd fucked with too many hoes in this area. Damn. "I'll talk to her when I find the time. Tell Noelle not to entertain that shit. Don't feed into it. Taylor just looking for some attention."

I started to tune them out as they spoke when I pulled up to a parking spot, seeing the door on the second floor open. I smiled as I stepped out, adjusting my letterman's jacket, and watched my date walk down the steps. Fuck, she was gorgeous. All I kept staring at were those hips and ass, picturing those legs wrapped around me as she smirked at me, coming down the steps in her heels.

"You look cute," she said, flipping her hair off her shoulders as I came to hug her.

"You look sexy as fuck," I told her, licking my lips at her. Girls eat that shit up when you give 'em the "I'm gonna dick you down" face. I mastered that shit well.

"Aye," Shiloh called into the phone. "I'll let you do what you do. Just be there tomorrow, nigga."

"A'ight," I said into the phone, opening the door for Cassie.

"Hey!" Noelle yelled out again. "Before you go, just remember the most dangerous type of woman is an emotionally hurt woman, Trent. You need to fix it."

"Chill out, Dr. Phil," Shiloh cut in before hanging up.

My mind was on one thing, and one thing only: Cassie and those hips, that mouth, and that ass.

As soon as she got comfortable in the car, looking around, she smirked cutely at me as I pulled out.

"What?" I laughed.

"Whose car is this? This isn't yours," she pressed.

I winked at her. "All mine, baby. Paid cash for it," I lied.

She bit her lower lip, flashing a little bit of the tongue as I smiled. She wanted the dick. Having a nice car as a man is like having a big dick and knowing how to stroke that shit. If you got both like me? Well, then, this is why I have issues like crazy-ass Taylor coming after me nonstop. I was going to just hold off on talking to her until after I finished with Cassie.

I took her out to eat at a basic-ass restaurant. You know, girls feel fancy as shit when you take them to Maggianos or someplace. Wasn't nothing for me, since Elijah gave me something for taking Jordyn to the clinic, and I just got paid yesterday, so I was straight. We went to the movies, with me keeping my phone off. I didn't want no calls, no interruptions that could fuck up this night. During the movie, I was the polite gentleman I know she wasn't expecting me to be. Didn't try to make a move on her. I wanted her to feel like I was truly wanting to be with her, and only her.

Shiiiiit, the moment we got to that car? I couldn't keep this bitch off me. All I could hear in my head was Shiloh telling me, "Don't fuck in my car." Even though it was mine, he said never fuck in that car. *Nah, bruh, I've already did it twice. This will be my third time.*

I didn't even make it out of the parking lot when I had to push my seat back a little to give her room. She dropped down and gave me head without so much as me spitting game to her.

"Shit!" I breathed, looking down as her head bobbed up and down on my dick. I loved my life. I never had a problem getting a female. Never will. My only issue with women is when they try to kiss you afterward. *Nah, you just put yo' mouth on my dick. I don't want to know what that mouth taste like. Fuck no.*

Yet, now as I watched her riding me in the front seat, breasts all in my face, knees hiked up as she gripped the back of my seat, hair bouncing, all I could think about was, I hoped I had another condom, and could it really get any better than this? You feel me? Why be in a relationship when I can get this on a regular from different women?

So, I was thinking everything was good with my life. Just had some decent grade-A sex and okay head. She could have done better, but since my ex had the tongue rings in her mouth and was into doing tricks and shit, no one would ever compare to her. I never had to work hard for a woman until I met Jade. She threw me completely off my game.

Back to the story. I'm thinking everything is good, right? You know, bad chick in the car with me, who is willing to spend the night. We in the car, heading back to the frat house as she's fixing her face, making sure that her makeup looks right. I can dig it. I cut my phone on and see a shitload of messages from Taylor, flipping out, cussing me out. There were seven voicemails from her and a few messages from my frat brothers about food tonight.

"You gon' make me breakfast, nigga?" Cassie asked in a sexy-ass voice.

I glanced at her, throwing a smile her way with a lick of my lips, keeping cool as I drove with one hand on the wheel. *Shit, if you step yo' head game up, you can get whatever the fuck you want.*

"I got you," I said instead as she smiled. "You beautiful, so I'ma do that for you. I don't often do shit like that, but for you, I'll make an exception."

"You better," she teased playfully as I laughed.

Bitch, I'm not making you fucking breakfast. You'll be out the house before I even let you use the fucking bathroom. Fuck outta here. Talking about breakfast. You ain't that cute.

Turning down the street, I spotted a few old heads that hung around the back of the campus yard, walking the streets like it wasn't cold as fuck out here in the beginning of December. They stayed trying to get at the college girls, even though the campus was about empty with the last of finals ending next week.

As soon as I took Cassie to the room after introducing her to the rest of the frat, we got it in. I'm talking bed, floor, against the wall. She was a runner, but I didn't tolerate that shit, not in my bedroom. *You gon' take this dick I'm giving you, and then you're going to get the fuck on. You know the game already. Come on now.*

So, when all was said and done, I was laid back against my headboard, smoking the last of my blunt, with home-girl beside me. Maybe she was pretending to be asleep so she could stay the night, but nah, that was not happening. I got up, throwing on some basketball shorts, and stepped out, walking up the steps to the living room to see Armond and AJ chilling on the couch, talking.

"What the fuck y'all getting into?" I asked, slapping hands with them as I grabbed a seat, pulling a chair from the kitchen. I was shirtless, sweat still on my back, one sock on, and comfortable as fuck. I was high out of my mind, but I was good.

"Shit, just talking about life, you know." Armond shrugged. "Where you getting these girls from, bruh? You stay pulling the baddest girls."

"I got it like that," I cheesed. "What can I say?"

"Man, you gon' catch the wrong female one day. I thought Jade might've tamed yo' ho ass down, but she might've enhanced it," AJ said as they laughed.

I remained silent, mind struggling to stay off Jade once the name was brought up, but I guess they noticed.

"Ahh, you still missing her?" Armond asked knowingly.

"I'm good, man. If she don't want to talk, then I can't force it. I'm going to continue to do me. She moved back up to New York anyway."

"Nah," AJ said, shaking his head. "She's just up there for the winter break. She's coming back."

I stared hard at him, and he already knew what the next question from me was going to be.

"Aye, we don't talk like that. I just follow her on Instagram and Facebook. Talking about she's ready to come back to Atlanta and shit."

"Nigga was about to go the fuck off on you!" Armond laughed, playfully punching AJ as I smirked.

Regardless of the fucked-up shit that I did to Jade, don't let it fool you. I was almost over the top, aggressive as hell when it came to other niggas looking at her, coming at her, or even mentioning her. I wasn't having it. That, I can truly say, is what Elijah and I had in common. We were crazy as fuck about our women. Shit, all the Carter men were like that. Our pops was crazy when it came to someone messing with any one of his baby mamas or kids. That's where we get it from. That's why we were so hard on Olivia. We were raised to protect, cherish, love, and appreciate women. Shit, we got the protection right at least.

I remember one time I was in the mall with her. Had to be Cumberland Mall. She liked to go there and buy oils and incense for her room when she smoked. So, we were walking, I was checking emails on my phone, with her occasionally stopping to eye the displays from different stores. She had on some leggings that made her little ass look thick as fuck. I don't know what was going on with her body that day, but she was thick with it. She had a loose-fitting long-sleeve top, with her blond dreads in a high ponytail. You could see hints of the tattoos on her arm, and her piercing on her lip that used to bother me, but I got used to it. She was pierced everywhere. Then to top it off, we wore matching Js. So, we were walking, with me trailing behind her, listening to her talk as I eyed my phone.

"So, I told the nigga, yo, fuck is you wilding for? We about to get it done," she continued as she stopped in front of the display in Forever 21. "What you think about this top?"

I looked up, eyeing the shirt, and shook my head no. I wasn't one of those dudes that didn't give a fuck what a female wore. I was into that shit. I liked people around me to look good at all times.

"So, did y'all do it?" I asked her, coming up close behind her as she continued to eye the outfit through the glass. She glanced at me, smirking. "Y'all ain't do it, did you?"

"Fuck no," she let out, and I laughed. "Turned in our project three days late because we were scrambling, trying to find shit off the Internet to pull. Still got a good grade, but never again will I work with them."

I wrapped my arm around her as we continued to walk, finally making our way into the store that sold all types of African-influenced art, paintings, books, and oils. As I looked back at my phone, checking for work-related emails, parties, and events, I didn't even notice a nigga who had the nerve to walk up to her.

Mind you, I was keeping a distance because I wasn't into smelling like sweet oils at the time. So, I hung around the entrance of the store. Just wasn't my type of place to be in, but if she was into it, I wasn't trying to knock her. Yet, the moment I heard her pop off at dude, my head shot up.

"Nigga, I'm not interested. Keep it moving, son," she snapped as this guy with long-ass dreads was trying to push up on her.

"I'm saying, though, you looking like you—"

I walked up slowly as he eyed me, throwing his hands up.

"Oh, I didn't even know you had a man, shawty. I was just trying to see what was up with you, throw a compliment yo' way."

"I'm good on that. I know I look good, nigga," she retorted, going back to smelling the oils as I stepped to him.

I could feel Jade grabbing my jeans pocket to lightly tug at it, letting me know to settle down, because she knew how I was. The only difference between Elijah and me when it came to women was he was reckless with it. I was of a different breed.

"Aye, man, I didn't know she was yo' girl," the guy said with an easy laugh. "You was standing all the way back there like you was scared to stand next to a beautiful queen like her. I was just showing some love to a woman who looked like she needed it." I could hear Jade about to go in, but I took that as the biggest insult I could ever hear a man tell another man—like I was not doing my job.

"She looked like she needed some love?" I repeated, and he smiled, hands still in the air to show he meant no harm.

"Aye, I'm just calling it how I see it," he said.

I nodded slowly. Without hesitation, I turned to firmly but gently pull Jade's locs, tilting her head to the side, and ran my tongue up her neck in a slow fashion as she laughed.

"Trent!" she shrieked in laughter, with me letting go before slapping her ass with a handful, looking at ol' boy, who couldn't say shit but look and hope he could find someone as bad as her.

"This right here is all me, bruh," I stated simply. "Don't ever in yo' fucking life walk up on mine again."

"You got it," he said, hands in the air as he walked out of the store with people looking at me with their mouths dropped. Nobody knew what to say after I just licked my girl's neck like that. What can you say after that? I was marking my territory.

Coming up behind her, I kissed her on the back of the neck, pressing my dick against her back.

"Lemme guess. You want some?" she said dully as I laughed against her skin, arms coming around her. "Shit, nigga, you better be glad I want some too after that nasty-ass shit you just did."

Damn, I missed her. Watching my two frat brothers on the couch talk and laugh it up some more, I pulled out my phone. I was about to call her before I realized she changed her number on me. All I wanted to do was talk.

BOOM!

BOOM!

BOOM!

BOOM!

BOOM!

The sound of someone banging on the door hard as fuck had us all alert as we jumped up from our seats.

"What the fuck? Who is—"

"Trent!" I heard Taylor's voice, and I damn near fell out. *Shit! I forgot to call her back.*

"Nigga, what the fuck you done did now?" Armond snapped as he rushed down the steps, looking out the peephole.

I came down behind him, slick feeling a little scared as I listened to her talk to herself.

"Got the fucking nerve to play me. You know I'm the wrong bitch to fuck with. After all that shit you said to me, and you wanna go back on yo' word!" she snapped. "Open this damn door! I know you're here!"

They both looked at me as I made my way to my room, ready to run and hide like a bitch. "Yo, just cut all the lights off, and don't open that shit!" I whispered harshly.

"Nigga, you can't have her banging on our door all night!" AJ snapped.

I went in the room quick, trying to grab some clothes to throw on. Cassie was laid up in the bed on her phone, taking selfies when she looked at me, eyes in panic.

"What's going on?" she asked.

"You gotta go, baby. I got a crazy bitch that's after me, and I don't want her to know you were here."

"So, yo' ass lied! You told me you didn't have a girl-friend!" she snapped as she stood up, ready to go off on me.

Fuck everybody. I was just trying to throw on some shoes and a coat.

"Nigga, how dare you use—"

"Trent!" Taylor yelled out again from outside as Armond and AJ came down, eyes wide in panic, matching mine.

"So, what's the fucking plan? Why we—"

"So, y'all knew he had a girlfriend but still let me come in here and get fucked? Y'all are some trifling-ass—"

"Shut the fuck up!" AJ snapped at Cassie, who started going in, threatening to call her brothers.

"Trent! If you don't open this goddamn door! We need to talk! I love you! I've always been in love with you! If you just open this!" *BANG!* "Fucking!" *BANG!* "Door!" she screamed in between hard kicks to the wooden door that was barely hanging on. Taylor had officially gone crazy.

"Just let her in. I'm about to sneak out through Rodney's room," I said, grabbing my phone charger. I was dressed like a straight-up bum in house shoes, coat, basketball shorts, and a tank, but fuck it. I'd brace the cold. Jordyn's house wasn't too far from there, just a block or so away. I was going to be cutting through backyards like hell, though.

I busted into Rodney's room as the other two went upstairs to hold a crazy Taylor off. Shit, I didn't even know what Cassie ended up doing. That wasn't my prob-lem. I immediately went for the window just as Rodney shot up from his bed, scared out of his mind.

"Nigga what the fuck—"

"Shhh!" I let out, trying to unlock his window that led to the backyard. Kicking the screen out, I could still hear Taylor yelling from around the front as I took off, hopping over the fence into another yard. I felt like I could hear her coming around the back, so I didn't stop running. I pulled out my phone as I tried calling Elijah, praying he would answer.

"Yeah, bruh?" he answered as I nearly tripped over a fucking big-ass rock. "Nigga, why you huffing and puffing in the phone like you—"

"Yo, if Taylor comes by, don't open that shit! Don't let her in!" I yelled, looking back at the house as I cut the corner onto the next street, thinking I was in the clear. I could hear Elijah saying something to Jordyn just as a big-ass pit bull came running out from behind the house, coming hard after me as I tried to run in those soft-ass house shoes.

"Shit! Yo! Unlock the door, E! Unlock the door when I—"

"What the fuck is yo' problem, Trent?" he yelled. "What's going—"

Headlights from a car came close up behind me, casting a shadow as I looked back, eyes wide in horror. I didn't know if it was Taylor, and I didn't take that chance as I dipped back into people's yards. The dog was no longer after me. I guess he went as far as he was willing to go. Running through another backyard, I felt myself slip, nearly busting my ass on some dog shit before getting up, feeling the chunk of it on the bottom of my house shoes. *Fuck!* I kept moving, though, because at this point, I didn't know what Taylor was capable of, and I wasn't trying to find out.

As soon as I spotted Jordyn's house, I ran up the short porch steps. Seeing the main door was open, I pulled back the screen door and nearly fell face first into the warm living room. The smell of fresh food being cooked from the kitchen hit me.

"Bruh?" Elijah laughed as I turned over on my back, chest heaving hard, looking at them. There they sat, simple as fuck, with her on the couch, glasses on, sipping something out of her mug. He sat on the floor in between her legs, shirtless, with his chains around his neck as she began to retwist his locs. "You smell like shit. Get the fuck on out this house smelling like that, nigga. Don't have my crib smelling like that! Go!" he yelled, kicking me as I sat up and tossed the shoes outside. They were ruined anyway.

Lying back down on the carpet, I closed my eyes, trying to calm myself down. I hadn't run that fast for that long in years. Hearing a phone go off, I looked at Elijah, who glanced at his phone, smiling hard at me.

"Taylor?" I breathed. He nodded. I shook my head frantically, pleading with my eyes, hoping he wouldn't rat me out. "Bruh, come on. Don't do that shit. I'm not ready to handle her crazy ass right now."

"So, what you want me to say?" He laughed, phone still ringing.

"Just tell her I'm somewhere else! Shit!" I started thinking. "I'm not in Atlanta right—"

"Hold up. I know what I'm going to say," he said, answering the phone. "Hello?"

I could hear her go off as he tried to keep himself from laughing. Jordyn just continued to twist his locs, occasionally pushing her glasses up like none of this even bothered her. "Yeah, Trent? He's over at Shiloh's crib right now. Just made his way over there. You know his girl be cooking them big-ass meals. Yeah," he said, nodding his head as he looked at me. "Oh, shit. Maybe he caught a ride with a girl. I'on know, Taylor, but you acting crazy. . . . I'm not calling you crazy, shawty, I'm saying you—"

Elijah looked at the phone before bursting into laughter. "Yo, she hung up. She not stupid enough to go over to Shiloh's place acting stupid. What the fuck did you do, bruh?"

"I don't know, man." I sighed, looking at my feet. I had one sock on, barely any clothes on, and I was still trying to catch my breath.

I looked around and noticed it was deadly quiet, with the exception of them two occasionally talking. Elijah made it seem like when he was with her, they be having these wild-ass nights, sleeping with different girls at the same time, drinking, and coming and going as he pleased. Yet, here I was with them on a Saturday night for the first time, and this was what he was doing. His eyes were closed as he took a pull on his blunt. She had a book laid out, reading as she twisted his hair. They were boring as fuck! No TV, no music, no nothing.

"Is this what y'all do?" I pressed, sitting up as they both looked at me.

Elijah smiled, blowing smoke out through his nose.

"Just sit in silence?"

"What? You want us to be running through backyards, rolling in dog shit, and having crazy bitches after us like you?" Elijah joked.

"Nah, but y'all just sitting here, looking bored."

Elijah shook his head. "I'm at peace, bruh," he stated simply, eyes closing slowly as she started on another loc.

Eyeing them once more, I smiled, feeling myself get envious at his content state. "Can I spend the night, Jordyn?" I asked, getting up to sit on the couch. I was tired as fuck, and I just wanted to have this night be over already. I was too old to be running from a crazy female, and too old to be fighting with my older brother. Everything would get squashed tomorrow.

"That's fine," she said softly. "There is some turkey meat left if you want to make a burger, and a bowl of salad already tossed." She pointed to the kitchen.

"Thank you, sis," I said, lying back on the couch, closing my eyes. I was enjoying the peace, hearing Elijah singing softly to himself. It reminded me of when we were little and you could faintly catch him singing on the low to himself. I needed to rethink a lot of shit, and this was the only place I could find the peace to do it. Closing my eyes as I leaned back, I let out a contented sigh, thinking this shit was over and done with—not even realizing this was just the beginning.

"Hey, um . . ." Jordyn let out, looking at her phone with an intense stare. "Taylor is on her way over here. She just texted me, asking if she can she talk to me."

"Whaat?" Elijah and I shrieked as I quickly got up.

"Yeah, she should be pulling up any second now." Jordyn shrugged. "To be honest, you put yourself in this situation, Trent, so you need to face reality and just deal with it. Talk to her. She'll respect honesty before anything else."

We both looked at her as Elijah shook his head, jumping up to close and lock the door. "Fuck that. You should have never messed with a damn virgin!" Elijah quipped as I looked around, trying to find a place to hide. "And why the fuck you got that crazy bitch's number in the first place, Jordyn?"

As soon as I caught a sight of headlights flashing in her window, I ran to the first room I knew of and closed the door. I tried to squeeze in the closet, but she had shit stuffed in there, along with Elijah's belongings. So, when that didn't work, I slipped underneath her bed with my back pressed against the springs. I laid my head down on the carpet, waiting, listening. I could hear the door open and see Elijah's bright red bandana socks as he stepped in the room.

You good, Haze?" he called out in a low voice, using the nickname Shiloh gave me when we were kids trying to hide from our parents. All four of us had nicknames. Mine was Haze, for the eyes.

"Yeah," I whispered back.

"Nigga, this is some stupid-ass shit," Elijah muttered with a laugh before walking back out, leaving the door open.

"Ah, what's the matter, Big Tay?" Elijah cooed, hearing her cry. "What did my brother do now? I thought you were past this shit."

"You know how long I've been feeling yo' brother?" she cried.

I closed my eyes. *Nobody told yo' stupid fat ass to like me in the first place!* I wanted to shout it, but I kept quiet and listened.

"I always told Olivia I wanted to be a part of y'all family so bad. I wanted to be a Carter, and the only person I wanted to be with was Trent. Been in love with him since I could remember," she mumbled. "So, to hear him tell me all this shit like we're going to get married and have kids, we're meant for each other, and he was always feeling me but just was too scared to say anything at the time . . . Like, nigga, why the fuck would you tell me all of that, break up with yo' girlfriend, tell me we're together, fuck me, and then the next fucking day, I don't hear from you? Ever! Like, who does that shit? I'm too old to be chasing behind niggas like that! I shouldn't have to—"

"Whoa, whoa, hold up," Elijah said, getting ready to come to my defense. "Taylor, listen to what you just said, baby. Niggas say shit. We always say shit to females just so we can get the pussy. That's it. We tell y'all what y'all wanna hear, how you wanna hear, when you wanna hear it, so we can get what we want, how we want, and when we want it. You feel me? You fell for the ol' okey-doke, shawty."

"So, you tell Jordyn what she wants to hear just to get—"

"Don't bring her—"

"Answer the question, Elijah," Jordyn said as I covered my mouth to keep from laughing. Now this nigga was getting caught up.

"Hold up! This ain't even my issue! I was just trying to keep it real with you! And nah, our setup was different. We knew what it was from the beginning."

"Jordyn, why must niggas be nothing but shit?" Taylor asked casually. I heard footsteps. "Come on. We need girls' talk. I don't have nothing to say to Elijah, because I'm about ready to swing on his ass. He's looking too much like Trent right now, so . . ."

I spotted Taylor's heels as she walked into the room. *Shit!* Jordyn followed behind, closing the door in Elijah's face.

"Aye! What about my hair?" he screamed out from behind the door.

"I'll finish in the morning, Elijah," Jordyn said as she sat down on the bed, mattress sinking in, with Taylor following behind her. I almost couldn't breathe, but I kept it together.

"Jordyn, I was so in love with that man." She laughed to herself. "I remember every year, beginning of school, I made it my mission to memorize his class schedule, so I could purposely bump into him. Start some shit. Now, as adults, when we had sex for the first time, he made me feel like I was the sexiest woman alive."

"The Carter boys seem to have a way of doing that," Jordyn said, and I could hear the smile in her voice. "Make you feel like you're their everything, like they'll protect and care for you as if you're all that matters. Then, you find out it was all a front. I know. Believe me, I know what you mean. Elijah is no different."

"So, what did you . . . how did you even deal with that? How do you still deal with that?"

"I honestly don't know." Jordyn laughed. "Our situation is a bit different from yours, so I can't really compare. Let Trent be. If he is grown enough to come to you and be honest about everything, then you can't be too mad at him for that. If he never says a thing to you, well, besides moving on, you don't need to look back. Go find a pretty girl to mess with. I always kind of picked up a gay vibe with you anyway," she teased, and Taylor laughed. "Girls are more fun in the bed anyway."

If my dick didn't get hard at that statement . . . boy, I was ready to slide up from underneath that bed and see what was up.

"Girl, stop!" she let out, and they laughed. "Can I spend the night here?"

"Of course," Jordyn said, getting up.

Hearing the door open, I watched Taylor walk out of the room, with Jordyn following.

Elijah walked in, closing the door. "Bruh, get yo' ass up," he whispered. "They in the kitchen. You can't stay underneath this shit all night. You need to talk to her."

The door opened again, and I watched Jordyn's feet walk in. She closed the door.

"Where is he?"

"Under yo' bed like a bitch," Elijah spat. "Just talk to her."

"I don't have shit to say," I retorted, hearing them groan.

"Man, I'm not about to sleep on this bed with my girl with you underneath, nigga. That's beyond gay as fuck to me."

"Taylor can have my bedroom. Elijah and I will sleep in the living room."

"Bitch, what?" Elijah flipped, and they started going at it. "I'm not sleeping on the fucking couch when I paid for—"

"Shut up, Elijah. Just shut the fuck up. We're sleeping in the living room. Rita's room has nothing in it, so would you rather sleep on the floor?"

"Man," he said, smacking his teeth as he walked out.

I hated that I was the one causing all of this, but I wasn't ready to face her. I felt nothing toward her. Did I lie to get inside the panties? Hell yeah, I did. It was too easy. She was too easy. But I didn't realize her feelings for me were that strong. Had I known, I would have never said what I said to her.

So now, here I was in this pitch-black room, trying to keep myself awake as Taylor snored lightly above me. Glancing at my phone, I saw it was going on 3 a.m. Fuck that. I was tired, hungry, and my body was hurting from being in this position for so damn long. So, I slid from underneath the bed and slowly opened the creaky door.

It was dark in the house, with the only light coming from the phones charging. I peeped Elijah and Jordyn laying together with a thin blanket on them. His mouth was wide open, dreads wrapped in a scarf, with a protective arm over her as she lay closer to his lower body. I started to make my way to the door when his head popped up, looking hard at me before rubbing his eyes.

"You out, bruh?" he asked in a low voice, sniffing.

"I'm gone. Good looking out, though." We slapped hands quietly then came in for a hug, careful not to wake Jordyn. "I owe you."

"Yeah, yeah," he mumbled, drifting back into his sleep as I stepped out of the house.

Walking down the dark street, my mind just went through everything I'd been through these past few months with females. Tia, Jade, Jordyn, and Taylor: all have or had an issue with me. Only one I did any harm to was my ex, and I wished on everything I could take it back, because all that shit was starting to kick back in and catch up with me.

Pulling my phone out, on my last 3 percent of battery, I texted Jahiem, explaining the situation between Tia and me. I told him it was one time, and I knew it was no way the baby was mine, because I knew for a fact I didn't nut in her. Even if I did, my pullout game is strong as fuck, so I wasn't worried at all. I apologized and told him I was ready to move on from this.

I texted Taylor and apologized, and I told her that I wished I would have done things differently. I told her I would always have love for her, but I couldn't be the man she wanted me to be. On my last percent of battery, I got on Facebook and called Jade out, telling her and the rest of the world I was sorry, I missed her, and asked her to please talk to me, call me. I learned my lesson. I was sick of being a selfish-ass nigga. I just wanted my girl back.

Looking up at the street signs as my phone shut down on me, I spotted a few people out walking around. They were drug addicts, most likely. I needed to hurry up and get back to the fucking house. It was too cold to be walking around in just shorts, a coat, and Elijah's shoes that I couldn't even fit.

Suddenly, I heard this car's loud engine. I turned back, seeing no headlights, just a small-ass car zooming up to the side of me. The windows rolled down. A nigga who had on a ski mask stuck his head out, and I immediately tensed up.

"Aye, you know where—"

"That's him!" I heard Cassie yell from the back seat of the car.

My mouth dropped. *Shit!*

"Oh, you the nigga that fucked my sister over, huh? Ain't you related to Olivia? You one of them Carter boys, ain't you?" the dude said with a laugh as the back window rolled down, showing another nigga with a ski mask on cough up a thing of spit, almost hitting my shoes.

"That's her brother," the one in the back seat said with a laugh. "Ahh, shit. We can kill two birds with one stone. You know yo' coked-out sister owe me some money and pussy? She stole from me—"

"Watch what the fuck you say about her," I warned, fists tightening up.

"Fuck you gon' do, pretty boy?" he asked.

I was just about to go in when he aimed a gun directly at me, causing my hands to go up in the air almost instantly. My heart was racing as I took a deep swallow. I'd never been so scared in my life.

"Look at this bitch nigga. The weakest Carter."

"Just handle his ass and come on!" Cassie snapped. "I got work in the morning!"

"Tell Olivia she got until next Friday to get right, or I'm knocking y'all down one by one."

"I ain't telling her—"

"Fuck it," the one in the front seat said as he pulled out his gun, aimed, and let loose a series of shots at me. I could feel my body jerk with the hits. I slumped to the ground, pain feeling like intense burns, almost numbing me completely.

"Nigga, you weren't supposed to really shoot him! Just scare him!" I heard a guy say.

The pain felt like it was on my legs, my arm, my chest. I couldn't . . . *Shit* . . . Last thing I heard was the car pull off before everything went black.

Noelle

I sat up quickly, seeing Shiloh nearly jump out of his sleep, chest heaving like he had just woken up from a nightmare. It wasn't even dawn yet, and we had literally just gone to sleep about an hour ago. Watching him stare blankly into space, I rolled my eyes and lay back down. I was too tired for a mood swing. I really was.

"Something isn't right," I heard him mumble as he got up from the bed to grab his phone. I glanced at the time on my nightstand. It was 3:52 a.m. I watched him start dialing numbers, but when no one answered, he just sighed to himself. I sat up and slowly went over to where he was, wrapping my arms around his neck, kissing the side of his face. He was so stiff, so tense. Physically, he was on alert.

"Baby, what's wrong?" I asked, kissing his ear. He moved his head out of the way but kept a soft grip on my hands around his neck. Both of us were naked in his bedroom as we sat there in silence.

"I don't know. I just don't feel right," was all he said. "I'm not going back to sleep, though, but you can."

I let out a sigh before pulling away to lie back down. "I'll try to stay up as long as I can," I mumbled.

He looked back at me, nodding before continuing to dial numbers on his phone, trying to get a hold of somebody. It was definitely going to be a long morning. *Ugh.*

Jordyn

The sounds of sirens going off outside woke Elijah and me from our sleep on the couch. Looking out the window, I could see the flashing lights zoom by as I heard another round of sirens go off. *What in the world is going on outside?* Elijah was fighting to stay asleep as my room door opened.

"What is going on outside?" Taylor yawned.

I got up from the couch, gently shaking Elijah from his sleep. We slept in our underwear, squeezing on this small couch together, while I allowed a sad Taylor to take the room. Long story on that one, but when he did wake up, we were already putting on some shoes and coats. I slipped on some jeans and a hoodie, grabbing my keys.

"What the fuck is happening?" he asked in a low voice as he sat up, taking his scarf off to shake his locs loose.

"I don't know, but I'm going to find out," I said as Taylor grabbed her keys.

"Hold up, baby," he grumbled, standing up to stretch as another round of sirens went off with blue lights flashing by the house. Taylor went on ahead and stepped out while I waited on Elijah to throw on some clothes. Yet, as he put on his jacket, he stopped—literally stopped moving as he looked at me with an intense stare, almost freaking me out.

"What?" I said.

His eyes shifted to the window before looking back at me. Shaking his head suddenly, he started to move with a quickness, looking around for his shoes before deciding to put mine on.

"What's wrong, Elijah?"

"Trent," was all he mumbled, grabbing the keys to his truck as he guided me out of the house, closing the door behind us.

It was a cold, early Sunday morning as we stepped out onto the streets, following the chaos, seeing other neighbors stepping out to see what was happening. Walking along the well-lit street, we could spot fire trucks, police cars, and an ambulance all together toward the end of the block.

"Hold my shit, baby," Elijah said, handing me his phone and keys.

"Where are you—"

He started to run in the direction of the lights. I followed, trying to keep up. The moment we reached the end where they were blocking everything off, with cops trying to back people up, I spotted the body. I instantly recognized who it was as they put him on the stretcher. Taylor was already standing there, mouth to her hand, crying as Elijah moved past everyone, screaming his brother's name. I could see the pool of blood on the curb, and my heart dropped.

"No, no, no, no," Elijah mumbled, moving underneath the yellow lines. "Not my brother, man. Not my brother," he cried, voice shaking.

"Sir, you're going to have to—"

"What happened? What happened to him?" Elijah frantically asked as the cops tried to calm him down. He gripped his head in a panic, watching them carry his brother's body into the back of the truck. He was hysterical at this point. I'd never seen him like this.

"Sir! You're going to have to ste—"

"That's my fucking brother!" he screamed, tears coming down as he snatched his arm away from the cop's grip. "Trent!"

I tried to go to him, but they were keeping me at a distance as I watched Elijah fight to get on the back of the ambulance. They finally let him in, closing the doors. Suddenly, as I watched the truck zoom past us, I felt I was in a position where I had to step up and take care of everything. I'd never had to deal with something like this before, but I was going to try for Elijah.

Grabbing Taylor's arm, I pulled her away, and we walked back to the house while I was trying to break into Elijah's phone. As soon as I remembered that lock code, I went through his contacts, trying to remember each sibling's name. Seeing a few missed calls from Shiloh, I decided to call him first. Although it scared the crap out of me just to talk to him, I had to suck it up.

"Hello?" He answered on the first ring.

"I, um . . ." I looked around as Taylor and I continued to walk. She was crying her eyes out. She could barely speak. "I—"

"Who the fuck is this?" Shiloh snapped.

I cleared my throat. "I'm with Elijah, and I . . . we . . . Trent's been shot, and Elijah just rode with the ambulance to the hospital."

"Shit." I could hear him hiss, and there was a bunch of noise in the background. "Which hospital, shawty?"

I started to panic, realizing I didn't even ask. But then I remembered hearing one of the officers say Grady.

"I think they're taking him to Grady. I can find out and call you back for sure."

He hung up immediately. I saw Jahiem had called Elijah a few hours ago, so I called him next as Taylor and I got in Elijah's truck.

"Hello?" Jahiem answered, sounding asleep.

"Hi, this is Jordyn," I said, turning the truck on as Taylor bent over in the seat, head in her hands, crying. "I'm sorry to wake you, but Trent's been hurt, and they're taking him to Grady Hospital."

"What!" He flipped, causing me to jump at the sound of his voice. "Hurt how?"

"He's been shot."

"What happened? Who did it? Do they know?" he asked frantically.

I could feel my anxiety about to take over, but I was fighting to keep it at bay.

Now is not the time to have a panic attack, Jordyn.

"They haven't said. I'm just trying to call everyone up. Elijah is already on his way down there with him."

"A'ight," he said, hanging up.

Going down the list of people, including his mom, I called as I started to drive, making my way to Grady. I felt myself trying to keep strong, even though this was too much for me to handle. The only person I couldn't get in contact with was Olivia, his sister. Taylor even tried, but to no avail, so she sent her a text message in hopes that she would get it.

When we got to the hospital, I spotted some of the siblings running around, trying to find the room. I hung back in the waiting room. I didn't do well with hospitals. I didn't even like being in one. So, I sat by myself, waiting and waiting. Occasionally I heard a doctor pass by, talking about Trent and his wounds. He'd been shot three times.

His mom, who was in tears, walked back in the waiting room with someone I guessed was her boyfriend. "It's okay, baby," he cooed, comforting her as she cried. "He's going to be okay."

More of the brothers came down, and Jahiem sat down across from me, fist to his nose as he closed his eyes. He said not a word. Anthony and his baby mama came and sat down along with Ontrell and his boyfriend. Talin and his wife sat down next to me as she talked him down, keeping him calm while she rubbed her belly. Nobody said a word until Shiloh and his girlfriend came in. His eyes were red, and his mom stared hard at him.

"I know you have something to do with it," Ms. Ava mumbled at Shiloh, who immediately cut his eyes at her.

"You better shut the fuck up talking to me. I don't have shit to do with my brother getting shot, and I ain't got shit to do with you period!" he snapped angrily.

"Don't talk to me like I'm one of your hoes, nigga. I'm yo' fucking mama."

"You ain't shit to me!" he spat, looking her up and down in rejection. "I don't fuck with you like that."

"Boy, I gave you life—"

"Take that shit away then!" he threatened, stepping up to her as the boyfriend stepped to him. Shiloh slowly backed up, smiling through the pain, eyes watering up. "Yo' li'l boyfriend can get got too, you feel me?"

"You're going to be respectful to her while I'm here," the man warned as Shiloh looked him up and down with his girlfriend pulling at his arm.

"Or what, mothafucka? Huh?"

"Nigga ain't finna do shit!" Jahiem spat as he jumped in the mix, standing beside Shiloh. That immediately started off a bout of yelling and arguing from the mom and her boyfriend versus the brothers.

Elijah slowly appeared around the corner, looking defeated. Everyone immediately became quiet as his mom wrapped her arms around his neck, trying to comfort her son. I was watching everyone get up to go to him while I sat nervously to the side. I didn't know what to do or how to react in this situation, because just being there in the hospital already had me on edge.

"Why they gotta do me like that?" Elijah cried as Shiloh grabbed him, holding him tight, letting his brother cry against him. "Why they fucking with me?"

Hearing him speak in first person wasn't unusual when it came to Trent. They considered themselves each other basically, including their sister. When one hurt, they all hurt.

"We gon' take care of it, E. Don't even worry about it," Shiloh promised. "This city ain't gon' sleep until them niggas do."

"You good?" Talin's wife asked as she looked at me. She was a pretty, light-skin girl with dreads tied up.

"I'm okay," I said softly.

Elijah looked up, eyes meeting with mine. I just slowly smiled, trying to keep positive when he walked over to me, causing me to stand up.

"I can't believe you stayed this long in a hospital," he mumbled as I wiped his eyes, smirking. He knew how I felt about them. I looked at the man I fell in love with, the one I met at the gas station who was sooo damn crazy, obnoxious, wild, and chaotic. Now he was trying to smile through the pain. His eyes and cheeks were wet from tears; his dreads were slumping down with his head as he tried to toughen up for me. He didn't want me to see this side of him. It just so happened that I had a man that would cry when he was angry, and I was just fine with that, even if he wasn't. So, instead of pitying him like everyone else, I wanted to show him that he was still my man, my protector, my everything, even though he was at his weakest.

"You remember that time we brought that light-skin girl back to the room?" I asked him softly, hoping no one else could hear us.

He nodded, smiling instantly. It was one of the craziest nights of our lives. It got violent on her end, and we had to call the cops to get her out of the house. I don't even know what kind of drug she was on, but she was definitely on something.

"Bitch was fucking crazy, J," he said as I laughed. "I already told yo' ass she looked like she was on some other shit, but when that weave came off, though? Bruh . . ."

"She was cute, though." I pouted as he shook his head, arms coming around my waist.

"Yo' taste in women is a hit or miss, shawty. Aye, but it's this nurse in Trent's room that is banging. Like, I'm talking phat ass and everything. She's yo' type," he said, and I smiled. Everyone else was silent, trying to listen to us converse about women.

"What does she look like?" I asked softly, wiping his face as he began to describe the girl to me.

"Where is he? Where is he?" I heard a voice say. We all looked up to see a light-skin man with hazel eyes, almost the spitting image of Trent and Jahiem, walk up. Elijah hadn't told me much about his dad, only that no one really messed with him for their own reasons. There was a lot of bad blood, a lot of issues with this family that I couldn't even begin to tap into, but that whole morning, it was nothing but family attempting to come together. Trent's fraternity brothers showed up in waves, a couple of female friends came, and the sister finally showed up, crying hysterically. It was my first time seeing her, but when our eyes locked, we instantly recognized each other. I'd seen her in too many gay clubs getting it on, and I almost slept with her at one point, but I was thankful that I hadn't. She was definitely the wildest one out of the group. I was sure her brothers had no idea who she truly was as a person.

With people in and out of the waiting room, wanting to see Trent, who I heard had finally woken up from his coma, the police came to ask questions and give a rundown of the process. He had survived three shots to the body. It was a miracle he was even alive, and the one girl that was by his side the entire time was Taylor—not the little girls he ran after on the yard, and not his ex-girlfriend.

Walking back outside into the cold Sunday afternoon, I spotted Jahiem sitting on the bench with a cigarette in his hand, looking at his phone.

"You're good for my li'l bruh, you know that?" Jahiem asked.

I smiled with a shrug.

"Y'all two were made for each other."

"I don't think one person can be made for another," I answered logically. "But I know what you mean."

He smiled before looking back at his phone. "You heard from yo' girl?" he asked, glancing at me as he took a drag off his cigarette, blowing the smoke out with a quickness. "Got me stressing out like a crazy nigga. I don't even smoke these things like that, but shit."

"Who's my girl?" I pressed curiously.

"Tia." He looked at me as I shook my head no. "I've been trying to call her, but her phone is cut off. I don't know where she is, and I can't find her homegirl."

"She's probably around the city somewhere," I mumbled, taking a seat on a nearby bench.

"Probably fucking around with the next nigga with her pregnant ass," he muttered with a smirk.

I smiled, watching him laugh to himself like he'd thought of something funny about her.

"If that's the case, then why are you so worried about where she is?" I asked.

He just looked at me from the side, taking a final pull before tossing the cigarette out, letting the wind catch the smoke. "I don't know." He shrugged. "I still love her ass, and I don't even know why. Ain't that some shit? I fell in love with a ho."

"We all did." I smiled.

Noelle

"Is there anything you want me to get?" I asked Shiloh as I came up behind him, hand on his shoulder. I needed to go home and change. I'd been at this hospital since 4-something in the morning, and now it was going on 8 o'clock at night. I needed a shower, a fresh change of clothes, and to get my life together in general.

He looked up at me with tired eyes, shaking his head in a silent no. He sat in the corner of hospital room, watching his younger siblings talk with Trent, who lay back on the bed, bandaged up on the shoulder, ribcage, and left thigh where he'd been shot. I don't even know how he was alive, but God was definitely looking out for him. Their mom stood at the end of the bed, smiling down at the three, but she kept her distance from Shiloh, as did he from her. It was just too much for me to handle: too many Carters, too much drama, and I hadn't even had a hot shower that day.

"Aye," Elijah said, turning toward Shiloh with a smile. "This nigga asked if he was a thug now that he's been shot. I told him I don't know too many pretty-boy thugs, so you'd be the first, bruh," he cracked as Shiloh smirked.

"Man, shut yo' ass up," I heard Trent mumble, and I laughed.

"I'm so glad you're okay, baby," their mom cooed softly as Olivia lay comfortably next to Trent on the bed. Shiloh stood up, placing his hand on my side to walk me out of the room. His eyes were empty and cold as usual, but his voice was tired.

"Go ahead and go home," he said, bringing me close for a hug and a simple kiss. "I appreciate you holding it together for me, queen."

"I got you." I smiled, kissing him softly on the lips.

The door opened, and his mom stepped out. Her low eyes immediately went to me with a warning glare. Even though she didn't get along with him, I could tell she didn't want me, or any other girl, pushing up on her son. I stepped back—just a little.

"Call me as soon as you get home, baby," he said against my mouth before kissing me again and letting me go. Without so much as a word to his mother, he moved past her to get back in the room, closing the door.

So, it was just her and me walking down the hall to get to the main level. In silence. She was dressed to a T; pretty, dark-skin woman with those signature eyes and short hair. She looked to be in shape for her age. Meanwhile, I had on a scarf, a hoodie, and some jeans with my only pair of Jordans and small coat in hand. I was ready just to go home and get out of this depressing setting. When I realized she wasn't going to speak, I kept it moving in the other direction, opting to take the stairs.

In the waiting room, I said my goodbyes to everyone, hugged Tyree, who kept everyone entertained, and walked out into the cold parking garage to find the truck. With Shiloh's keys in hand, I hopped in the big Escalade and cut it on, letting the engine warm up as I looked around. I felt so small in there.

As soon as I pulled off, my phone rang. Looking down at the caller ID, I smiled.

"Helloooo," I greeted.

"Gurl! What the fuck is going on? Did you hear about that boy that got shot—"

"I just left the hospital," I said, cutting her off.

"So, it was Shiloh's brother. I was thinking it was maybe another Carter. Damn, how many of them is it?"

"Too many to count," I mumbled.

"Any of them single? Shiiit, help a girl out here. I'm trying get like you," she joked.

We chopped it up for the rest of the ride, until I reached my house. I saw a familiar car parked outside. *What in the world?*

"Oh my God," I mumbled, hearing Layla chew on her food.

"What's the matter?"

"Girl, this man is at my house again." I sighed, parking the truck at Shiloh's place and hopping out.

"Who?"

"Michael," I said, closing the door. I stepped over the yard to get to mine and saw that his car was empty. *What in the world?*

"He's parked at my house, but he isn't in the car."

"Bitch, that nigga might be in yo' house while you playing. Did you leave yo' doors unlocked?"

"No, I would never do that," I said slowly, looking down the street in both directions before looking at the house. It was getting dark, and I just . . . ugh. This was like the weekend from hell. It really was. My birthday was so wonderful, so amazing, only to fall on the worst weekend imaginable. "Can you stay on the phone with me?"

"Yeah, yeah, of course," she said. "Girl, he probably just sitting in yo' living room with flowers and a fake-ass wedding ring, ready to marry yo' scary behind."

"And you don't think that's weird that he's even in my house in the first fucking place, Layla?" I snapped as I walked up the steps, looking for my keys. I ignored her laughter as I glanced at my door and the lack of a door knob. My shit was wide open!

"Oh my God," I breathed. "I'm about to call the police. I can't do this."

"Wait, don't—"

I hung up as I pulled my door back gently and stepped inside my house, almost scared to blink for fear of missing something. Looking around, I saw nothing was out of place. Everything was how I'd left it. There was no trace of someone being there, but I did hear music—soft Erykah Badu playing from my room. I didn't leave anything on in this house. No radio, no music, and on Sundays, I only listened to Gospel, so I knew somebody was in there.

The kitchen light was on. I crept toward it, but it looked like . . . exactly how I'd left it. I grabbed a frying pan, unhooked my earrings off, and laced up my shoes tighter. If this wasn't Michael, this mothafucka had another thing coming. If it was Michael, then he had about five seconds to explain what the fuck his problem was.

Walking to my room with my heart beating loudly, I lightly pushed my room door open, seeing no one, just the music being played. *What the fuck?* I looked around as I stepped farther into the room, and I nearly screamed when I felt hands come down on my shoulders.

"Surprise!"

I turned around, horrified to see Michael, smiling at me, in a plain V-neck graphic T-shirt, jeans, and some Timberland boots. His chocolate face was glowing with that smooth, low haircut.

"What the fuck are you—"

"Don't be mad, Noelle!" he quickly let out, handing me a bunch of roses. "I thought I would come by and surprise you."

I dropped the pan, gripping my chest, trying to calm my heart down. I was ready for battle; I swear I was.

"How did you even get in my house, Michael?" I snatched the roses from him and tossed them on the bed. I wanted answers, and I wanted him to leave before I called the cops. This was way beyond crossing the line.

He just smiled, licking his lips at me. "I was calling, but I see your boyfriend made you block my number, so—"

"I blocked your number, Michael! You can't keep—"

"I'm not finished," he said, cutting me off. "I came by, and I saw your door was fucked up, so I decided just to stay until you got here, to make sure no one would come in. I was going to explain everything to yo' boyfriend. Come on. I wanted to see you since I didn't see you at church today."

"I didn't go, and I'm not going there anymore." My hands were still shaking as I cut the music off. Sitting on the edge of my bed, I buried my face in my hands, tired, stressed, and just beyond scared out of my mind. All I could hear was Aunt Alice saying, "Something ain't right with that man." *Well, yeah, now I know.*

"Is everything okay?" he asked softly, sitting down next to me on the bed, hand coming to my shoulder. I quickly got up, backing away from his touch as I looked at him.

"Michael, you need to leave," I said in a low voice, letting him know I was serious. "This is beyond invasion of privacy, and I'm trying real hard to keep the peace."

"Noelle, calm down," he said, walking toward me as I backed up against the wall, shaking my head as my body tensed up. "I'm not going to do anything to—"

"Get out, Michael! I'm serious! It's not funny anymore. It's not cute. I will never fucking like you, even if I wasn't with Shiloh! I told you this!"

He tilted his head to the side in a sadistic kind of manner, smiling as he looked me over, licking his lips. "You're just saying that, Noe," he said.

My eyes grew wide. Nobody called me Noe except for Shiloh. Nobody knew he called me that, because if anyone outside of Shiloh called me that, I was quick to correct them.

"Don't call me that!" I let out a scream as he came at me, grabbing me by the waist, trying to kiss me, gripping my body tight.

I tried pushing his forehead back. Grabbing both my hands, he held them behind me as he came for my neck. I was screaming out as loud as I could, trying to knee him where it counts.

"I just want to taste you one time. I've been wanting you since I first—"

"Let go!" I screamed, feeling him pull my sweats down along with my panties.

Fuck no, not today. You got the wrong one on the right day. I started clawing at his face, screaming and spitting, while moving my legs to keep him from getting hold of me. Then I heard the voice of my savior walking in that front door.

"Hellooooo, Noelle!" Tyree sang, and I started screaming for help. Michael immediately let go.

Tyree rushed to my room, tote in hand, eyes wide in horror. "Nah, nigga! Get the fuck on! Not my bitch!" Tyree screamed in his signature high, dramatic voice. He slammed his bag on Michael, who laughed.

"What you gon' do, punk ass? Huh?" Michael pressed, stepping to Tyree, who didn't back down. He just cocked his head before tossing his bag on the bed.

"What's good?" Tyree said, voice dropping low as they sized each other up.

I slowly reached down for my frying pan, aiming it like I was in the game, ready to hit at any moment.

Michael's eyes were bloodshot red with rage as he looked at the two of us, smirking. He knew he couldn't take us both on. Tyree was a big man, and this frying pan was pure iron. *Try it if you want to.*

"I'm coming back to get what's mine, Noe," Michael said, blowing a kiss at me before walking out, pulling his pants up. "You'll be mine, baby! We belong together, shawty!" he let out, vernacular changing completely. There was no uppity white boy tone in his voice. He went straight hood on me in a matter of seconds, and he sounded comfortable with it, like it was natural.

Tyree rushed to the living room to look out the window, making sure he pulled off, while I stayed near the door of my room.

"Girl!" he let out, looking back at me with a smile. "Is that the nigga that gave you the plastic necklace? Damn! You got niggas going crazy over yo' ass! You need to tell Shiloh what the fuck just—"

"No," I said, cutting him off with a shake of my head. I wiped my eyes and face. "I'm not trying to bother him with this shit. We took care of it."

"But he—"

"He got a lot going on right now with his brother, Tyree. Just keep this between you and me and the Lord," I said.

He nodded slowly before coming to me with open arms, hugging me. "Did you let him in the house?" he asked as I looked up at him.

"This man broke into my house. You see my door knob?" I flipped as Tyree laughed.

"Gurl, you and these Atlanta men. Ain't no telling how he would have reacted once he got inside them chocolate walls, boo."

"Eww, Tyree," I said, moving him back as he laughed. "Anyway, I came here to see if you wanted to grab a bite to eat. I couldn't sit in that depressing-ass hospital any longer."

"We can go." I sighed.

I wasn't used to men like this. At any point in time did I ever lead Michael on? Did I put myself in this situation? I just . . . I needed to go home. I needed a break from this city, from these people, from this lifestyle. Shiloh was no better. It was like dating violence himself. Even though he never put a hand on me, being with him caused me so much stress in my life. I just wanted to go home.

When I got home, I was feeling a little bit better about today. I had my takeout food in hand, ready for a good book and then a night's rest for work in the morning. The weekend was finally over, and I just wanted Monday to hurry up and come. I needed a normal day, please.

Walking up the steps as I waved bye to Tyree, I came to the front door and noticed that it was cracked open again. I dropped my head in defeat. Pure defeat.

What the fuck! We just went to fucking Wal Mart to fix this shit.

"I can't do keep doing this shit," I mumbled, swinging the door open in anger. I looked around, seeing no one. Putting the food down, I walked back to my room and saw Shiloh sitting on the bed in deep thought. I let out a sigh.

"You ever heard of waiting until I fucking get back home?" I snapped.

He looked at me, expression colder than usual. He sat in his sweats and hoodie, eyes falling hard on me as if he was trying to read me.

"What's the problem, Shiloh?" I asked with a sigh.

"Where's my money?" he asked casually.

My eyes grew wide, looking at the closet where he'd told me he was going to keep some money for safe-keeping. He'd specifically told me not to touch it. I had honestly forgotten it was there until now.

"What are you talking about, Shiloh? Shouldn't it be in the closet some—"

"It's not fucking there," he snapped, standing up as he eyed me hard. "Again, where the fuck is my money, Noe?"

"I don't have it! I didn't touch your money! I forgot it was even—"

"You ain't forget shit," he spat, walking back to the closet.

I followed him, watching as he tore through it like a tornado. Brand new dresses, shoes—everything was out of place and on the floor.

"Oooh, baby girl," he sang slowly as my heart started to beat faster. "We got a problem, queen."

I instantly thought about Michael being here in this house alone while we were at the hospital.

"Michael was here!" I blurted out. "He was here when we were at the hospital."

Shiloh cut his eyes to me before continuing to go through the closet, ripping apart brand-new shoe boxes with the heels falling out.

"I'm serious, Shiloh!"

"Three things I told you I don't play about, Noelle."

"I'm not lying! He came here! I had to fight him off of me! Shiloh, I'm not—"

"Three things! My money, my loyalty, and my family! Two out of three has been fucked over!"

"I didn't touch it!" I cried, feeling like a little girl. "I swear I didn't touch your money, Shiloh! Michael was—"

He grabbed me by the shoulders, slamming me hard against the wall. His eyes were soulless as he looked at me, not an ounce of love in his expression.

"Last time a bitch took money from me," he started.

My eyes grew wide as my mind flashed back to everything that had happened to me: the gun in my face, Aunt Alice's house, Michael, and now this. I couldn't keep leaving myself open to this bullshit.

I felt myself just sort of snap. Pushing him back, finding the courage to stand up to a man I thought I loved, I went in my purse, pulling out all the money I had.

"Here! Take yo' fucking money and get the fuck out!" I screamed, throwing change at him as he tried to block his face. "I'm sick of this fucking city! I'm sick of the crazy-ass men I seem to attract! I'm sick of people taking my kindness for weakness, wanting to take advantage. You know I wouldn't steal from you!" I cried.

He said nothing, just stood there, eyeing me hard as I threw my purse at him, hoping to hit his face.

"Get out!"

"Where's my money?"

"I don't have yo' stupid-ass money, Shiloh! If you're going to kill me or shoot me, do so now, because I'm done! I give up! I gave you so many damn chances! All the shit you put me through—yo' crazy-ass family, yo' brothers! You can have it, because I want nothing to do with it or you! Go!" I pointed to the door.

He grabbed his phone and walked out, with me following behind him.

"If my money don't turn up in three days—"

"Then what, nigga?" I snapped, cutting him off.

He turned to look at me.

"What? You gonna flash your gun at me, thinking I'm going to be scared? I'm right with the Lord. I know where the fuck I'm going once you do it, so please!" I begged with a laugh and clap of my hands. His eyes grew wide. I stepped up to him closer, showing no fear, my blank face matching his shocked expression. "Do it! Point the fucking gun at me, nigga. You so quick to whip it out on everyone, so easily placing fear into everyone's heart. Well, I'm not afraid of you! I laid with you. I gave you the closest thing to me! I—"

Feeling like I was about to choke up, I told myself, *Not now, bitch. Don't do it in front of him.*

"I'm not afraid of you, Shiloh Cameron Carter, and never will I ever be again. So, if you want to keep threatening me about money, end this shit now and kill me," I said.

He backed up, almost looking scared himself. No words. He just turned and walked out of the house, never looking back as I slammed the door shut.

I'm getting the fuck out of here by Tuesday. I'm sick of this place.

Taylor

"How you feel?" I asked Trent, who sat up in the hospital bed. It was a Wednesday afternoon, a few days before his big party, which I didn't think he would be able to go to. He was still trying to recover, but he was showing great progress. I took off from work and remained a constant by his side. The only time I went home was to bring a change of clothes, food, drinks, and shit to clean myself with. I was not leaving this nigga's bed for nothing until he was healed.

We sat in the room, with me sitting on the chair next to the bed, while he sat up, flipping through the channels, looking sexy even while bandaged up. He sat strong, with his beard starting to grow in from lack of shaving. Diamond studs in each ear, his hazel eyes glistened as he looked at me with a flirty smile. He was still the same charismatic nigga like before. He had I don't know how many girls handing him cards, balloons, and teddy bears, but best believe I collected that shit. I kept it off to the side so he wouldn't be distracted by it.

"I feel a little better than last night," he said, cutting the TV off as he leaned back on the bed, left shoulder wrapped up. He was shot in the upper, middle, and lower half of his body, and he still managed to live. I kept telling him how blessed he was, because that doesn't happen often. All it takes is one shot.

"You good? I know you gotta get ready to go soon," he said.

I shook my head. I was sitting comfortably in my jeans, cute flats, red sweater with pearls around my neck, and my hair in a poof-ball ponytail. I wore little to no makeup. I wasn't going to look like a bum by his side. Fuck no.

"I'm off for a week, so I don't go back until next Monday," I told him with a smile.

"You don't have to do this, though, Tay," he mumbled, looking hard at me.

"I want to, Trent. Regardless of how we ended up, I'm still going to be there for you till the end," I stated, hoping he could see me staying by his side was dedication and proof that I was the one for him. His brothers were out of town but would check in every couple of hours to see what was up.

"So, what you tryna watch tonight, shawty? I don't see nothing on," he said, flipping the TV back on as I went through my phone, looking through the TV Guide app.

"They got a lot of Disney movies playing. A lot of Christmas movies are coming on tonight," I told him.

He laughed. "You think they got porn?"

"Nigga, now is not the time!" I said, and we both laughed.

"Shit, I can still get hard and still manage a stroke or two," he said, trying to move his hips before wincing in pain. "See?"

"You need to stop before you hurt yourself." I giggled, standing up to check his bandaged ribcage, making sure no blood was seeping through his wound, or that he didn't rip his stitches. Feeling his hand come to my waist as I looked him over, I smiled.

"Thank you, Tay," he mumbled as we looked at each other.

Without hesitation, I leaned in and kissed him gently on the lips. I thought he would pull away, but he just deepened the kiss. I moaned, pulling away gently as our eyes locked. I still felt that spark, and I knew he did too. He had to.

"Damn, you trying to fuck with a nigga while he's down, knowing I can't respond right now," he groaned, and I laughed.

"I'll be there when my nigga gets back up," I said with a wink before heading to the main door. "I'm about to get me something to drink from the machine. I'll be back."

"A'ight," he said.

I walked out of the room, closing the door behind me. I felt so . . . so elated at the thought of us being together. There was no other man I could see myself with. Shit, I got so happy, I wasn't even watching where I was going. I nearly bumped into this dark-skin girl with a bag in her hand.

"My bad, yo," she said coolly.

"You're good," I responded with a smile before I kept moving down the hall, all smiles. I had the nigga of my dreams. He was all I ever wanted.

Jade

"My bad, yo," I told this light-skin girl, accidentally bumping into her in the hospital hallway. She smiled. That was something these Southerners had me doing every time I saw someone now.

"You're good," she said as we continued in opposite directions.

I was looking for Trent's room, checking the number on each door. I let out a sigh, hoping I was ready to see him in this state, because I didn't know what to expect. I had gotten the phone call that Trent had been shot, and I came straight back down to Atlanta a few weeks before my scheduled time. I didn't even notice the Facebook status he'd made until after the fact.

Flipping my dark brown locs off my shoulders, with my bracelets jingling loudly, I let out another sigh before opening the door.

"Aye, they got *A Christmas Story* playing on—" He stopped as he looked at me, eyes wide. He tried to sit up in the bed like he was about to get down, only to realize he couldn't move like that. "Jade?"

I smiled, feeling my heart drop at the sight of this man bandaged up like this. Closing the door, I dropped my bag on a chair and walked over to him. My Tims were fresh, with my leggings and a long-sleeve red flannel shirt, and my locs were hanging freely. I stood at the edge of his bed, looking him over with a small smile.

"Yo, why you in the bed playing like you hurt, nigga?" I snapped playfully, tapping his foot.

He smiled. "I was waiting on you to nurse me back to health," he responded coolly, leaning back on the pillow.

"Son, I'm still mad at you, yo. You might not want me to nurse you back to health," I said.

He laughed, licking his lips. We sat in complete silence, taking each other in. I felt myself about to choke up. I thought I could handle seeing him, but old feelings were coming back, new feelings were surfacing, and seeing him bandaged up like this only made it worse.

"I would have came sooner, but my flight wasn't—"

"You came, and that's all that matters," he said, cutting me off. "I'm sorry."

I shook my head and put my hand up.

"I really am."

"We not talking about that right now," I said as the door opened.

"Trent, can you believe they only had . . ." The girl I bumped into walked in slowly, eyeing me hard. She kept the door open like she was ready to show me the way out.

So, this was her. She was the one that took him from me. Eyeing her, I could see why he would choose her over me. She was your typical pretty girl, probably in a sorority, light-skin with a cute face, and dressed like she had sense.

"Who are you?" she asked abruptly as I cut my eyes to Trent.

"Taylor, give me a minute with—"

"Is this the ex-girlfriend?" Taylor asked with a laugh, pointing at me as she looked me over like I was garbage.

Bitch better know where the fuck I grew up at. When someone looks at you in that kind of way, you get cut on sight. They too friendly down here in Atlanta. Too friendly.

I kept it cool, because this wasn't the place to act up and act out *Jerry Springer*.

"I see why you stepped out on her," she said, closing the door with a smirk as she sat down in the chair closest to him.

I looked at Trent, who had a pleading look in his eyes, almost like he was begging me not to take it there. He knew how I was. He knew my mouth and he knew my rap sheet. But I wasn't fighting over a nigga that ain't mine.

"I'm not here to cause any trouble, regardless of how you feel toward me, Taylor," I said, putting emphasis on her basic-ass name. "I'm here for Trent, just like you are. He's not mine no more, so I'm not fighting over the nigga. You got him. I just wanted to check in on him, because I still love him," I said to her before realizing I'd never even told him I loved him. His eyes grew wide as I silently cursed myself.

Fuck! Why I gotta run my mouth like that? Shit. Trying to sound all noble and mature. Fuck outta here.

"You love me?" he said.

I rolled my eyes. "Nigga, chill with it," I said, hand in the air to kill any thoughts he was trying to have. "I got love for you—"

"Nah." He laughed with a shake of his head as he sat up, reaching his arms out. "You love me, Jade. Don't you? Admit that shit."

"Nigga, get the fuck outta here, yo." I laughed, looking up at the ceiling as I walked over to the other side of the bed before looking at him. Those fuck-ass hazel eyes.

He pulled me close to him as he looked me in the eyes.

"I mean, that don't change the fact we not gon' ever be together again, but yeah, I love you."

"I can't believe you're capable of love, shawty," he mumbled in awe.

I rolled my eyes, trying not to smile. "Son, you can still get cussed out. Don't get it fucked up, nigga. We still not cool, pretty boy," I stated as he pulled me closer to him.

"Trent," Taylor called out, standing up in panic.

I backed away from his touch. I wasn't going to allow myself to get caught up with him.

"I'll let y'all do what you do," I said, backing up some more. "My sister is going to pick me up. I can check on you tomorrow, though."

"I'll still be here," Taylor stated.

I resisted the urge to roll my eyes. "I'm sure you will be." I smiled sarcastically.

Dumb broad. Fuck outta here. I said you can have the nigga. Not my fault he still wants me.

"Jade!" Trent called out as I headed to the door. "Jade!"

"What, nigga? Fuck is you screaming for?" I snapped, grabbing my bag as I turned around to look at him.

"*The Breakfast Club* is yo' favorite movie. Red is yo' favorite color. You're an Aries, and Aria is your first name," he let out, and my mouth dropped. "I forgot the other questions, but I just . . . I wanted you to know, Aria."

We stared at each other as my eyes started to water up before I looked at Taylor, the woman he cheated on me with, by his bedside, hand in hand. She stared hard at me, but his eyes remained on me.

"I'm sorry, Aria."

I walked out of the room without another word and tried my hardest not to look back. That night, though, sleep was hard to come by. I had to fight the urge not to text him, because I knew his security guard Taylor was watching that phone.

With the little sleep I did get, I managed to get up the next morning and get dressed. Pulling my locs back in a ponytail, I threw on some sweats, a low-cropped hoodie that only showed skin if I raised my arms, no bra, and my boots. I was bold like that. Dead middle of winter, and that's what the fuck I was wearing.

It was early morning, and I had just finished eating a small breakfast when I made it to his room. Opening the door slowly, I saw he was knocked out on the bed, but no Taylor in sight. Looking around, I quietly stepped in, hearing this nigga's monster-like snore before closing the door. I watched him stir out of his sleep. He looked at me with a weak smile.

"Where's yo' girl at?" I asked, coming to the bed, sitting on the end of it as I looked his body over.

"She went home to change, sleep a little bit before coming back."

I nodded slowly as I looked around the room. "They couldn't find you a better—"

"Aye, she's not my girl," he said, cutting me off.

I looked at him, smirking. Watching him wince in pain, though, caused me to be alert. "What's wrong?"

"Nothing. I gotta take a piss." He sighed, closing his eyes. "You gotta help me. I need to shower and all of that."

"Is that what she did for you?" I asked with a laugh before getting up. "Dedicated broad, I see. Come on," I said, helping him out of the bed. I became his support to stand up. The leg where he was hit was his weakness. Because he was so much taller than me, I almost collapsed under his weight as I wrapped my arm around his side.

"Hold up, baby. Hold up, baby," I let out quickly, seeing him wince as he put his foot down.

We made it to the bathroom, and I held onto him with my back turned while he pissed.

"Aye," he mumbled, glancing at me with a smile. "I missed you."

"I know you did."

"You remember how we used to go to McDonald's every morning, sit in that parking lot and eat? Talk about going to class, and then soon as we get back to the room, we fucked ourselves back to sleep?"

"Nigga, I remember," I said with a small laugh as he finished up.

We started taking a sad trip down memory lane as I helped wash him. He brushed his own teeth, and he cleaned his own dick, because if I touched it, we weren't getting out of that bathroom. Knowing him, he was going to try and fuck me handicapped.

By the time we walked out of the bathroom, a nurse was just finishing up with the changing of his sheets. I walked him back to the bed, lifting that leg up so he could lay back. I reached up, touching his small faded beard that was trying to come in, loving the rugged look on him. It made him look like a fine grown man instead of a cute young boy.

"You like it?" he asked, hand on my wrist as I continued to touch his jaw, feeling the smooth hairs. I nodded, seeing him smile before scooting down on the bed. "Come lay next to me."

"Nigga, I'm not doing that!" I laughed at his desperate expression.

"Why not?"

"Because yo' girlfriend might come in here."

"She's not my girlfriend. I'm single," he stated as I rolled my eyes. "Are you single, or is there some nigga back home that I don't know about?"

"I'm single," I muttered, looking down at the sheets.

"Why can't two single people get in the bed with each other? Come on," he said, patting the empty space next to him.

Shit, fuck it. I kicked my shoes off and got up on the bed, careful not to cause any pain. I slipped underneath the thin sheets, resting my head on his chest as his arm came around me.

"Jade?" he started, grabbing the remote.

I looked up at him. "Well, don't just stare, nigga. Say what you got to say," I retorted, and he smiled. *Me and my damn mouth.*

"You already know I'm going to try my hardest to get you back, right?"

I stayed quiet, looking back down his body as I closed my eyes, letting my head rise and fall to his slow breathing.

"I know I fucked up with a lot of things pertaining to us. A lot of shit I wish I could do differently, and if I wasn't in this bed right now, I would be trying my hardest to win you back with all my moves."

"Yo' moves?" I laughed.

"The dinners, the roses, everything. I been through hell and back. I kind of just want to start over again with you."

"Why now, Trent? You had all this time to say something."

"You changed yo' number on me!"

"Nigga, don't blame the number change. You clearly found Facebook and spoke yo' damn mind, so miss me with that number bullshit," I snapped as he sighed. "Now that you all shot up and hurt, looking for some attention, I bet you think I'm just going to sit here and fall for that shit like a dumb ass, like yo' dumb broad that don't know you still got feelings for me. But as soon as you recover, you probably gon' be fucking more girls than ever. Nah-uh," I said, sitting up as I looked down at him. "I'm not about to be yo' pity love like yo' girl Taylor."

"Jade, it's not like that," he groaned. "I don't feel the same for her like I do—"

"So, why did you sleep with her?" I snapped, feeling the tears come down. Looking up at the ceiling, I shook my head, trying to keep it together. "Nigga, I wasn't even trying to bring this up right now, because it's more important things, like yo' health, we need to focus on. You fucking around with this girl who is still here is the last thing I want to talk about, Trent."

"I'm sorry."

"Yeah, you are. I know that," I said, cutting him off as I wiped my eyes.

He watched me with a pained expression on his face. Pulling me gently by the collar of my hoodie, he brought me down to his face, and right when I tried to back away from his crazy ass, he sat up, wincing in pain, and kissed me. I gripped his ears, taking it deeper as he lay back down with me coming down on him, our mouths moving. My tears were hitting his face. This nigga, this pretty boy, the one I gave such a hard time to, had me falling harder than a skydiver. We were polar opposites, but somehow, we kept the attraction between us live.

"I'm sorry, baby," he said against my mouth before kissing me again. "I'm sorry. I love you, Aria. I'm in love with you, Aria. The moment you came up on my doorstep going in on me, I knew you was something different." His hazel eyes looked deep into mine. My heart responded with rapid beats to that statement. "I want another chance. We never got a chance to be friends, just jumped right into it," he said, and I nodded in agreement.

Pulling back, I sat up as we looked at each other, hand in hand.

"So, friends?" I pressed, licking my lips, feeling his thumb rub my hand affectionately.

"Friends," he said. "You can't be talking to no other nigga, though."

"Yo, kill the noise. You need to check yo' self before you come at me. You the one with mad broads lined up and down the block waiting on you," I said, and he smiled. "I can talk to whoever I want to talk to. I'm single, nigga."

"We'll see," he said.

The door opened, and Taylor walked in with a bag of food. Her mouth dropped as she looked at us, then cut her eyes at Trent.

"Really, Trent? Like, seriously—"

"Taylor, chill."

"I sat by yo' side day in and day out! You don't even like her! You said so yourself. None of yo' friends or family likes her!" She flipped.

I looked at Trent, mushing him hard in the face. "You been talking shit about me too, nigga?" I asked with a grin as he smiled. "I should beat yo' handicap ass down now."

"You ain't finna do shit," he tested.

I laughed, trying to mush him again, but he grabbed my wrist to keep my hand steady.

"The only way you can beat me is when I'm down."

"Nigga, how many times have I whooped yo' ass?" I flipped, shocked he would even lie like that. Then again, he was a proven liar.

"You got me one time in the gym, but—"

"Lies!" I called out as we both laughed, almost forgetting Taylor was even standing there until the door slammed shut. We both looked up, seeing she'd left the room, food on the ground.

"Was she better in the bed than me?" I asked curiously.

He smiled, his hand coming to my thigh. "She was a virgin."

"Ahhh! You low-down, dirty nigga, taking her virginity away!" I laughed. "I bet she's been after yo' ass hard ever since too. Niggas ain't shit. I swear, yo," I said, smacking my teeth as he rolled his eyes.

"You have no idea what the fuck I been through these past few weeks without you," he groaned.

"Tell me about it. And who the fuck shot you, nigga? You of all people?" I teased, lifting up the sheet to see his bandage-wrapped ribcage.

"It's been a lot of dumb shit I got caught up in, and my sister, I don't even know what the fuck she got going on," he said, shaking his head with a sigh.

I never told him because it was his family, but I knew about Ms. Olivia Carter for a minute now. None of it was good, either. My sister had a few girls that used to roll with her, and they fell out because of her attitude, her ways, and her lifestyle—whatever the fuck that means. All I knew was, if I ever met the bitch and she came at me sideways, I was swinging. No fucks would be given that day just because she's Trent's sister.

"Where do I even begin?" he asked, looking at me as he sat up, ready to tell me what had been going on.

"Start by telling me why you decided to step out of what we had to sleep with that girl," I said blatantly.

Jordyn

"It's about that time tonight! It's going down at the Spring Lounge! The last and final hot party of the year! We doing it right!" te DJ yelled from the radio. "The Carter Boys are swinging through. So, ladies, come dressed to impress! The men of Kap—"

Elijah cut the radio off as he turned over in the bed, groaning with a yawn before wrapping his arm around me. It was Friday, late morning, and he had just flown back to Atlanta about an hour ago. We were trying to catch up on lost sleep before this big party tonight.

So much had happened this past weekend that this week just felt like a much-needed vacation. I had rehearsal for Christmas concerts coming up, Elijah had radio and TV appearances, studio sessions, and he'd filmed another music video. We wanted to do normal stuff, because that's what we needed right now. We were at his house, in the bed, wrapped in these covers like burritos, trying to keep warm during the freezing cold that made its way into the house, regardless of the heat being on. Since I wasn't able to have sex for at least two weeks, Elijah and I made up for it in other ways. There's always other things you can do besides that and still get off. Come on, now. It's me we're talking about. So, we lay naked next to each other in a deep slumber, breathing opposite each other. When I inhaled, he exhaled. But my mind was slowly starting to come to consciousness. I mentally felt myself waking up before my body did.

It was a crazy way to end the year. My life had changed so drastically in a matter of months, just from meeting this man. Feeling him stir in his sleep, I opened my eyes, watching him turn his head to face me, one eye open.

"What you doing up, bae?" he asked in a groggy voice.

"I just am," I said, yawning with a stretch. My legs sat comfortably between his as he moved closer to me, kissing my chest repeatedly.

"Tonight is going to be crazy, isn't it?" I asked.

"Hell yeah. One last time for the end of the year, and then I'm slowing the fuck down until January. I can't keep turning up like this, shawty," he said in between kisses as I smiled.

"Your brother calls Noelle his queen," I noted randomly.

"And?" he asked, looking up at me with those droopy eyes.

"And I want you to call me something sweet and romantic like that," I stated.

He snorted, with his eyes turned up in defiance. "Ain't no mothafucking queens in this house, nor a damn king. I am a god, baby," he stated.

Now it was my turn to roll my eyes.

"You can be my goddess."

Neither one of us was overly religious like that, but it still sounded silly.

"You don't like that?" he asked knowingly.

I shook my head, feeling him make his way in between me, coming up to kiss my neck. "What about wet-wet?" he groaned as I laughed.

"Elijah, we can't, and you know this," I reminded him, feeling his hands gripping my ass as he sighed.

"Shit, I'm used to getting some in the mornings from you on the regular," he muttered, getting off. "We definitely not doing this abortion shit again if you get pregnant. I don't like how it made you feel afterwards, and I don't like not having sex for three fucking weeks."

"You'll be okay," I said softly, watching him sit up.

Shaking his locs loose, he adjusted the chains around his neck. They never came off unless we were in the shower.

"What all do you have to do today?" I asked.

"We about to sneak Trent out that hospital and get him to this damn party," he said, getting on his phone as my mouth dropped. I was not expecting that. "How you gon' be in the hospital on yo' own damn party? Nah, nigga, we'll have him back by morning, but he's going."

"So, are you going to get a wheelchair or something? Because—"

He waved at me to be quiet as he started talking on the phone.

"Aye. Everybody know what the plan is for tonight?"

"Yeah," Jahiem answered on speaker phone. "Talin and Toni and her people are gonna hold it down outside, having the truck ready for when we bring him. Taylor told me his ex-girl showed up."

"Ahh, shit. Nigga got drama already and ain't even left the fucking room. Where Shiloh at?"

"You know he go ghost for a couple of days after doing what he do," Jahiem mumbled.

My eyebrows came together, confused. *What did he do?*

"Nigga will be here, but don't nobody know where he at? Trell got the wheelchair ready, but this nigga needs to be on crutches."

"How, Jahiem?" Elijah snapped sarcastically. "Nigga was shot in the shoulder. What the fuck you want a piece of wood shoved underneath that same shoulder for, bruh?"

"I'm saying, though, a wheelchair? He ain't that handicap—"

"Trent will make the most out of that shit, trust me," Elijah mumbled, looking back at me, eyes wandering.

Teasing him, I started to rub my body down gently before proceeding to pretend like I was about to play with myself.

"You hear me?" Jahiem snapped as Elijah's mouth dropped in awe.

"Yeah, um . . . nah, what you say?" he muttered, hand already on his dick as I laughed. We were nasty like that.

I got up without so much as a word and went into the bathroom, coaxing him to follow.

"Aye, I'm about to get it in. Let me call you back," he said, hanging up, tossing the phone on the bed as he followed me. "Don't tease a mothafucka then walk away, shawty. Not in my house!"

After enjoying some "us time," we started to get ready for the party. The closer it got to the party, the more chaotic it became around his house. Everyone started showing up, including Trent's fraternity brothers, a couple of sorority girls, and his family, of course. Elijah had a full house, but the drinks were already lined up, music was turned up, and the only one missing was Olivia. Once again.

I was fresh out of the shower, hair straightened, waiting on Elijah to finish picking my outfit out because . . . I don't know. That's what he liked to do. It was one of the things I didn't care too much for but tolerated. Music was bumping downstairs, and he had on his thick black sweatshirt with the red A on it, black straight-leg jeans, and black-and-red Gucci high top sneakers with a red bandana tied around his head like a headband. His dreads were loose, with rings on his fingers, chains, and just his usual flashy, reckless attire.

"A'ight, try this on. I bought this for you a while back, but you wasn't filling it out like how I needed you to." He handed me some black leggings that zipped up in the back, and a long-sleeve black crop top that showed way too much breast. I slipped the ensemble on with no panties. A small line of flesh showed between the high-waisted leggings and the top.

"Hell yeah," Elijah mumbled, sitting back on the bed, looking me over. "Turn around so I can see the back and you can look in the mirror, bae."

I turned around, looking at myself in the mirror as I fixed my hair, feeling him come up and tap my ass. "God damn, J! You looking like Selena in this bitch! Shit, I'm gon' have to fight niggas off yo' ass tonight, boy, I swear."

"Hush, Elijah," I cheesed, feeling him come up behind me, smoothing my hair out as it fell to my waist. If he could, I was sure he would marry my hair before me. "You want to do my makeup too?" I asked as he bent down, biting my ass hard. "Elijah!"

"I'ma chill." He laughed.

As soon as I finished up, with him picking out my shoes and me managing to do a little makeup that I learned from the video shoot I went to, we stepped out hand in hand and made our way downstairs to the pre-party.

"Yooo! Y'all ready?" Elijah let out as everyone turned their attention to us, eyes falling hard on me.

"Nigga, you felt like you had to make a grand entrance with yo' bitch?" one of his friends asked.

Elijah checked him. "Nah, bruh. She can't help but look that good. But what you not gon' do is call her a bitch, especially in front of me. Apologize," he said, taking a cup as his friend apologized to me.

"Aye! Can I get everyone's attention?" Ontrell shouted as he stood on top of a table. Elijah damn near had a heart attack, fussing at him about his furniture, causing

Trell to get down with a laugh. "So, look! This is what we doing! We need everybody to bum rush that hospital and cause the biggest fucking distraction of a lifetime while we get Trent out. Soon as we get him in the car, we meet back up here to start the pre-party; then we rolling out! Any questions?"

I looked around. There had to be over thirty-something people squeezing into this townhouse. A couple of girls from school were eyeing the Carter boys, especially Elijah, but they couldn't see him without seeing me, because he kept me close.

"What time we leaving?" Jahiem asked as the front door opened.

Shiloh appeared in the doorway with about twenty guys and girls behind him. Oh, this was serious. I didn't even know how he managed to find a space to park.

"Ahhh, shit! You know it's about to be some shit when this nigga show up with the gang! Hell yeah! We need to go now!" Elijah hollered out, making his way over to Shiloh as they slapped hands.

"Uhh, it's too many damn people up in here," Tyree complained, cup and small tote raised in the air as he made his way through. "Nah-uh, y'all got pregnant bitches struggling to breathe and shit. I'm standing the fuck outside."

I smiled, following him out. We stepped out onto the yard, hearing the music continue to play.

You could tell who was who. Trent's fraternity brothers balanced out against the street boys, wearing red and dressing nice, while the guys with the Carters were either over the top, extremely hood, or quiet and just observing. Somehow, the two groups didn't clash, but blended in well. The girls, on the other hand, you couldn't tell the difference between one groupie and another. As far as I was concerned, they were all there to get a closer look at the Carter boys.

"You good, Toni?" Tyree asked, hand on her shoulder as she nodded, holding her stomach.

"I'm good. We need to hurry up and fucking do this before I change my mind," she mumbled.

I looked back at the house, seeing nobody was moving nowhere.

"So, you the one that locked Elijah Jodie Carter down. I've been meaning to talk to you at the hospital but haven't found the chance," Tyree said as he eyed me. "I guess we related now," he said, flashing his ring in my face.

"Congrats on the engagement." I smiled.

"Nigga, she don't give a fuck either way." Toni laughed. "She looking like how I'm looking, ready to get the fuck on. I'm tired and I'm cold."

"Exactly!" I laughed.

"Where is Noelle at?" Toni asked Tyree, who sighed.

"I don't even know. I haven't spoken to—Shiloh!" he called out, waving the quietest brother over.

He stared at us for a second before shoving his hands in his pockets and walking over slowly. He always freaked me out; never said a word to me, rarely spoke to anyone, so him having a girlfriend was shocking in itself. I bet he was mute in the bedroom, too. *Ughh. That's the worst. Quiet sex is a turn-off.* He stood next to us, low eyes hard on Tyree, wearing a black thick coat with the fur on the hood.

"Where is my chocolate princess at?" Tyree asked abruptly, hand on his hip.

"I don't know where that bitch is at, and I don't give a fuck," he spat in a low voice.

Tyree gasped, hand to his chest. "Nigga what the—"

"She stole from me, and out of love for her, she better be glad I didn't pop her on sight or put a hit out on—"

"She what?" Toni and Tyree shrieked at the same time.

Tyree started shaking his head. "Nah, nigga, we not talking about the same girl. Where is Noelle at?"

Shiloh remained quiet, just stared at him, occasionally glancing at me, letting his eyes roam with ease. He made me so uncomfortable; I just took a few steps away from him.

"She told you about that dude being in her house—" Tyree started.

"I don't believe that shit. She probably was talking to him this whole time."

"Uhh, no, I was there, nigga. He slick tried to rape her. She said he had been posted up in that house for hours before she got there. You didn't see the door knob? He tore that shit off!" Tyree laughed. "If I wasn't there, she would have still been screaming."

"You didn't tell me that!" Toni flipped, punching Tyree in the arm.

"Well, the girl held up that frying pan with her country ass, ready for battle! Ready to wop that nigga in the head! I told her to tell you, but she said you got enough going on with Trent being in the hospital and whatnot, so she said to say nothing about it. We took care of it, but I doubt if my girl stole yo' money, nigga. You need to rethink that with yo' quiet ass and go find her and apologize," Tyree demanded.

Shiloh just stared at him, almost as if he had zoned out, jaw working slowly, looking exactly like Elijah before turning to walk away.

"He is so weird to me," I mumbled.

"Girl, that is just sex appeal you have yet to understand," Tyree moaned, eyes following Shiloh's every move. "I would let him destroy my ass if I had the chance."

Toni scrunched her face at him in disgust. "Nigga, you sick as fuck. I don't want to hear nothing like that," she said, walking off as I laughed.

"A'ight! Let's go! We moving out!" Anthony called out from the house. "Who blocked my truck in?"

Everyone started to pile out. I felt a hand on my lower back. Looking up, I saw one of Trent's fraternity brothers smiling back at me.

"Hey, you probably don't remember me," he said as I smiled politely back.

"Vaguely," I responded to the nice-looking, brown-skin guy with a small fro and perfect teeth.

"I used to see you around the yard a lot with yo' books, heading into that library. How did you do on your finals?" he asked as we continued walking, his hand still on my back.

"I'm pretty sure I aced them with ease," I boasted with a smile as he laughed.

"You're probably the type that doesn't have to study," he guessed.

"Oh, I'm always studying, constantly wanting to learn new things. It's a habit." I shrugged as we stepped out onto the street, holding a basic conversation about school.

"Aye! College boy!"

We both looked up to see Elijah standing at the edge of his yard, looking dead at us, legs wide as he pointed at the guy I was with. *Great.*

"He talking to me?" the guy asked.

I sighed. "I really don't know," I said, backing away, feeling embarrassed.

"Bruh! I'm talking to you! Don't look at me like you don't know what the fuck I'm about to say, nigga! You had three years to get at her! That pussy belongs to me, nigga!"

"Elijah a fool, bruh." Someone laughed as I started walking back to the yard.

"What is the matter with you, Elijah?" I snapped as he made his way toward me. "He wasn't even—"

"Get yo' fast ass in the truck. I ain't got shit to say to you right now, shawty," he retorted, opening the door to get in. "Walking off with that nigga at my own damn house. Fuck is wrong with you?"

"We weren't even talking like that!"

"Yeah, okay." He laughed sarcastically as I got in the front seat, with his friends hopping in the back, laughing. I just sighed, clearly irritated by his display of ignorance. *Boys.*

The moment we rode into downtown, everyone was lined up, car after car trying to get into the parking garage of the hospital or lined up on the side of the street. There were just that many of us. I switched shoes, wearing all black Jordans that Elijah had gotten me, and I hopped out with him, heading toward the entrance. It took all of a few seconds for everyone to walk inside in waves and start disrupting the quiet peace. Someone was filming the whole thing as a few people went up to the desk to disconnect the phones, while others went down the hallways to make sure it was cleared out. Jahiem pushed the wheelchair, with Elijah sitting in it, singing, "We turning up tonight with them Carter Boys. If you here with us, then shawty, make some noise," over and over with a touch of soul in it.

We made our way to Trent's room. I had to admit it was kind of exciting. I felt the adrenaline pumping as we covered the hallways with our people. As soon as we entered his room, we saw Trent and Jade lying in the bed. His mouth dropped at the sight of us.

"What the fuck are y'all—"

"Get yo' ass up, bruh. We going to this party tonight!" Elijah hollered, getting up to help his brother out of the bed. "This yo' fucking graduation party. What you look like not being there? I wasn't gonna leave you hanging, twin."

"Yo, y'all niggas is straight wilding right now," Jade said in awe as she grabbed Trent's things. There was no sign of Taylor.

As soon as they got him in the wheelchair, they rolled him out and made a run for it. Everyone cleared a path as Jahiem took off, while the rest of us followed, laughing the entire way. Jade caught up with me, struggling to carry the bags. I took one to help her out.

"What the fuck is going on?" she asked.

"Just go with it," I told her with a laugh as we all hopped on the elevator. Some people took the stairs, screaming "Allll the waaaay turned up!" and ending it with "Aaaye!" before repeating it once more. This right here felt like the true ratchet essence of Atlanta.

The moment we made it to the car, with his brothers helping Trent inside, we pulled off with such speed. Everyone was trying to get out at the same time, knowing the cops had probably been called.

When we made it back to Elijah's house, everyone really started to enjoy themselves. Jade helped Trent shower and get dressed. His brothers carried him up and down those steps until finally, he was dressed in his usual pretty-boy fashion in the wheelchair, enjoying a drink, laughing it up with everyone.

"Y'all niggas are straight-up fucking crazy!" Trent laughed as people posed for pictures. The sorority girls all crowded around his wheelchair, fighting to see who was going to sit on his good thigh, while his brothers acted a straight fool, throwing up gang signs that strangely looked almost identical to the frat signs.

I hung back, leaning against the wall with a drink in my hand, watching everyone else have fun. Parties and me had never really gone hand in hand, but I tried my best to be a good sport about it. I watched Elijah interact with a few girls. He glanced at me, low eyes glossy red as he made his way over. Taking my drink, he sipped it, standing close up against me.

"What, Elijah?" I said softly, just a little under the music. He leaned in and kissed me on the side of the mouth repeatedly as my hands gripped his sides, trying not to laugh.

"Why you all the way over here being antisocial on me?" he asked, stepping closer in front of me as I moved a loc out of my face.

"Gee, I don't know," I said sarcastically. "You think it's got something to do with half the men in here are scared to approach me, and the females in here are staring at you and your brothers like meat?"

"A'ight, chill with all of that, shawty." He laughed, taking another sip of my cup. "They not scared to approach you—"

"Yes, they are, Elijah. You are too territorial sometimes. You just need to—"

"I just need to get my dick wet. That's what I need to do," he said, coming to my neck, trying to bite it as I laughed. He was drunk and barely even trying to listen to me, so I let it go. Elijah was going to always be Elijah, and nothing more.

"Are any of your brothers leaving the party early? I have rehearsal tomorrow for my concert on Sunday," I told him.

He lifted his head up to look down at me with those low eyes. "Shiloh is usually the first to leave. You want him to drop you off?"

I immediately shook my head no, and he laughed.

"You acting like you scared of that nigga."

"I am!"

"Ahh, come on!" He laughed sloppily. "Probably won't even say shit to you. I'll get him to drop you off back at yo' place."

"Elijah don't—"

"Shi!" Elijah called out in front of everyone as I covered my face in embarrassment. "You got my girl scared to ride in the car with you, nigga. Can you drop her off?"

Shiloh laughed as I quickly silenced a drunk Elijah.

"Yo! We need to roll out! It's time to go!" Ontrell yelled. "Time to celebrate!"

With that being said, everyone started to pile out of the house, with people wanting to ride with other people. Too many girls were trying to ride with Elijah, but with me driving because he was too drunk to drive, they were hesitant to even ask. They waited around that car like groupies. Outside in the yard, with dozens of people trying to get their cars started, warmed up, and ready to go, Ontrell and Tyree made their way over to us.

"Aye, we riding with you since my car is up front. I don't feel like waiting for everyone to leave just so I can pull out," Ontrell said, hopping in the back seat, with Tyree following.

"Can we get a ride?" a girl asked as I started Elijah's truck. She and her three friends stood out there in their dresses, with weaves done to perfection, eyebrows drawn on like artwork, looking like they were freezing.

"Honey, how the fuck did you get here in the first place?" Tyree asked.

I continued to ignore them, looking over at Elijah, who was messing with Ontrell, acting like a little boy.

"Nigga, quit hitting me!" Ontrell snapped with a laugh before popping a quick one upside Elijah's head.

"Our ride already left us, so we just trying to—"

"Mm-hmm," Tyree cut in knowingly. "Get y'all asses in the trunk."

"Aye, nah! They can ride! Let 'em sit in the back seat with y'all!" Elijah blurted out. The girls immediately climbed in at his admission.

"Nah-uh! Hold up!" Tyree screamed as they climbed over him just to get close to Ontrell and Elijah. There were five people in the back, with one sitting on Ontrell's lap.

"Are y'all ready?" I asked softly, hearing Tyree snapping on one of the girls. There was too much going on, with Elijah already turning around to flirt. So, I just backed out and started going, following behind the long line of cars all heading to the same place.

When I say this was the most stressful ride anywhere? I almost pulled over to get out myself.

"Nigga, you can get the fuck out if that's how you feel," one of the girls said. "Ain't nobody disrespecting you, but if you keep talking to me like you—"

"What the fuck are you gonna do, bitch?" Tyree snapped.

I sighed, watching Elijah collect a number from one of the other girls right in front of me. It never failed. Drunk or not, he held his alcohol well, so he knew exactly what he was doing. He was just trying to push me again, to see how far he could push me before I snapped.

"Aye, both of y'all chill out. It's no space in here for y'all to be arguing."

"That's because it's too many fish in this damn truck," Tyree mumbled as I pulled up to a red light. Elijah rolled his window down, yelling out to the car beside us.

"Nigga, where the fuck you going?" he yelled out.

I leaned forward to see Anthony and his load.

"We going to the Spring Lounge to party with them Carter boys. Where the fuck you going at, bitch-ass nigga?" he responded with a laugh.

"Ahh, shit! We trying to fuck with them Carter niggas too!" Elijah laughed as Anthony sped off, ignoring the red light. "Drive, Jordyn! Catch up to that nigga!" he yelled, trying to take the wheel as I smacked his hand away.

"Elijah, you need to stop!" I snapped just as another girl leaned forward.

"I wanna sit on your lap, Jodie!" she whined with a pout.

"Ahh, hell no," Tyree muttered. "I'm sorry, boo, but you a fucking ho with no manners or respect. You see his girlfriend sitting there."

"She's not his girlfriend." The girl laughed. "Not what he told me in the house—"

"I don't have a girlfriend," Elijah let out.

I looked at him, seeing him smirking to himself. He was trying to see how far he could push me. At least that's what it felt like. I let him get away with so much, because he thought I would never leave him.

"Bruh, you better chill, man," Ontrell warned.

"No, let the girl sit in his lap," I said softly as I continued to drive peacefully. "Elijah thinks he's cute right now, acting this way in front of other girls because he knows I won't do anything."

"Couldn't be me, boo. Let any one of these hoes in this car try me—"

"You gon' do what?" another girl snapped as they started going at it with the arguing.

The girl who was pouting made her way in the front seat, straddling him as his hands came around her waist.

"Oh, nah-uh! You gon' let him do that, Jordyn?" Tyree shrieked, and Ontrell shushed him.

"He can do whatever he wants," I mumbled, feeling my heart racing as I continued to drive, not once looking in the passenger's seat.

"Jordyn won't do shit 'cause she don't give a fuck like I do. Any ho can come up to me and get at me, and she'll just be standing there on the side like, uhhhh," Elijah mocked, and the girls laughed.

I continued to drive, a small smile on my face as we came to another red light. He was definitely trying it tonight, but it was cool. You should know me by now in this story and how I reacted to his childish bullshit. I didn't. Rarely did I ever pay attention to it.

"You just gon' sit there and take that, Jordyn? Couldn't be me," Tyree said again, stirring up the pot some more.

Glancing at Elijah, I watched him playfully pretend like he was going to kiss the girl, who played with his dreads as she tried kissing him back.

"So, you really about to do this in front of me, Elijah?" I snapped angrily.

He looked at me with a sly grin.

"You ain't finna do shit no way," the girl retorted, popping her gum at me.

"What you want me to do, J? Yo' walls all scratched up from that abortion. I can't fuck with you for a few weeks, so where am I gonna find some—"

"Bruh!" Ontrell snapped, slapping him hard against the head.

All the girls gasped, and I felt my entire body become numb. Nobody but Trent was supposed to know about . . . fuck it. I unbuckled my seat belt so fast and got out of the truck as the light turned green.

"Jordyn, hold up! He didn't mean it!" Ontrell yelled as I slammed the door shut.

I watched the girl climb in the driver's seat as the car horns from behind started going off. The girl waved at me with a smile before pulling off just as I started walking toward the nearest gas station. I left my coat in the truck, so I was out there with no money and no phone. I didn't care. I was done. Regardless of him loving me or not, I wasn't about to take that from anyone. Elijah had become too comfortable with me and my nonchalant nature. He always wanted me to react and be dramatic like him, but not everything in life called for that.

Being careful not to get hit, I looked around for a payphone before deciding to go inside, needing a place to stay warm. The man obviously looked at me suspiciously, but what was I going to steal with this skin-tight stupid outfit on? Walking around the store for a bit, I looked around for a public phone on the counter, or maybe a wall, before deciding to walk back outside, hoping no one would try anything.

I should have never got out that damn truck. Fuck!

Looking around the small gas station, I could see a payphone far off, but just as I started to walk up to it, a truck pulled up in front of the store, nearly blocking me off. With my arms folded across my chest, I continued walking to the phones, hearing the truck door slam shut.

"Aye, the fuck are you doing out here?"

I turned around, seeing Shiloh standing there in his coat, hands in his pockets, legs wide as he looked at me, confused. As if my night couldn't get any worse.

"Where is my brother?"

"I got out the car and they drove on," I muttered, teeth chattering as I continued to walk to the payphones.

Hearing the bells chime, I figured he must have gone inside the store, so as I made my way to the phones, I checked to see if any loose change was inside.

"Jordyn, you are better than this. Look at what the fuck you got on," I mumbled, looking down at myself. I would never be caught dead in something like this, but I wore it because he wanted me to. Everything down to my hair, nail color, and shoes were all Elijah. Leaning against the phone post, I watched Shiloh walk out of the store. He looked around before spotting me. He stared; I stared back, watching him get back in his truck.

He backed up to where I was and rolled the window down. I heard jazz music playing softly throughout the truck. He was staring at me with those droopy eyes. I folded my arms across my chest once more.

"So, you need a ride or nah?"

I nodded as I pulled the door open and slipped inside the warm vehicle. We sat in silence for a few minutes, coming to another fucking red light, because suddenly, Atlanta didn't want anyone to fucking drive.

"What's with these red lights?" I snapped to myself before looking at Shiloh, who glanced at me. In that moment, in that second, all I saw was Elijah—the exact same stupid face. Without warning, I hauled off and hit him dead in the face, right on the cheek. I gasped, seeing Shiloh was too late to block the punch.

"What the—"

"Oh my God! I'm so sorry!" I shrieked. "I didn't mean to—you looked like Elijah, and I'm just so—"

"The fuck?" Shiloh flipped loudly as he touched his jaw, cheek turning red. "I'm not that nigga! Twice the nigga's age, and twice the nigga's complexion! Fuck is wrong with you?"

"I'm sorry," I cried.

He grew silent. He was still upset, but I don't know; something in me just felt like I was ready to let it all out.

"Why is it that if I do the same thing he does to me, it's a problem?" I asked.

He looked at me, eyes squinting. He remained quiet.

"He let it be known that I had an abortion, saying my walls were scratched up," I mumbled. "Picked out my outfit, won't let me talk to certain people anymore, and I let him do it because I thought I loved him. I thought that's what love is about," I said, looking at Shiloh.

"I really don't give a fuck about this, shawty, to be honest with you," he said blatantly in a dull voice, switching lanes. "I got my own fucking problems to deal with. Where am I taking you? I got a couple errands to do, so you're just gonna have to ride, but am I taking you home or nah?"

"Take me home," I answered softly. "I don't—"

"Don't gotta talk," he said, cutting me off.

I nodded and leaned back in the seat. He was the only brother I didn't like. Now you can see why. It was like talking to a brick wall on fire. If you even get close to it, let alone touch it, you're going to get burned.

I watched him get on the highway. He touched his jaw again, and I rolled my eyes. *Get the fuck over it, dude. I didn't even hit you that hard.*

"You lucky my brother got a thing for you, shawty," he said, rubbing his jaw.

"That's what they keep telling me. I'm lucky, yet here I am in the car with you, watching what I say so I don't make you upset, while he's off partying with God knows who," I let out sarcastically, hands thrown in the air in defeat. "Real fucking lucky."

He said nothing, but I continued, feeling ready to vent again.

"What the fuck is wrong with you all? All of you Carter boys! Trent is so shallow. He can't see when he hurts someone if they were crying in front of his face. Elijah takes advantage of someone's kindness for weakness. Manipulates me into thinking I'm all he wants when really, he just wants sex. Do you know that he brags to all his friends about me?" I let out as Shiloh kept his face stone cold, looking forward. "Brags to them about how I let him have multiple girls in the bed with us, and how I'm the best he's ever had, blah blah. I know my sex is good; I've mastered the art form. I could have fucked anyone. I could have had Trent, because Lord knows he's tried it! A couple of times! You!"

He looked at me with wide eyes, mouth slightly open. "Hold up, shawty. You ain't even gotta worry about me coming on to you. I don't even find you attractive," he stated.

I sarcastically laughed. *But you couldn't stop staring at my body? Oh, okay. What do the cool people say these days? But that's none of my business? Sips tea? Yeah, you don't find me attractive. Okay.*

"I don't even know what your problem is, but you are the rudest person I ever met! How can you talk to your own mother like that? You have brothers that look up to you, and to see all of them gang up on her in that hospital because you did it? That was disgusting!" I spat, feeling like I was on a roll.

He sat up straight, looking back before switching another lane.

"I don't know who your girlfriend is personally, but I consider her lucky she doesn't have to put up with you—"

"Aye! Whatever the fuck you got going on with E? Leave me and my girl out of that shit. Don't put her name in yo' mouth; don't put my mama name in yo' mouth; and don't ever lay yo' fucking hands on me again. If I call my mama a bitch, that shouldn't have shit to do with you."

"It says a lot about your character," I mumbled.

He cocked his head back before nodding slowly. Suddenly, he slid over to the far-right lane and pulled over. I sat up, looking around, wondering why I even ran my mouth. I wasn't like this with Elijah, so why did I suddenly feel the need to be like this with the scariest brother?

Cutting the truck off, he turned and looked at me. His eyes were low but hard as he stared at me.

"Who the fuck are you?" he asked abruptly.

My eyes grew wide, with my mouth struggling to find words.

"Huh? Who are you, shawty?"

"I'm not anyone—"

"Let me tell you something," he continued. "Growing up, I watched my dad beat on my mama for all the reasons he could think of. When the triplets were born, he abused the fuck out of Elijah and Trent in every way possible!" he spat as my eyes grew wide. "When they were little babies, shawty. You fucking with li'l babies like that," he let out, voice cracking. "Nigga, you sick as fuck in the head!"

I felt my eyes water up as he continued.

"They don't remember that shit, but I remember everything. I tried telling my mom what I seen this nigga do almost every night, and she wouldn't believe me, until one day, she saw that shit for herself. What did she do? She confronted that nigga, with my li'l ass right behind her, ready to fight. On and on again, he would go after her.

"I tried defending her, until I became of age, when I was looking like I could be a threat to this nigga. I already knew how to work a gun, knew how to make money, and had Elijah following behind me. Everything I learned, I watched my pops do it. How to make, sell, spend, and double whatever I had, I watched him do it. Despite how I felt towards him, I told myself I was going to be bigger and better than him. I was gonna raise them niggas to be a man, even though I was still learning my damn self. But I didn't want my pops nowhere near the triplets. If they were going to be influenced by anyone, it was going to be me.

"First time getting locked up, my mama called the cops on me, because I almost beat that nigga to death. They asked me was I trying to kill him. I said, 'Hell, yeah. And if y'all don't lock me the fuck up right now, I will make sure I finish the job.'

"Why I call my mama a bitch? She let that shit happen. She decided to believe that nigga, even though she saw it with her own eyes!" he finished.

"They don't remember any of this?" I asked, barely above a whisper.

"Nothing. If you ask them what they were like when they were five years old, they couldn't tell you shit. Any normal person could remember when they were four or five. They somehow blocked that shit. Nigga would lock them in the room for days at a time, shawty. Only time he would let them out was to take them somewhere, and they'd be gone for several more days. Only them two. He didn't fuck with Olivia.

"My mama was running behind after him on the streets. When our grandma got us, shit started to change, and I told her I wasn't going back, and I wasn't allowing the triplets to go back either." He shook his head at the thought.

"Was he on any type of drug?" I asked, watching him sit back in the seat, eyes closed as he calmed himself down.

"Cocaine. Runs in the fucking family," he let out sarcastically in a low voice. "That's what we sold back then: cocaine, weed, crack, and pussy."

"Did your dad sexually abuse you?" I asked, watching his jaw clench as his closed eyes tightened up. My chest began to grow stiff with nerves for him. I felt tears building up as I immediately leaned over the seat, wrapping my arm around his head to bring him close. I didn't know this man from a can of paint, but I pressed my forehead against his and held it, wishing I could take away whatever weight he was carrying for him and his brothers.

Softly, I began to speak in Spanish, telling him everything would be okay. I told him to keep strong and let go of whatever he was holding inside. He quietly gripped my wrist, pulling from my body, with us connecting with the eyes. I would like to think I took some of his pain away, even if temporarily, but everything he said still had me in shock.

Hearing the cars zoom by on the highway, we sat in silence. I took his hand, grasping his tight fist.

"He should be in jail," I stated, watching him smirk as he opened his eyes.

"Nigga should be dead. Jail is a luxury to niggas like us. He should be dead. You see how the fuck Ontrell is. Ask him how he knew he was gay. The nigga will say he was always like that. Nah, bruh! You were forced into that shit! Ain't nobody just born fucking gay!" he snapped angrily.

I begged to differ, but this wasn't the time to state that.

"Do the other brothers know?" I asked.

"Anthony and Jahiem know, because that's who I was with all the time when we were out running the streets. Ant don't bring his kids to see that nigga, and he never will. He saw that shit for himself, too, but Ontrell don't remember, and we don't ever plan on telling them, because it will fuck with yo' head if you know some shit like that."

"I understand," I said, letting go of his hand. These men were walking around, living it up, having no idea they were messed with when they were younger. Yet, Shiloh had to carry that burden with him always, because he saw it firsthand. And the simple thought of him not knowing if he was ever touched in any manner made it worse. I couldn't even imagine. It made me look at him in a whole new light. He was protecting them in so many ways by keeping that with him, and that gave me so much newfound respect for him.

Looking at him, I could see he had his eyes closed in deep thought.

"It wasn't all bad, though," he said suddenly, looking at me. "Just like every other big-ass family, we have our demons and shit."

"What was Elijah like when he was younger?" I asked curiously, switching the topic. I didn't want to hear any more about that, because I wasn't sure how to even respond to it.

"Ahh, that li'l nigga was wild," Shiloh said with a smile, thinking back. "He stayed wearing my shit, tried to walk and talk like me. Trent was doing his own thing. He never been the following type, but Elijah was up underneath me constantly. So, I sat that nigga down one day and was like, 'You trying to be put on, li'l man?'"

"How old were you?" I asked.

He rubbed his chin, thinking. "Probably like fifteen or sixteen. He told me he wanted to make his own money, so I said I'ma teach you how to turn ten dollars into twenty, and fifty into a hundred in one night. He was with Ant, Jahiem, and me every chance we got, but Grandma didn't play those games," he said with a smirk. "One night, E and I was sneaking back in the house when she woke up and whooped his ass. I'm thinking I'm good to go, but she grabbed me and started hitting me too!" he let out as I laughed. "That's who I was on my way to go see, to check on her, because I heard she was sick."

"Ohh," I said slowly, mouth dropping. "Can I meet her?"

He looked me over slowly before reaching in the back, grabbing this pink-and-green blanket. "Cover up if you going in her house. I don't know how she's going to act when she sees you," he said in a low voice.

I quickly wrapped the sorority blanket around me, almost feeling like I was somehow sinning by having this on me. Looking him over again, I felt even more curious. Not that I was attracted to Shiloh in any shape or form. He looked too much like Elijah, and I was barely attracted to him when we first met, but I could see what Tyree was talking about.

"So, you're not attracted to me, or I'm not your type?" I asked.

He glanced at me. "You a pretty girl and all, but—" He shrugged as he cut the truck on. "I prefer my women dark. Always have."

I smiled, thinking about his mom being dark-skin, then remembering his girlfriend at the hospital. She was just as dark. Interesting how attraction works. It always seems like light goes for dark, and dark goes for light.

As soon as he merged onto the highway, he got on the phone. I watched the cars go by, wondering what Elijah was doing and if he even thought about me.

"Yeah, a'ight, bet," he concluded, hanging up. "Did you already eat?"

"Not really," I said softly as we pulled off the exit ramp. "What is your grandma doing up this late anyway? It's almost one o'clock in the morning."

"She's probably smoking a joint." He shrugged as my mouth dropped. *Of course.*

We pulled into this small neighborhood and turned into the driveway of the first two-story house on the left that sat on a slight hill. There was a small white car sitting outside. The porch light was on, and I heard a dog barking loudly in the back. She had the metal bars on her windows like most houses in the hood.

"Come on. We're going to make this quick," he said, getting out.

I hopped out of the truck and followed him with the blanket wrapped tight around me. He rang the doorbell. I could hear Marvin Gaye playing as the door swung open. This tiny, dark-skin woman with a blunt in her hand, wearing a long T-shirt and some basketball shorts with house shoes, stood with a wide grin. Her face was barely aged, with those signature low eyes that ran strong in the family. *Good grief.*

"Boy, you ain't tell me you was coming!" she let out as she quickly opened the screen door to hug Shiloh, bringing him down to her height as he kissed her cheek.

"Heard my ol' lady was sick," he said.

She smiled before glancing at me.

"Mama, this is—"

"Noelle! Baby, the moment I heard about you, I was telling Ava I had to meet this woman for myself! Come here. Step inside so I can get a look at you. Take off that hot-ass blanket, too," she demanded.

I quickly looked at Shiloh, who was trying not to laugh. We stepped in, and I immediately started trying to explain myself.

"I'm not Noelle. I'm—"

"So, who are you?"

"Mama, this is Elijah's girlfriend. I was just trying to take her home, but I wanted to stop by and see you first," Shiloh cut in.

The woman squinted her eyes at me as if she were trying to remember.

"I'm with Elijah, ma'am," I said with a nice smile.

Her gaze shifted from Shiloh to me. "Welp, you look better with Shiloh, baby, and that's the God's honest truth," she huffed. I laughed, looking crazily at Shiloh.

"Mama, you can't be saying that when you meet my girlfriend."

"I can say what the hell I want. Y'all two," she said, pointing at Shiloh and me, only to then nod her head with a smile like she knew something we didn't know.

Shiloh cut her crazy ass off. "What you still doing up anyway? You got a birthday celebration this weekend. I told you we turning up over here."

She turned her attention back to him with a huge grin, excitement in her weary eyes. "I was telling yo' uncle I wanted to throw a BBQ, and I want all my kids and grandchildren here. I want all of y'all here this Sunday after services," she demanded, and he nodded. "Bring yo' women, too. I want to meet everybody for my nine-tieth birthday."

My mouth dropped. Ninetieth? She barely looked seventy.

"My time is coming soon. I can feel it. I want to see everyone before the Lord calls on me," she said.

Shiloh rolled his eyes. You could tell he wasn't the religious type.

"I'll get everyone, Mama," he said, taking the blunt out of her hand, trying to take a pull on it. She smacked him so hard he had no choice but to give it back.

"Boy, ain't no smoking in this house. I done told you that."

"But you—"

"It's my house. I do what I want," she retorted, and he grew silent.

She turned her attention back to me, smiling. "Child, you look hurt. What has my grandbaby been putting you through?"

"What? I'm fine," I said, shaking my head quickly.

She put her hand on her hip. "I can see the pain in your eyes, baby. Come on." She took my hand.

The blanket slipped. She took one look at me and my outfit, shaking her head. "Go upstairs to Olivia's old room and find some clothes for this girl, Shiloh."

"Yes, ma'am," he obliged, rushing up the steps.

Sitting down in the well-decorated living room, I started telling her everything from the moment we met until now. I left out the sex, of course, but that was like eating a sandwich with nothing on it. Our relationship was based on sex and only sex. She kept her hands over mine as she stared me down, giving out the best advice I could ever ask for when it came to dealing with these men.

"I helped raise these men to the best of my abilities, and one thing I can say about each and every boy, including those boys who aren't mine: they love hard, baby. They love hard, and they hurt harder. They need strong women to bring 'em in every once in a while; strong women to protect their feelings, care for them when they need it, and make them feel like they're your everything. Even though we can protect and provide for ourselves these days, these boys like to feel wanted. When they get out of line, though? You gotta check 'em that first time. Sometimes you gotta put your foot down and say enough is enough." She slammed her fist down on her thigh for emphasis. "Take my oldest, Shiloh. Li'l boy used to talk back so bad to his mama when he was younger. You want to know what I did? I told him if he don't start respecting her, my daughter," she said, pointing at herself, "you and I, we're going to have a problem. I don't play that shit, not with my kids. Don't give a fuck who you are."

"So, what did you do?"

She smiled, taking a pull on her blunt before blowing the smoke out through her nose. "I grabbed his li'l ass by the shirt, took him outside in front of everybody, and gave him a whooping, making him apologize. He was crying, everybody was laughing, but I bet you he didn't say nothing else to my daughter again. I told him if you don't have nothing nice to say, don't say nothing at all. So, he didn't. Hasn't spoken since," she said.

I swallowed a gulp of nerves. This family was too much for me.

"I did it because he has such an influence on his siblings that when I see Elijah, who don't know no better, calling his mama a bitch because he sees his big brother doing it, I got a problem. Put your foot down one time, baby girl, and I promise you, you will start to see a change. If you let these Carter boys walk all over you every chance they get, you are just going to end up losing yourself in the end."

"Yeah," I mumbled, looking down at myself. I touched my face, feeling the makeup and lack of glasses.

She got up from the couch, feet sliding across the carpet as she grabbed a few pictures from her mantel before sitting back down. The moment I looked at the first picture of all the men and boys who were in the first row, my mouth dropped. Elijah, Trent, and Shiloh were at the bottom, wearing suits and ties, looking so cute.

"This was a picture for Easter. They wanted all the Carter men to pose together," she said thoughtfully as I spotted Ontrell, who smiled. There were so many of them.

"How old were they?" I asked, pointing at Elijah.

"Oooh, chile!" She sighed, looking up before looking back at the picture. "Had to be six years old at the time. Shiloh was probably ten, maybe eleven, meaning Ontrell was still a toddler."

She showed me another picture of all the women, and the only one I recognized was Olivia, who smirked a devilish grin, her hazel eyes bouncing off her dark complexion. There was another photo of all the uncles and aunts, with a small baby in the arms of the women. They were standing outside of the church, with the oldest woman in the middle, dressed in white.

"Whose baby? Why is he the only baby in the picture?" I asked, pointing curiously at the small body hugged up tight on the woman.

"This is their aunties and uncles on the Carter side of the family. Big family." She nodded proudly even though she wasn't a part of it. "Big family. And the baby? That's Junie boy," she said.

She showed me picture after picture. I got to see what Elijah and Trent looked like as kids. Nothing had changed, except for Elijah growing locs. All three triplets dressed alike up until a certain age, which I thought was cute.

"Olivia one day said she wanted to wear pink." She laughed, shaking her head at the memory. "So, we said,

'Okay, let's get you some pink.' Well, at that age, the triplets were still dressing alike, so we made the boys wear pink too."

"Oh God!" I laughed.

"Honeeeey, them boys did not leave their room that entire day, crying and complaining about what they had on," she said as we both laughed.

"So many good times with my grandbabies. There was this other time, Shiloh had the nerve to sneak a girl in this house, thinking I wouldn't know. Chile, please," she said, waving me off as I looked at a baby picture of Shiloh, seeing him cheesing with no teeth. He had a head full of curly black hair. "Olivia came rushing to my room to tell me a girl snuck in the house, and with my broom in hand, I bust that door open, seeing he was butt-ass naked in that bed with her. Girl! I nearly beat the ho out of her. I told her, 'Get yo' fast ass out this goddamn house!' He was embarrassed, and the triplets, of course, were watching, laughing at their older brother. I told him, 'I ain't having no great grandkids, nigga. Not in my house you ain't.' Them girls know they loved them some Shiloh," she said, shaking her head. "Mmmph. That was Ava's pride and joy, whether he wanted to believe it or not. But that was her everything when he was first born. He—"

Shiloh came walking down the steps with three black shoeboxes in his hand, face twisted up in confusion. "Grandma, where did these come from? I found these in Olivia's closet," he said, voice cold as we both stood up.

"Boy, I don't know. She was just here a few days ago with her li'l friends." She waved him off with her hand. "Did y'all eat? Want me to fix you some leftovers?"

She walked in the kitchen as I walked toward him, seeing him place the boxes on the dining room table, looking through them.

"Everything okay?" I asked, seeing stacks of money in each box. One box was already halfway empty.

"Nah," was all he muttered. "Grandma! We about to go! You good?"

"Now wait a minute! You just got here!" she let out, walking out of the kitchen as he quickly ran up to her, hugging her and kissing her on the cheek.

"Love you, Mama. I'll get everyone to come by Sunday. I promise," he said before taking the boxes. "Come on."

I followed him out to the truck. The moment we got in, he cut the light on, looking through the boxes as he handed me one.

"Start counting," he demanded. I could tell he wasn't in the mood for games, so I did as told, coming up to about fifteen thousand dollars. The other two boxes total had twenty thousand in them.

"Where did you get all this money from?" I gasped, handing him the box. He looked at me, eyes hard. "What's wrong?"

"I had over a hundred thousand dollars in these boxes," he mumbled, jaw muscles flinching as he let out a hard sigh. He was definitely trying to calm himself down. Elijah was the exact same way.

"Soooo," I said slowly, "is this the money you said Noelle stole?"

"These are her shoeboxes," he said.

My mouth dropped. "How did it get in Olivia's room then?"

He started the car, nearly backing into the mailbox as he pulled out in anger without so much as a word. We made one last stop at a gas station before he finally dropped me off at my house. I spotted Elijah's truck parked in my driveway, and a figure sitting on the porch steps in the dark. *Great.*

"Shiloh, thanks for—"

"Get out," he said abruptly.

I quickly opened the door, definitely not in the mood. I got out of the car, leaving the blanket, and started for my door, knowing I didn't have my keys on me. When Elijah's head popped up, dreads a wild mess, eyes blood-shot red, all I could think about was what his grandma had said: *care for them when they need it most.* Luckily, he was only drunk and didn't need me. I could smell another woman on him from a mile away—not talking about perfume, either. I knew he had sex with someone else, because I could smell her body odor on him.

That's why he's on my porch now, ready to cry and whine like a baby. Not tonight.

"Jordyn?" he started, standing up with the keys in his hand.

I just took the keys, feeling his cold fingers as I unlocked the door. I remained quiet as I opened the door. With him trying to follow behind me, I turned around and closed the screen door in his face before closing the main door shut with a lock.

"Jordyn!" he yelled, banging on the door. "I'm trying to say I'm sorry!"

I tossed the keys on the couch, tied my hair up, and went into my room, closing the door behind me without so much as a thought of the man outside my door.

Tia

"Who knows?" I said to Porscha over the phone as I lay back in my bed. Friday night, I was in the middle of nowhere, rubbing cocoa butter on my growing belly. My hair was wrapped up, and I was sitting in a T-shirt with some silk pajama bottoms and thick socks on my feet. I knew there was a lot of shit going on up there in Atlanta, but for once, I didn't give a fuck. I wasn't having a bad time down here in Albany, but I wasn't turning up and balling out like I usually did. I was just chill. I took Noelle's room, and I'd been relaxing, helping clean up around the house and cook dinner at night. First night, I felt like a stranger because I didn't even know Noelle, but her overly nice ass got me here with her overly nice family, and I felt like, for once, I belonged somewhere. I wasn't even thinking about going to Atlanta no time soon. I could see my daughters being raised out here; or maybe I would move to Florida since I wasn't that far from there.

"Oooh, it's so packed out here, you really are missing out. This party is about to be something serious," she said as I heard the car door slam.

I just looked around my quiet room—no TV, everything decorated in pink and yellow, fan blowing in my room to cool me down because I was running hot constantly. I was always running hot for no reason. Yet, there was still peace and quiet. Everyone else in the one-story house was asleep, while I kept my lamp on, staying up, running my mouth on this phone.

"Who is out there that I know of?" I asked, hearing her talk to a few people.

"Umm, oooh! You remember that bitch from biology class last year? Girl, she trying too hard in that dress I know she got from Rainbow. Them heels looking like they giving up on life itself," she joked, and I laughed.

"She was always a lame anyway."

"Right?" she said as we both laughed. "Oh, hey, girl!"

"Hey, Porscha!" someone responded back.

"Fake-ass bitch," Porscha muttered as I shook my head. "Oooh, you are not going to believe this, but they are pulling up as we speak."

"Who is they?"

"Them Carter boys," she stated, and my heart started to pound.

"How you know it's them?" There was silence as I listened to the background. "Porscha!"

"Because they always come in numbers. It got to be like fifteen to twenty-something fucking cars. Damn! They got everybody stopping to see who the fuck about to come out. Look at this shit, pushing Trent in a wheelchair. They oughta be ashamed of themselves!" I rolled my eyes as I listened. "I see Jahiem now getting out his car with a few girls. You want me to call that nigga out?"

"Porscha, don't—"

"Jahiem!" she yelled as I buried myself underneath the covers in embarrassment.

Oh my fucking God, Porscha. Why do I have to have a best friend like you? Why? Showing out at the wrong damn times.

"Porscha, stop!" I hissed.

"Nigga, you ain't shit!" she continued. "Tia, this man had you sitting outside his apartment door in the cold, and you telling me I can't—bitch, *whet*? Oh, I'm gon' call that nigga out like it's roll call in the classroom. Jahiem!"

"You are too much, Porscha." I laughed softly, careful not to wake anyone up. After all, I was on their house phone, running my mouth.

"Shit, he act like he can't hear me, but that's okay, because I'm gonna catch that nigga in the club, and watch me accidentally spill my drink on his face."

"You are crazy!" I laughed.

"You would do it for me, and you have. Remember that time you saw Derek in the club? What did you do when I wasn't there?"

"Slapped the shit out of him." I sighed, knowing my ass loved to fight some-damn-body.

"Uh, he gon' call me later on that night, crying, talking about he sorry. Nigga, boy bye!"

"Walked right up to him, didn't even give him a chance to speak, just slapped him in the face and dared his bitch to try it," I said with ease, looking at my nails before proceeding to rub the cocoa butter in once more.

"Mm-hmm. Bitch, if I'm crazy, I get it from you. We ride or die, shawty. Till the end."

"Till the end."

"Jahiem!" she called out as I laughed at her ghetto ass. "Shit! He's coming over here, too."

"You should have took yo' ratchet ass inside the damn club al—"

"What the fuck is yo' problem?" I heard him ask. I sat up in the bed, ready to defend her before realizing I was too many cities away from Atlanta right now.

"Nigga, you know my problem with you and how you did my friend!"

"Who the fuck is yo' friend?"

"Oh, nah-uh! Girl, he wanna play dumb like he don't know!" Porscha said to me as I sighed. "You ain't shit, nigga! She is lying in the bed pregnant with yo' babies, and you acting like—"

"Where she at?" he asked suddenly. I could hear the rumbling of the phone before hearing Porscha voice far off in the distance.

"Hello?"

I froze, feeling stuck. "Who is this?" I said.

"Tiana, where are you?" Jahiem asked, and I heard a car door open. "Aye! Aye, chill out. Let me talk to her for a minute, shawty. You'll get yo' phone back, I promise. Go inside and tell 'em DC put you on, shawty. I'll come find you."

"You better, or we gon' have a problem, nigga," Porscha threatened.

I heard a car door close shut, followed by a sigh.

"Tiana, where you at? I know you been laying low, so just let me know where, and we can fix this shit," he said.

I cocked my head back. "Fix what?" I asked in a dull voice. If he thought I was going to even . . . ha! I was not one of those little pathetic, looking-for-love bitches in the books y'all reading about. Once a nigga is done with me? After I chased behind his sorry ass? Best believe I was done with him. I don't walk backwards, I don't eat backwards, and damn sho' don't date backwards. Always moving forward.

"Fix whatever we got going on. I'm sorry I didn't hear you out, and I think we should get back together and figure out what the fuck is the next step," he said easily. "I still want a DNA test, but I'm not going to leave you hanging while you pregnant, shawty. I was fucked up for putting you out like that, but understand I was mad and hurt."

"I understand," I said softly, nodding my head as I closed the lid of the cocoa butter jar.

Did I mention I had a job now? I worked at the local daycare, answering phones and shit. Yeah, got the job as a favor of Noelle's dad, who treated me like his own daughter. The whole family was steady buying little-girl outfits and things I would need.

"You hear me?" Jahiem asked as I tuned back in.

"I hear you."

"So, just stop playing around and come on. You know I love you. You still love me, so let's just work this shit out," he said with a smile in his voice.

"Jahiem? You know I met this girl at a train station who didn't know me from nowhere? She took me to the doctor's office on her appointment time, and I found out I was having three girls," I said, hearing him almost choke up in a cough.

"Three!" he shrieked.

"Mm-hmm. She ended up feeling sorry for me because I told her I had no place to go, so her family took me in," I continued.

"A'ight, so tell them thank you, but you need to come on. You out there with three kids that are mine, and—"

"Nigga, don't be rude," I cut in. "I was still talking," I said, smacking my teeth. "So anyway, I've been with her family for almost a week now, and they got me a job, and they buy things for the babies, and I'm fed on a regular. Learning how to cook real country-ass meals, too, because her grandma don't play." I laughed.

"Why you telling me all of this, Tiana?"

"I'm telling you this because I don't need you. I don't need your help. I am going to do this myself."

"What? You can't—"

"I can, and I will, nigga. Don't test or try me. You had me sitting outside that fucking apartment all night, while these complete strangers took me in their home without even a second thought! I slept with you, I fell in love with you, but you so easily just—"

"You hurt me, Tia! Do you not understand hearing that you slept with my younger brother was some shit I wasn't prepared to hear?"

"I said I was sorry. I should have told—"

"Nah, nah! Don't be fucking rude. I'm talking now. It's my turn to talk, shawty. Shut the fuck up!"

I grew silent, biting my tongue, and all kinds of bullets at this point.

"I never fell for nobody as hard as I fell for yo' ass! Even when you didn't want my dog ass, I had my eyes on you ever since I saw you at that party. I gave it a chance, Tia. I got used to the idea of having to come home to a girl with a baby. I liked having my own family to take care of, and you about to take that away from me because of something you did—not me! I don't care how hard any nigga tries to act, nothing is worse than hearing the woman he fell in love with slept with someone else. Especially my younger brother! I hurt too, Tia. You know that?"

I felt the tears about to come down.

"You not the only one, shawty. Yeah, yo' ass sat outside that concrete floor because I was mad as fuck that you lied to me, to my face, that entire time. All I was thinking about was you pushing my brother's kid on me."

"Jahiem, I—"

"Shut the fuck up!" he snapped, and I dropped my head, feeling the tears come down. "I may be a fucking fool for this, but I still want to be with you. Bruh, I swear I might be going crazy, because I shouldn't want shit to do with yo' trifling, two-faced ass, but here I am about ready to beg. Bring yo' ass back the fuck home so we can talk and work this out like adults, Tiana."

"No, Jahiem," I cried softly, hearing him sigh.

"So, you just gonna let it end like this? Not let me see my own seed? When you were the one that fucked up? Not me! How did you expect me to react, Tia?"

I remained quiet as he grew silent on the phone. We just sat there listening to each other's breathing for a few seconds.

"I tried talking to you, Jahiem. I tried to—"

"I wasn't ready to fucking talk then!" he let out as I wiped my eyes. "Where are you? What the fuck area code is this?"

"I'm in Albany, and I plan on staying the remainder of my pregnancy," I stated softly. "I am going to finish up my degree down here and hopefully find a place of my own to stay. I'm not going back to Atlanta. Yeah, nigga, I fucked up by not telling you about Trent and me. Yet, you putting me out your apartment the way you did, threatening to call the cops on me, threatening to beat my child out of me? Nigga, *whet*?" I snapped sarcastically, voice full of attitude. "Where they do that at? Love don't make niggas do shit like that."

"Nah! You right! A broken fucking heart makes niggas do shit like that, Tia. Stay the fuck down there then with yo' dumb ass. I don't want shit to do with you."

"That's fi—"

He hung up. Staring at the phone, I let out a deep sigh, trying to fight back more tears. Nigga was not about to have me shed anymore tears over him.

Taylor

"Look at this nigga," I mumbled to myself as I stood a few feet to the side, watching Trent enjoy a lap dance from some random ho. I had just arrived at this party at the Spring Lounge, and when I say this shit was packed? I mean, this shit was thick, shoulder to shoulder, people trying to dance with little to no space. VIP was full of the Carter boys. I'm not just talking the brothers; they had cousins, close friends, and other music artists that filled up the VIP booths while everyone else looked on in amazement. Elijah had girls dancing on him, while the rest of the brothers danced behind a girl. Tyree, of course, kept an eye out for Ontrell, standing on the side with his arms folded across his chest.

Then there was Trent. Focusing my attention back to him, I sighed. *How the fuck can you tell me one night we should think about being together again? You're the only one that's been by my side. You're a constant in my life. We have so much history . . . Then! The ex-girlfriend shows up, and you forget that I'm here. Fuck you, nigga!*

"Hey, you trying to dance, pretty lady?" a guy asked, hand on my lower back as I turned around to look up at him.

I shook my head no, and he put his hands up in defeat before moving on to the next girl. I wasn't interested in dancing with no one. I just kept my eyes hard on Trent, who had all the girls surrounding him in his wheelchair. I mean, of course I was looking cute with my blue body con

dress on and my hair in a twist-out with the big hoop earrings, but I felt like it was all for nothing when the main
nigga I wanted barely noticed me as he was surrounded
by other women.

"Yo, we about to play this for my boy, Trent Carter! He
just officially graduated college!" the DJ called out. "I see
ya over there getting it on, playa! We about to drop this
for the ladies! I want y'all to show him some love!" The
song switched to Usher's "I Don't Mind" as girls started
putting their hands up with a series of, "Dis my song,
beetch!"

Rolling my eyes, I was about to walk toward Trent
before feeling a hand on my shoulder. I turned around,
seeing his ex-girlfriend shaking her head at me. She was
a little shorter than me, with her locs hanging freely and
wearing a red dress with gold heels. I nearly smacked her
fucking hand off me.

"What the fuck you got to say?" I snapped, turning fully
to Jade, giving her that warning look. "We not cool like
that."

"Yo, first off, we will never be cool. You slept with my
nigga. Second, I was trying to stop you from making a
fool of yourself like you did at the hospital." She laughed
sarcastically. "Let that nigga be, ma. He's not interested
in you, and he's not interested in getting back with me.
That nigga likes attention and for women to feed that ego.
If you let him get to you like that, then the only person
that's going to lose in the end is your mama. That's all
I'm saying." She shrugged. "I'm not trying to fight or
argue with you, because I'm not trying to fuck nobody up
tonight. I was just helping you out."

Swallowing my emotions, I turned to look back at
Trent, seeing him kissing on some girl who was barely
covered. "He said he wanted to be with me when he was

at the hospital," I said to her as she stood next to me, blunt in hand.

She just shook her head, looking at me before passing it my way. I took a strong pull, needing to calm my nerves before passing it back to her.

"Yeah, the nigga told me he was in love with me and was going to work on getting me back, but do you see me putting any thought behind a man's words?" she asked knowingly. "Actions speak louder than words. 'Specially with a man. Always remember that. We here at this party that cost thirty dollars to get in, and we got in for free! There are mad niggas in here that are looking for a broad to fuck with, and you bitching over the one nigga who hasn't glanced your way." She laughed.

One of her guy friends stepped up toward me. He was a tall, lanky guy, smiling hard as hell at me. "Come dance with me, shawty," he said, hand out.

I smiled. "Nigga, I don't even know you. I look like I could break yo' li'l ass in half," I said as they laughed. He just licked his lips at me, adjusting his fitted cap.

"I'm not intimidated, shawty. I prefer my women thick like you. Come dance with me, and I'll show you just how easy I can handle you," he said smoothly.

"Oooh! KD putting that game on her!" one of the other boys yelled out over the music as Jade laughed. "Nigga spitting that crack!"

"Go have fun, ma. Let that nigga go. Trent is a dog-ass nigga and will always be one until someone does the same shit to him," Jade said, waving me off with her friend.

Looking back at KD, I decided to let him lead me out to the main dance floor. Without so much as a glance back, it was time to move on from Trent. I was done chasing behind that nigga. I'd been doing it for years, and I was tired of running. Let this be the end of my story.

Michael

"We them boys in the hood, sell anything for profit!" I yelled, going along with the song as I drove down the dark streets, trying to head up to Shiloh's house. I was feeling good, just got back from this dope-ass party. I got some head from some random ho in the club who was all for it. I had a little buzz and a high going. Life was straight. Money was not an issue. After robbing this dumb-ass nigga who was getting too old to see when niggas was trying to come up from underneath him, I blew my share on the strip club, a new whip, and clothes. Olivia had to pay back some people, but my share was strictly blown on materialistic shit.

Hearing my phone go off, I glanced at it, seeing my home boy Kev was calling me. "What's good? I'm almost there," I answered, whipping the Mustang like I stole it down a street. It was early Saturday morning, probably like three something, and niggas was still out, trying to make that money, fuck a bitch, or just continue on with their high. Regardless, people were out.

"Something ain't right with this nigga Mayes," Kev said, sounding worried.

I snorted. Just about everyone was scared of Shiloh Carter. Nah, not me. I just stole a hundred thousand dollars from his ass and almost fucked his bitch. I was far from scared.

"I'm almost there. Chill out, nigga." I laughed. "Find yo' balls and man up."

"Fuck you," he spat as I laughed, hearing him hang up. It didn't make sense that a grown man was scared of another man.

When I came to the last house on the street, I could see cars parked as I pulled mine to the side. Getting out with my coat on, I smiled at my new whip. I was loving my Mustang. You know how many bitches I pulled with this car? Man!

"Life is good." I smiled to myself before walking toward the small house.

Shiloh had at least four places that I knew of where he could stay. This one was for everyone to stay and hang out at, mostly for the high-school niggas who were trying to bang under him. The one next to Noelle was just a place he went to when he wanted to be alone, but I knew he had a big, fancy-ass house somewhere up north. I hadn't seen it, but I heard about that shit.

Walking up to the black door, I pulled it back, already smelling that thick, powerful shit. Music was playing, with a few of the girls sitting in the corner, rolling joints and talking, all of them banging to the right. They had tattoos on their faces and arms, and they were as rough as men. I kept on walking past the kitchen, and I spotted Shiloh sitting on the chair in sweats, with a hoodie on, smoking. My eyes immediately went to the three black shoeboxes on the table. *Shit!*

He just watched me with low eyes before sitting up. "Nigga, sit the fuck down," he said, blowing smoke from his mouth.

I took a seat, glancing at Kev, who shrugged. "What's good, big homie? You looking like you stressed." I laughed, trying to play it cool.

"I am, nigga. These females about to run me to the grave, I swear," he said, shaking his head. "I ain't never been this off my game."

"Noelle still didn't admit she took yo' money, huh?" I asked knowingly.

He cut his eyes at me hard, and I immediately wished I could take it back. *Shit!*

"Nah," he said slowly, leaning back in his seat, taking another pull. "I need you to take care of something for me, though. That's why I called you two here. I'm about to—"

"Aye! Look at this nigga carrying a thong in his pocket!" someone yelled out.

I quickly turned around, feeling one of the young niggas pull Noelle's black thong out of my pocket, laughing. "You wearing thongs now, Mayes?"

"Lemme see! It's probably some girl's thong. Let me smell that shit!" another asked as they started tossing it around.

"Y'all quit playing!" I screamed, fighting, trying to get it back.

"Ohh! Yo, I swear to God, this got Shiloh's name on it!" another yelled.

My heart stopped. I felt like all the air escaped from my chest as everything came to a hard silence.

"Bruh, what?" Shiloh retorted as he stood up.

They all started crowding around the boy with the thong, while Shiloh stood off to the side, face confused. Kev looked at me with his eyes wide, shaking his head like he was about to try to escape from even being associated with me.

"Yeah, see, that shit says Shiloh on the tag," one said, showing Shiloh, who cut the light on.

"Yo, cut the music off. Cut that shit off!" he snapped, and the music became silent.

Everyone started looking at me as I backed up, watching Shiloh look at the thong before glancing at me.

"What you doing with my girl's panties, nigga?" he asked.

"Oh, shit," someone mumbled as Shiloh tossed the thong to the side, along with the blunt, and stepped to me.

"I didn't—"

"I bought her this, and she put my name on it in front of me, so ain't no fucking mistake in who they belong to. So again, what the *fuck* are you doing with Noelle's shit in yo' back pocket?" he screamed, fists balling up.

I felt my body become numb with nerves. Everyone looked at me, ready to back him at any cost. "She gave those to me."

"Nah, no the fuck she didn't!" he screamed, pushing me back hard against the wall.

"She gave them to me! I'm not lying about that!"

"Maybe she gave them to him, big homie. Females ain't shit these days," one guy said, trying to stand up for me.

Shiloh kept his eyes on me before backing up, nodding his head with a smirk. That smirk was the last thing I wanted to see. Nigga was sarcastic as fuck, so I knew it wasn't over. This wasn't the end of it.

"You right. Bitches ain't shit these days," he agreed, hands in the air. "What's yo' first name, Mayes?"

I said nothing. I couldn't even speak. I was struggling to find the perfect lie to protect me. He continued to stare at me, waiting.

"Ain't that nigga name Michael?" someone muttered from a distance.

Shiloh's head turned so quick in that direction that I started to back up, realizing I had no other place to go but the corner.

"Michael?" Shiloh repeated. He stared at me as the room became even more intensely quiet. "Nigga, you the one that's been harassing my girl. You the one that's been calling her and showing up at her fucking house this whole fucking time!" he screamed, causing me to flinch at the sound of his voice. He shook his head, dragging both hands down his face. "You tried to fuck my girl. It was you this whole time."

"I didn't—"

Without warning, he struck a blow to my face so hard, causing my head to bounce off the wall before he grabbed me and slammed me to the ground. I tried to block myself, tried to fight back, but the nigga was over me, not letting up.

Feeling them pull him off me, I laid limp on the ground, bloodied up, trying to find the strength to speak. I couldn't see out my left eye, and I barely saw out my right.

"Shiloh, calm down."

"You put yo' hands on my girl, nigga. Why would you try me like that?" he asked with a groan, trying to calm himself down. "You took my fucking money, too! You knew where that shit was the entire time!"

"Olivia," I let out, blood spilling out of my mouth.

"Get that nigga up. I just put new carpet in this shit!" Shiloh spat. "Take him outside. Don't want him in my house."

Feeling them lift me up, I cried out as the pain started to overtake my body. I was dropped hard on the cold grass.

"Who else knew about this?" he asked.

No one spoke up, but I could hear Kev being dragged out of the house before being tossed on the ground with me. Both of us were lying on the grass together.

"You the closest nigga to him, so I know you knew he—"

"I didn't know!" Kev pleaded.

I watched in horror, seeing Shiloh pull out his gun and shoot Kev on the spot before letting out a thing of spit as he kicked his body to the side.

Nah. Fuck, nah. Olivia is taking this blame. It was her idea in the first place. I was just the nigga dumb enough to fuck with her calculating ass.

"Olivia did," I said, coughing up blood as I struggled to breathe.

Shiloh came up to me and kicked me hard in the face. I felt myself losing consciousness.

"Olivia . . . It was yo' sister's idea."

Shiloh bent down to my level, grabbing my head as he stuck the gun inside my mouth. His eyes were cold and soulless. I started crying, pleading for my life.

"I hope everybody is fucking watching this and taking notes!" he announced to the crowd standing behind him. "I am the wrong nigga to fuck with on any level! My woman is off limits. Don't even look her way! My money is off limits, and my family is off limits!"

"Olivia—"

He pulled the trigger.

Elijah

"Nigga, get up!" Jahiem let out, hitting my leg hard as I groaned. "Get these mothafuckas out yo' house, bruh."

Turning over slowly, I could feel a thick arm next to me as I quickly, eyes still closed, reached over to feel for a face. *This nigga here.* I opened my eyes, seeing Trent lying on the other side of my bed, mouth wide, looking handicapped like fuck.

"Why is this nigga in my bed?" I asked in a groggy voice as I sat up, shaking my locs loose.

"He was already here when you got back I think. I don't know," Jahiem said, shrugging as I stood up, head pounding, stomach growling. Cold air hit my bare chest hard as I reached down for my hoodie, throwing it on with my basketball shorts.

"Last night was crazy as hell. I don't think I drank that much since last year at Mansion Elan," Jahiem said.

"What people are still in my house?" I asked, yawning as I followed my older brother out of the room, closing the door behind me.

"Shit, I don't know. I just woke up in the other room, but I heard voices. All these people made their way back to this house and passed out, I guess." He laughed as we went down the halls, opening doors, getting every female out.

Whether they were clothed or not, they were leaving. I didn't even know how niggas made it back to this house, but they was laying up in my kitchen, eating shit out of my fridge, looking at me like I was the fucking stranger. Black people don't do shit like that. Only niggas. There's a difference.

"Get out," was all I had to say. Clearing out my house, I let my dogs inside to make sure they ran everyone off before sitting down on the couch with a tired sigh. All I wanted was Jordyn at this point. I didn't want my brothers there; didn't want my house to look like a tornado blew through it. I just wanted my girl. That's how I had planned this night: turn up, and then wake up in her arms, like always.

"You good, li'l Carter?" Jahiem asked as he sat down, carefully trying to roll up a joint.

"Nah, these women in Atlanta are a trip, bruh." I sighed, rubbing my face to wake me up.

He smirked with a jump of his shoulders as he cut his eyes at me. "Only if you let them be, E," he said as Ontrell came around the corner, rubbing his eyes.

"Where the food at, E? You ain't got shit in this fridge," he complained.

"Y'all black mothafuckas ate all my shit."

"Where yo' nigga at?" Jahiem asked, taking a light to the joint before taking a pull on it.

"He in the room, 'sleep still," Ontrell said, sitting down as Jahiem passed him the joint.

I let out another groan at the thought of him and Ty fucking in one of my guest rooms.

Shit, I'm gonna have to change everything about that damn room—sheets, pillows, walls, everything. Love 'em both, but hell nah. Not in my house.

"I want my Jordyn," I mumbled, closing my eyes, thinking about what she was doing at this time of the morning. I was so used to being around her peaceful ass that just sitting in the room with my brothers alone was chaotic for me.

"Where Talin at?" I asked.

"Home with the wife. They left early. You know he not about to have her out that late with a baby," Jahiem said knowingly as Ontrell passed me the blunt.

We sat in silence, thinking about all that had happened, passing back and forth, when Tyree came down wearing a robe—my robe, at that.

"Bruh," I started, hearing him smack his teeth.

"Don't even start, Elijah. I don't have nothing on under here, and I can't find my clothes, so I got to wear this," he said as Jahiem and I groaned in protest. Ontrell just laughed, pulling him down next to him on the floor.

"Keep that shit," I mumbled, grabbing my phone off the coffee table, trying to call Jordyn. I knew she wouldn't answer.

Fuck! Why do I have to fuck up so many times with this girl?

"Aye, we need to get something to eat," Ontrell said, blowing smoke out his mouth. "I know Ant should be up by now," he said, pulling out his phone.

The phone rang loud on speaker, and then we heard the sounds of kids in the background.

"What's good, Trell?"

"You making some breakfast?" Ontrell asked.

I tapped Jahiem on the shoulder, already knowing what Anthony's response was going to be.

"Why? So your begging ass can come over and eat all my kids' food off they plates?" he snapped, and we laughed.

"Well damn, nigga! Make enough for me and it won't be a problem!" Ontrell went in.

"Uncle Trell!" We heard Baby Girl in the background. "Uncle Trell, I gotta show you what I made in daycare!"

"Tell yo' daddy to let me come over."

"First Shiloh, now you. If anyone else come over eating up my food, I'm going the fuck off," Anthony retorted. "Hurry up and come on, Trell." He hung up, and we all looked at each other.

"Shit," Jahiem started, standing up. "Time to go eat a meal for free then."

"Leh go!" I laughed as we all made our way upstairs. I woke Trent up, opting to be his caretaker for the day, since we still hadn't taken him back to the hospital.

"Where is Taylor at?" he asked as I helped him in the bathroom. "I ain't all the way comfortable with you doing this shit for me."

"And you think I want to be here?" I laughed, turning my back so he could take a piss. The things you do for your family. "I don't know where Taylor is at, though."

"Has Jade called me? Or—"

"Nigga, I don't know," I snapped. "They not here. That's all we both know at this point—Taylor, Jade, or Jordyn."

"Well, you fucked up with Jordyn. I didn't mess up with Taylor or—"

I quickly backed away, dropping my shoulder from his grip as he hollered out in pain, trying to balance his weight on the counter.

"A'ight! I'll shut up!" he pleaded as I smirked. "Fuck!" He couldn't stand on both legs without support, and the moment he stretched that arm out, his side and shoulder was fucked, so really, he needed to learn to keep his mouth closed.

Soon as everyone was dressed, they helped me get Trent into the truck, and then we all piled inside before pulling off. It was rare when we had a whole weekend from the music, but we were about to take full advantage of it.

"Aye, so, only ones left now to have kids are E, Trent, and Shiloh," Jahiem noted from the back seat as Tyree cleared his throat. "And Olivia."

"Uh, what, we can't have no kids then?" Tyree pressed with an attitude.

"I mean, unless y'all plan on adopting or something," Trent pointed out.

"We will in about two years or so," Trell said with a yawn. "I want a daughter. He doesn't want no kids, but honestly, nigga really don't have no choice."

"Aye! Like a boss! Tell him like it is," I called out, and they laughed. "Nigga putting that foot down."

"Whatever. I want kids one day," Tyree said with a smack of his teeth.

I turned down a street that led into Anthony's subdivision, tuning them out as I pulled up to the two-story brick house, seeing Anthony. Shiloh's truck was parked outside. Nigga had no idea we were coming. I blew the horn, bringing the truck to a park just as the front door opened. All four of his bad-ass kids came rushing out, barefooted, pajamas still on, with Baby Girl carrying her nappy-headed Barbie doll in hand, stomach poking out of her little Winnie the Pooh thermal shirt. Anthony stood in the doorway, shirtless, with an apron on, looking like Rick Ross' mama with dreads.

"This nigga ain't got no type of tact in front of these white people." I laughed, hopping out of the truck.

"Uncle Jodie!" they all screamed as I grabbed my nephews, hugging the boys before picking up the one girl.

"Trell, I'ma beat yo' fucking ass!" Anthony screamed as we all laughed.

Trent was helped by Jahiem, who placed him in the wheelchair as we made our way in, with the kids tugging at each of us. Shiloh was sitting in the dining room, giving us a heads up in greeting as we grabbed seats. Baby Girl climbed from one uncle's lap to another, while her brothers went back to playing video games in the huge living room. Anthony went back in the kitchen, occupying the stoves as he continued to cook. When I say this nigga can throw down? I mean, him and Noelle probably were neck and neck. I ain't never had her breakfast, though, but this nigga here, though? Shiiit.

"Aye, you remember when we all got high together for the first time?" I asked as everyone laughed.

"We came straight to this nigga's house in the middle of the night and started cooking up everything he had in the kitchen." Jahiem laughed.

"Anthony was always the nigga made for the kitchen," Trell said as Anthony threw a dish rag at him, hitting Baby Girl instead.

"Daddy!" she cried.

"Hit yo' uncle for me, Baby Girl," he demanded.

Trell shook his head, pleading to his niece, who laid the tiniest hand on his face before smacking him hard.

"Daamn!" I let out as we laughed. It felt good to be with the family. We were just missing one other brother, but I knew he had his wife to look out for.

"A'ight, so what's the problem?" Anthony asked, setting the last plate of food down on the table before sitting down himself at the head. We had pancakes, eggs, bacon, sausage, orange juice, and waffles. The little boys demolished their shit while playing video games, but Baby Girl sat in Anthony's lap, eating alongside him. She was a true daddy's girl at heart.

"What you mean, what's the problem?" Trent asked as Ant looked at him knowingly.

"Y'all don't come here unless it's a problem. Usually it's a one-on-one type thing, but all of y'all here at the same time? Nah," he said, shaking his head. "Who did what?"

"I got a baby mama who is on the other side of Georgia and doesn't plan on coming back, if that counts as a problem," Jahiem said sarcastically. We all looked at him. "I told her to stay down there. Not trying to raise no damn kids anyway. Even though she was in the wrong. She lied, and somehow, I'm being punished for it. My life would have been over if I had kids anyway, so I'm better off."

"Nah, kids don't ruin yo' life, bruh. I hate when people say that." Ant sighed, looking at his daughter, who was eating. "Aye, y'all watch this," he whispered. He turned his fork upside down and started picking up the food that way, with his daughter no doubt watching. Sure enough, she turned her fork upside down and started to imitate. "Kids are a beautiful thing, Jahiem. One baby ain't gonna ruin yo' life, nigga."

"Try three girls," Jahiem said, and we all damn near choked on our food.

"Three?" we shrieked together.

He nodded. "She's having three girls."

"And you just gonna leave her by herself?"

"She don't need my help! She said so herself!"

"You tripping. I would have dragged her ass back up here if it was me," I stated, taking another bite.

"Oh, but what about you then? You and Jordyn, since everybody wanna judge me?"

"Hold up. All y'all got women problems?" Ant asked, looking at everyone.

Shiloh shook his head with a huge grin on his face, like he was trying not to laugh.

"Fuck is so funny about that?" I snapped at him.

"Yo' girl left you on the doorstep," he said, pointing at me. "Yo' baby mama is a ho," he said, pointing at Jahiem, who snorted. "My girl don't want shit to do with me no more, and you treated the females that was holding you down like shit," he said, pointing at Trent before laughing. "Now we all sitting up in this house, looking like some lonely-ass Carters. I came over here to get some advice from this nigga on how to get Noelle back, but if I think about this shit, Ant is the wrong person to ask, because he got three baby mamas that can't stand him, and another kid on the way." Shiloh laughed as we all looked at him. He just shrugged.

"Nigga, you wanna try wearing a fucking condom or something?" I let out, and he laughed.

"I don't know what a condom is, bruh," he said, getting up to unlock his front door before sitting back down with his daughter.

"The one person we need to ask is the main nigga not here—the only one married with a kid on the way," Jahiem said.

"Somehow, Grandma wanna see all of us, including the girls, over at her house tomorrow for her birthday," Shiloh said with a sigh. "She wanna meet Noelle so bad, and I can't even get the bitch to answer a text back."

"So, go get her. You know where she stays and where she work," Tyree chimed in for the first time. "Go after her."

"I don't chase after no female, bruh. Never have; never will."

"See! That's y'all problem!" Tyree snapped. "Y'all too proud, thinking that Carter name is supposed to get y'all somewhere. Noelle don't care who you are or where you come from or what you do. You did wrong; you need to fix it. She won't come to you, and the longer you wait around, the faster she is going to move on, nigga. Stop acting like you too cool to care, nigga, and show some actual emotion for once."

"Elijah," he said, looking at me. "You so scary, boo. I don't know why you so scared to fall in love with that girl. You did yo' best last night to push her away, and she was holding out until you said the abortion thing in front of them girls. You ain't shit, nigga," he said, rolling his eyes as I dropped my head.

"Trent, you a dog, and I hope one day you find a girl that's going to do to you what you done to others. Jahiem, I think you should drag that bitch back up here, simple. There," he said with a quick smile before continuing to eat as we all looked at Tyree.

"What you think yo' uncles should do, Baby Girl?" Ant asked as we all looked at her.

She put her finger to her chin, pretending she was thinking hard, with her afro puff ponytail resting on Ant's chest.

"I want . . . I want you guys to be happy," she said in a soft voice as I smiled.

"The only Carter in the room that makes sense. Damn shame," Tyree mumbled as Ant kissed his daughter on the head.

Suddenly, the front door opened, and Olivia stepped in the house with shopping bags. "Hellooo!" she greeted, taking her shades off as the kids ran to her.

"Auntie!" Baby Girl shrieked, rushing into her arms.

She looked at us with a smile, looking like she was trying to cover up her hangover. "Y'all looking so depressed over there!" She laughed, coming to the table, picking food off my plate.

Looking her over, I watched her jerky movements. My sister could dress better than most females in Atlanta, and she was classy about that shit, but she was high as fuck right now. Her clothes were barely on, and her movements were too erratic. She was hype for no fucking reason.

"What you on right now, Livie?" I asked, folding my arms across my chest with a smirk.

"What are you talking about, Elijah?" She laughed, sitting down in the chair next to me, nearly scooting me off of it.

"Yeah, she high as fuck right now. I can tell." Jahiem laughed. "Around the kids, though? Like, really?"

"I have a hangover, but I'm not high. I swear!" She giggled. "Honest, I'm just happy to see y'all all together. I don't even do drugs like y'all do. Weed occasionally, but that's it. Besides!" she shouted, hand in the air as I cut my eyes at my brothers knowingly.

They might have fell for that shit, but I knew she was on something other than weed. I'd fucked with cocaine, pills, acid—all of that—a couple of times in my day. My sister was on something, because this was my first time seeing her like this.

"Grandma's birthday is tomorrow. We can—" Shiloh pushed himself away from the table to stand up, grabbed his coat, and walked out without another word to any of us.

"What's wrong with Shiloh?" she asked, hazel eyes looking at me.

"I don't know. I never know," I said. "The nigga stays mad at the world."

Noelle

"Hold on! I'm coming!" I screamed, wrapping the towel around my soaked body. *Who in the world would be knocking on my door this late in the evening anyway?* "Shit!" I hissed, touching my wet hair. I didn't want to open this door, letting the cold in, knowing I had nothing on underneath the towel.

The knocking went off again, and I snapped, "I said hold on! Who is it?" I cut the lights off, so I could look through the peephole without any distraction. The moment I saw Shiloh standing out there, I rolled my eyes, crossing my arms over my chest to keep the towel close.

"Noelle, can we talk?" he asked in a low voice.

"Looking for your money still? Huh?" I let out. "Still think I stole it? I got a couple of dollars in my bag now that I can—"

"This is serious, shawty," he groaned. "I'm not the type of nigga to beg and chase behind no female, but can you just please let me in?"

I remained quiet, looking at the door before deciding to unlock both main and screen doors. He stepped in with a bouquet of roses in his hand, dressed like he was ready for war—camouflage pants, cream-colored long-sleeve shirt, with a black Polo coat on and brown Polo boots buckled and strapped. I could see the imprint of his gun in the front as I closed and locked the door.

He turned to look at me with those sleepy eyes and curly hair trying to grow back in, holding the flowers out.

His eyes, for once, showed some type of emotion. It was fear.

"I got these for you," he said softly.

I took the roses, opened the door, and tossed them out in the front yard before closing the door back to look at him. Noelle London was not playing any games that night.

"What the fuck do you want, Shiloh?" I asked, sitting down on the couch, keeping the pink towel close. "You want to talk, so talk."

I watched him take his coat off. He sat down with a heavy sigh on the opposite couch, looking at his hands in a nervous state. Talking wasn't his strong point with me, so I planned to make him as uncomfortable as possible by just being silent.

He looked at me with sad, puppy-dog eyes. "I'm sorry, Noelle," he said. "I apologize for my actions last week and for accusing you of taking something that belonged to me. I should have had more trust in you."

I remained quiet, just looking at him, watching him take that deep gulp.

"Can you say something, shawty?"

I just stared at him, my face blank. I had all the time in the world. It was Saturday night, and I planned on watching all the seasons of *Living Single* and eating a bowl of ice cream. I had originally planned on being caught in my feelings, but this was much better.

Getting up, seeing he wasn't going to say anything else, I just pretended like he wasn't there. I continued on with my nightly rituals in the bathroom, coming out with my hair wrapped, wearing a T-shirt and panties. I slipped on my socks and cut the TV on.

"So, you just not gonna say shit back?" he asked.

Cutting the kitchen light off with my bowl in hand, I plopped down on the couch and started watching my favorite show. It really did feel like he wasn't there, to be honest.

"I need to fucking talk to you, Noelle. You ignoring me ain't gonna get us nowhere," he snapped.

I paused the TV and looked at him with a soft smile—fake, of course. "I'm listening," was all I said, and his eyes softened up.

"I don't . . ." he started, dropping his head. "Can you stop acting like this? Go off on me, yell or scream. Something," he begged, looking back at me.

I just stared. It was time for me to talk now. Delicately placing the bowl on the table, I cleared my throat. "You honestly think you can walk in my house, apologize, give me some cheap-ass roses in the dead middle of winter, thinking I want to watch that shit die in my house, then give me some weak-ass apology? Nigga, you antisocial, mood-switching-having ass, scared to open yo' mouth around me unless it's about money, mothafucka can't cook but stay begging for food, think I'm supposed to be scared of you because of your fuck-ass last name, dick-curving-having . . . all yo' brothers lame like you! How dare you step in my house and tell me to talk? Tell me we not going to get nowhere if I'm ignoring you. I'm not trying to get nowhere with you no more! Get out!" I screamed, throwing the remote. He was shocked. "I said get out! Don't sit there acting like you don't know fucking English, nigga! You got that GED in prison, nigga, so I know you can read, write, and hear correctly! Get out!"

He looked so hurt, I had to check myself, because I was about to give in to that face, but seeing he wasn't moving, I stood up to stand in front of him. "I'm not playing with you tonight, Shiloh. You—"

"I said I was sorry, Noelle!" he let out, taking my hands.

"You can't possibly love me if you don't trust me, Shiloh!" I cried, feeling him pull me down toward him on

the couch, wrapping his arms around me. "I wasted so
much energy and time with you."

"No, you didn't. I—"

I pushed him away from me before sitting on the couch,
facing the opposite direction of him. Arms crossed, I
stared him down. He just kicked his shoes off, propped his
feet up on the small love seat, and grabbed my feet.

I'd been wanting him to massage my feet for the longest.
After seeing Talin do it for his pregnant wife, I wanted in
on that action. I used to tell him real men did it, but he
refused. It's amazing what guys will do to get back on their
woman's good side.

"Can you forgive me?" he asked, rubbing my left foot.

I felt myself calming down. "I'm assuming you found
out who took your money," I stated in a dull voice, watching his hands.

"Not important, shawty. Can you forgive me? I won't
ever question your trust, love, and loyalty again, baby.
I made that mistake, and I'm trying not to make the
mistake of losing you for good," he pleaded, sounding
sincere.

Resting my head against the couch, I pulled my feet
from his hands with a sigh. He leaned forward onto my
body, bringing me close as he kissed the side of my face
repeatedly.

"Shiloh!" I shrieked, trying not to laugh. "I am still mad
at you!"

"But you love a nigga, right?" he pressed, kissing my
neck. "Long as you love me, I know you not going nowhere,
just like I'm not going nowhere," he mumbled against my
skin before kissing my chest.

"Shiloh, it shouldn't be that easy," I breathed, closing
my eyes as he playfully bit at my nipple through the thin
shirt. I should have worn a bra. It was a small percent
chance I knew this was going to happen.

Lifting his head up, he looked at me before sliding up to kiss me on the lips. It was our first kiss since our first big fight. The spark was still there, and the emotions were still there, if not stronger than before, since we'd been apart for so long.

"I love you, and I'm sorry, baby," he said against my mouth, looking me in the eyes.

"I love you too," I said, touching his hair as we kissed again.

Turning over, he laid his head on my stomach, placing himself in between my legs, with my thighs up, as he reached for the remote that I threw at him. He pressed PLAY.

Looking down at the man I love to hate and hate to love, I smirked. "You would watch *Living Single* with me?" I asked curiously.

"Maxine is my bitch," he said casually, and I smiled.

I have a man that watches Living Single. *Wonder if he's into* Sex in the City.

"Was there something else you wanted to talk to me about?" I asked.

"Yeah, but not now. We'll talk about it later on. Let me enjoy being with you."

I smiled as I turned my attention back to the TV, rubbing his head. We didn't last ten minutes without us going to my bedroom and making it up to each other in the best physical way possible.

Slow, steady, and sensual was his mood that night as he repeated over and over how sorry he was. My nails dug into his back, with my legs wrapped around his body. We rocked up and down together slowly, kissing and apologizing to each other.

This man was probably the craziest person I'd ever met. He had a temper unlike any other, yet he was the only man I saw myself with for the rest of my life.

Protector, provider, and a lover was what I needed in a partner. I was the right amount of sweetness against his cold personality, but I could stoop to his level if I ever needed to check him. We were perfect together.

Eyes locking once more, he pressed hard in me as we both released at the exact same time, our eyes never leaving each other.

"I love you, queen," he said in a shaky voice, kissing me as my body jerked against his.

I love it when men go out of their way to be so nice, so overly romantic, to stay on your good side. It's the best feeling in the world.

The next day, Shiloh, his grandmother who I finally met, and I went to church together. All three of us were in the car, with me allowing her in the front seat as I listened to them talk.

"Yeah, I told yo' uncle I wasn't having all them fancy drinks at my house. We gon' have babies walking around there, too?" she said, hand on Shiloh's arm as he drove smoothly out of the church parking lot. "Noelle, you went to Bible school when you were younger, right?"

"Yes, ma'am," I said, and we began passing Scriptures back and forth, with Shiloh rolling his eyes every so often.

I could tell he was not a believer in God. He claimed no religion. I guess he rolled one too many times, because she caught him out the side of her view and popped him hard in the face.

"What I do?" he shrieked as I laughed.

"Boy, don't be rolling yo' eyes to the Word. I see you over there!" she retorted. "Honey, these boys here about to make me crazy. They used to run me ragged."

"Oh, I bet." I smiled, with Shiloh glancing back at me.

We continued to drive, until we made it to her house, seeing cars were already parked. It was such a beautiful Sunday, with the sun shining and somewhat warm weather on this winter day. I had to bring a change of clothes. I wasn't going to be wearing this dress all day. I wanted to be comfortable.

"Noelle, baby, when you get changed, I want you to meet everybody," she said as Shiloh helped her out of the truck.

I could already hear the music going, and I could tell this was going to be a good old-fashioned old folks' get-together, just like back home. Yet, the moment I walked through the door, I was sadly mistaken. These people were literally attempting to turn up. Earth, Wind, and Fire were playing. I could smell weed in the air, and the grill was going on in the back, with people dancing. There was a table for the older guys playing spades.

Shiloh greeted everyone, introducing me as his woman. All the women sitting together on the couch were swapping stories, and the kids were running in and out of the basement. I followed Shiloh up to his room, where he closed the door so I could change.

"Your family is so beautiful," I said as he sat down on the bed.

"Shit, that's just one side. You ain't seen the Carters yet." He yawned, laying back on the full-size bed. "That's when the bullshit begins."

Looking around the dark room, I smiled at all the basketball posters and pictures of naked women. Just like a boy's room. I wondered how many girls he brought in there. I looked back at my man, seeing his eyes were closed, and he had slipped his shirt off, just leaving his jeans and socks on. I smiled.

"How many hoes did you sneak in here?" I asked, slipping out of my dress.

"Not as many as you would think." He laughed.

Putting my hair in a ponytail, I slipped on some dark blue skinny jeans and my sorority T-shirt, and I swapped my heels for pink Air Max sneakers. Removing the church makeup, I applied just a basic eye color and foundation, with Shiloh no doubt watching me.

"What, babe?" I said, fixing my hair.

"Just watching you," was all he said as the door opened.

One of the little kids that had gone with us on our date barged in before running back out, laughing. I heard the feet paddle down the stairs.

"Let the bullshit begin, shawty. The Carters are here." He sighed, getting up.

"Does your family not get along with your dad's side?" I asked.

"My daddy got three baby mamas, Noelle," was all he said, and I nodded. "They love all the kids as one, but nah, fuck nah."

Following him down the steps, my mouth dropped at the wave of people I'd never seen before come walking in with drinks in their hand. Some were arguing, while the kids nearly knocked people over with their running. Shiloh grabbed one of the little boys to reprimand him as I hugged his brothers.

"Noelle! I'm glad you decided to take this foolish nigga back!" Anthony said with a laugh as we hugged. "Came to my house in the middle of the night, crying over you, shawty."

"Bruh! You know goddamn well I wasn't—"

"Are you serious?" I laughed just as an older woman stepped in between us, resembling Anthony.

"Since my boy is so goddamn rude, can't introduce me to—"

"Mama, I was finna do it." Ant sighed. "Noelle, this is Ontrell and my mama—"

"Heeeey, people! Where the drinks at?" I spotted Elijah's mom walk in, with Trent in the wheelchair and Elijah pushing him. "Where's the birthday girl at?"

"Oooh, I can't stand this bitch," Anthony's mama mumbled with a roll of her eyes.

Oh my Lord, what have I gotten myself into?

Everything started happening at once. People were talking over each other, and the men claimed they could throw down on the grill. The spades table got a little violent, but once I realized there were some old Greek heads in the house, I started to build on that. As soon as they played "Atomic Dog," all the guys who were Greek got in on it.

I was sitting on Shiloh's lap outside in the backyard with a beer in his hand as I watched his uncles start to hop, with Trent hyping them up.

"Pretty boy over there can't move in that wheelchair! Look at ya!" one of them cracked, and Trent laughed.

"I can call up my people now if you want me to, Unc! You know I would do it!" Trent laughed.

"Nah-uh!" one of the aunties said as she started to stroll.

I instantly recognized it, jumping up behind her, following her lead.

"Ayyyeee!"

"Where is Olivia at?" someone called out.

I locked eyes with Shiloh, who was smiling, watching me.

"Y'all really about to have a stroll-off without the best sorority?" another lady asked. I was eyeing that royal blue shirt she had on.

Taylor, with her plate in her hand, joined in, too, and we all strolled around the yard, doing our calls like the old times.

"Bruh, I will never understand this shit," Shiloh said to Elijah, who shook his head.

I watched Anthony, Jahiem, Trell, and Talin walk out the back door to find a seat. Shiloh dug in the cooler to pass them each a beer. As soon as the song changed, we all laughed it out, catching our breath. I took my seat back on Shiloh's lap.

Everything came to a calm as the evening started to take over the sky. We were listening to the older generation tell stories. The men on both sides of the family got along well, but the women barely spoke.

"Oh, yeah, I remember back in my day when people sold that shit because they had to. Not because it was a cool thing to do," one of the men said. "You sold dope back then to make ends meet."

"But you selling it to your own people," another argued as they tossed some wood into the center of the yard. Giant rocks were placed in a circle as someone set the wood on fire, creating a bonfire.

"It doesn't fucking matter who we selling it to, youngin'," the man snapped. "That was the game back then. People nowadays doing that shit because they think it's cool, but don't know the first thing about dope, crack, any of it. All they know is sagging their pants and listening to this tired-ass rap music."

I looked at Shiloh, who was listening closely before glancing at me.

"Who is he?" I asked.

"My dad's brother Christian," he said softly, smoothing my hair back.

"He sold drugs too?"

"We all did. It was the family business for the longest. Still is," he said, pulling my hips closer to his waist to adjust my weight. "You just haven't seen all of them yet. This family shit runs deep as fuck, baby."

"Wow," I said, amazed, as I tuned back in to the heated debate.

Glancing at Elijah, I saw that he had his head down, with a beer bottle in his hand. He was keeping quiet, with Jahiem trying to talk to him. I guess Shiloh looked back at him before looking at me.

"He missing that girl," he said.

"E!" one of the men called out, tossing a napkin at him. "Boy, you sick or something?"

"Nah, Uncle," he mumbled, barely looking up.

"You some big ol' fancy superstar now, but you sitting here looking like yo' cat died."

"His girlfriend broke up with him," Trent snitched easily as Elijah cut his eyes at him.

"Boy, all this pussy running around here and you worried about one girl?" The man laughed. He was definitely a Carter. If that didn't give it away, the gun tucked behind him did.

Before anything else could be said, we heard this loud commotion, followed by a scream, coming from the house.

"Get out! Get out my house!" their grandma cried.

We all quickly got up to see two grown-ass women having it out on the floor. It was Elijah's mom and Anthony's mom. The men broke them apart, and you could see wigs on the floor, broken furniture, and clothes halfway off.

"That's why he never wanted to be with yo' ass!" Anthony's mom cried as he pulled her away.

Ms. Ava, I think was her name, turned to Shiloh, looking like she expected him to help her. He just turned and walked back to his seat like it was nothing. Elijah moved past her and headed upstairs, so I thought I would reach my hand out to help her get herself together. I thought wrong, clearly. She smacked my hand away at the same time Shiloh chastised me.

"Don't help her, Noelle. Let her look stupid," Shiloh snapped, sitting back down in his chair as Ms. Ava's eyes started to water.

"Boy, I told you about talking to yo' mother like—"

"Grandma, I don't care! You hear me? I don't give a fuck!" he let out angrily, immediately setting off the biggest verbal jump I'd ever seen take place with Shiloh.

"Nobody told you to disrespect yo' own mama like that! She gave birth to you! She—"

"No! He don't wanna hear nothing like that!" Ms. Ava cried as she pushed me aside to step out of the house so she could confront her eldest son. "He don't wanna hear that I carried his ungrateful ass for nine months, fed him, clothed him, bathed him! Wiped and cleaned his nasty ass for years! I could have—"

"You wasting yo' time on me, Ms. Ava," Shiloh said in a low voice as he stared at her, eyes cold and dark as night.

His uncle, out of nowhere, took his apron off, hauled off, and hit Shiloh hard in the face, causing the biggest reaction I'd ever seen. I couldn't react fast enough when Jahiem, Trell, and Talin all jumped in, ready to defend and fight with Shiloh. His mother started crying, pleading with her brother not to hit him again.

Okay, so he isn't a Carter? I can't keep up with this shit.

"You talking all that big shit, nigga! Fight me! You not about to talk to my sister, yo' mama, like that, boy! I'm sick of her crying to me about yo' ungrateful ass!"

"Aye! Aye, you not about to touch my nephew, big dawg," another man said, stepping in between the two groups. "You already know I'm not about to let you lay a hand on these kids."

"They grown men, Christian!" Ms. Ava said. "Let them fight with grown men, since Shiloh wanna run his—"

"Hold up! Hold up! Let me set this straight, because I'm sick of this. Every time I see you, it's always some bullshit, so I'm going to be grown about it," Shiloh said, moving past everyone to get to his mother, jaw red from the hit his uncle gave him.

He stood in front of her, eye for eye. She immediately broke down in front of him, crying as we all watched in heartache. She was pleading to have her son back. He wasn't moved—far from it.

"I respect you for raising me up until Grandma got me. I respect and appreciate all the things you did for me and the triplets," he said, hand on her shoulder. "But I don't want nothing to do with you. When I marry that girl," he said, pointing at me, "don't show up at my wedding. When I have my firstborn, you will be nowhere near my kids, and you know why! Don't sit here and act like you so innocent, because nobody else knows what the fuck you let happen!"

She dropped her head in defeat, tears flowing. Nobody else said a word. They were just looking on like I was, in shock, confusion, and hurt.

"This is my last time saying this. I don't want it to be an issue every time we all get together. Just act like you don't know me, because that's exactly how I'm going to treat you." With that, he turned back and sat in his chair as everyone looked at his mom.

Trent was the first to speak. "Bruh, I don't think you should—"

"Nah, let that be the end of it!" one of the uncles said, turning his attention back to the grill. "Tired of the bullshit myself. Whatever they got going on is between them two. So much goddamn drama in this family, I almost forgot it was Sunday. Go cut the TV on and see who's playing!" he called out.

"Bruh, what the fuck did she let happen?" Elijah asked, coming to the doorway, looking irritated. "You never said why you don't want shit to do with her."

"Mind yo' business, E," Shiloh warned, eyes only for his mom.

"She's my mama too, nigga! What the fuck are you always so angry for? 'Cause she called the cops on yo' violent ass? I would have too! You need to learn to—"

"It don't have shit to do with you," Jahiem cut in.

"You not even related to her, so why the fuck are you even talking?" Trent asked as Jahiem stood up once again.

"Stay yo' cripple ass down in that seat, nigga," Jahiem snapped as Ms. Ava shook her head, walking back in the house, crying.

I looked at Shiloh, who showed absolutely no compassion. None whatsoever. Hearing the front door open and close, I looked back, seeing their sister with her two friends walking in.

"Hellooo?" she sang. She was wearing riding boots with a cute brown leather jacket, hair straightened with that side bang swoop as she walked in, all smiles. Her friends? I couldn't even describe them to you. I could see why Taylor didn't hang around her as much.

"There goes my baby girl!" one of the uncles let out as she shrieked in excitement, rushing up to the men. They were all babying her and hugging her like she was the ray of sunshine during this dark time.

"I need to sit down." I sighed, walking back in the house, needing time to process everything that had just happened.

Taylor came in behind me, flat out ignoring Trent, who was calling her name as we walked closer to the front door, sitting down in the dining room. The grandma, whose birthday celebration this was supposed to be, just walked upstairs, cussing to herself, following after her daughter.

"Girl," Taylor said with a roll of her eyes and a deep sigh. "This has been pretty calm compared to what it can usually get to."

"Are you serious?" I gasped, hearing the sounds of arguing once more.

She nodded, afro bouncing as she looked back down.

"Why aren't you and Olivia speaking?" I asked.

"Because the bitch is not who I became best friends with. I don't know this Olivia," she said hatefully. "I don't deal with—"

The front door opened, and a girl walked in with a gift bag, wearing a beautiful black gownlike dress with a coat on. Her hair and makeup were done to perfection.

"Jordyn!" Taylor yelled out as she quickly got up to hug her. "I'm glad to see you made it."

"Yeah, I thought I was almost too late," she said, closing the door.

I politely smiled.

She started to look around. "What's going on? I thought it was like a party or something."

"Girl, you right in the middle of—"

"Nigga, do something!" I heard Elijah yell, and we all scrambled to crane our necks down the hall, seeing Shiloh and Elijah about to go at it.

"Oh my God," I groaned, making my way over.

"Elijah!" Jordyn called, and he quickly turned around, eyes wide as he looked at her.

He nearly tripped over his feet to rush over to her. "You—" He wrapped his arms around her neck so quick, nearly knocking her back, and he immediately started begging forgiveness.

"Y'all are so cute," Taylor cooed.

I went to grab Shiloh. I was ready to go. This place was nothing but drama everywhere I fucking went. Luckily, Shiloh was on the same page, along with the rest of his brothers.

"You out?" Jahiem asked, slapping hands with Shiloh as he grabbed our things.

"Yeah. I should have never come here."

"Don't even worry about it, bruh," Jahiem said. "I'm about to make this trip to Albany tonight. Yo, Olivia got some bad-ass friends. You seen ol' girl with the tattoos?"

"She was looking at me," Trell boasted as Shiloh put his hand on my lower back to guide me out of the house.

"Lemme take a walk. I need to calm myself down," Shiloh mumbled.

I slipped my coat on and followed him, keeping quiet, so he could have his own thoughts. Hearing the car engines start up as people started to leave, I looked at my man, seeing the pain and hurt in his eyes. What the hell happened between him and his mom that caused him to act like that toward her?

"You okay?" I asked softly as we walked down the hill, using the streetlights to guide us. I stopped him from walking as we stood next to a curb. I looked up at him.

"I'm sorry you had to see that," was all he said, eyes on the ground, looking like a little boy who was hurt.

Cupping his face to bring his eyes back to me, I could see him trying to hold it in, to block off any emotion. Yet, the moment I caught those eyes watering up, I immediately used my thumbs to press down on his eyes as he closed them. Wiping away any stray tear, I brought him close for a hug. He needed to let it out, whatever it was. He needed to release it, so he could move on from it. I wasn't going to ask questions. I wasn't going to speak; just let him release it.

Jordyn

"Can't believe I'm doing this," I mumbled to myself, pulling up to this two-story brick house. I'd just finished my Christmas concert, and I felt like ignoring Elijah wasn't the right thing to do. Plus, he had my phone in his truck. We needed to actually talk and work through some things, instead of me pretending everything was okay all the time.

Parking alongside the curb, I got out, lifting my dress up so it wouldn't drag. My signature long-sleeve black gown hugged my body just enough to see a peek of the curves. I wore a simple silver necklace, and my hair was done in a bun as I walked up to the house, hearing music playing. With a simple birthday card and a gift card to Barnes & Noble since I heard she liked to read, I pushed the already open door, hearing the commotion from the back.

"Jordyn!" Taylor screamed out as she got up to hug me. "I'm glad to see you made it."

"Yeah, I thought I wasn't going to make it," I said, glancing at Shiloh's girlfriend, who gave me a tired, fake smile. "What's going on? I thought it was supposed to be a party or something?" I asked, looking at Taylor before glancing at the chaos out back.

"Girl, you right in the middle of—"

"Nigga, do something!" I could hear Elijah scream. Noelle and Taylor quickly got up to see what I was seeing. Shiloh and Elijah were squaring off. I sighed. Noelle started to go toward them, but I decided to cut it short.

"Elijah!" I called to him, and he turned around, eyes wide, mouth dropped. I shyly waved to him with a slow shake of my head. Almost tripping on his own two feet, he ran up to me, nearly knocking me down as his arms came around my neck.

"Elijah, you're about to make me fall!" I laughed.

"I'm sorry, Jordyn. I'm so sorry," he repeated over and over as Taylor cooed. He looked back at me before kissing me hard on the mouth, and I tasted beer. "I fucked up, and I shouldn't have—"

"We can talk about it later. I have a gift for your grandma," I said, seeing all his brothers making their way out. Shiloh and I locked eyes, and he gave me a heads up in greeting. I smiled back just as their grandma came down.

Elijah introduced the two of us, with his mom right behind her. Even though I wasn't there, I could tell a lot had happened. Everyone looked mentally drained.

By the time we got in my car, since he rode with his mom and Trent, I was curious to know what had happened in there. Letting him drive, I popped open a bottle of beer, taking a swig as we shared, enjoying the night ride to his favorite wing spot.

"So much shit, baby." He sighed, rubbing his head as he glanced at me. "So much deep-rooted issues between everyone. Only person that don't have no drama is Livie. She's peaceful all around with the fam."

"Mmm," I said. "I bet."

He looked at me with those hopeful, sleepy eyes. I already knew what was coming next. "Can you come over tonight? Stay the night with me? Let me make it up to you?"

"Elijah." I sighed, turning to him. "We have so much we need to figure out between us before we even begin to think about—"

"I know," he said, cutting me off as he got on the highway. "I know that, Jordyn."

"Sooo, I mean, we can't just not talk about it or ignore it. I'm tired of acting like everything is okay with us. I let you get away with so much shit, Elijah, and you know it. You take advantage of my soft, quiet nature, expecting me to—"

"Hold up." He laughed with a shake of his head. "You far from quiet, shawty."

"I am!"

"No the fuck you not, Jordyn. I do apologize if you feel that way, but you far from quiet. Get that shit right."

"This isn't funny! I'm trying to tell you how I feel, Elijah! You sleeping with these girls in front of me, telling everyone about the abortion, and . . . and . . . I'm sick of how you talk to me like I'm just some random bitch in the club. You think everything is fucking funny. You refuse to tell me you love me, but you have no problem scaring my boyfriend into breaking up with me, and . . ." I sat back in the seat with my arms crossed. "That's all I have to say." I took another shot of the beer angrily.

He looked at me with that tongue sticking out the corner of his mouth and a goofy-ass smile because once again, everything was funny to him.

"Jordyn?"

"What, Elijah?" I snapped, watching him pull into the parking lot in front of the small wing shop. He leaned in and kissed me sloppily on the lips. "Ew, Elijah! Move!" I freaked, trying to push him away, but he stuck that tongue out, trying to lick all over before coming to my neck. "Elijah!" I laughed. "I was being serious!"

Pulling away, he eyed me with a small smile as I wiped my soaked mouth and neck.

"You're so fucking disgusting, Elijah. I swear I don't even know how I deal with you," I mumbled.

"I'm about to knock all yo' issues out the park right now, shawty," he said, and I cut my eyes at him. "Will you be my girlfriend?" My mouth dropped. "My one and only girlfriend."

"Yes." I smiled.

"Will you forgive me? Because I am just a simple-ass nigga who is too dumb to see the girl he was meant to be with has been in front of my face this entire time, grandma glasses on and everything," he teased.

"Yes, I forgive you, Elijah," I answered, moving his wild locs out of his face as he smirked at me.

"Will you move in with me? My house looks a fucking mess, and I don't want to clean it by myself," he said. I outright laughed before nodding my head.

He continued, "When the day comes and I pop that question on whether or not you want to marry a nigga, will you say yes?"

I gasped. *Not even . . . I don't . . . how in the hell did he even word that question?*

"I will say yes," I said with a soft smile.

His eyes lit up like a little kid as he leaned in and kissed me gently on the lips.

"You know I've been in love with you since the moment you told me you was bisexual, shawty," he teased, and I laughed.

"Yeah right, Elijah."

"Real talk, I've been in love with you longer than you have with me, baby," he said, kissing me. "A nigga is straight-up crazy about yo' nerdy ass, baby. You got my heart, my soul, my everything. All you. I'm just a simple man without you."

"That was so sweet, Jaja," I cooed, using the pet name I gave him when I caught him sleeping with fingers in his mouth like a pure baby.

"You ready to go home, baby?" he asked. "This is my last night before I get back to work, so we gon' make this count; you feel me?"

I nodded. Sure enough, we stopped and got the wings, grabbed a bottle of E & J, went to his house, straight to his room with his two dogs chilling on the floor, and watched *Scandal,* starting from Season 1. That's how we turned up on a regular, watching shows on Netflix. Rarely did we have wild sex with other women. It happened, but this was mostly what we did when we were together. He'd smoke, we'd eat naked, and then watch these shows.

"Aye, look at this." Elijah laughed, showing me a text message. His brother Anthony sent a picture of his car scratched up with the windows broken. The caption read: 2nd baby mama did this.

"Your family is something else." I sighed with a shake of my head as he leaned back.

"They are," he agreed. "Carter boys stay in some mess, baby. Always have, always will."

Tia

Sunday night, I was sitting in the bed, rubbing cocoa butter on my stomach once again. I could barely get any sleep, even after a full meal. Glancing at the clock, I saw it was going on 1 a.m. Shit, I guess it was Monday morning then. Sitting in the bed with my thick socks and shorts, with my shirt raised above my protruding stomach, I sighed. I was content. Not happy, but I was good. Blessed.

"I do want me something to drink, though," I mumbled, getting up. Walking down the hallway, I headed for the kitchen, seeing headlights pulling in the driveway.

"Who the fuck is coming here at this time of night?" I walked toward the front foyer and peeped out the window, spotting a red—

"No the nigga did not just pull up to this house," I said, mouth dropped. I started to unlock the door but realized this door creaked so damn loudly it was bound to wake everyone in the house. Hearing the car door slam and the alarm sound off, I quickly opened the window, seeing Jahiem look around the area, looking lost.

"Nigga!" I hissed, and his head turned toward the door. "What the fuck are you doing—"

"Tia?" he questioned, heavy-ass boots stepping up to the porch. "You need to—"

"What are you doing here?" I whispered loudly.

"Fuck you mean, what I'm doing here? You—"

"Lower your voice!" I snapped before looking back, knowing I was loud as shit just then, and hoping I woke no one up. "Meet me around the side of the house, Jahiem. That side window."

"Just come out."

"Now!" I snapped, hearing him groan. I quickly ran to my room, careful not to cause too much commotion, and popped up my window, pushing the screen out as he appeared. He stood there with his thick red coat on, looking at me like I'd lost my mind.

"I'm too old to be sneaking through windows."

"Nigga, I'm pregnant with no damn clothes on. I'm not coming outside."

"So, just let me in the front door."

"Jahiem, we not about to sit here and argue. Either get in, or I'm calling the cops on you."

He bit his tongue as he tried to lift his thick leg up to get inside. With me holding onto his arm, I tried pulling his stiff-ass body in the small window before nearly falling back on the floor as he fell back on the ground, hollering out.

"I shouldn't have to do this shit!" he screamed as I quickly got up, trying to help his loud, ignorant ass in the room.

As soon as I got him inside, I closed the window. His eyes went to my stomach, and he immediately dropped his mouth. He hadn't seen me in a while, so the growth was shocking to him. Yet, looking at him, I couldn't help but feel the rush of emotions I had for him, standing tall with his trimmed beard, dark pink lips, and dark brown eyes, looking hard at my stomach. He had a red coat on, looking like a fashionable Blood out of New York with those boots. I gently sat back on the bed, lifting my shirt, and continued on with my cocoa butter as if I didn't just sneak this man into my room.

"You been getting regular checkups down here?" he asked, looking around the room before sitting on the edge of the bed.

I reached down below to grab the pictures from the 3D ultrasound I had the other day, showing all three bodies perfectly placed in my stomach.

"Here," I said without looking at him.

He took the photos and stared with such an intense look that he could have burned a hole through the damn thing.

"Three girls, already named. First and middle."

"You not gonna give 'em my last name?" he asked, eyes on me.

"I thought about it," I said, shrugging. "Still thinking on it.

"Why she off to herself?" he asked, pointing at one baby, who was separate from her sisters.

"Nigga, I don't know." I laughed softly, watching him smile as he continued to look.

"So, what now?" he asked, looking at me as I continued to rub this cocoa butter on me. Shit was the most relaxing thing I could do, like therapy.

"You tell me, Jahiem. All I know is right now, I'm about to rub this butter on my stomach before I go to sleep. I got work in the morning," I said.

He glanced at his phone. "You won't come back to Atlanta?"

"I won't. Not until after the babies are born."

"So, you really about to make me come all the way down here every time I want to see yo' fuck ass?"

"Yep," I said, cutting him off. "And *whet,* nigga? What's the problem?"

He kicked his shoes off, put his feet up on the bed with me, took his coat off, and brought my legs down closer to him, spreading them out over each thigh. Without another word, he took the cocoa butter jar from me, placing it on his side as he started to rub my stomach with it.

"You been doing the yoga I showed you?" he asked as I lay back, closing my eyes. I nodded. Told y'all Jahiem was into that organic, all-natural type of lifestyle. When people looked at him, all they saw was a nigga gang-banging, gun tucked, and some local rap star. When people knew him, they would see he was into meditating, eating healthy, reading books constantly, and always the one to talk about what the black community needs to do as a whole to improve. Y'all see how he get on me about wearing weave and makeup around him. He hated it. Nigga was a tree hugger to a T. We were so opposite, clashing constantly, but here we were about to bring three girls into the world.

"Shouldn't be putting this stuff on you, shawty," he said, reading the ingredients of the jar. "Shea butter is better for your skin. I keep telling you that."

"Jahiem, why are you here?" I questioned. "I'm not leaving to go back to Atlanta with you, so you really wasted a trip."

"Nah, but I wanted to see you, so I came. Been through too much shit these past few days, and I'm tired, Mama. I'm tired," he said with a sigh. "I can't—and refuse—to let you raise three kids on your own, especially if they're mine."

"If?" I snorted with another roll of my eyes.

"I know they're mine."

"Oh, now you know, nigga."

"Chill out, Tia. Wrong nigga, wrong night," he warned, and I immediately grew quiet. He was the only nigga I let check me. Only one. Anyone else would have been popped in the face, but Jahiem got it.

"You—"

The door swung open as Noelle's dad came in with the bat in hand, wearing nothing but some damn briefs, with that stomach poked out.

"It's not what it looks like!" I shrieked. "He's my—"

"Get on out of here, boy!" he yelled to Jahiem, who quickly got up, hands in the air.

"Aye, I'm not here to—"

"Get out! We don't tolerate that kind of foolery in my house! Not under my roof!" he yelled as Jahiem quickly got his things.

Needless to say, we were both kicked out of the house. So, with my things stuffed in the back seat, I texted Noelle, telling her what happened and telling her I would see her in Atlanta.

"And you wanted to stay down here?" Jahiem laughed, looking over at me.

I hit him hard on the arm. "It's not funny. They took me in—"

"And kicked yo' ass out. You should have just let me in through the front door like I said earlier."

"Whatever, Jahiem," I mumbled, looking out at the dark sky. It was going to be a long-ass drive with just us two in the car. *Ugh.*

"Aye, you hungry?" he asked, pointing to a field of trees. There was nothing on the road for miles and miles. We probably passed only one or two houses every so often.

"What are they besides trees?" I questioned as he pulled over to the side of the road.

"Come here," he said, getting out.

I followed him, wrapping my coat around me as he stood in front of the small wooden fence.

"Peach trees."

"Get me one!"

"Get me a bag out the car or something," he called out, hopping the barrier as I quickly went inside the car to find a plastic bag.

As soon as I came to the fence, watching him jump up to pull a few down, I smiled. I couldn't believe this nigga here was stealing peaches from somebody's land. A porch light came on from the house nearby, and I nearly dropped the bag as I rushed back to the car.

"Shit!" Jahiem blurted out, trying to climb the wooden fence before falling flat on his face.

"Jahiem!" I laughed. "Baby, are you okay?"

He got to his feet and ran to the driver's side, slipping into the car with ease as the peaches fell out of his hands, onto his lap.

I quickly grabbed them all as he took off, wiping dirt and grass from his face.

"Damn! You see how big these things are?" he asked excitedly, holding one up before taking a bite. I grabbed one to take a bite and smiled. I guess since it was slightly warmer down here than Atlanta, they were still able to grow before taking them in. Whatever the case, it was good.

"You so damn clumsy, nigga," I said with a laugh, remembering that fall.

"Aye, I'm too big to be doing all this 007 shit," he said, picking up speed on the lonely highway.

We sat in silence for a while, just enjoying the peaches, throwing out the pits, and occasionally looking at each other.

"*Whet*, Jahiem?" I snapped, seeing him smile. "*Whet* you gotta say now, nigga?"

"What the fuck is *whet*?" he mocked, and I laughed.

"It just comes out. I don't mean to say it on purpose." I giggled as he smiled at me.

"You ghetto as shit, Mama."

"But you carry a gun with you, and walk around with yo' red flag like it's nothing, but I'm ghetto? If I'm ghetto, nigga, you hood as shit then. Fuck outta here," I retorted.

He stopped the car dead in the middle of the highway. I looked back, seeing no cars coming, before looking at him.

"We about to have three kids," he said in a low voice, looking at me. Suddenly, reality hit him hard. "Three at once."

"It was always a possibility," I said.

He leaned in and kissed me. It was our first kiss since breaking up. Cupping his face gently, I pulled away to look at him. He was the man that tricked me into sleeping with him, and I was so glad he did. That dick was made for me. I swear it was.

"Shit is going to be hard with my job and everything. Small-ass condo, neither one of us have parenting experience—"

"I'm going to have my job once I graduate," I chimed in.

He cocked his head back, looking hard at me. "You not working—"

"Nigga, *whet*? I'm not working?" I repeated with a laugh. "I did not go to college to get a degree and not put it to use, nigga."

"So, who is going to watch the kids?"

"Babysitters, daycare, and—"

"Nah," he said, sitting back in his seat as he continued to drive with a shake of his head. "I see now we already gonna have a problem. I don't want no stranger watching my kids, Mama. I don't believe in that daycare shit."

"I'm not gonna sit at home like no housewife and do nothing. I want my own money too."

"So, wait until they get in school, then—"

"We not about to have this conversation," I said, cutting him off.

We sat in silence as he continued to drive.

"I love you, Jahiem," I mumbled, still hearing him huff and puff about daycare to himself.

"Love you, too."

Just like that, our bipolar asses continued on with the drive without so much as a hate bone in our body.

Trent

"So, you just gonna leave a nigga here by himself?" I complained, watching Ontrell get his things together. I was back at the hospital on a Sunday night after leaving from my grandma's house. I didn't feel like I needed to be here, but physical therapy for walking and healing my scars was something nobody in my family wanted to put up with or had the time to deal with, so I was back at this depressing-ass place—white walls, white sheets, few channels on the TV, with a window looking out at nothing but another building.

"Bruh, we got so much shit to do tomorrow. Working on this new album, and I'm trying to dip into my own solo shit." Ontrell sighed, coming to the side of my bed. His hair was starting to grow in on the sides from where he shaved that shit. He was wearing a thick black trench coat with a new piercing on his left ear. "You gotta hold it down on yo' own, big bruh. Time is money, and—"

"Money is time," I mumbled, repeating what our dad used to tell us all the time, meaning put the time, energy, and effort into your investment, and in time, you'll see it come back to you.

"Where yo' girls at? Taylor not coming by?" he asked, checking his phone as I grabbed mine.

"Nah, she won't speak to me, but I know how to handle that easily." I smirked, knowing just what to say to get Taylor back in my hands, back on team Trent.

"A'ight, well, I'm out, big bruh," Ontrell said, coming to me with a quick hug. "Get better, nigga."

"I will," I said, watching Ontrell walk out.

I started to scroll through my phone, looking for Taylor's number and calling her on speaker.

"Hello?" she answered.

"What you doing, beautiful?" I asked with a grin, licking my lips. Whether it's over the phone or not, ya boy got the charm.

"I'm actually—"

"Aye, come on. We about to miss the movie," I heard a man say.

My body stiffened up, eyes coming close together in confusion.

"I have to go Tre—"

"You not gonna come to the hospital? I still need help," I let out. "Who the fuck is with you right now?"

"I'm on a—"

"Taylor, what you want to snack on?" the man asked as they started to talk. "You want those? Yeah, lemme get the Milk Duds for my girl. She likes chocolate and popcorn together." Nigga was talking like he knew her forever.

"It's so good, KD. You have to try it." Taylor laughed, and I cleared my throat, letting her know I was still on the fucking phone.

"Sounds nasty, shawty," he replied.

I looked at the phone before hanging up on her. "Didn't like yo' fat ass anyway," I muttered, scrolling through the phone to find Jade's new number. As soon as I found it, I pressed down with a smile.

"Yo?" she answered with that thick New York accent.

"Come see me in the hospital. I miss you," I said easily.

There was a moment of silence, then I heard her blow out her breath like she was smoking. Of course she was.

"I'm good, nigga," she responded softly.

"You what?"

"I said I'm good," she repeated more clearly. "Why you back in the hospital if you was already—"

"Come on, Jade," I groaned, frustrated. "I don't want to sleep alone in this place, and I don't want to be by myself. Can you just stop by for a minute? You not too far from here anyway, so I don't understand the problem," I snapped, trying but failing to keep my attitude in check. Last thing I wanted to do was argue when all I was trying to do was to get a female in my room.

"You right." She sighed. "I'll stop by in a few minutes to check on you."

"You know I love you, right?" I cheesed, trying to sit up in the bed.

"I love you too, baby," she cooed before hanging up.

"Hell yeah!" I shouted, feeling like I'd won the fucking lottery. You'd never catch me without a female by my side. Even when I was at my lowest and weakest point, I was going to have a chick with me.

Two Hours Later

I should have known she was lying. Should have fucking known. After repeatedly calling her back with her not answering, I gave up. I tried calling Taylor again, but she cut her phone off. No female was trying to deal with the nigga in the hospital bed. I called Elijah, my blood, my twin, my partner for life, but guess who answered?

"Hello?" Jordyn said softly.

"What y'all doing?" I asked, looking at the time. It was going on 12 o'clock at night.

"Elijah fell asleep during *Scandal*, and I'm not sure I want to wake him."

"Nah, nah, it's cool," I said quickly. "Talk to me, Jordyn. I feel like the loneliest nigga in Atlanta right now. I'm not used to this."

"Well, um . . . I was trying to go to sleep myself," she said, clearing her throat. "Maybe you should use this time to think about your year. Think about the things you've done, or what you could have done differently."

"For what, though?" I laughed. "My life is perfect, shawty. I don't need to rethink nothing. I'm good on this end. I survived bullets, I graduated school, and I got women that will do whatever just to get with me. I'm good on this end."

"Said the loneliest nigga in Atlanta right now," she retorted with a laugh. "Look, I'm going to sleep. It's inappropriate to be talking on the phone with you while your brother is sleeping next to me. So, on that note, good night, Trent. Use that time to reflect."

"Yeah, whatever," I mumbled, hanging the phone up. Lying back on the hospital bed, I looked up at the ceiling. *Fuck everybody. Shit.*

The Ending

Jade

So, we finally reached the end of this damn book. Since I started this shit, I'm going to be the first to end it.

Now that we hit the new year, I can honestly say my life hasn't changed much. I learned a lot from dating the prettiest Carter boy. Learned that I need to calm down all my dominance and know my worth as a woman. Still single, but I got a couple of dudes I'm talking to. Nothing serious. I wanted to use this new year to focus on me, school, and my art.

Haven't spoken to Trent since I told him I was going to see him in the hospital. Can't be around that type of energy. Nigga is so full of himself. The girl that he's meant to be with, I hope she makes it hard for him; make him work for it, because he needs to be taught a lesson. Getting shot wasn't enough for him. Just made him feel—Shit, why the fuck am I talking about this nigga on my story? Anyway! Spring semester is starting soon. New niggas, new places to see, and new vibes to mesh with. I'm ready for the new year. Time for me to do me.

I'm out.

Jordyn

"You were absolutely wonderful, Jordyn," a woman said, coming up to me to shake my hand.

I smiled, responding back in kind, while secretly looking around. *He said he would be here.* It was a New Year's Eve concert in New York that I was asked to play in. Of course, I never turned down money or a chance to showcase my skills on the violin to the world. It's always a great way to bring people together.

"Beautiful. She is absolutely amazing," a man said, coming up behind me as we shook hands. "I want to talk to you about having you perform in France for the ballet."

"There she is!" someone else called out.

I looked up, seeing two guys walking up to me with all smiles. Everyone was dressed in their finest gowns, tuxedos, and suits, looking stunning in the concert ballroom hallway as I mingled with the guests, all wanting to meet me. I had on a red gown to stand out in front of the all-black orchestra that accompanied me, with my hair pulled back and glasses on. Elijah broke my granny glasses in half by crushing them during sex. I think he did it on purpose, but he bought me another pair, slimmer and a bit more stylish. Yeah, pretty sure he broke them on purpose.

Looking around again as I pretended to listen to the conversation, I spotted a tall black man with dreads walking to the glass doors. I smiled, feeling myself getting excited. *He came. Elijah actually came.* I knew he wasn't going to make my performance due to scheduling differences, but he said he would dress up for me.

"Jordyn?" someone called out as I tuned back in, looking at Dale, the man who made this all happen. "Why don't you play something for these lovely people? Give them a taste of your imagination."

I smiled, holding the violin up in position as I began to play, eyes watching Elijah as he hung back, coat in his hand, watching me. To be honest, I had no idea what I was playing. I just knew that certain notes sounded good when played together, so I went with that as he came closer.

I wanted to scream. Seeing him in a suit for the first time was not all that I'd imagined. His locs were braided back into a ponytail, and he was wearing all black, including a tie, as he stepped closer with a lick of his lips. He knew he looked good, too. I wished he would have covered up the tattoos on his face, but I saw he tucked the chains in, keeping it simple with an all-black Rolex.

As soon as I stopped playing, I thanked everyone who clapped, raving on and on about my name, before I walked up to Elijah. My mouth dropped as I looked him all the way over.

"I look good, don't I, shawty?" he asked, licking his lips. His low-lid eyes were smiling just as much as his mouth with that cheesing grin.

"You look amazing," I said, arms coming around his neck as we hugged.

"We still going to the peach drop, or whatever the fuck fruit they dropping?" he asked, kissing me on the side of the face.

"Just a ball I think." I laughed, kissing him on the mouth before taking his hand to introduce him to some of my people. He wasn't able to transition like Trent, unfortunately, but it was funny seeing their reaction when he spoke.

"Elijah is a beautiful name," one lady commented. He nodded with a smile. "Do you two have plans later on?"

"Shiit," he let out, looking at me.

The lady's face nearly froze on stiff, giving that infamous white-person smile when they're uncomfortable around black people but trying not to show it. "She already know what my plans are for the night. She trying to see this whatever drop in Times Square, so I said I'm down with it, but she already know what the fuck I'm trying to do." He smiled sneakily at me.

"Oh, wow," a man said awkwardly, looking at both of us as I tried my hardest not to laugh.

On that note, I said my goodbyes and dragged Elijah out of there. The parking was unbelievable, and the crowd was even crazier. I had to take the train to get there, since certain streets were closed off.

People started recognizing him and wanted to take pictures as we stood in the freezing cold, waiting for this ball to drop. I had something I wanted to tell him the moment it hit midnight. So, as the countdown began, I grabbed his hand, seeing girls were trying to get close to him, sneaking pictures. As soon as the ball hit, the fireworks went off, lighting up the sky.

He turned to me. "I love you, Jordyn," he said, kissing me, cold lips hitting mine as we held it together, his hands gripping my lower back close. "Let that shit last you the whole year, because I ain't saying it no more," he said, and I laughed.

"I love you too, and I'm pregnant again," I said quickly, kissing him once more.

He pulled back with a shake of his head and a smile. My mind was already on another abortion and a better birth control option. Not only did we use a condom to prevent it from happening again, but we even said we couldn't go through another abortion, so no pregnancies could happen with us. Yet, here we were.

"I don't know how it happened, though!" I shouted toward him over the loud crowd.

"We'll just have to deal with it, shawty," he said, shrugging with a weak grin.

I looked hard at him, wondering if he knew something I didn't. Before I could even ponder on the thought, he leaned in and kissed me once more.

"We having a baby, Jojo!"

"We're having a baby," I repeated, barely whispering it over the loud noise as we smiled at each other. God knows I wasn't ready to have a damn child. Neither was he, but . . . wow.

I'm going to be a mother with the man I met at the gas station.

Tia

"Do you think she will like me?" I asked, smoothing my hair back.

Jahiem looked at me as he drove down east Atlanta, hitting close to Little Five Points near Moreland Ave. It was the beginning of January, and my man was only here for a day. He was going back to California tomorrow morning with his brothers.

"You'll be a'ight, Tia. My mama is cool. She don't have a mean bone in her body," he said with a shrug. "Told you to wear something comfortable, though, because she'll probably have you sit on the floor."

"Even though I'm pregnant?" I asked dully, looking at him. Nobody was going to allow a pregnant woman to sit on the damn floor.

"Okay!" He laughed, hands in the air. "You know Tonya Hayes better than me. Where you think I be getting half my shit from? All that organic stuff in the fridge, the soaps, and lotions? The yoga? She teaches that shit."

"That don't have nothing to do with her having basic furniture in the house," I snapped as he shook his head.

"You'll see," he mumbled.

We stayed quiet as I nervously looked out the window, wondering what she was like. I mean, I made up my mind a while back that Jahiem, although we had a rocky start, was the man I wanted to spend the rest of my life with. Even though there was a small chance that these kids weren't his, he came to terms with it. At least, that's what he said. He had no problem throwing that shit in my face when we argued.

All in all, though? I'd say last year taught me so much. I grew up so fast. I left some friends in the past and made some new ones for this year. Noelle and I hung out when we could. Porscha was still, and would always be, my bitch, but she was going in a different direction than me. My mind was on finishing school and maintaining a household with this nigga. She was still trying to turn up.

I became close with Jahiem's brother's wife, Toni, who was only two months ahead of my pregnancy. Turns out, we both didn't take shit from neither one of these niggas, and we had no problem expressing that. We already said that as soon as these babies were born, we were both going to go celebrate by smoking a blunt and having a girl's day out while the men took care of the kids.

Jordyn still wasn't fucking with me. We barely talked, even though I heard she was pregnant. Since she wasn't speaking, Elijah's following ass didn't speak either. I told Jahiem about it, but he just said he worships the ground that woman walks on. If Jordyn wasn't with it, neither was he, and there was nothing he could do about it. As long as he was respectful about it, that's all that mattered. Whatever, though. She didn't have to speak, but we were the women to be raising the next generation of Carters. At some point, her scary ass would want to speak, so I wasn't bothered.

I hadn't heard from Jade, and I didn't give a fuck. I—

"Aye, you hear me?" Jahiem asked as he turned the car off.

I looked around the thick neighborhood with houses lined up on hills. There were all kinds of houses in different colors, with the patio porches in the front instead of the back. The house we were at had a porch that wrapped around to the sides, and multiple cars lined up alongside it.

"This is where you grew up at?" I asked, looking at the giant tree in the front yard—no leaves on it, but it was decorated with Christmas lights. I could see an older man sitting on the porch, smoking a thick-ass blunt, maybe a cigar. He was sitting in that rocking chair, straight chilling.

"Yeah, most of the time anyway. I was always with Shiloh and Ant," he said, getting out of the car.

It was one of those random days in Atlanta where the weather seemed like it was trying to give you a sneak peek at spring. So, I had on a light hoodie with some cute jeans and riding boots that went perfect with my top underneath. My hair was in an afro puff, and I wore no makeup and hardly any accessories.

I took Jahiem's waiting hand, and we walked up to the porch, opening the door before stepping onto the wooden plank. I saw the man in the rocking chair had his eyes closed.

"Who is he?" I whispered, looking up at Jahiem. I watched him squint his eyes at the man before shrugging.

"Shit, I don't know. My mama pick up stray niggas from the street all the time," he said, opening the door. "Mama!"

I gasped in awe of her house when we walked in. The smell of incense burning hit my nose hard as I looked at the lack of furniture, the wooden floors that were shiny, and colorful decorations that hung from the ceiling. Pictures of Jahiem and Talin when they were kids hung on the wall. I even spotted Toni and Talin together in a few pictures when they were in middle school. So much African art decorated her space. Tall statues, and even a man-made water fountain sat in the corner of her dining room.

"In here, baby," she called out as we walked toward the living room.

Her living room was spacious, with pillows and mats lined up everywhere for people to sit. Three girls were sitting with their legs crossed, eyes closed. A brown-skin woman with thick locs laying on the floor turned toward us, smiling before standing up.

"Oh my God, your mom is beautiful," I mumbled, watching her push her pepper locs back as she held her arms out for Jahiem. She was a tiny woman, slender frame, with long, knee-length locs. She was wearing all types of bracelets, beads, and rings, with beautiful skin. She looked more like Talin, but I could see Jahiem in her face for sure.

"Let's go in here and let them meditate," she said, pushing us back toward the dining room as she dropped a beaded curtain barrier down to block off the living room.

"Who you got up in here with you, Mama?" Jahiem teased, moving her locs back as she playfully hit him. "And who the fuck is that man sitting out there?"

"He's been sitting out there for days now," she said, waving him off as my mouth dropped. "I make him breakfast and dinner, and he just stays. Never leaves. I told him eventually he would have to go."

Jahiem walked toward the front door, opening it, and looked to his left at the man. "Nigga, get the fuck on from my mama's porch. She's not feeding you no more."

"This boy here," Ms. Tonya and I said at the same time before we looked at each other and laughed.

"So, tell me, Tiana," she said, linking arms with me as we sashayed into another side room. It was decorated the same, with huge sitting pillows and rugs, with multi-colored curtains and artwork. There really was no furniture.

"Yes, ma'am?" I pressed as she looked at me, both of us the same height, before rolling her eyes.

"Honey, it's not that serious. You can call me Tonya. What I want to know is, when are you going to let me cut your hair?"

My mouth dropped. She started touching my 'fro, twisting at the ends. "It's a lot of heat damage and dryness, baby. You need to let this go, or it's not going to grow."

"Cut it all off?" I freaked.

"Just to give you a low cut. You have the face for it." She smiled. "What are you using on your skin?"

"Oh God, you sound like Jahiem." I sighed, and she laughed. I saw where he got it from, the constant nagging about my appearance.

We spent five minutes talking about what I used on my hair and how I should maintain it, along with my skin. I started telling her about the yoga he'd been having me do, when he walked in, hugging his mom once more. Kissing her on the cheek, he looked just like an overgrown mama's boy. It was even cuter since he was twice her size, towering over her small frame.

"Where the food at? I know you got some," he pressed as she pushed him away.

"Go look in the fridge upstairs. I brought some stuff back from home for you to take, since I knew you were coming."

As soon as we were alone again, she had me sit down on the pillows as she sat in front of me. The ray of light hitting through the curtains was just enough to shine on both of us.

Smiling at me, she took my hands. She was definitely a spiritual older woman. I could feel it, more so than look at her and know.

"You love my son. That I do know," she said with a soft smile. "I can see it in the way you look at him."

"I do," I said, nodding.

"I know he loves you just as much, and he is very excited about the three girls coming into his life. Nervous, but excited."

I continued to nod, eyes never leaving hers.

"So, all I'm going to ask of you is to protect him. I know he's grown and thinks he knows the world, but protect him, because he is still reckless at times. I see a little bit of that in you as well, so maybe you two need to protect each other from this fucked-up society we live in. Protect each other from outside pain and heartache, and protect your family. I raised both of my sons to love and respect everyone, but to stand up for their beliefs and not to take shit from no one. You understand?" I nodded. "I expect the women, their partners, to be the same way, if not stronger."

"Can I ask a question?" I asked hesitantly.

She nodded, eyes never leaving mine.

"How is it that two brothers that are extremely close grew up completely different?"

"Oh, man!" She laughed. "His father, Marion Carter, got a hold to Jahiem's mind before I knew any better. I was too busy chasing after the hot niggas on the street—the dope dealers and the niggas with the fancy cars," she said.

I laughed. Sounded like me.

"So, when Talin was born just a few years behind, I was coming into my own, and I'd gained so much knowledge from my past mistakes. Well," she said thoughtfully, looking up. The hood chick definitely came out of her then. "I was still fucking with Marion, but even so, I knew being with a man like him wasn't good for me. Jahiem already made up his mind he wanted to be like his daddy, so I said, 'Go on then, since you think you grown. Get locked up and arrested, give the white man a reason to talk shit about us. Whenever you ready to get some damn sense, bring yo' ass home. Until then, don't come around my house with that foolishness, nigga,'" she said easily. She really was cool as hell.

"Now, both sons are preparing for fatherhood, and I couldn't be more excited. Welcome to the family, Tiana," she said with her arms out.

We hugged, and I promise y'all, I could have cried. I'd never felt like I was a part of my own damn family, but here she was, taking me as her own.

"Thank you." I smiled, pulling back.

"Only thing I will say, and I told Toni this, even though I considered her a daughter long before her and Talin were together. If you hurt my son in any way, shape, or form," she said, looking hard at me, "know that I am the wrong mama to cross when it comes to my boys. I will fuck you up my damn self if you fuck with my kids. You hear me? Don't let these beads and this spiritual shit fool you. Born and raised in Atlanta, just like you, and I can get back to those roots if I need to. The wrong bitch to cross, and the wrong mama," she said as I quickly nodded.

She smiled before helping me stand to my feet. "Now, let's go cut this hair. I can't stand looking at damaged hair, honey."

Noelle

So, I guess, everyone is giving a snippet of their life now to end the book, huh? Everything is good on my end so far. New year, new attitude, new beginnings.

Shiloh and I spent Christmas together with my family, who had a hard time accepting him at first—or just my dad did. But my mom and grandma loved him. Dad barely spoke two words to Shiloh, who didn't care either way.

I started a new job, and I was in the process of moving into a better neighborhood. I was constantly praying for Shiloh when he got taken to the police station on a regular. They were trying to accuse him of murder, with three charges against him, but they could never find the evidence to prove it. Either that, or the cops working for him were the same ones pretending to hold him in. I don't know. I never asked. Only thing I said to him was, "You are close to thirty fucking years old. Stop the madness, Shiloh. It's time for a change, because I don't want my life to be surrounded by that type of drama. I can deal with your wild brothers; I can even deal with your crazy family, but this? No. SMH. Hell, no. We are grown and way better than that. Too old to be fighting and shooting people and trying to live that lifestyle. Get it together, babe. Seriously."

I was in the car with Tyree, on our way to Layla's house. I had a bone to pick with her. It was Friday night, cold as heck in the beginning of January, with Tyree driving my car, trying to hype me up.

"I told you she wasn't really down for you like that! Girl, I know how to sense a ho from a mile away! You can smell them bitches before you see them! Layla has been wanting our nigga for the longest!" Tyree said as I cut my eyes at him. "Bitch, he's my man just as much as he's yours. Don't play."

"I can't believe she would do something like that this whole time." I sighed, looking at a message from Shiloh, asking me not to go over to Layla's house.

Fuck that. Y'all know when I start cursing I mean business.

Turns out, Shiloh has been holding secrets from me about Layla getting his number and sending him naked pictures. He never responded, but he never told me anything, because he didn't think it was that serious. Yet, as I read the messages she sent him, she was dogging me out, telling lies about me, all while spreading her legs for my man in a text. This had been going on for two months now. Trust me, I went off on Shiloh, because he wasn't innocent in this at all. Far from it. He had an earful from me, but as we pulled up to Layla's place, seeing she was walking outside on the phone, running her mouth, I smirked. She had no idea that I knew.

"Look at this trifling bitch," Tyree mumbled, cutting the car off. "Go beat her ass, Noelle!"

"Tyree, you know I'm not the fighting type. I just want to ask why."

"Fuck that! This girl has been smiling in yo' face this whole time, laughing, and a kee-keeing with you like life is good! All while sending yo' man naked pictures and videos to his phone, talking about what she wanna do to him! Gurl, please, beat that bitch down!"

I got out of the car, tuning him out as she waved to me.

"Girl, you don't ever come over here!" She laughed. "Baby, let me call you back. My besties just stopped by," she said, hanging up.

I could feel my anger trying to reach its limit, but I was going to conduct myself like the classy woman that I am.

"Hey, girl! Shiloh must have gotten arrested again," she concluded as I slowly walked up to her. My hair was wrapped up in a scarf, I had on boots, and I was wearing all black, with my cute Free People leather jacket with the hoodie coming out of it.

"Beat that bitch down!" Tyree yelled from the window of my car as Layla's eyes grew wide, looking at him, then me.

"What the fuck is he talking about?" She laughed.

"Soooo," I started, looking down at my feet before stepping closer. "You been sending naked pictures to Shiloh for over two months? To his phone?"

Her eyes grew wide as she stepped back. She had taken her braids out of her head, only to replace it with a weave that went to her waist. She had UGG boots on, with the house phone in hand. She was still living at home with her mom. She continued to stare.

"You can't speak now? You did so much fucking talking about me to him, so now that you have the chance to say that shit to me, you can't open yo' mouth?" I asked.

"Beat that bitch, downnn!" Tyree yelled. "She ain't tryna talk, Noe! Get her ass!"

"I didn't—"

I flipped the switch just at the sound of her voice. Coming for her, I reached for that weave to bring her down, dragging her along the grass while pounding her face and throat. I wanted to prove my point without having to say a damn word—beat the face in one time and leave.

And that's exactly what I did. I left her on that grass in the cold night, crying with a bloody nose as I got back in the car. I ignored Shiloh's calls. Nobody, and I mean nobody, better not come for that man on any level.

Like I said when I began this story, I can get just as crazy if I'm pushed far enough. Don't come for my man, and that's all I'm going to say. It's been a blessing. Have a wonderful year, everyone.

Tyree

Shiiiit, I don't have a damn thing to say.

My life was good. I was getting married in four months, and after that, Ontrell and I were moving to California in the summer. Both of us were working hard to make that money so we could maintain a certain lifestyle. Although we were both still in our early twenties, we were sharp when it came to business. With Shiloh helping him, Ontrell started investing in a couple of business ventures and taking things to the next level, while I expanded my business. I didn't know how we were going to pull it off, but within the next two years, he was going to go to school to get a degree in business, while I was going to try to start working fashion weeks around the world. I wanted to eventually have my own clothing line for men, with my man as my main model.

I grew closer to the women of the Carter brothers, especially Jordyn. I wasn't so much fond of Tia, because I thought those triplets were Trent's babies. I'm just saying what everyone else was thinking, but the truth would come out when the DNA was given. Jordyn, Noelle, and I put money on it. Damn, we ain't shit, but it was all in good fun.

Be blessed, tricks, and keep it moving. No drama on my story or in my life. That's what females are for.

Taylor

So, I had a boyfriend! Oddly enough, it was Jade's best friend, KD. In turn, her and I hung out more often than we should have. She was actually cool as hell, and I could see why Trent was with her in the first place. I didn't have not one bad thing to say about anyone but Olivia. Fuck her. She was a bitch and would always be one. I moved out into my own place and left it at that. Over twenty years of friendship gone down the drain because she lied. Any-who!

Trent didn't speak much to me when we did see each other, but I was trying to keep my distance from that family as much as I could. My whole life was centered on them. It was time for me to enjoy my own damn last name and have my own friends.

So there. That's all I got for ya. LOL.

Elijah

Was I crazy for getting my girl pregnant on purpose? Nah. Fuck nah. I was just making sure no other nigga would try to come for her. Not while she was pregnant with my seed, they wouldn't. So, yeah, I was that nigga to poke a hole in the condom and trap my bitch. I did it. Say what you want, but I was straight-up crazy about her. I knew it; she knew it, and any nigga that was feeling like they wanted to test my crazy and try her would know it too. Straight up.

But! We all still met up every Sunday as a family, leaving all the girls out but Livie, and we just chilled. The music was taking off bigger this year, and I even convinced Shiloh to get on a track. A lot of y'all don't know it, but he can sing, if not better than me. Shit runs in the family, too, on our mama's side. Other than that, shiit, I don't have nothing to say. Life is good, shawty.

Trent

I don't have much to say.

I was in school to get my masters, single, and running these streets wild, getting into every female I could. I was enjoying myself. Last year made me realize that life is way too short to be fucking up with these girls. My wounds had healed nicely, and my mind was focused and driven. There was still a lot of bad blood between the families, and now Olivia and Shiloh had something going on. No clue what the fuck was going on there, but as my brother said above, life is good, shawty. Can't complain. What's up!

Jahiem

I fell in love with a ho. That's my story, and I'm sticking to it. Fuck what everyone else thinks. Can't help who you fall for. She was my ride or die baby mama, and I wouldn't change her for the world.

Nobody else's opinion mattered at this point. I came home to a beautiful girl, working on her school shit, food was cooked, and she was right by my side, ready to fight my battle with me, no matter the situation. She had my back, and I had hers. Period.

I suggest everyone in the new year get healthy, watch what the fuck you put in yo' body, and remember that black lives matter. These white people don't, and will never, give a shit about us, so do what you got to do to survive in this society, and surpass expectations set by yourself and by others. At the end of the day, as long as you happy, that's all that matters.

Shiloh

Don't really have shit to say. I don't feel the need to explain how my life is, and it's only been a few fucking weeks into the new year. My life, my woman, and my way of doing shit is my business. Keep it moving, nigga. End of the story.